PASSIONATE RITUAL

When Shadow entered our lodge, I was standing beside the fire, a red blanket draped around my shoulders. He had told me once that when a man was courting a woman, he would play his flute outside her lodge in the evening. Later, if the girl was interested in the man, she would stand outside her lodge wrapped in a big red courting blanket. If she looked with favor on the man, she would hold out her arms, inviting him to stand inside the blanket with her. Now, as Shadow walked toward me, I held out my arms. He smiled, the expression spreading to his eyes when he saw I was naked beneath the blanket.

I smiled up into his darkly handsome face as I wrapped the blanket around the two of us. "If we were courting, would you still offer my father many horses for my hand in marriage?"

"That is a silly question," Shadow said, his hands caressing my back. "Surely you know the answer."

"Yes, but sometimes a woman likes to hear the words."

"I can offer you more than words as proof of my love," Shadow said huskily, drawing my hips against his strongly muscled thighs. "Shall I show you how much I love you?"

MADELINE BAKER

RECKLESS LOVE

LEISURE BOOKS  NEW YORK CITY

Harley—
this one's for you.

A LEISURE BOOK®

November 1995

Published by

Dorchester Publishing Co., Inc.
276 Fifth Avenue
New York, NY 10001

I

1883

It was summer in the valley once more, the time of year the Indians called Many Leaves. The trees were green and full, the sky was a warm vibrant blue, the berry bushes were thick with dark purple fruit. Animal life abounded in the wooded hills and valleys, and I smiled as I saw a deer and her twin fawns glide soundlessly through the underbrush across the deep, fast-moving river that ran through the middle of the valley. Blue jays called to one another from high in the leafy tree-tops, gray squirrels scampered back and forth between the pines, while beady-eyed lizards sunned themselves on the rocks scattered along the riverbank. Now and then a speckled fish jumped after a fly.

Sitting in the shade of an ancient oak, I was happily content. My three-and-a-half-year-old daughter, Mary, named for my mother, slept peacefully on the blanket next to me. My son, Heecha, now four and a half and tall for his age, was out hunting with his father. Our only neighbors and best friends, Calf Running and Flower Woman, had taken their three-year-old, Nachi, for a walk in the woods to pick blackberries.

We had lived in the valley since the winter of '78 and life had been good. The winters had been mild; we had never wanted for food or shelter. Truly, we had been blessed by Maheo, the Great Spirit of the Cheyenne, and by Usen, the god of the Apache. Almost, it was as if we were the only seven people on the face of the earth, so isolated were we from the rest of the world.

It had taken a lot of hard work to establish our residence in the valley. Shadow and Calf Running had spent many long hours hunting so that we might have enough hides to cover our lodges, make clothing, and feed our children. Once, Shadow had raided a homestead many miles to the south, stealing seed so that we might have a garden. Flower Woman and I had put in long backbreaking hours planting and hoeing and weeding, but our efforts had been amply rewarded. Our vegetables were growing beautifully in the rich brown earth; we had corn, beans, pumpkins, squash, beets and tomatoes. The surrounding hills were thick with game: deer, turkeys, quail, rabbits, an occasional elk. The river provided fish. Calf Running and his family would not eat the fish, however, for the Apache believed the fish was related to the snake and was therefore cursed and unfit to eat.

We had wild plums and berries, honey and sage, wild onions and squaw cabbage, as well as many other herbs and roots, some of which we used for food and seasoning and others which were used for medicinal purposes.

Sometimes, when I had a few leisure moments, as now, I missed living in a house surrounded by friends and neighbors who shared my background and heritage. I missed shopping in a store and being able to attend church on Sunday. But only sometimes. Still, there were times when I could not help wondering what was going on in the rest of the world. Who was president? What were the latest fashions like? Had the Army finally subdued all the Indians? Occasionally, when Shadow and Heecha were away and Mary was asleep, I wished for a book to read. As a young girl, I had loved nothing more than to curl up before the fire with a good book and let it carry me away to distant lands.

Nothing in my life had turned out as I had planned, I mused, smiling faintly. Once I had dreamed of marrying a rich man, of living in a big house in Bear Valley

where I had grown up. I had dreamed of
having lots of children, of traveling to
New York where my husband would buy
me dozens of dresses, all silk and satin and
lace. We would dine in the finest
restaurants and go to the theater and ride
around in an elegant carriage drawn by a
team of matched black stallions. How
frivolous those dreams seemed now.

I laughed softly as I looked at the hide
lodge I shared with Shadow. It was not a
big house, but it was home, and surprisingly comfortable. It was waterproof
and windproof. In the summer, we left the
lodge flap open and raised the sides and
the air moved in and out, exiting through
the smoke hole, cooling the lodge and its
occupants. In wintertime, with the flap
closed and a fire burning, the lodge stayed
cosy and warm.

Pensive now, I fingered the hem of my
skirt. It had been a long time since I had
worn the cumbersome attire of a white
woman. Gone were the petticoats and
pantalets, the shoes and long stockings of
my girlhood days. Now I wore a doeskin
dress and moccasins and little else. My
bed was a pile of soft robes, my home a
lodge of skins, my stove an open fire, my
bathtub the river beyond. We were not
rich in material possessions, but I was rich
in Shadow's love, and that was enough for
me. I did not have silks and satins and
servants, but I had a wonderful husband,

two happy healthy children, and dear friends. I had never been happier in my life and my only wish was that all my tomorrows would bring the same joy as today.

Daily, I thanked God for a husband like Shadow. He was tall and strong and handsome. He was kind and tender and considerate. He was reliable and resourceful. Shadow. He had been a part of my life for almost as long as I could remember, and I smiled happily as I recalled the first time I had seen him . . .

I had been a skinny child of nine at the time; Shadow had been three years older. I had met him near the river crossing close to our homestead in Bear Valley. I had been frightened of him at first, expecting him to take my scalp because he was a Cheyenne and I was a white girl. Instead, we had become friends. Back then, my parents and I had been the only white people in the valley and Shadow had been my only playmate. Of course, Shadow did not really play. He thought "girl things" were foolish and a waste of time and refused to do anything he considered silly or undignified—which was practically everything I wanted to do. So he taught me to read trail sign and how to read the moon and the stars. He taught me how to skin a deer and tan the hide, and how to speak his language. Of course, Shadow was learning, too. His English grew less stilted, and he picked up some swear

words from my father, but my mother was
his best teacher. She taught him to read
and write and how to behave at the dinner
table. When Shadow turned fourteen, his
visits to our place tapered off and then
ceased altogether as he devoted himself to
the task of becoming a Cheyenne warrior.

By then, other white families had
moved into our valley and when I was
fifteen, I fancied myself in love with
Joshua Berdeen, a good-looking young
man who lived nearby. It was in my mind
to marry Josh when I turned sixteen, only
Shadow entered my life again and turned
my world upside down. Knowing my
parents and neighbors would not approve
of my friendship with an Indian, Shadow
and I met in secret and as the days passed,
we fell hopelessly in love. I yearned to
marry Shadow, even though I knew my
parents, and especially my father, would
never approve and that my friends would
shun me. I begged Shadow to take me
away with him, but he was a man of honor
and he refused to go against my father's
wishes. And so, quite shamelessly and
deliberately, I seduced the man I loved,
knowing that once he had taken my
virginity, he would marry me, for honor's
sake. Shadow had been secretly pleased
and amused by my obvious tactics.

"I suppose I shall have to marry you
now," he had lamented in mock resignation. "That was your intent, wasn't it?

To tempt me into marriage with your irresistible woman's body?''

I had happily admitted my guilt, and he had promised to return for me the next day. But Shadow did not appear the next day, or the next. Three days later, Shadow arrived at our place, badly wounded. He had been whipped and knifed by some of the men in Bear Valley. Feelings had been running high for several weeks. Homesteads had been burned, John Sanders had been killed, his six-year-old daughter, Kathy, had been kidnapped by the Sioux, and when the settlers had encountered Shadow riding toward our place, they had dragged him behind their horses, pistol-whipped him, slashed his leg, and left him for dead. That same week, Joshua's homestead was attacked, his father, mother and brother killed. Josh stopped at our place on his way to Fort Lincoln. He was going to join the Army and fight Indians, he declared vehemently, and nothing we could say would change his mind.

When Shadow recovered from his wounds, he left our place to join his people in their fight against the increasing flock of whites moving west. I had been heartbroken to think Shadow's loyalty to his people was stronger than his love for me. My father had stated it was for the best, and mother agreed.

In the spring of 1876, the minor skirmishes between the Indians and the settlers turned into a full-fledged war. Our homestead was attacked. My mother was killed, and it seemed that all was lost when Shadow arrived on the scene. He bargained for my life with the chief of the attacking Indians and they agreed to let me go. I had not wanted to leave my father behind, but my father, who hated Indians with every fiber of his being, had pushed me out the door, insisting I go with Shadow if it would save my life. I had never seen my father again.

That night, I made the decision that had brought me to this place. Shadow had not tried to influence me. I can see him as he was that night, kneeling before me, his arms outstretched, his face impassive, as he waited for my decision. Would I go with him and live with his people? Or would I go to Steel's Crossing and stay with Pa's friends? That night, for the first time since I had fallen in love with Shadow, I saw him as an Indian. The hideous red paint on his face, the eagle feather in his long black hair, the wolfskin clout that covered his loins—all bespoke Cheyenne blood. How could I spend the rest of my life with this man, this stranger? How could I ever forget that he was an Indian, and that it was an Indian who had killed my mother? I thought of all the people in our little valley who were dead because of Indian hatred and Indian vengeance.

I gazed into Shadow's eyes, but I saw nothing there—no trace of love to persuade me—and I knew that this was a decision I had to make on my own. Only Shadow's outstretched arms betrayed his inner feelings.

For endless seconds, I did not move. My parents were dead, killed by Indians. My friends, everyone I had ever known, had been killed by Indians, and hate for the whole red race churned in my breast. But wrestling with that hatred was my love for Shadow, for love him I did, and I knew that no matter what happened, my love would remain unchanged. Our people might turn the sun-kissed grassland red with blood in their efforts to slaughter each other, but I knew our love for each other would survive. With a sigh, I had gone into Shadow's waiting arms and from that night on Shadow was not an Indian and I was not white. We were simply two people desperately in love.

For a time, Shadow and I had lived with his people. I grew to love the Cheyenne, especially Shadow's father, who was a kind, warmhearted man. But then, in the summer of that year, Custer came to the Greasy Grass. His defeat at the hands of the Sioux and the Cheyenne outraged whites everywhere and the Army began to hunt the Indians with a vengeance. Sitting Bull fled the Dakotas and took his people to Canada. But

Shadow would not leave his homeland and when, after many battles, the Cheyenne decided to go to the reservation, Shadow refused to surrender. I can still remember standing alone on the prairie, just Shadow and I, watching his people begin the long journey to the reservation.

For awhile, Shadow and I had lived alone near the river crossing in Bear Valley, but then, by some magical Indian method of communication, the word spread that Two Hawks Flying—that was Shadow's warrior name—had not gone in. By twos and threes, warriors from various tribes came to Shadow, the last fighting chief on the plains, begging him to lead them in their fight against the whites. Calf Running was one of the first to find us. To my chagrin, Shadow had agreed to lead the rebellious warriors and so we went to war once more. I had fought at Shadow's side until I grew heavy with his child. Even now I shuddered to remember those days, for they were filled with terror and bloodshed. We had been hunted by the Army day and night, driven ever westward until we crossed into the land of the Apache. At last, when there were only thirty warriors left in our band, Shadow said it was time to quit.

The last night we spent with the warriors had been a sad time. Shadow's men, made up of warriors from many tribes, had developed a strong bond of love and respect for one another. Together, they had shared many hardships. There were no formal farewells that last night. The warriors left as they had come, in small groups of two or three or four until, at last, Shadow and I were alone again.

I put my memories aside as they began to grow more unpleasant and centered my thoughts on my husband instead. Shadow. He was an integral part of my life, the best part. He had been there to comfort me the day my mother was killed. He had been there when our first child was born dead, he had been at my side when Mary was born.

Shadow. I felt my heart flutter with excitement as I saw him striding toward me now, a deer slung over his broad shoulders. I had known this man most of my life and I marveled that he seemed to grow more handsome, more virile, with each passing day. Or did it only seem that way because my love for him daily grew stronger?

I gazed at his face, a face I knew as well as I knew my own. His forehead was unlined, his cheekbones high and proud, his nose as straight as a blade, his jaw firm and square. His thick black hair, parted in the middle, fell to his waist. He wore only a clout and moccasins, revealing a broad chest, skin that was a deep bronze, and arms and legs that were long and well-muscled. His flanks were lean, his stomach hard and flat. And his eyes—they were as black as ten feet down, shaded by sooty lashes that women would have died for. Just looking at him thrilled me down to my toes.

"Nahkoa, look!" Heecha cried, running toward me on strong, sturdy legs. "See what I caught?"

I smiled proudly at my son as he showed me the fat gray rabbit he had killed.

"You have done well, little warrior," I said, beaming.

Heecha grinned from ear to ear as he held up the rabbit so I could see it better. My son was a handsome child, all Indian this day. He was dressed in buckskin pants and a buckskin vest. Moccasins hugged his feet, a beaded headband held his shoulder-length hair from his face.

Heecha gazed at the rabbit in his hands. "I set a trap to catch it," he boasted. "My father taught me."

"I am proud of you both," I said solemnly. "I am the most fortunate of women, to have two fine hunters in my lodge."

Heecha nodded gravely as he thrust the limp carcass into my hands. "Skinning and cooking are squaw work," he declared with just a hint of male arrogance.

I stared into his darling face, choking back the laughter that bubbled in my throat. He sounded just like his father! I glanced up at Shadow and saw that he, too, was remembering the day he had spoken similar words to my mother.

"You shall have the rabbit for dinner this very night," I told my son. "But now it is time for you to water your father's horse."

Heecha smiled as he ran toward the peeled pole corral located behind our lodge. Caring for Shadow's spotted stallion was a chore our son dearly loved. Already, he could ride like a seasoned Cheyenne brave.

Scooping Mary into my arms, I walked back to our lodge beside Shadow. I went inside and placed Mary on her bed, then went back outside to skin Heecha's rabbit while Shadow butchered the deer.

"The man will never learn," lamented a male voice, and I turned to see Calf Running and Flower Woman approaching our lodge while their son, Nachi, ran off to join Heecha at the river.

Calf Running was a Chiricahua Apache. He was short and stocky, as were many of his race. He had dark skin and coarse black hair. A long scar, souvenir of a Comanche blade, ran the length of his left cheek. He had a deep and abiding hatred for white men, who had murdered his family in cold blood. Calf Running had been but a boy of twelve at the time, but he had tracked the men who slaughtered his family and killed them all while they slept. He was a proud warrior, a ruthless fighter, a kind and gentle husband and father.

"More and more I find him doing squaw work," Calf Running went on. "I fear Hannah's influence has weakened his manhood."

Shadow scowled at his long-time friend as he sliced off a section of deer haunch and began to skin the hide from the meat.

"Look at him," Calf Running continued, shaking his head in dismay. "He does not even have the decency to look ashamed."

"I would welcome a man who was not afraid to lend a hand with the butchering and the skinning," Flower Woman remarked. "I find it a fine quality in a husband."

"Do you?" Calf Running accused with mock anger. "Perhaps I should sell you to Two Hawks Flying."

"Perhaps you should!" Flower Woman retorted. Her words were harsh, but her eyes were filled with laughter.

Shadow stood up, wiping his bloody hands on the sides of his buckskin pants as he looked from Calf Running to Flower Woman. "I am very fond of you, Flower Woman," he said gravely. "But one wife is all I can handle."

Flower Woman nodded. She was a pretty woman, with a slender figure, long black hair and luminous black eyes. "I understand," she said with feigned regret, "but if you ever change your mind . . ."

She broke off, giggling, as Calf Running caught her to him, his good arm pulling her close. His left arm, shattered by a cavalryman's bullet years ago, hung limp and useless at his side. It was, he had once told me, a small price to pay for freedom.

With a smile, Calf Running planted a kiss on Flower Woman's cheek. "Never mind, woman," he growled. "I have decided to keep you after all."

"I think you are all mind-gone-far," I said as I skewered Heecha's rabbit and placed it over the fire to cook.

"I think you are right," Calf Running agreed good-naturedly. "Come, woman, let us go to our own lodge. I am hungry."

"He is always hungry," Flower Woman remarked with an exaggerated sigh. "Some day he will be as big and fat as an old buffalo."

I smiled as the two of them went off toward their own lodge, which was set up a short distance from ours. They were a happy couple and very much in love. I knew many white people thought the Indians incapable of love and laughter, but Calf Running's lodge overflowered with both.

When they were out of sight, I turned to face Shadow, troubled by something Calf Running had said.

"Do you mind helping me with the butchering?" I asked, frowning. "Does it offend your manhood?"

Shadow grinned as he took me in his arms. "Do not make sounds like a foolish woman," he chided, kissing my eyes and the tip of my nose. "I am a Cheyenne warrior. Skinning a deer cannot change that."

"I love you," I murmured as I lifted my face for his kiss.

"Do you, Hannah?" he asked, only half kidding. "Have you never regretted the kind of life we live? Have you never longed for your own people, your own customs?"

"Never," I said firmly. "You are my people. I have never been sorry that I chose to live with you and follow your ways."

Shadow's smile warmed me through and through. It was so good to see him smile. There had been many times in the past when we had little to smile about. There had been the awful days when I had ridden the war trail at his side, the times when we had gone without food or shelter, times we had huddled together, shivering, in the rain and snow. Deep in my memory lingered the faces of the dead warriors we had left behind, the tiny unmarked grave in Arizona where our first son was buried. A son I had never seen. Even now, six years later, I could remember how my arms had ached to hold my firstborn child, the tears I had shed when I stood at his tiny unmarked grave. And yet, for all the misery of the past, I knew I would gladly live it all over again to be here now with the man I loved.

Shadow and I stood together for several moments, our bodies pressed close as we remembered the bad times that made the good times all the more sweet. Then Mary emerged from the lodge, clamoring for her father's attention, pulling on his pant leg until he lifted her in his arms. Mary squealed with pleasure as Shadow swung her high in the air. She was a pretty little thing, with dark brown hair and fair skin. Her eyes were gray, like mine. No one, seeing Mary, would ever guess her father was an Indian. Not so Heecha. He was the spitting image of Shadow, with the same black hair, the same copper-hued skin, the same black eyes. No one, seeing my son, would guess he was anything but pure Cheyenne.

Shadow's dark eyes glowed with pleasure as he tossed Mary in the air, then caught her safe in his arms, and I thought what a beautiful picture the two of them made.

Heecha returned shortly and demanded to be tossed in the air, too. He shrieked with delight as his father continued the game, tossing him higher and higher.

When Heecha and Mary tired of that game, they began to wrestle with Shadow, jumping on his back, pulling on his arms and legs in an effort to hold him down. Shadow's deep laughter filled the air as he grabbed a child in each arm and lifted them off the ground. Heecha and Mary wriggled and kicked to no avail and finally declared Shadow the winner.

"Dinner's ready," I called, and Heecha slid out of his father's grasp, eager to taste his first kill. Heecha generously shared a bite of the rabbit with each of us, and we all agreed it was the best rabbit we had ever eaten.

After dinner, Shadow played with Mary and Heecha while I washed the dishes and banked the fire for the night. While I put the children to bed, Shadow went outside for his evening walk.

I was changing into my sleeping gown when I heard it, the faint melodical notes of a Cheyenne courting flute. I paused, everything else forgotten, as I listened to Shadow serenade me.

The Indians were a musical people. There were songs and chants for every occasion: religious songs, prayer songs, healing songs. There were songs of mourning and songs of bereavement.

There were love songs and war songs. There were soft lullabies and rousing songs of joy. There were animal songs, some prayerful in nature, others a plea for good fortune. A particular song, known as the horse song, could be sung over a favored horse to make it strong and sound for a particular fight or journey. There was a morning song hummed by the men upon awakening. Often, it was the first sound heard in our lodge.

In my many years of living with Shadow, I had heard them all, yet none was more beautiful than the melancholy notes of Shadow's flute. The music permeated our lodge, surrounding me like invisible arms, telling me that I was loved.

When Shadow entered our lodge, I was standing beside the fire, a red blanket draped around my shoulders. He had told me once that when a man was courting a woman, he would play his flute outside her lodge in the evening. Later, if the girl was interested in the man, she would stand outside her lodge wrapped in a big red courting blanket. If she looked with favor on the man, she would hold out her arms, inviting him to stand inside the blanket with her and they would stand close together, the blanket over their heads and bodies, lost in a warm red cocoon. Now, as Shadow walked toward me, I held out my arms. He smiled, the expression spreading to his eyes when he saw I was naked beneath the blanket.

I smiled up into his darkly handsome face as I wrapped the blanket around the two of us. "If we were courting, would you still offer my father many horses for my hand in marriage?"

"That is a silly question," Shadow said, his hands caressing my back. "Surely you know the answer."

"Yes, but sometimes a woman likes to hear the words."

"I can offer you more than words as proof of my love," Shadow said huskily. His hands cupped my buttocks, drawing my hips against his strongly muscled thighs. "Shall I show you how much I love you?"

"Yes, please," I murmured, and lifted my face for his kiss.

Shadow's mouth closed over mine as he lifted me in his arms and carried me to our bed. He placed me gently on the soft robes, then stretched out beside me.

How wonderful to lie in Shadow's arms, to know he loved me as deeply as I loved him, to know that tomorrow would bring the same happiness as today. Time had not dulled our joy in each other, or lessened the thrill that erupted in the center of my being whenever Shadow caressed me. Sometimes we made love tenderly, with Shadow caressing me with light and gentle hands, as if he were afraid I might shatter at the slightest touch. At those times, he made me feel as if I were the most cherished woman in all the world. He coaxed me and petted me, holding back his own release until he was certain my wants and needs had been satisfied.

At other times, he took me boldly, dominating me, exerting the strength and masculinity I so adored. He was masterful then, demanding, arrogant. His hands roamed my body, kneading my flesh, molding my shape to his as his tongue boldly raped my mouth, firing my blood until I thought I should explode or melt in his arms.

This night, I gloried in the subdued strength of his hands as he stroked my breasts and thighs. His lips and tongue traveled over my face and neck, nibbling, tasting, scorching my skin like a dancing finger of flame.

I moved restlessly beneath him, begging him to make me his, to satisfy the yearning he had created.

But he was in no hurry this night. Drawing back, he let his gleaming black eyes wander over my body, his long brown fingers following the same path as his eyes, until I was on fire for him.

Wanting him, eager for him to possess me, I rolled over on my side, my fingers stroking the hard wall of his chest, moving slowly, purposefully, toward his flat belly, down toward the thick nest of black hair between his thighs.

I grinned triumphantly as Shadow's desire flared to match my own, his need as great now as mine.

Whispering my name, he covered my body with his. My hands moved restlessly up and down his back, reveling in the muscles bunching beneath my fingertips. I grasped his buttocks as he surged into me, drawing him closer, closer, knowing I could never get enough of him.

I closed my eyes as he moved inside me, lost in the wondrous pleasure of my husband's embrace.

Shadow whispered love words in my ear, the phrases coming in a mixture of Cheyenne and English as he told me he loved me, needed me, wanted me. I was caught in the web of his voice, loving the sound of it, deep and husky with passion as he cried my name.

I returned his love with every fiber of my being, giving all I had to give, wanting to please him, to pleasure him in every way.

Later, wrapped in his arms, I drifted into a peaceful sleep, never dreaming that the future would hold anything but the same blissful contentment as today . . .

II

Summer-Winter

1883

The summer days skipped by one by one, each as long and serene as the day before. Shadow and Calf Running roamed the wooded hills every day, hunting meat for the coming winter. Flower Woman and I sewed the skins into warm shirts and leggings and moccasins for our husbands and children. We made tons of pemmican, that tasty Indian dish concocted of dried meat, animal fat and berries ground together, as well as jerked deer meat.

One lazy afternoon in late summer, Shadow ran into camp, smiling hugely. He had sighted a small herd of buffalo! This was indeed cause for excitement, for the buffalo that had once roamed the prairie in vast herds had been hunted almost to extinction by the whites.

Moments later, we were mounted and riding toward the herd. Heecha and Nachi were fairly bursting with excitement as they waited for their first glimpse of the great shaggy beasts which the Cheyenne called pte. The boys had grown up listening to their fathers tell of hunting the buffalo. Their eyes had grown wide as they heard stories of warriors who had been crushed beneath pte's cloven hooves, of horses who fell and were pounded into the dust.

Flower Woman and I stayed downwind with the children while Shadow and Calf Running stalked the herd on foot. Shadow hunted with his bow; Calf Running used a rifle because he could not manage bow and arrow with one hand. Heecha and Nachi watched their fathers in awe as first Shadow and then Calf Running brought down a buffalo. The rifle shot spooked the herd and they broke and ran, their hooves churning up a great cloud of yellow dust. As always, I was fascinated by the sight of the buffalo with their great shaggy heads, black curved horns, and beady black eyes. A full-grown bull might weigh as much as two thousand pounds.

When the dust cleared, Flower Woman and I began the monumental task of skinning the carcasses. It was hard, dirty work, but no one complained. All of us were eager to taste the rich red meat. The hides would furnish new robes, the hair would be woven into rope, the horns would be used for spoons or cups, the ribs, lashed together with rawhide, would provide a sled for use in the snow. The meat would see us through the winter. The small intestine would be filled with meat and made into sausage.

That night we feasted on hump meat and tongue, laughing as we licked the rich red juice from our lips. Oh, but it was good to be alive on such a night, to gorge ourselves on food that Maheo had provided, to sit under a sky alight with a million stars surrounded by family and friends.

Later, sated and content, Shadow began to tell Heecha, Nachi, and Mary of the old days, when the buffalo were numbered in the thousands. There were no white men in those days, save for a few trappers and mountain men. Those were the good days, the shining times, when the Indian ruled the land and Man Above smiled down on his red children.

It was near midnight when Calf Running and his family returned to their own lodge. I tucked Heecha and Mary into their beds and then went out to sit beside Shadow, who was staring into the smoldering embers of the fire, a brooding expression on his face. He had turned strangely quiet and I wondered what had spoiled his good mood.

"Shadow, what is it?" I asked after awhile. "Is anything wrong?"

"No, Hannah," he answered

tonelessly. "I am only sad that our son will never know the thrill of stalking pte. I fear that, by the time he is old enough to hunt, the buffalo will be gone. Heecha will never know what it is like to be a warrior, to raid the Crow or steal Pawnee horses, to listen to the old men tell the stories of our people. He will never know the pain and the wonder of the Sun Dance. Our way of life is gone forever. When he is a man, perhaps the Indian will be gone forever as well."

"Shadow . . ."

"My heart is heavy for my people. I miss the land where I was born, where my ancestors are buried. I miss the buffalo hunts. I miss the warriors I grew up with. It all seems so long ago. Tonight I feel old, so very old . . ."

"Are you sorry we did not go to the reservation with your father and the others?"

"No," Shadow said quickly, firmly. "I would not want our children to grow up surrounded by soldiers, to never know any freedom at all."

My heart ached for my husband. I did not fully understand what he was feeling; I could never really understand what it meant to lose everything you had known and loved all your life. True, I had lost my childhood home and my parents, but I had not lost forever the entire fabric of my life. I could always go back to my people and

live like a white woman again, if that was
my desire. I could celebrate the holidays I
had always known, attend the church of
my choice, come and go where and when I
pleased. But Shadow's people would never
again roam their homeland, would never
again be free to live as they had always
lived, to practice their religion as they saw
fit. For the rest of their lives, the Indians
would be imprisoned on a reservation,
subject to the care and goodwill of people
they considered the enemy.

Not knowing what to say, I put my
arms around my husband and drew him
close. Shadow buried his face in my neck,
his strong arms circling my body in a grip
of iron, as if he would never let me go.

"Hannah . . ." Shadow whispered my
name, his voice thick with emotion. A long
shuddering sigh ran the length of his body
and I held him tighter, hoping the
strength of my love would somehow help
to ease his heartache.

I thought of all the times Shadow had
comforted me, of the many times I had
turned to him for solace . . . the day my
parents were killed, the awful days following the death of our firstborn child, the
time when I had been a prisoner of the
Army and one of the soldiers had raped
me. It had been the strength of Shadow's
unconditional love and support that had
carried me through those trying times and
made me want to go on living.

Turning my head, I kissed Shadow, letting my lips linger on his. With a low groan, he returned my kiss, his mouth hard and warm, sending shivers of delight racing along my spine. He whispered my name again and again as his strong brown hands caressed my face, my hair, the curve of my back. As always, his touch filled me with a wondrous sense of peace and contentment even as I felt my body began to tingle with desire.

Soon we were lying naked beneath our sleeping robes, our bodies pressed close together. There was no room for sadness now, no time for regrets or sorrow or thoughts of what might have been. My hands moved restlessly over Shadow's firm flesh, loving the sleek smoothness of his copper-hued skin, loving the way his muscles bunched and relaxed beneath my questing fingertips.

I ran my hands along the insides of this muscular thighs, smiled as he groaned low in his throat. His manhood throbbed against my leg, hard with desire, exciting me.

Wanting to see him, I threw back the buffalo robe and sat up, letting my eyes wander over his broad chest, flat belly, and lean flanks. I grinned as my eyes lingered on the evidence of his growing desire.

Shadow looked up at me, his dark eyes dancing with amusement as my eyes boldly roved over him. When he tried to draw me down, I batted his hand away and straddled his hips. Slowly, I bent down and kissed him, my breasts rubbing against his chest, the soft abrasion of flesh against flesh igniting my longing for the man lying passive beneath me.

I ran my tongue across Shadow's lips, and he swore softly as he reached up and grasped a handful of my hair, his mouth grinding against mine as he pulled me down on top of him.

I gave a gasp of pleasure as he thrust into me and our bodies began to move in the magical, age-old rhythm of mating. I closed my eyes, lost in the scent and touch of the man I loved above all else . . .

The changing leaves announced the changing seasons as late summer, which the Apache called Thick with Fruit, gave way to fall, the time When the Earth is Reddish Brown.

I loved the glorious golds and reds and rich browns of autumn, the sound of leaves crackling merrily beneath my moccasined feet as I gathered firewood. The air was brisk, exhilarating, the sky a deep and vibrant blue.

Flower Woman was pregnant again, and we began sewing things for the new baby, which would be born the following spring. Calf Running was thrilled with the prospect of having another son; Flower

Woman hoped for a daughter. I shared my
friend's joy in the coming child and
secretly hoped that someday soon, I, too,
would carry a new life under my heart.

It was hard to believe that my babies
had grown so fast. Mary was a delightful
child, always cheerful, her eager hands
always exploring, her dove-gray eyes
alight with the joy of each new discovery.

Heecha had turned five in October,
yet it seemed like only yesterday when I
had held my son to my breast. Where had
the years gone? Already, he was learning
many of the skills a boy needed to know to
become a warrior. Daily, Shadow and Calf
Running took the boys into the hills,
teaching them to hunt and track, to read
the moon and the stars and the signs of
the seasons. Heecha had been strutting
around like a veteran warrior ever since
the day he killed his first rabbit. Young as
he was, he already showed signs of being a
proud warrior and I wondered if that air of
manly pride and self-assurance was an
innate quality common to all Cheyenne
males.

As the nights grew longer, we spent
more time inside. Calf Running, Flower
Woman, Shadow and I passed many a
night playing poker after our children
were asleep. The Indian people loved to
gamble and both Calf Running and
Shadow were excellent poker players.
Shadow won the most often as he had a

wonderful knack for bluffing. There were
many times when he won a hand on guts
alone. I usually lost. But then, I could not
keep a poker face when I had three aces
and a fourth in the hole. Maddeningly, my
Indian husband and friends had been
trained since early childhood to conceal
their emotions so I was at a decided dis-
advantage, never knowing if they had a
pair of deuces or a full house. Calf
Running hated to throw in a hand and
would bet heavily even when he knew he
was beat.

When the snow came, we had snowball
fights and built huge snowmen. We went
sledding on sleds made from the bones of
the buffalo we had killed in the summer.
Heecha and Mary and Nachi loved the
snow and they played in it like frisky
puppies, running and jumping in the
drifts, or digging long tunnels.

When Christmas came, I insisted on a
tree and we decorated it with pine-cones
and rawhide cutouts dyed red and green. I
told Heecha and Mary the Christmas
story, and Mary cried softly because the
baby Jesus had no home. Our gifts to the
children were homemade. Shadow made
Heecha a small bow and a half dozen
arrows, as well as a deerskin quiver. He
worked on the bow and arrows for weeks
prior to Christmas. The bow, a smaller
version of Shadow's, was made from
juniper wood. The bowstring was made

from sinew. The arrows were made from the straight shoots of the red willow. Shadow labored over these small shafts as carefully as he labored over his own, making sure the proportions between the shaft, head, and feather were just right. An arrow too light in the shaft would not fly straight, an arrow that was too heavy would not carry far enough.

Mary's gift was a rag doll and several dresses for the doll. I also made Mary and her doll matching dresses and ribbons for their hair. I made new moccasins for everyone.

We sang "Silent Night" and other carols and ate wild turkey with sage dressing for dinner.

Later, as we sat around the fire, Heecha pestered Shadow for a story. "Tell about Heammawihio and how he created the earth," Heecha begged. "It is a good story."

Shadow smiled fondly at his son. Then, gathering the children to his side, he began.

"Once, many many years ago, a Person was floating on the water which covered the whole earth. There were no other people, no land, just water and many kinds of ducks and geese and swans. The Person called to the water birds and asked them to look for some earth. One after another the different birds dived into the water to try and reach the bottom so they could find some earth for the Person, but none was successful until a little mud hen dived very deep and came back with a little mud in its bill. The Person took the mud from the bird and worked the wet earth in his fingers until it was dry. Then he placed little piles of dry earth on the water around him and these little bits of earth spread out and became land.

"After the earth had been made, a man and a woman were created and placed upon it. The creator, Heammawihio, made the man from a rib taken from his own right side. The woman was made from a rib taken from the left side of the man. After the man and the woman were created, they were separated. The woman was placed in the north where it was cold, and the animals and birds which were made in that part of the world were different from those made in the warmer part of the world where the man was. The woman was given control of Hoimaha, the storm. She had gray hair, but she was not old, and she never grew older.

"The man in the south represented summer. He was young and he grew no older. The woman in the north controls the cold and snow, sickness and death. The man in the south controls the thunder. He gave man fire as a weapon against the cold. When the woman and the man went to the north and the south, Heammawihio was alone again, so he created other people. These people multiplied and became the Tsi-Tsi-Tsas, which means those related to one another. Later, our brothers, the Dakotas, would call them, Sha-Hi-Ye-Na, meaning people of alien speech. The white man would pronounce it Cheyenne, and that is what they call our people to this day."

Heecha sighed as the story ended, his eyelids fluttering down. Mary was already asleep, her head pillowed on Shadow's lap.

Carefully, I lifted Mary and placed her on her own bed while Shadow carried Heecha to his bed on the other side of the fire and covered him. My heart swelled with emotion as Shadow stood there for a moment, his dark eyes warm with love for his son. He was a good father, patient and kind. He never got angry with our children, never punished them, never raised his voice. When they did wrong, he explained why their behavior was not acceptable. Always, he was gentle and understanding, listening to their questions, giving them honest answers they could easily understand.

Bending, Shadow reached under Heecha's bed and withdrew a beautifully embroidered shawl. "Merry Christmas, Hannah," he said, and kissed me as he draped the shawl around my shoulders.

I knew the shawl had been stolen from some store or clothesline across the border, but I did not chide Shadow for

stealing it. Once, long ago, I would have
been shocked at the very idea of accepting
stolen goods, but the Indians considered
raiding and stealing from the enemy an
honorable trait, and so I smiled at my husband as I murmured my thanks.

My gift to Shadow was a new shirt. I
had tanned and worked the deerskin until
it was the color of fresh cream, as soft as
velvet. Footlong fringe dangled from the
sleeves. The back was embroidered with
a red-tail hawk, wings outstretched in
flight, talons curved.

"It is beautiful, Hannah," Shadow
said, pleased. "Truly a fine gift."

"Put it on."

Shrugging out of his old shirt, Shadow
slipped the new one over his head. My
heart began to flutter wildly as I looked at
him. How handsome he was! The soft
cream-colored buckskin emphasized the
blackness of his hair and the dark bronze
of his skin. The soft cloth hugged his
broad shoulders and powerful arms, and I
felt a quick surge of desire as he bent his
head over mine.

"Haho." He whispered the Cheyenne
word for thank you as his lips brushed
mine.

I clung to him, feeling my knees go
weak and my blood turn to fire as his kiss
deepened. Once I had thought such
volatile feelings would mellow with age
and the passage of time, but I knew now

that even when I was old and gray, Shadow's touch would still have the power to ignite the passion in my soul and leave me breathless with desire.

I protested when he took his lips from mine, but he only grinned at me as, carefully, he removed his shirt and neatly folded it and put it away. Then, dark eyes alight with desire, he reached for me again. I melted in his arms and as his mouth closed over mine, I had the best Christmas present of all.

III

Spring 1884

It was the Time of Little Eagles when they rode into our valley, forty warriors ranging in age from sixteen to fifty, and one woman. The Indians were mounted on weary ponies, their copper-hued faces streaked with dust and old war paint, their lances and rifles glinting in the light of the rising sun.

I felt a cold chill skitter along my spine as I recognized the squat, flat-faced warrior riding in front. Geronimo. I glanced at Shadow, standing beside me, my fear plainly etched on my face and in my eyes.

"Stay here," Shadow cautioned, and went out to meet the fierce Apache chief and his men.

"Welcome, Geronimo," Shadow said, raising his right hand in the universal sign for peace. "What brings you to our valley?"

I did not need to hear Geronimo's answer to know they were on the run. His warriors had the wary look of hunted men about them. It was a look I had seen many times in the past.

"We are seeking shelter on our way to the Cima-Silkq," Geronimo replied, confirming my fears. His flat black eyes moved over our lodge, missing nothing, then darted to Calf Running's wickiup, which was set up a short distance from ours.

"Ho, brother," Calf Running called as he emerged from his lodge. "It is good to see you again."

"It is good to see you, Calf Running," Geronimo replied in greeting.

"Come, step down and eat with us," Calf Running invited. Unconsciously, he slipped into his native tongue as he spoke to Geronimo. It was a harsh, guttural language, one I had never fully mastered.

Geronimo nodded curtly as he stepped down from his paint pony. This was a man who had known war for most of his life. He was a Bedonkohe Apache who had lived a life of peace until his family was murdered by Mexican troops, and then he turned into a man of vengeance. It was the Mexicans who gave him the name Geronimo. In the 1860's, he had married a Chiricahua woman and lived with her people, according to Apache custom. When Cochise decided to try the path of peace, Geronimo left the Chiricahuas and continued to ride the warpath, raiding into Mexico and Arizona. Now, at the age of fifty-five, he was still at war.

His warriors and the young woman warrior known as Lozen, dismounted and squatted on the ground, their faces devoid of expression. Lozen, I later learned, was so honored and respected by the Apache warriors that she was granted a place in their tribal councils. A rare honor, for an Apache woman.

Flower Woman came to stand beside me, her lovely black eyes mirroring my own concern. Geronimo was on the war trail again, and his presence in our valley could only mean trouble for us sooner or later.

While Flower Woman and I sliced and cooked a deer Shadow had killed the day before, the men sat in the shade, smoking and talking. Life on the reservation was no good, Geronimo said, his voice bitter. Apaches were meant to live free in the Cima-Silkq, the Sierra Madre Mountains, not to live like cattle penned up on a reservation waiting for the white man to feed them. There was never enough food or blankets. The old people died of sickness, the children cried for food, the women grieved for their dead. And the warriors—they chafed at the enforced inactivity. Denied weapons of any kind, they could not hunt for meat to alleviate their hunger. It was a bad way to live. It was not honorable, to sit passively by while your women and children cried and your old ones died of hunger and disease. A man had to defend his honor, to fight for his freedom, or he was not a man. And Geronimo meant to fight. He had left the San Carlos Reservation in the fall of 1881, taking 310 men, women, and children with him. Among those who had fled the hated reservation with him were Victorio, Old Nana, Juh, and his son, Delshinne. They had been raiding on both sides of the border ever since, using the Cima-Silkq as their base. In the two years since their escape, Victorio had been killed in a Mexican ambush at Tres Castillos, and Juh had drowned while crossing a stream. Many warriors had been killed.

But the fighting went on.

"Will you join us, Two Hawks Flying?" The question came from Geronimo, and I felt my insides turn to ice as I waited for Shadow's reply.

Slowly, Shadow shook his head. "No. I will fight no more. We have made a good life here, and here I will stay. Nohetto."

Geronimo did not like Shadow's answer. His displeasure was clearly reflected in his flat black eyes, and in the way his mouth went white around the corners.

"And you, Calf Running," Geronimo asked gruffly. "Will you fight with your

people, or have you grown soft and weak
like this yudastcin Cheyenne?''

Shadow's face grew dark at the brazen
insult. His hand moved toward the knife
sheathed on his belt, and only Calf
Running's restraining grasp on Shadow's
arm prevented violence from erupting in
our valley.

Calf Running's dark eyes met
Geronimo's in a bold stare. "I will stay
here," he said clearly, "with my Cheyenne
brother and his family."

Geronimo glared at Calf Running. For
a moment, I thought the war leader would
kill us all. Then, slowly, he turned his bull-
like head toward the hills.

"This is Apache land," he said curtly,
his eyes burning into those of Calf
Running. "You will not tell anyone we
have been here."

"I will not tell."

Shadow's eyes narrowed thoughtfully
as he glanced from one trail-weary warrior
to another. "You are being followed." His
voice was thick with accusation and anger
as he faced Geronimo.

The old Apache chief nodded.
"Nantan Lupan trails us. He is using
Apache scouts to track us."

Nantan Lupan meant Gray Fox. It
was the name the Apaches had given to
General George Crook. Crook was a
formidable opponent, a renowned Indian
fighter, yet it was said he was sympathetic

to the plight of the Apache.

"And you led him here!" Shadow glanced at our snug lodge, at our garden growing along the riverbank, at the meat drying on the rack beside our lodge. And then, with one hand shading his eyes against the bright morning sunlight, he glanced into the hills. Whatever he saw made him swear under his breath, and I could not help smiling faintly as I heard him mutter one of my father's favorite cuss words.

"Hannah, pack whatever you can carry. Flower Woman, you had best do the same."

The note of urgency in Shadow's voice sent a ripple of unrest through Geronimo's warriors. They rose to their feet, their weapons at hand, their hooded eyes scouring the countryside.

My heart was pounding with an old familiar fear as I ran into our lodge and began to stuff our clothing and cooking utensils into Shadow's war bag. Heecha woke up as I moved about the lodge.

"What's wrong?" he asked sleepily.

"Get up," I said, trying to keep the panic out of my voice. "We're leaving. Can you catch up the horses for me?"

"Yes, nahkoa."

"Put on your heavy shirt first."

Wordlessly, my son did as bidden. I felt a quick surge of pride as his stout legs carried him out of the lodge. How grown

up he was! He did not waste time asking
questions as so many boys his age might
have. Instead, he went quickly to do as
told.

I packed a change of clothing for each
of us, some jerky and pemmican, the shirt
I had made for Shadow, the shawl he had
given me. When I had packed everything I
thought essential, I went outside. Mary
trailed at my heels, one hand entwined in
my skirt. Geronimo and his men were
mounted, their faces inscrutable. Lozen
swung aboard her calico pony, her face set
in fierce lines.

I searched for Shadow and Calf
Running and saw them standing near Calf
Running's wickiup, their heads close
together. Flower Woman threw me a
shaky smile as she gathered Nachi in her
arms, and I knew she was as nervous and
upset as I was.

The tension in our little valley was so
thick I wanted to scream. Someone was up
in the hills, waiting, watching. Was it
Crook? I knew George Crook only by
reputation. He was a redoubtable Indian
fighter, feared and respected by all the
tribes. In 1852, he graduated from West
Point, ranking 38 in a class of 43. In '76, he
had fought the Sioux and Cheyenne at the
Rosebud and been defeated. The Indians
had considered it a great victory, to out-
fight "Three Stars." It was said that
Crook rarely wore his Army uniform, pre-

ferring to wear a canvas hunting suit. He
had one other peculiarity in that he preferred to ride an old gray mule, appro-
priately named "Apache," rather than a
horse, maintaining that mules had more
sense than horses, were better gaited, and
more sure-footed.

I glanced up into the hills surrounding
our valley and saw nothing. What had
Shadow seen?

"Are you ready, Hannah?"

Shadow had come up behind me, his
moccasined feet making no sound on the
soft grass.

"Yes."

With a nod, Shadow swung effortless-
ly aboard his spotted stallion. Bending
from the waist, he reached down and lifted
Heecha up behind him. I felt a shiver of
apprehension race along my spine as I
stared at the paint streaked across
Shadow's face and chest. Sometimes, I
forgot how savage he could be. Living in
our little valley, I had seen only his gentle
side—the loving husband, the caring
father, the good friend. Now, staring up at
him, I saw Two Hawks Flying, the
Cheyenne warrior. A single eagle feather
was tied in his long black hair; fringed
leggings, deerskin clout and moccasins
were all he wore. The red paint streaked on
his chest reminded me of blood . . .

I felt an ache in my heart as I watched
Shadow ride to where the Apache warriors

were gathered. If there was a fight, I knew
Shadow would be in the thick of it. And
Heecha with him.

Flower Woman came to ride beside
me. Nachi rode behind her, his chubby
arms tight around her waist. Mary rode in
front of me, her doll clasped to her side.

Single file, we rode out of the valley,
heading south, toward Mexico. A handful
of scouts rode ahead, Geronimo and the
rest of his warriors rode behind us.

We had not gone far when gunshots
sounded behind us. Instantly, the scouts
riding point came racing past us. I fought
down a rising tide of panic as my horse
lined out in a dead run. Mary began to cry
and I held her against my breast,
shielding her tiny body with my own.

We ran for what seemed like miles,
until our horses were lathered with sweat
and then, to my horror, I heard gunshots
from somewhere up ahead. I jerked back
on my horse's reins as soldiers streamed
out of a stand of trees. Fearing for Mary's
life, I guided my horse toward a thicket
and stayed there, hidden from view, while
the fighting raged all around me. I had
lost track of Flower Woman. Now, as I
tried to soothe Mary, I prayed that my
friend had also found a place to hide, that
Shadow and Calf Running would not be
killed, that we would be able to return to
the valley.

The Apaches were badly outnum-

bered, yet they fought valiantly. The air
was filled with the sound of their ferocious
war cries. Dust swirled around the com-
batants, adding an unreal quality to the
scene of death and destruction. I searched
through the wild melee for Shadow and
Calf Running, felt my throat tighten as I
saw Shadow and a burly soldier grappling
over a long-bladed knife.

The rest of the battle faded away as I
watched Shadow wrest his knife from the
soldier's grasp. My husband's face,
streaked with crimson paint, was awful to
see. I did not often think of Shadow as an
Indian. He was my husband, the father of
my children, the man I loved. The color of
his skin had never been a problem. I knew
what he was, what he believed in, and
loved him the more for it. But sometimes,
as now, his Indian heritage was brought
vividly to mind.

Eyes blazing with hatred, mouth open
in a feral snarl, Shadow plunged the knife
into the soldier's neck. Blood spurted from
the man's severed jugular vein, spraying
over Shadow's hands and arms. Raising
his fist over his head, Shadow voiced the
Cheyenne cry of victory.

Sickened by the sight of so much
blood, I turned away, suddenly conscious
of an abrupt quiet. The battle was over.
The Indians had surrendered.

Shadow came to me while the soldiers
were rounding up the Apaches and looking

after the wounded.

"What happened?" I asked, trying not to notice the blood drying on Shadow's hands and arms.

"Crook has captured Geronimo. They are taking us to San Carlos."

"San Carlos! But we're not Apaches. Won't they let us go?"

Shadow glanced at the blood staining his hand. "I do not think so," he muttered ruefully.

"Where is Flower Woman?"

"Dead." There was a world of sorrow behind the single, softly-spoken word.

"And Nachi?"

"Dead." Shadow's dark eyes glittered with hatred as he glared at the soldiers milling about in the distance.

"Does Calf Running know?"

"Yes. He has vowed to kill the man responsible."

Tears pricked my eyes, but I could not cry here, not in front of our enemies. Biting down hard on my lower lip, I forced myself to stare straight ahead, but all the while I was seeing Calf Running and Flower Woman walking hand in hand beside the river while Nachi skipped alongside. How happy they had been! I remembered the day Flower Woman's child had been born. I had been the first to see the child, the first to hold him. And now he was dead, his bright black eyes forever closed, his happy laughter forever stilled.

"Heecha!" Panic tore through my breast as I realized I had not seen my own son since the battle began.

"Hannah, be still. He is all right."

"Where is he?"

"Riding with 'Three Stars.' "

"With Crook?"

"The man saved his life. Heecha fell off my horse while I was fighting with one of the bluecoats. Crook rode by and carried him to safety."

"Thank God," I murmured, drawing Mary close. At least my children were safe and well.

In a short time, the dead were buried, the wounded had been cared for, and we began the long trek to San Carlos.

That night, after putting Mary and Heecha to bed, I met General George Crook. He was a man to inspire both fear and confidence. I could see why the Apache called him the Gray Fox, for his hair, eyes and beard were gray. I liked him immediately, for he seemed a kind and caring man. He spoke well of Heecha's courage during the battle.

"And you, ma'am?" Crook inquired politely. "Are you a captive?"

"No. My husband is Two Hawks Flying, of the Cheyenne."

"Cheyenne?" Crook glanced thoughtfully at Shadow sitting quietly beside me. "I thought you were a bit tall for an

Apache," Crook remarked to Shadow. "How come you to be riding with Geronimo and his broncos?"

"They came to us," Shadow replied curtly.

Crook nodded. "Well, I'm afraid you'll have to go to San Carlos with the others for now. I imagine, in time, you'll be shipped to Pine Ridge or Red Cloud."

Shadow's face betrayed no sign of emotion, but I could feel the anger rising within him. I knew he would not go willingly to a reservation, any reservation.

"And you, ma'am, do you have relatives hereabouts?"

"No."

"Back east, perhaps?"

"No."

"I see." Crook stroked his beard thoughtfully. "I can take you to Fort Thomas with me, if you like."

"I prefer to stay with my husband."

Crook looked doubtful, but before he could say anything, there was an outraged cry from across the camp as Calf Running sprang at one of the soldiers, his good hand reaching for the man's throat. I knew without being told that the soldier was the person responsible for Flower Woman's death, and Nachi's, too.

A gunshot rang out, echoing in the stillness of the night, and Calf Running went suddenly limp as a dark red stain blossomed across his back.

Instantly, Shadow was on his feet, a shrill war cry issuing from his lips as he hurled himself at the trooper who had shot Calf Running in the back. Shadow's hands went around the soldier's throat, his momentum carrying both men to the ground. Shadow's eyes were narrowed with fury as his strong brown fingers tightened around the white man's neck, slowly choking the life from his body.

I screamed as a soldier wearing the stripes of a sergeant pulled his sidearm and fired at my husband. Shadow turned when he heard my frightened cry and the bullet meant for his back grazed his rib-cage instead. Two other troopers sprang forward, grabbing Shadow's arms, pulling him away from the unconscious man on the ground.

"Bind him!"

The words, harshly spoken, were Crook's. "How's Fenton?"

"He's coming around, sir," answered one of the troopers.

"Have the sawbones take a look at him. Sergeant Higgins, I want two men standing guard over Geronimo and this Cheyenne at all times. Rogers, pick a detail to watch the horses."

When Crook had finished issuing his orders, I asked if I might tend Shadow's wound. Crook agreed with a curt nod of his head, warning me not to try to free

Shadow's hands or feet or sneak him a weapon.

I obtained a clean cloth, salve, and bandages from the Army doctor and then went to see Shadow. Kneeling beside him, I saw he was wearing what I called his Indian face, that peculiar expressionless mask that hid his feelings as effectively as a shroud. An armed soldier stood behind him, rifle at the ready.

Wordlessly, I began to wipe away the blood smeared across Shadow's ribs. I knew the wound was painful, but he never flinched, not when I wiped away the blood, not when I applied the thick yellow salve, not when I wound the bandage around his middle.

I looked at my husband as I tied off the bandage, willing him to acknowledge my presence, willing him to feel my love, but he refused to meet my eyes. Instead, he stared, unblinking, into the distance. Briefly, I touched his shoulder. Then, head high, I went to sit beside our children. Mary was still sleeping peacefully, her doll tucked under one arm, but Heecha was awake.

"Nahkoa, why is my father tied up like that?" my son asked, a puzzled expression furrowing his brow.

"Because the soldiers are afraid of him," I said, wondering how best to explain what had happened to Heecha.

"They know your father is a mighty warrior chief like Geronimo."

Heecha smiled proudly. He could understand that.

The rest of the journey to San Carlos passed uneventfully. Shadow was silent and withdrawn, reminding me of another time, long ago, when he had been a prisoner of the Army. I remembered those days as we traveled mile after mile. Shadow and I had taken refuge in a cave high on a hill when a troop of the Seventh Cavalry found us. I had been in labor with our first child that day and very frightened, not only of the soldiers, but of delivering my baby in the wildnerness with no doctor to help me, no woman to assist me. Filled with doubts and fears, I had started to cry . . .

Shadow whispered my name as he took me into his arms. Oh, the strength and comfort in his embrace, the magical solace I found as he held me, gently rocking me back and forth as if I were a child.

Outside, a light rain began to fall. It was soon over, and the world was deathly still, as if every living creature were holding its breath. And then, from some-where in the distance, a horse whinnied. Quick as a cat, Shadow was at the mouth of the cave.

"*Major Kelly's scouts have found us, haven't they?*" *I asked.*

"*It is not Kelly.*"

"*Not Kelly. Who, then?*"

"*It is the Seventh,*" *Shadow answered quietly, and then he laughed.* "*I suspect they have come to get even for Custer. I knew they would never forgive us for that.*"

"*Shadow, you've got to get out of here!*" *I cried, frantic for his safety.* "*Go now, before it's too late.*"

"*It is already too late,*" *he replied tonelessly.*

Rising, he removed his buckskin shirt. Then, while I watched, he began to paint his face and chest for war. My pains were temporarily forgotten as I watched him apply vermilion paint to his torso, the broad zigzag slashes like ribbons of blood across his flesh. Smaller, similar slashes marked his cheeks.

That done, he reached for his warbonnet. And Shadow, the man, became Two Hawks Flying, the warrior. I knew he was going out to meet the soldiers, that he intended to die fighting like the proud Cheyenne warrior he was, with a weapon in his hand and a last prayer to Man Above on his lips. And though I knew he didn't have a chance in a million if he went out of the cave armed and ready to fight, and though I knew he would surrender if I but asked him to, I could not voice the words.

When he was ready, he took my hand in his, and I felt my heart swell with love for the tall, handsome man kneeling at my side.

"I love you, Hannah," he said quietly. "See that our son grows brave and strong. Never let him forget that he carries the blood of many great Cheyenne warriors in his veins."

"I won't," I promised, choking back a sob as he left the cave without a backward glance.

I heard him call Red Wind, and in my mind's eye I saw Shadow swing aboard the tall stallion with the effortless grace I had always admired. And suddenly I knew I had to see him one last time.

Teeth clenched, I struggled to my knees and crawled to the entrance of the cave. I had to stop twice as pains doubled me in half, but I went determinedly forward. I was breathing hard when I reached the mouth of the cave... Lead whined into the hillside around Shadow, gouging great chunks of dirt from the earth, and my mind screamed for him to run, to hide. But he might have been a statue carved from stone.

And then the soldiers were too close to miss. I saw one of them line his sights on Shadow's chest and I screamed, "Josh, no!" and stumbled out of the cave.

And then I was falling head over heels down the icy hillside. A terrible pain stabbed through me, followed by a rush of warm water, and I screamed Shadow's name as I felt myself being torn in half. And then I was falling again, falling into a deep black void . . .

I shook my head, clearing the images from my mind. The next few weeks had been awful. I mourned for my stillborn child, buried while I was delirious. I ached inside for Shadow, who was under heavy guard, his arms and legs tightly bound as they were now, his face an impassive mask.

Joshua Berdeen had been all kind concern in the next few days, hovering over me, making certain I was comfortable and warm, reminiscing about the good old days back in Bear Valley.

Josh had vowed he still loved me, that he wanted to take care of me. Shadow was going to hang, Josh had told me, as if the matter were of little importance. The Army wanted him out of the way once and for all. I had begged Josh to think of some way to save Shadow from hanging. And he had. He had promised to arrange for Shadow to escape from the stockade. All I had to do was become Mrs. Joshua Berdeen.

I could not believe Josh meant what he said, but he did, and in the end, I had married him. To have refused would have meant Shadow's death, and I could not allow that, not when I could stop it. My marriage to Joshua had been a failure from the beginning, but I had consoled myself with the knowledge that Shadow, at least, was alive and free. It was not until much later that I learned Josh had deceived me . . .

My reverie came to a halt as Crook brought the column to a stop for the night.

The next day we reached the San Carlos Reservation.

IV

The San Carlos Reservation, nicknamed Hell's Forty Acres, was the most dismal plot of ground I had ever seen. The land was flat and gravelly, dotted here and there by the drab buildings of the Agency. Cottonwood trees, shrunken and scrawny, marked the course of a shallow stream. Rain was infrequent in this part of the country; when it came, it was almost a miracle. Hot dusty winds swept across the flat ground, destroying vegetation. Temperatures soared in the summer—110 degrees in the shade was considered a cool day. Flies and gnats and a host of other bugs swarmed in the air.

I saw hungry, dirty, frightened Indian children darting behind bushes or into their wickiups as we approached, and I held Mary closer to me. Surely we would not have to stay in this awful place; surely my daughter would not have to live like these poor children.

As I glanced around, I met the sullen, hopeless, suspicious gazes of grown men and women. Their black eyes grew bright with hate as they watched the soldiers ride up. Geronimo's chains were removed and he walked haughtily toward a brush-covered wickiup and ducked inside. Several warriors turned and followed him.

Shadow was also released. I went to stand beside him, uncertain of what we were going to do. Crook had gone to his headquarters at Fort Bowie, promising to try and get us transferred to another reservation.

Shadow's face reflected the horror of what he saw as he glanced around the reservation. Warriors sat cross-legged in the scant shade of their wickiups, a few women stood together holding a listless conversation. I shuddered at the thought of remaining in this terrible place. The Indians stared at us impassively, betraying no sign of curiosity or friend-liness.

With a resolute sigh, Shadow swung Heecha to his shoulders, took me by the hand, and led us toward the stream. He stopped at a level area shaded by a stunted cottonwood. This was to be our home.

I cannot describe the misery of the next few days. No one spoke to us. We had little to eat, no shelter from the blazing sun. Mary cried constantly, begging to go home. Heecha stayed close to his father, his eyes frightened though he tried to put up a brave front.

Little by little, we heard about life at San Carlos. The government had some hazy idea that the Apaches should take up agriculture. I could only wonder how the men in Washington expected the Indians to farm when there was no irrigation, no tools, and no seed. The Indians might have raised cattle, but no cattle ever came. They refused to raise hogs because hogs ate snakes, and snakes were taboo.

The longer we stayed at San Carlos, the more I could understand why the Indians were so miserable. Day after day they were left with nothing to do, nothing to occupy their hands or minds. Geronimo, who was naturally suspicious and surly, grew more and more resentful of the conditions of his people. He began to drink heavily, consuming great quantities of tiswin, which was Apache beer brewed from corn.

The summer passed and fall was in the air. Shadow grew more and more despondent. Heecha grew thin. Mary was too listless to cry. Daily, I went to Agent Tiffany and begged him to let us leave the reservation. I never told Shadow that I was pleading with a white man for our release, knowing he would be furious.

Daily, Agent Tiffany said no.

Finally, in late autumn, word came from Crook that we were to be transferred to the Rosebud Reservation in the Dakotas. The good news was dampened by the fact that Shadow was to travel in the prison wagon under heavy guard, his feet shackled. One of the officers at Fort Bowie had recognized Shadow's name and informed Crook that the man known as Shadow was, in reality, the Cheyenne war chief known as Two Hawks Flying and was considered to be quite dangerous and should be treated accordingly.

My heart grieved for Shadow. He was a proud man and I knew being in chains wounded his fierce pride. He did not resist when the chains were locked around his ankles. He stood tall and straight, his eyes heavy with disdain. Word that he was considered dangerous spread quickly and three men now stood guard around him while a fourth checked the irons on his feet.

One of the soldiers prodded Shadow in the back. "Get in the wagon, redskin," the man ordered brusquely, and jabbed his rifle barrel into Shadow's back a second time.

Shadow whirled around, his black eyes filled with rage, and the soldier took a step backward, cowed by the anger in Shadow's eyes.

The other three soldiers chuckled,

amused by the man's needless fear. After all, the Indian was in chains and the frightened trooper was holding a rifle. But then Shadow's dark eyes swept over the other soldiers and the laughter died in their throats. Unarmed and in chains, Two Hawks Flying was still a formidable presence.

Shadow's lips curled down in contempt as he climbed into the back of the prison wagon and sat down on the raw plank that served as a makeshift seat. Agent Tiffany said my children and I could ride in front, but we chose to ride in the back with Shadow.

The trip was uneventful. I was glad to be leaving San Carlos behind. Surely conditions at the Rosebud Reservation would be better. And even if they weren't, at least we would be among Shadow's people. I wondered what had become of his father, Black Elk, and of his wives, Fawn and New Leaf. I remembered how kind they had all been to me, how they had shared their lodge with us before Shadow and I had enough skins for a lodge of our own. I remembered Crazy Horse, the mighty war chief of the Oglala Bad Face Band. He had been one of the major leaders in the battle against Custer. He had been killed at the Red Cloud Agency in September of '77. The commander of Fort Robinson had tried to have the Sioux chief arrested and when Crazy Horse resisted, a soldier had thrust a bayonet into his side.

Shadow said little on the journey to Rosebud. Often, I saw him gazing at the familiar landscape, a melancholy expression on his handsome face. I knew he was dreaming of the old days when he had lived in these hills and valleys as a free man.

Heecha and Mary were confused and upset. Heecha did not understand why we had left the valley, or why his father was in chains. He said little, but his dark eyes mirrored his confusion. Mary clung to me, refusing to let me out of her sight for even a moment. Often, she woke crying in the night and it took hours to quiet her.

One morning the wagon passed near Bear Valley and my heart ached for those wonderful carefree days when I had been a young girl in love, with my whole life ahead of me.

At last, we reached the reservation. Shadow was freed of his shackles and we made our way toward the Indian lodges that were scattered at random. I looked at each person we passed, hoping to see a familiar face, and almost fainted dead away when I saw a big man dressed in buckskins coming toward us. A man who was not an Indian. A man with curly brown hair and a graying red moustache.

"Pa!" The word erupted from my throat in a hoarse cry of joy and disbelief.

My father stared at me for a long moment, his eyes riveted on my face. "Hannah!" he exclaimed jubilantly. "My God, is it really you?"

I nodded, and then we were in each other's arms, hugging as if we would never let go. Tears of happiness flooded my eyes and cascaded down my cheeks as I laid my head against my father's chest. All these years I had thought him dead and now he was here, very much alive. It was a miracle.

When we could finally tear ourselves apart, we took a long look at each other. I could not stop smiling as I studied my father. He had changed little since I had seen him last. He was still tall and broad, his shoulders as wide as a barn door. His hair, though graying, was still thick and curly. His sideburns were still long, his eyes remained a deep bright blue. And yet he was different, and I knew he was still grieving for my mother who had been dead for almost nine years, killed by the Sioux back in Bear Valley.

"Pa, you remember Shadow?" I said at last.

"Of course." Pa's voice was warm and friendly.

Quite a switch from the old days, I thought, surprised and pleased.

"I knew I could count on you to look after my girl," Pa said, offering Shadow his hand. "It's good to see you again."

Shadow looked at Pa's outstretched hand for several moments, obviously remembering the many quarrels they had had in the past. Then, with a nod, Shadow shook my father's hand.

"And who might these young'uns be?" Pa asked, smiling down at Heecha and Mary, who were standing quietly beside Shadow.

"This is Heecha," I said proudly. "And this is Mary."

"Mary." Pa choked on the name as he caught Mary into his arms and gave her a hug. There were tears in his eyes, when he looked at me, and I knew he was remembering my mother.

"Come along," Pa said gruffly. Pivoting on his heel, he led us to a squat wooden cabin located near a slow-moving river. An Indian woman emerged from the house as we drew near. Her hair was long and gray, her face lined with age.

"Sunbird, this is my daughter, Hannah, her husband, Two Hawks Flying, of the Cheyenne, and their children, Heecha and Mary." Pa's face flushed a bit as he put one arm around the old woman's shoulders. "This here is Sunbird, my adopted mother."

I blinked in astonishment. Mother! I looked at Shadow and saw the same surprised expression on his face. My father had hated all Indians for as long as I could remember, but then, he had good reason.

His parents, a sister and two brothers had been killed by Blackfeet Indians when Pa was just a little boy. Pa had been left for dead and would surely have died of starvation and exposure if a kindhearted old mountain man hadn't happened along and found Pa wandering around the charred ruins of his family's covered wagon.

Pa smiled sheepishly. "Let's go inside," he suggested. "I think we have a lot of catching up to do."

The cabin was small, a parlor, a kitchen, and two bedrooms, but it was clean and well cared-for. Colorful Indian rugs covered the floor and decorated one wall. Two overstuffed chairs were placed before the fireplace, a square oak table between them. There was a small table and two chairs in the kitchen. There was no stove, so I assumed Sunbird preferred to cook Indian-style over an open fire. Bright blue and white gingham curtains fluttered at the open windows. A Sioux lodge could be seen through the East window and I knew somehow that it belonged to Sunbird.

My father and I sat in the chairs before the fireplace. Shadow sat cross-legged on the floor. Sunbird sat on the edge of the raised hearth stirring a large pot of stew. Heecha and Mary curled up on the rug before the hearth and were soon asleep, lulled by the fire and the conversation.

My father's story was quite amazing. After Shadow had come and taken me away, the fighting had resumed. Hobie Brown and his sons, who had taken refuge with us after their homestead was destroyed by marauding Indians, had all been killed as the battle went on. Pa, enraged, grieving for the loss of my mother and his friends, had fired round after round into the midst of the Indians, killing many warriors. When the Indians decided to burn him out, Pa had charged out the front door, a pistol in each hand, a mighty shout on his lips.

The Sioux had pulled back until he was out of ammunition; then, apparently admiring his courage and fighting spirit, they had taken him prisoner. He had been at the Greasy Grass when Custer was killed, bound and gagged inside a Sioux lodge. So close, I thought, and I had never known he was there.

After the massacre, he had been taken, still captive, to the Dakotas where he had been a slave to a warrior known as Standing Elk. It had been a hard life for my father. He had been mocked and reviled, abused and beaten, but his hatred had kept him strong. He had tried to escape many times, but each time he had been caught and whipped. And then, unexpectedly, Standing Elk's mother had decided to adopt the white man to take the place of another son who died from pneumonia. Eventually, Pa had been accepted by the tribe as one of them. When Standing Elk's band was taken to the reservation, Pa had gone with them. By then, Standing Elk was dead, having been killed by a bear, and Pa did not want to leave Sunbird alone.

At the reservation, Pa had opened a small trading post where he sold a wide variety of supplies to the settlers moving west. He used a good part of the money he made to help feed and clothe the Sioux.

I was speechless as Pa finished his story. Imagine, my father living with the Indians of his own free will. It was beyond belief and yet, he was here.

"Tell me about you, Hannah," Pa urged. "What brings you and Shadow here after such a long time?"

As briefly as I could, I told Pa about my life with Shadow, how we have lived with his people for almost a year after the Custer massacre, how Shadow had refused to go in when his tribe surrendered, how we had lived alone for a short time, and how he had come to lead a band of renegade warriors against the whites.

Pa listened intently as I told of those dreadful days, his eyes darting from my face to Shadow's and back again. I told how Shadow's men had disbanded when we ran out of food and ammunition, how the soldiers had continued to trail Shadow, how they found us at the cave where I lost our firstborn child.

"Josh was very kind," I said.

"Josh!" Pa exclaimed. "Josh Berdeen?"

"Yes. He was in command of the soldiers who found us. He took us to Fort Apache. I . . . I married him."

Pa's eyes grew wide. "Married him?" Pa glanced at Shadow, who had remained silent during my tale.

"Yes. Josh blackmailed me. Shadow was to be hung. I begged Josh to free him and Josh said he would, if I would marry him. So I did."

Pa looked at Shadow again. "And?"

"He did not keep his word," Shadow said flatly. "Like all white men, his words were filled with treachery."

"Not all white men," Pa refuted quietly. "Go on, Hannah."

"Josh freed Shadow from the stockade, but he left him bound in the woods to die of starvation. Two men found Shadow and took him back East where they exhibited him as Two Hawks Flying, the last fighting chief on the plains. Shadow was their prisoner for many months. I didn't know any of this at the time, of course. I thought Shadow had gone back to the Dakotas."

"Where's Josh now?" Pa asked.

"Dead." Shadow spoke the word, and it was filled with satisfaction.

"I was pregnant with Shadow's child

when I married Josh. Josh was outraged when he discovered the baby wasn't his. He threatened to give the child away. I knew he meant to do it and I ran away. Josh came after me. He found me in the same cave where he had found us before. Josh was going to make me leave Heecha in the cave to die. But Shadow came and changed all that."

Pa looked at Shadow again.

"I left him wounded in the wilderness, as he had left me," Shadow said flatly. His dark eyes moved possessively over my face. "And I took back what was mine."

Pa nodded. I could see by his expression that he understood why Shadow had done what he had done to Josh. Once, Pa would have been outraged by such seeming cruelty, but no more. He had lived with the Sioux long enough to become acquainted with their beliefs, their way of life. Indian justice was rarely as civilized as white justice, but the punishment always fit the crime.

"We went to Mexico after that," I went on. "Shadow fought with Geronimo for a little while, but when Geronimo decided to winter at the reservation, we left. Shadow and I and another Indian couple lived in a little valley at the foot of the Sierra Madres until this summer when Crook came through rounding up Apaches. We spent the last few months at San Carlos. It was horrible."

Pa nodded. "We've heard a lot of bad things about San Carlos. The agent, Tiffany, was recently indicted by a Federal grand jury for keeping eleven men in confinement for fourteen months. The men were innocent of any crime. Hopefully, conditions will improve now that Army officers have taken over running the place. If they can get rid of Sieber and Mickey Free, maybe the Apaches will settle down."

I had heard of Al Sieber. He was a big Pennsylvania Dutchman who was a natural gunman and utterly ruthless. It was reported that he had once gunned down an Apache prisoner in order to save on rations. He was hated and feared by the Indians. Mickey Free was half Mexican and half Irish. He had been raised by Apaches and often acted as an interpreter, though he could not be trusted. The Indians despised him.

"So," Pa said. "You're here. You'll stay with us, of course, until you can get a place of your own."

I looked at Shadow. "Is that all right with you?"

"If it is what you want," Shadow answered tonelessly.

"We'll stay," I said, grateful at the thought of living in a house and sleeping on a bed.

Later, after we had eaten and the children were tucked in for the night, we four adults sat outside drinking coffee.

"I never gave up hoping that someday I'd find you," my father remarked. "Every few months I went around to the other agencies, hoping to hear news of your whereabouts."

Shadow leaned forward. "Did you ever hear anything about my father?"

Pa nodded slowly. "He's dead, Shadow. He died at the Red Cloud Agency two years ago."

"And his wives?" The question was mine.

"The young one died of a fever quite some time ago. I think the older one lives at Standing Rock with her sister's family."

We were suddenly silent.

Images of Shadow's family drifted across my mind. I remembered his father, Black Owl, as I had seen him the first time: a tall proud man wrapped in a red blanket. The moment I saw him, I knew he was Shadow's father. He had the same hawk-like nose, the same stubborn set to his mouth, the same fathomless black eyes. I remembered seeing Black Owl standing under a starry sky, his arms raised in prayer as he pleaded with Maheo for the life of his son. I remembered the last sad day when Black Owl decided to take his people to the reservation. Tears had burned my eyes as I watched the two warriors embrace for the last time, deeply moved by the love and respect they had for one another.

"Come with us," Black Owl had urged. "You cannot fight the white man alone."

Shadow had laughed hollowly. "I am not foolish enough to try," he had said. "But neither will I surrender my freedom."

I remembered standing at Shadow's side as his people left Bear Valley for the last time . . .

I thought of New Leaf, Black Owl's wife. She had been kind to me in the days when Shadow and I had shared her lodge. She had been about forty then, with a wide expressive face and a tendency to be plump. Her eyes were always sad, even when she smiled. Later, I had learned that New Leaf had lost two children. She was quiet and soft-spoken but she had a quick mind and I had often overheard Black Owl discussing tribal affairs with her late at night. She had given me my first pair of moccasins.

Black Owl's second wife, Fawn, had been one of my dearest friends. Seeing how awkward and cumbersome my long skirt and petticoats were, she had given me one of her dresses to wear until I could make some of my own. She had been a changeable creature, her moods shifting from merriment to anger and back again, sometimes in the space of a few moments.

I had often seen Black Owl scowling at her as if trying to decide whether to scold her or hug her.

In the beginning, I had been shocked to learn that Black Owl had two wives, more shocked to think that a girl of seventeen could be married to a man close to fifty. Fawn did not seem concerned that her husband had another wife, although I found such an idea shocking and immoral. Fawn, however, seemed quite pleased with her situation.

"Why should I not like it?" she had asked. "Black Owl is a brave warrior and a good provider. We always have meat in our lodge. And the work is not so hard when there are two to do it."

Later, I realized there was nothing immoral or sordid in a man having two wives. It was, in fact, a practical solution to a major problem, for the women far outnumbered the men and a warrior often married an aged squaw or a widow simply to provide her with shelter and protection.

And now Black Owl and Fawn were dead.

Shadow rose silently to his feet and moved soundlessly down the porch stairs out into the darkness beyond the house. My father and Sunbird and I made small talk for several minutes, and then I went to look for Shadow.

I found him standing under a windblown pine, his face lifted toward the sky, his arms upraised in prayer. I came to a halt some twenty feet away, not wanting to intrude on such a private moment. How beautiful he was, standing there in the dappled moonlight. His black hair hung loose to his waist, as smooth as the hide of a panther, as black as the night around us. His profile, outlined in the light of a full moon, was clean and perfect. His body, clothed in dusty leggings, clout, shirt and moccasins, was tall and straight and strong.

Several minutes passed before he lowered his arms, and then he stared into the distance, his eyes dark and brooding.

"Shadow?"

He turned slowly to face me, and I saw the moisture shining in his eyes. I had never seen my husband cry—not when he was wounded in battle, not when our first-born son was born dead, not when his people were defeated for the last time. But he was crying now, for his father, and for a way of life that was forever gone. It was a sight that tore at my heart, and I felt my own eyes fill with tears as I went to him and took him in my arms.

"I'm sorry about your father," I said earnestly. "He was a fine man."

"He is better off dead," Shadow said bitterly. "We would all be better off dead."

"Shadow . . ."

"I cannot live like this!" he said

vehemently. "I would rather be dead my-self!"

"No! Don't talk like that. Please, Shadow, don't give up hope. Things will get better. I know they will."

"They will not."

It frightened me to hear the discouragement in his voice. He had always been the strong one, someone for me to lean on. How would we survive if he gave up now?

The next few weeks were not as bad as I thought they would be. My father and Shadow formed a close friendship that warmed my heart. It was wonderful to see the two men I loved the most walking together, talking without arguing, smoking in companionable silence on the porch in the evening after dinner. Shadow found many old friends on the reservation and his spirits lifted.

Sunbird and I quickly became friends. She was a dear sweet woman, one who loved to be of help to others. She often went calling on those who were sick, taking them a pot of soup, a bit of candy, some fresh baked bread. She also acted as a midwife, staying with the Indian women through their labor, making sure the mothers were comfortable, the babies healthy and able to suckle. She sat with the dying, giving them the warmth of her smile and the strength of her presence.

She quickly grew to love my children as if they were her own blood and before long, Heecha and Mary were calling her grandmother and trailing after her.

After San Carlos, the Rosebud Agency seemed like Heaven, to me at least. I knew Shadow still felt keenly that he was no longer a free man, but I hoped, in time, he would come to accept our new way of life and find happiness.

It was wonderful to be able to bathe in a tub again, to have sweet-smelling soap and hot water and fluffy towels. It was a rare treat to have sugar and cream in my coffee, to be able to munch an apple, to satisfy my sweet tooth with a piece of hard candy.

I bought several yards of material and made dresses for Mary and myself, as well as several shirts for Shadow and Heecha. It seemed strange to wear petticoats and a chemise again. Strange, but nice. I felt feminine again, though I refused to wear stays or a corset. I kept my moccasins, as well. Tight, hard-soled shoes seemed like some kind of Chinese torture after the comfort of Indian footwear.

Shadow continued to wear his buckskins, refusing to don the garb of a white man, Heecha, copying his father, also refused to abandon his buckskins in favor of corduroy and cotton.

I enrolled my son in school at the Fort. Heecha protested loudly, but Shadow insisted he learn to read and write, as he had been taught. It was a useful talent, Shadow said, and Heecha stopped complaining.

"The day will come when you will need to know these things," Shadow had explained. "A wise warrior is one who learns everything he can, even if he must learn from an enemy."

Heecha had been going to school only a few days when he came home with a bloody nose and an eye that was swollen and already turning black.

"What happened?" I asked, horrified.

"Some white boys were making fun of my name," Heecha said. "So I hit them."

"And they hit back?"

"Yes."

"Perhaps we should give you a white name," I suggested. "Then you will not be so different."

"No," Heecha said, lifting his head proudly. "I am not ashamed to be Cheyenne."

"But you are white, too," I reminded him gently.

Heecha looked at Shadow. "Should I change my name, nehyo?"

"If you wish," Shadow replied. "But it must be your decision."

"Do you have a white name?"

"No."

"Have you ever wanted one?"

"No."

Heecha pondered that for a moment. "Will I be able to seek a vision when I am older?" he asked at length.

"I do not know," Shadow answered. "I do not know if the white men will allow you to go into the hills to seek a vision. I do not know if there will be any ancient ones left to guide you in your quest."

"Tell me of your vision, nehyo," Heecha coaxed.

A vision was sacred and not to be bantered about, but Shadow had shared his vision with us several times. It was a story Heecha and Mary never tired of hearing.

"I was sixteen summers," Shadow began, "when I went to Elk Dreamer for instruction. When I had learned the things I needed to know, we went to the sweat lodge to purify ourselves. My father was there also. It was a scared time. I tried to empty my mind of everything as I prayed to Maheo to grant me a vision.

"The next morning, I went to the mountain alone. Morning and evening I made an offering to Man Above and to Mother Earth and to the four directions, pleading with the spirits to grant me a vision. Three days passed and nothing happened, but on the fourth day . . ."

"The hawks came," Heecha interjected, his voice swelling with excitement.

"Yes. The sun was high overhead when it seemed to split in half and out of the middle flew two red-tailed hawks.

" 'Be brave,' the male hawk cried in a loud voice. 'Be brave, and I will always be with you. You shall be swift as the hawk, wise as the owl.' "

"What did the female say?" Mary prompted.

"She said, 'Be strong and I will always be with you. You shall be smart as the hawk, mighty as the eagle.' "

"And that was how you got your name, Two Hawks Flying," Heecha finished.

"Yes."

"Tell about the Sun Dance," Heecha said, his dark eyes glowing as he envisioned himself following in his father's footsteps.

"Elk Dreamer slit my skin, here, and here," Shadow said, touching the scars on his chest. "Skewers were inserted under the skin, and then rawhide thongs were attached to the skewers and I was lifted high into the air to hang from the sacred pole. The pain was great, but it is a pain a man must bear if he would truly be a man. The sun beat upon my flesh and my sweat mingled with my blood as I offered my pain to Man Above, praying that he would accept my suffering."

"And then the hawks came," Heecha said. "The same hawks that came before."

"The very same. 'Be brave,' the male admonished. 'Be brave and you shall be a mighty leader among the People.' "

Shadow smiled at his daughter. "The female said, 'Be strong and everything you desire shall be yours.' "

"Do you have everything you desire?" Heecha asked.

"Yes, naha," Shadow answered, his eyes moving from Heecha's upturned face to mine. "I have everything I ever desired."

"Did the hawks come again?" Heecha asked.

"Once, when I needed them."

"I would like to see them," Heecha said, and Mary nodded a vigorous agreement.

Shadow nodded slowly, a faraway look in his eye, and I knew he was thinking that the hawks would not come to a man who was no longer a warrior.

"I will keep my Indian name," Heecha decided. "And if the white man will not let me go away when it is time for me to seek my vision, then I will run away and go anyway!"

"And I will help you," Shadow vowed.

"And I," I promised, smiling fondly at the men in my life. "But now it is time for dinner."

One afternoon I went to the sutler's store at the fort and came face to face with Kathy Sanders. I stared at her for several minutes, wanting to be certain it was really Kathy. And it was. The same blond hair, the same blue eyes. She was seventeen now, and as pretty as ever.

"Kathy?"

She turned, frowning when she saw me, and I realized she did not recognize me. And who could blame her? I bore little resemblance to the young girl she had known in Bear Valley.

"Kathy, do you remember me? Hannah Kincaid? I lived at the trading post in Bear Valley."

"Hannah!" she cried, and put her arms around me. "Of course I remember you. You used to give me candy whenever I came into the store. What are you doing here?"

"It's a long story. My father is here, you know."

"Yes, I've seen him," Kathy said. "He lives with an old squaw."

There was no mistaking the contempt in Kathy's voice.

"What are you doing here, Kathy? How did you get away from the Sioux?"

"I didn't get very far away," Kathy said bitterly. "The warrior who kidnapped me lives on the reservation."

"Are you still living with his family?"

"No. When his tribe surrendered, the commander of the fort, General McKay, took me away from the Indians. He and his wife took me in. I've been living with the General and his family ever since."

"Are you happy with them?"

"I guess so. Hannah, where's my mother? I wrote to her when the McKays took me in, but I never got an answer. Is she all right? Did she go back East after my father was killed?"

I looked away, unable to meet Kathy's eyes. Florence Sanders had been a lovely woman, deeply in love with her husband. When he was killed by the Sioux, she had withdrawn into a world of her own. From that day on, she never spoke. The Walker famlily took her in. I remembered as clearly as if it had been yesterday going to visit Mrs. Sanders. She had never known my mother and I were there. Stony-faced, she sat in a straight-backed chair staring out the window, one of her husband's shirts clutched tightly to her breast. She never recovered. When the talk of war turned to acts of war, the Walkers packed up and left for Oregon, taking Florence Sanders with them. They never made it.

"Hannah?"

"Kathy, I'm sorry."

"She's dead, then?"

I put my arms around Kathy while she cried. Several women paused to stare at us, then hurried out of the store.

"Can we go someplace and talk?" I asked.

Nodding, Kathy led me through the back of the store into a small room packed with crates and boxes. A worn sofa stood against one wall. Kathy sat down, still weeping softly, and I sat next to her.

When her tears subsided, she dried her face on the hem of her skirt. Smiling faintly, she looked at me. "I'd like to hear your long story now."

Her eyes were wide by the time I finished. "You actually married an Indian? How could you marry a savage? I hate them all."

"I understand how you feel, Kathy, truly I do. After all, the Sioux killed my mother, too. But you can't spend your whole life hating. In the end, you're the only one who suffers."

"I can't help it. I don't see how you could possibly love an Indian. They're nothing but heathen savages. As soon as I turn eighteen, I'm leaving this place and never coming back. I never want to see another Indian as long as I live."

"Well, as long as you're here, you will come to dinner tonight, won't you? I know my father would love to have you. And I want you to meet Shadow and my children."

"I don't know . . ."

"Please. It's been so long since I've seen anyone from home."

In the end, Kathy relented and came to dinner. She looked like a princess out of a fairy tale. Her hair was piled regally atop her head, revealing a slender neck and creamy shoulders. Her dress, of pink tulle, was frothy and becoming.

Pa welcomed Kathy warmly and our meal was congenial and pleasant. Kathy was coolly polite to Sunbird, but she was completely smitten with Shadow. Watching her, I could see all her prejudices fading fast. I could not blame the girl for being infatuated with my husband. He was, after all, incredibly handsome. At twenty-eight, he was every inch a man—strong, self-assured, and very, very male. Kathy hung on his every word, asking him countless questions about the Cheyenne, just to hear the sound of his voice. When we went outside for coffee, she stuck like a cocklebur to Shadow's side, smiling up at him as though he were the most wonderful man in the world, laughing softly when something he said amused her.

I was suddenly sorry I had invited Kathy Sanders to dinner.

Later, alone on the porch with Shadow, I threw him a stern look. "Well?"

Shadow lifted one black brow. "What is wrong?"

"You seem to have made quite a conquest tonight."

Shadow frowned. "What do you mean, a conquest?"

"Kathy Sanders. She couldn't keep her eyes off of you. I believe the girl fancies herself half in love with you already."

"Do not talk foolishness."

"It isn't foolishness."

"She is just a child."

"Some child," I muttered petulantly.

Shadow stared at me, and then he grinned. "You are jealous!" he exclaimed.

He was right, but I didn't want to admit it. Kathy was so pretty, so young. Her figure was slim, shapely, and girlishly feminine. How could I possibly compete with her youthful freshness and innocence? I was not old or fat, by any means, but I had given birth to three children. And I was twenty-five years old, hardly an innocent young girl any longer.

"Hannah."

I refused to look at him, not wanting him to see the jealousy burning in my eyes.

As always, Shadow knew what I was thinking and feeling even better than I did. "Hannah." He smiled down at me, his eyes warm with love as he drew me close. "Do not be jealous of Kathy Sanders or anyone else. It is you I love. Only you. Nothing will ever change that. You are a part of me, of my life. The best part."

His words, softly spoken and sincere, chased all my foolish fears away. I closed my eyes as he kissed me, the familiar longing stirring in my blood as his mouth closed over mine. His hands cupped my buttocks, pressing my hips against his solid male flesh. The stirring of his desire

fired my own and I sighed happily as he
lifted me into his arms and carried me
down the steps into the darkness. I did not
question him as he carried me down the
path that led to the river, content to be
held in his strong arms, my head pillowed
against his broad chest.

He stopped at a secluded place beside
the river, gently lowered me to the ground.
Then, his eyes never leaving mine, he
began to undress. My heart began to beat
faster and faster as he removed first his
shirt, then his moccasins, then his fringed
buckskin pants. I was breathing heavily
as he slowly shed his clout to stand naked
before me, his desire plainly evident.

I lifted my arms, silently urging him
to come to me. His eyes, black as ten feet
down, burned with a fierce light as he
knelt beside me and began to remove my
clothing. I shivered with anticipation at
his touch, wanting him to hurry, wanting
to feel his flesh against my own. But he
was in a teasing mood, and he undressed
me with infinite care, his lips brushing my
skin as he removed my dress.

"White woman wear too many
clothes," he complained softly as he began
to remove my chemise, and then my
petticoat, his mouth caressing each area of
skin he exposed. He chuckled as I let out a
low moan and then, as I arched upward,
pressing my breasts against his chest, he
stilled his gentle laughter and drew me

close. The game was over and we clung together, arms and legs entwined as the love we shared forged us together.

Later, lying in Shadow's arms, I knew I need never be jealous of anyone.

Kathy Sanders made many excuses to come to my father's cabin in the days that followed. She came to see Heecha and Mary. She came to see me. She came to ask Pa about a horse she wanted to buy from one of the Indians. She came to talk about old times in Bear Valley. She came to ask Shadow to teach her to speak Cheyenne . . .

I was amused at first, but the more I saw Kathy with my husband, the more irritated I became. Kathy was learning the Cheyenne language, but she was also learning to love Shadow. You could see it in the depths of her clear blue eyes whenever she looked at him, which was often. I knew Shadow loved me, that he would always love me, but I wondered how long he would be able to resist Kathy's advances which, as the days went by, became more and more bold. She found countless excuses to touch Shadow's arm, his shoulder, his cheek. Once, she leaned forward, apparently intent on what he was saying, her hand lingering on his thigh.

Pa and Sunbird thought it amusing. Harmless, but amusing. I did not think it was harmless and I did not think it was

the least bit amusing. And when my
patience wore thin, I began to get angry.
Who did that little snit think she was, to
openly flirt with *my* husband? To think, I
had once given her candy and thought she
was cute!

It was on a day in late November that
things came to a head. Walking to the
river to fetch water for Sunbird, I spied
Shadow and Kathy Sanders standing
together beneath a cottonwood tree.
Kathy was wearing a sky blue dress that
perfectly complimented her honey blond
hair and fair skin. The bodice was square-
cut and edged with lace, revealing a
generous expanse of flawless white skin.

Kathy was gazing intently at Shadow,
her head tilted back, her blue eyes shining
with love, her pink lips slightly parted.

They had not seen me and I quickly
ducked out of sight behind a bush, my
ears straining to hear what was being said.

"Isn't it true that Cheyenne men
sometimes have more than one wife?"
Kathy was saying.

"Sometimes," Shadow replied.

"Have you ever thought of taking a
second wife?"

"No."

"Oh." Kathy was obviously disappointed.

I smiled, foolishly thinking that would
be the end of it.

"I would like to be your second wife,"

Kathy said boldly. Standing on tiptoe, she pressed her lips to Shadow's. "I would do anything to make you happy," she murmured breathlessly. "Anything."

Shadow looked momentarily surprised, then flattered. And then he smiled. "I am honored that you want to share my lodge," he said gently. "But I cannot take you for my woman. You are not an Indian, and your people do not allow a man to have more than one wife."

Well, I thought, that was tactful.

"I don't care what people would think," Kathy murmured sullenly. "I want you."

"We cannot always have what we want," Shadow replied.

Kathy thought Shadow was lamenting the fact that they could not be married, but I saw the wistful look in Shadow's eyes as he glanced into the distance and I knew what he was yearning for. He was not wishing he could have Kathy for his wife, as she supposed. He was longing for his freedom.

Tears filled Kathy's eyes as, standing on her tiptoes, she kissed Shadow a second time and then ran back to the fort.

Shadow sighed heavily and then smiled broadly. "You can come out now."

I gasped in surprise. "How did you know I was here?" I demanded, stepping out from my hiding place.

"I always know when you are near."

Drat the man, he had ears like a lynx and a nose like a bloodhound.

"I do not think we will be seeing much of your friend in the future," Shadow mused.

"You don't have to sound so sad about it," I retorted.

"Well," Shadow said, grinning, "you cannot blame me for being flattered. She *is* very pretty and she thinks I am wonderful."

"Oh, you!" Playfully, I punched him on the arm. "You're despicable!"

Shadow frowned at me. "I am not sure what that word means, but I do not think it was a compliment."

"It wasn't."

"Do not be angry, Hannah," he chided. "You are also very pretty, and you also think I am wonderful, and that is why I have no need of a second wife. Why, I will never need anyone but you."

How could I stay mad at such a man?

Shadow and I went for a swim in the river later that night after we had put Heecha and Mary to bed. The water was cold, invigorating. Shadow's skin glistened like wet bronze as he swam up-river with long effortless strokes, his hair streaming behind him like a dark shadow.

I paused to watch him, admiring the way he sliced cleanly through the water, his strokes smooth and even. He made hardly a ripple as he disappeared under the water. A few moments later I felt his hand on my leg as he pulled me under. I came up sputtering and splashed him in the face. He quickly retaliated by dunking me a second time, and the battle was on.

Like children, we splashed and teased and wrestled in the chill water. I was no match for Shadow's easy strength and he soon had me pinned down in the shallows near the riverbank.

"Impudent wench," he murmured. "I shall have to teach you to show me more respect in the future."

Wrinkling my nose, I stuck my tongue out at him, and he pushed my head under the water a third time. I took a mouthful and when he let me up, I blew the water in his face.

With mock anger, he scooped up a handful of sand from the river bottom and washed my face with it and I began kicking and thrashing about and the battle was on again until Shadow dropped his mouth over mine. Wet skin rubbed against wet skin, creating a delightful sensation that was slippery and exciting.

I felt the heat rise in Shadow's loins, felt his swollen manhood press against my belly, and I was on fire for him. My arms went around his neck and I clung to him as the only solid thing in a wet and turbulent world, moaning with pleasure as he parted my thighs. The throbbing heat of his manhood filled me, making me complete, and I

closed my eyes, lost in a world of sensation. The water swirling around us was
no longer cold; I did not feel the cool air,
for Shadow's body covered mine, warmer
than any blanket.

The water lapped around us, primal,
buoyant as a mother's womb. I whispered
Shadow's name, my nails raking his back
and shoulders, as wave after wave of
exquisite pleasure washed through me.

Later, we crawled out of the water,
feeling deliciously weary and content,
almost as if we had been reborn. Dressing,
we snuggled beneath a blanket and spent
the night under the vast starry sky, the
only two people in all the world.

V

Winter 1884-Spring 1885

Our life settled into a pleasant routine on
the reservation, and I was content. Pa and
Shadow worked at Pa's trading post
together, causing me to remember a time,
long ago, when I had envisioned just such
a thing. Many of the Indians who had been
reluctant to deal with my father now came
to the trading post because Shadow was
there. Everyone had heard of Two Hawks
Flying, and they knew he could be trusted
to give them a fair deal.

Sunbird looked after Pa's house and
did the cooking; I looked after Heecha and
Mary and did the washing and ironing,
made the beds and changed the sheets.

Winter came, bringing snow and rain.
And then it was Christmas once more, one
of the happiest I had ever known. It was
so good to be with my father again, to
reminisce about Christmases we had

known in Bear Valley when my mother was alive.

Between Christmas and the new year, there was a dance at the fort. I longed to go, to dance and laugh and listen to the music. I had made a few friends at the fort. General McKay's wife, Leona, was my favorite. She was a motherly sort and she took me under her wing as she did everyone she met. I also liked Thelma Byers, the schoolteacher. She was a rather plain, middle-aged woman with light brown hair and nondescript features. She was sympathetic to the Indians and had offered to come and teach the children on the reservation, but the Indians wanted no part of the white man's learning for themselves or their children.

When I mentioned the dance to Shadow, he refused to go, but when he saw how disappointed I was, he relented and agreed to accompany me.

I had not reckoned with Army prejudice. Leona McKay met us at the door of the mess hall where the dance was being held. Her expression was troubled, her eyes sympathetic.

"My dear," she said, blocking the door. "I . . ." She cleared her throat as she glanced nervously at Shadow. "Hannah, there's just no nice way to say it. The ladies have asked me to tell you you're not welcome, that is, you are, but . . ." Leona McKay's face turned bright red as she glanced at Shadow again and quickly looked away.

"Are you trying to tell me my husband is not welcome here?" I asked bluntly.

"Yes. You do understand, don't you, dear?"

"I understand," I replied curtly. "Good night."

Hurt and angry, I turned on my heel and walked away from the music and the dancing. Leona McKay was supposed to be my friend. She was the General's wife. If she had insisted that Shadow be made welcome, the officers' wives would have acceded to her wishes.

My anger evaporated as quickly as it had surfaced, and I was suddenly glad that Leona McKay had not made an issue of it. I did not want people to accept my husband because they had to. If they could not see what a find man he was, that was their loss, not mine.

When we were out of sight of the mess hall, Shadow laid his hand on my arm.

"Hannah?"

"What?"

"I am sorry."

"It's not your fault."

"No?"

"No."

Shadow cocked his head to the side as the post band struck up a waltz.

"Would you care to dance?" he asked,

holding out his arms.

"I'd love to."

I stepped into Shadow's arms and we stood close together, swaying back and forth in time to the music.

"It's time you learned how to dance the dances of my people," I remarked, and when Shadow didn't object, I taught him how to waltz. He quickly caught on and we danced around the parade ground under the stars, twirling and dipping and swaying until I was breathless.

When the music stopped, Shadow pulled me close and kissed me, a deep passionate kiss that made my knees weak and my heart beat wildly.

Let Leona McKay and the other so-called ladies shut me out of their dance, let them gossip and look down their noses at me because I had married an Indian. I wouldn't have traded my life, or my husband, for anything the world had to offer.

I smiled up at Shadow, seeing the love in his ebony eyes. "Let's go home."

In the spring, Kathy Sanders surprised everyone by announcing her engagement to one of the lieutenants at the fort. I was even more surprised when Kathy asked me to be her matron of honor. The wedding was set for late June.

It was about this time that I began to notice one of the men at the fort. He was a sergeant in his early thirties, with slicked down black hair, brown eyes, and a sweeping, cavalry-style moustache. His name was Joe Mattlock. He seemed nice enough. He always smiled and touched his hat when he saw me. Sometimes we exchanged a few words about the weather or some happening at the fort.

I thought nothing of it at first. Most of the men at the fort lived alone as only those with the rank of lieutenant or above were permitted to have their wives with them. A woman out west, any woman, was a welcome sight, and treated with respect.

As the days went by, I seemed to see Joe Mattlock wherever I went. He came often to the trading post to buy tobacco, or browse through the mail-order catalogs, or buy a handful of candy. Sometimes he spent the better part of the morning in the store, just talking to Pa.

I was down at the river early one April morning, washing a few of Mary's things, when Joe Mattlock sauntered toward me.

"Pretty weather we're having," he remarked congenially.

"Yes." I soaped one of Mary's dresses and scrubbed it on a flat rock. My little girl was a terrible tomboy and loved nothing more than playing in the mud or wrestling with the Indian boys her age. I had made her several pretty dresses, and it took a good deal of washing to keep them clean.

"I thought maybe you'd like to take a little ride with me," Mattlock said.

"A ride?"

Mattlock shrugged. "Yeah. Maybe take a picnic lunch and ride out on the plains away from all this. There's some pretty country beyond the river."

"Yes, I know."

"Well, what do you say? Tomorrow, about noon?"

"I'm sorry, I can't."

"Why not? The old squaw will keep an eye on your young'uns."

I rinsed Mary's dress and laid it on the grass to dry, then stood up, my hand massaging the small of my back.

"Thank you for your invitation," I said, coolly polite. "But I'm a married woman."

Mattlock made a sound of disgust low in his throat. "A marriage to a redskin is no marriage at all."

"It is quite binding, I assure you," I retorted. "Excuse me, I have to go now."

Mattlock stepped in front of me, backing me up against one of the cottonwood trees that grew along the riverbank.

"Come on, honey," he coaxed. "I know you must be yearning to be with a white man after living so long with that Cheyenne buck."

I gasped as his hand snaked around my waist and yanked me forward, so that my breasts were crushed against his

chest. His mouth was hot and wet,
disgusting as it ground into mine. I put
my hands against his shoulders and
pushed as hard as I could, trying to get
free of his hold on me, but his arms grew
tighter, cutting off my breath. His mouth
traveled from my lips to my neck, and
then he was kissing my breasts, his lips
searing my skin through the bodice of my
dress.

"I knew you'd be sweet," he rasped.
"Real sweet."

"Let me go!" I demanded, hoping he
could not detect the rising panic in my
voice.

"Relax, baby," Mattlock purred, his
voice smooth and silky. "Let Joe show you
how it should be done."

"My husband will kill you for this," I
cried, striking Mattlock's face with the
palm of my hand. "Let me go, damn you!"

"I like a woman with spirit," Mattlock
said, grinning as he caught my hand and
twisted it behind my back. "But not too
much spirit."

I winced with pain as he gave my arm
a sharp twist. I was frightened now. A fine
layer of cold sweat broke out across my
brow as I stared at Joe Mattlock.

"That's better," he drawled. With a
low chuckle, he pressed the length of his
body against mine, letting me feel his
rising desire.

Trapped between the tree and his

body, I was helpless to resist when he
began kissing me again, his tongue raping
my mouth. He howled with pain when I bit
him. Jerking back, he slapped me hard
across the face.

"You little wildcat!" he snarled.
"You'll pay for that."

I opened my mouth to reply, but
before I could utter the words, Mattlock
was grabbed from behind and I had a
glimpse of Shadow's face as he hurled Joe
Mattlock to the ground.

Mattlock sprang to his feet and the
two men came together, knotted fists
striking flesh. Sunbird and my father
arrived a few moments later.

"Pa, do something!" I cried fran-
tically.

"Best to let them fight it out here and
now," Pa muttered, his eyes intent on the
two men grappling in the dirt.

Men, I thought disgustedly. There
wasn't a one of them that didn't like to see
a good scrap now and then.

Joe Mattlock was a big man, strong as
an ox. But he had met his match in
Shadow. I cringed as the flat sound of
flesh meeting flesh filled my ears.
Mattlock's left eye was swollen almost
shut, Shadow was bleeding from his nose
and mouth. Both men were panting
heavily, and I wondered how much longer
the fight could go on.

With a mighty roar, Mattlock

knocked Shadow aside and leaped to his feet, his hand drawing the pistol from the holster at his side.

"You damn savage!" he sneered. "You'll never hit a white man again!"

Shadow glared at Mattlock, his face horrible to see in its anger. Slowly, deliberately, Shadow advanced toward Mattlock, his dark eyes blazing with fury.

Joe Mattlock was a seasoned trooper. He had seen the killing look in Shadow's eyes before and he knew what it meant. Muttering an oath, he raised the pistol and leveled it at Shadow, his finger growing white around the trigger.

The shot rang out loud and clear. I screamed as the bullet tore into Shadow's left side. Blood quickly stained his shirt front, and still he moved toward Mattlock.

"Damn!" Mattlock exclaimed.

He was going to shoot again and at such close range, I knew he could not miss. Before anyone could stop me, I stepped between the two men.

There was a terrible burning pain beneath my left breast, and then nothing but a deep black void . . .

VI

Shadow

Shadow watched in horror as Hannah spiraled slowly to the ground, and then his eyes moved to the face of Joe Mattlock. With an animal-like snarl of pain and rage, Shadow lunged at Mattlock. Tearing the pistol from the cavalryman's hand, he put the gun to the man's head and pulled the trigger. The face of Joe Mattlock dissolved in a sea of blood and brain matter as his body slowly crumpled to the ground.

Throwing the gun aside, Shadow ran to Hannah. She lay where she had fallen, unmoving. Her eyes were closed, her face pale as death. A lock of her hair, red as flame, fell over one shoulder. A thin trickle of blood oozed from a small hole just under her left breast.

"My God," Kincaid murmured brokenly. "She's dead."

Shadow raised tormented eyes to his father-in-law's face, but before he could speak, there was the sound of horses coming fast.

"Shadow, you've got to get out of here," Kincaid urged. "General McKay will have your head in a noose before nightfall when he finds out you've killed one of his men."

"No." Shadow's voice was thick with pain. "I will not leave her."

"You can't help her now," Kincaid said with a shake of his head. "Go on, make a run for it. I'll look after the kids until this blows over."

There was a rattle of spurs and harness as a dozen troopers drew rein some twenty feet from Hannah's body.

"What the hell's going on here?" demanded the sergeant in charge.

"Shadow, go!" Kincaid shouted.

With a last look at Hannah, Shadow turned and ran for the river. He hated to leave her, but Kincaid was right. There was nothing he could do for Hannah and his children needed him alive. Tears burned his eyes as he thought of Hannah throwing herself in front of Mattlock. She had sacrificed her own life for his.

A volley of shots followed Shadow's fleeing form. One struck the ground at his feet, another passed through the flesh of his upper arm.

With a cry, he dove into the river and

let the rushing water carry him down-stream until he came to an abandoned beaver lodge. Diving, he sought the entrance of the lodge and took shelter on a small ledge inside.

Listening, he could hear the soldiers riding up and down along the river, searching for him. He heard the reservation police talking softly as they dismounted and scouted for his trail. Surely they knew where he had gone to ground. But they were old friends, and they passed by his hiding place.

At dark, Shadow crawled out of the river. Keeping low, he made his way down-river. The wound in his arm was of no con-sequence. The bullet had passed through his flesh, the cold water had stoped the bleeding. But the wound in his side con-tinued to ooze blood with every step he took.

Teeth clenched against the growing pain in his side, he walked until he could walk no more and then took shelter in a tangled thicket. He had no food, no weapon save for the knife at his belt. Shivering convulsively, he dug a shallow hole, curled into it and fell instantly asleep.

When he woke, it was dark. Was it the same night, he mused, or the next? His side was stiff, the pain constant, but not as terrible as the ache in his heart. Hannah, his beloved, was dead. With a hoarse cry, he drew his knife and raked the blade across his chest—once, twice, three times. Had he been a woman, he would have cut off a finger, but a man did not sacrifice a finger to show his grief. A man must have two good hands to hunt and to fight.

Overwhelmed with pain and grief, he stared at the knife in his hand and then at the bullet wound in his side. The bullet was embedded in his flesh. If it did not come out, the wound would fester and he would die. For a moment, he contemplated dying, but then he thought of Heecha and Mary. He must live, for his children. Someday, he would return and claim them. Someday . . .

He felt himself growing weaker as he searched for the proper sticks to make a fire. When he found what he was looking for, he gathered a small pile of tinder-dry leaves and twigs. Then, with great patience, he began to twirl the greasewood stick in the palms of his hands. In time, the greasewood ignited a tiny flame in the softer cottonwood. He blew on the small fire gently, coaxing it to life as he added more leaves and twigs. When the fire was burning steadily, he passed the blade of his knife through the flames.

Waiting for the blade to cool, he lifted his eyes toward Heaven. "Hear me, Maheo," he prayed in a voice raw with pain. "Give me the strength to do what I must do. Hear me, Father of Spirits, guide my woman safely to the After World. . . ."

The blade was cool enough. Taking a deep breath, he began to probe his flesh for the ounce of lead embedded in his side. Sweat poured from his brow, dripping down his face and neck as he guided the slender blade deeper into his side. His vision blurred. Nausea rose in his throat. And still he probed his flesh, fighting the urge to vomit, willing himself to stay conscious until, at last, the slug was dislodged. His last act before darkness overtook him was to press the re-heated blade across the wound.

He tossed restlessly when the fever came. His desire for water drove him out of his hiding place toward the river and he slid down the grassy bank, burying his face in the cool water. After drinking his fill, he slid into the river, letting the icy water wash over his fevered flesh as he raised his voice in prayer.

"Help me, Man Above, lest I perish."

He laid in the shallow water for a long time, only dimly aware of his surroundings, his eyes closed against the sun's glare, until the sound of rushing wings roused him from his stupor. Opening his eyes, he saw a pair of red-tail hawks gliding toward him. He smiled faintly as they hovered near his head. It was good to see his old friends again.

"Be strong," cried the male in a voice

like thunder. "Be strong, and you will prevail."

"Be brave," the female admonished. "Be brave, and all you have ever desired shall yet be yours."

All you have ever desired . . .

"Hannah." He whispered her name as the two birds climbed into the sky to disappear into the sun, and then he loosed a terrible cry of rage. Hannah was all he had ever desired, and she was dead.

Pain knifed through his heart as he remembered the first time he had seen her so long ago. Even as a child she had been lovely, special. He remembered how he had taught her to hunt and track and fish, and how pleased she had been when he praised her efforts. He recalled the day he had eaten the raw heart of a buffalo calf and how embarrassed she had been when she threw up all over him.

Time telescoped and Hannah was sixteen and so very beautiful. Her hair was as red as flame, her eyes a soft warm gray, her mouth ever curved in a smile that was his and his alone. He remembered the day he had seen her bathing in the river back in Bear Valley, her skin sleekly wet, her breasts full, her hips nicely rounded, her legs long and shapely. He had known from that moment that she would be his. Their love had blossomed into a rare and beautiful thing, undimmed by hardship or the passage of time.

He remembered how she had ridden valiantly at his side when they had gone to war against the whites even though they knew it was a fight they could never win. He remembered how she had nursed the wounded, grieved for the dead, comforted the dying. He remembered how beautiful she had been the day Elk Dreamer had made her his wife at the war camp on the Rosebud River.

Hannah. She had endured much to be with him—hunger, cold, war, the death of a child. And now she was dead, because of him . . .

The next several days melted into one another. Waking, he drank frequently from the river, his thirst increased by the amount of blood he had lost. He ate wild licorice and blackberries and once, a snake that passed too close. He chewed the raw meat slowly, the simple task of eating making him weary.

Asleep, he dreamed of Hannah, always Hannah. Sometimes she was young and vibrant, her smile warmer than the summer sun at midday, her dove-gray eyes merry with laughter as she played with Mary. And sometimes he saw her as he had seen her last, lying still and silent upon the ground, her lifeblood staining her breast. At those times he woke in a cold sweat, her name a cry on his lips . . .

The wound in Shadow's arm healed quickly; the wound in his side took longer. His legs seemed to grow weaker with the passing of each day, and he knew he needed meat to strengthen his limbs. Roots and berries did not provide the nourishment a man required.

With great effort, he trapped a rabbit, and then another. The meat restored a part of his strength. He waited at the river one whole day, waiting patiently for the game that came to drink there each evening. At last, three doe made their way to the water's edge. Holding his breath, Shadow hurled his knife at the one doe that didn't have a fawn at her side. The blade caught the animal in the throat, killing it almost instantly. The other doe bounded away from the river, their tails flashing white as they ran.

Lacking the strength to drag the whole carcass to his shelter in the thicket, Shadow sliced the hindquarters into sections. He made three trips to the thicket, storing the meat high in a tree. The fourth time he returned to the carcass, he found several vultures tearing at the deer's remains.

Wavings his arms wildly, Shadow spooked the big black birds long enough to take the last hunk of meat. The birds and the wolves could have what was left.

While he waited for his body to heal and his strength to return, he fashioned a

bow of hickory wood. Deer sinew served as
the bowstring. It was not as strong as a
bowstring made from the large tendon of a
bull buffalo, but it would do.

That night, he sat under the stars, his
eyes gazing into the distance. It was quiet
on the plains. Once, the buffalo had
covered the land like a great brown
blanket. Once, the Indians had roamed the
endless prairie, their conical lodges
dotting the landscape, their vast horse
herds grazing on the thick buffalo grass.
Once, the sound of drums had filled the
air. But now a great silence filled the
earth. No more did the buffalo migrate
across the plains, their hooves churning
up clouds of yellow dust, their bellows
echoing like thunder. No more did the
Indian move across the land, following
pte. No more did the hills ring with the
happy sound of a free people. There was
only silence, and a vast emptiness.

VII

Samuel Kincaid sat at his daughter's bedside, his large calloused hand enveloping her smaller one. For ten days she had lain in bed, drifting in and out of consciousness, her breathing shallow and uneven. Miraculously, the bullet fired by Mattlock had passed through Hannah's body without striking any vital organs. However, there was a large lump on the back of her head, sustained when she fell, that was causing much concern.

The Army doctor came every day. And every day there was no change in Hannah's condition.

Kincaid prayed as he had never prayed before, begging God to spare the life of his only child, if not for his sake, then for the sake of his grandchildren. Heecha spent hours at his mother's side, his dark eyes sad and brooding. Mary clung to her grandfather, her gray eyes, so like Hannah's, filled with bewilderment.

"Namshim," Heecha said, using the Cheyenne word for grandfather, "will my mother die?"

"I don't know, son," Kincaid answered. "It's in God's hands."

"Whose God?" Heecha asked. "The white man's god, or Heammawihio?"

Kincaid knelt down so that he was face to face with his grandson. "They're the same God, Heecha. It doesn't matter by what name you call him."

"I do not believe that."

"But it's true nonetheless. There's only one God, or Great Spirit, and he loves all his children."

"My father's friend, Calf Running, said the white man's god was stronger than the red man's god. He said Heammawihio was displeased with his children and that was why the Indian was being driven from his land."

Sam Kincaid let out a long breath. How did you explain gold and greed and Manifest Destiny to a child?

"If I prayed to the white man's god, would he hear me?" Heecha asked hopefully.

"Yes, son, he'd hear you."

"Will he make my mother well again?"

"I don't know. But it wouldn't hurt to ask."

"Can we ask him now?"

"If you like."

"Me, too," Mary said. "I want to pray for nahkoa."

Sam Kincaid blinked back his tears as the three of them knelt beside Hannah's bed to pray.

Another week went by, and Heecha's faith in the white man's god began to dwindle. He had expected a miracle, and nothing had happened.

When two weeks passed without any improvement in Hannah's condition, Kincaid decided to take her back east. The Army sawbones was good at sewing up torn flesh and mending broken bones, but he was at a loss to know what ailed Hannah. Perhaps a city doctor would know what to do.

Sunbird understood why Sam was leaving, but she would not go with him. She belonged with her own people, in her own land. Kincaid did not argue. He left Shadow a letter, telling him that they were going to New York City to find a doctor who could help Hannah.

As he signed his name to the short note, Kincaid wondered if Shadow were still alive.

They went by flatbed wagon to the nearest railhead. Kincaid booked a private car for Hannah so they could travel alone and undisturbed. He did not want people staring at her, wondering what was wrong, wondering why she stared blankly into the distance.

Sitting beside her, Kincaid looked out the window as the train began to move. He was glad to be leaving it all behind. He should have taken Shadow's advice years ago and left Bear Valley before it was too late, before the Indians claimed the life of his wife and destroyed their home. But for his stubbornness, Katherine Mary Kincaid would still be alive, and Hannah would not be lying beside him as still and silent as death . . .

VIII

Shadow

It was on a dark moonless night that Shadow started across the prairie bound for the reservation. It was a strangely eerie feeling, walking across the yellow grass, alone. Nothing moved on the face of the land, not even the wind.

It was long past midnight when he padded quietly toward the small cabin that belonged to Hannah's father. He knew, even before he stepped inside, that it was empty.

Outside once again, he rounded the west corner of the house to where a single lodge made a dark outline against the darker night. He scratched softly on the hide near the entrance and in a few moments Sunbird lifted the flap. She did not seem surprised to see him.

"Welcome," she said, gesturing for Shadow to enter the lodge. It was roomy

and comfortable inside and Shadow
breathed deeply, relishing the scent of
sage that rose from the fire.

"Where is Kincaid?" he asked.
"Where are my children?"

Sunbird nodded her head as she pulled
a white envelope from beneath her
sleeping robe and handed it to Shadow.
"Kincaid, he is a good man. He left this for
you in case you came back."

The letter was brief, but no words had
ever thrilled Shadow more. Hannah was
alive! Alive but not well. He quickly read
on.

"I don't know if you have survived
your wounds," Kincaid wrote, "or if you
will ever read this. However, I have taken
Hannah to New York City to see a
specialist. I cannot tell you where we will
be staying, for I have no relatives in the
city and have not been to New York in
over 40 years. The children are well. I pray
God you are the same."

His heart filled with joy, Shadow bid
the old woman farewell and ducked out of
the lodge. Hannah was alive!

Noiseless as the night, he made his
way to where several horses stood hipshot
in a peeled pole corral. Taking a bridle
from one of the posts, he slipped into the
enclosure, speaking softly to the horses.
Gently, he slipped the bridle over the head
of a good-looking calico mare and led the
horse out of the corral.

Once clear of the corral and the nearby Indian lodges, he swung onto the horse's back and headed east. New York City, Kincaid had said. Shadow knew little of the cities of the white man, only that there were many of them across the wide Missouri. He had seen some of them when he was an attraction in Hansen's Traveling Tent Show. He had thought them noisy, overcrowded places populated by countless people—people of all colors, people who had come to the carnival to gawk at him: little yellow men with strange eyes, big black men with kinky hair, Mexicans, mulattoes, Germans, Irishmen, Swedes. But no Indians, he mused wryly, save for one half-naked Cheyenne warrior in chains and feathers.

It was a part of his life he rarely thought of, a time of humiliation and shame. He had been mocked and laughed at, poked and prodded. And whipped, he mused ruefully. His back still carried the scars. Finally, he had escaped. Though badly wounded, he had killed the three men who had kept him in chains. He had dipped his hands in the blood of the last man, and it had been a good feeling. It was the last thing he remembered before he blacked out. When he woke, he was in the house of a white woman and her daughter. The woman's name had been Rebecca Matthews, and she had saved his life. She had been afraid of him at first, but later she had come to his bed, wanting him in the way a woman wants a man. And he had obliged her because she had saved his life and he had nothing else to give.

That night, bedded down near a shallow waterhole, Shadow thought of Rebecca. Perhaps she would help him find Hannah.

IX

"Hannah. Hannah, wake up. We're here."

The sound of a man's voice penetrated the mists of darkness and I opened my eyes. Turning my head, I saw a big man with broad shoulders and curly brown hair smiling down at me. He was dressed in dark blue twill pants and a white shirt.

"How are you feeling, honey?" he asked, giving my hand an affectionate squeeze.

"Fine," I answered, wondering who the man was, and where I was.

"Good. Your dress is hanging on the door. Your, uh, underthings are there, too. Let me know when you're dressed. I'll wait outside. You can, uh, call me if you need help."

"Get ready for what?" I asked, frowning.

"We're at the train station, in New

York. I've got a carriage waiting."

I stared at the man. New York? A carriage? "Excuse me," I said politely. "But who are you?"

"Who am I?" The man looked at me strangely. "I'm your father."

"He's dead," I said softly, wondering why I could remember that and nothing else.

"Is he?" the man asked. "How did he die?"

"I don't remember."

The man's brow furrowed and a look of worry spread over his face. "Do you know who you are?"

Slowly, I shook my head. A faint stab of fear pierced my heart. I didn't know who I was. Or where I was. New York, the man had said. I glanced out the window. People milled about the station: ladies in fancy dresses and wide-brimmed hats decorated with fake flowers and colorful plumes, men in suits and ties and derby hats. A Negro porter walked by, several bags under his arm. In the distance, I could see houses and carriages and a few shops.

"Hannah." There was a barely concealed note of despair in the man's voice. "Your name is Hannah . . ." He paused, a deep frown puckering his forehead.

"Hannah what?"

"Berdeen," he said heavily.

"Berdeen." I repeated the name

slowly. It meant nothing to me, nor did it sound the slightest bit familiar. "Who are *you*?"

"I'm your father, Samuel Kincaid."

"Kincaid?"

"Yes. You were married, but your husband died. You have two children."

"Children!"

"Yes, Heecha and Mary."

"Heecha? What a strange name?"

"It's an Indian name."

I laughed humorlessly. "Why would I give one of my children an Indian name?"

The man sighed heavily, as if he wasn't sure what to say, or how to say it. "It's a long story, Hannah, and quite complicated. Let's save it for later, when you're feeling better. Why don't you get dressed now? The train will be pulling out soon."

The man looked suddenly old as he left the compartment and closed the door behind him. I got up slowly, feeling weak and a little lightheaded. My mind was in turmoil as I pulled on the underthings hanging on the door and then slipped into a dress of flowered blue muslin.

"Hannah." I said the name aloud, but it struck no chord within me. I felt so strange. I could walk and talk and think, but I could not remember a single thing. It was odd and a little frightening.

The man was waiting for me when I stepped out of the car. Two children stood beside him. The boy was handsome, with straight black hair, black eyes and dark, coppery skin. The girl was a charming little thing, with wavy brown hair, wide gray eyes, and a fair complexion. They both stared at me uncertainly, and I guessed the man had told them about my condition and warned them not to say anything.

"Ready, Hannah?" the man asked kindly.

"Yes."

He handed me into the rented carriage, lifted the children into the opposite seat, and flicked the reins over the backs of the two-horse team.

It was a big noisy city. The streets were crowded with people, and they all seemed to be in a hurry. There were uniformed policemen on horseback, Chinese men in long flowing robes. Negroes driving beer wagons and fancy carriages. It was a bustling town, and I had a vague memory of a childhood dream that involved New York and a dark, faceless man.

Mr. Kincaid drew the carriage to a halt before a large hotel. The building was painted white with dark green shutters on the windows. Two large potted palms stood on either side of the entry. A patterned carpet covered the floor of the lobby. Several sofas and chairs, all covered in dark burgandy velvet, were placed at intervals. A large chandelier hung from the middle of the ceiling.

In a matter of moments, Mr. Kincaid had secured a suite of rooms and we were climbing the staircase to the second floor.

"You rest, Hannah," Mr. Kincaid said, patting my hand. "I'll look after the kids." Pulling a silver watch from his pocket, he checked the time. "It's four o'clock now. I'll pick you up at six for dinner."

I nodded, content to let him make the plans. Feeling suddenly tired, I sat on the edge of the bed and removed my shoes and stockings. Sighing, I fell back on the bed and closed my eyes. Gradually, the sounds from outside faded and I drifted to sleep, and sleeping, began to dream . . .

I was wandering through a dark land, alone. Ahead of me, through a hazy gray mist, I could see a man. Deep within my heart, I knew I would never be happy unless I could reach the mysterious man who loomed ahead of me. I ran and ran, but I could not close the distance between us. Once, he paused on a low hill. Turning, he looked in my direction. I peered into the murky darkness, trying to discern his face, trying to call his name. But his face was in deep shadow, and no sound emerged from my throat. Abruptly, he turned away and was gone. A great sadness filled my breast as I lost sight of him. Bereft, I traveled for miles and miles through the deepening darkness, but I could not find him . . .

When I woke, my face was wet with tears.

Mr. Kincaid came for me a half hour later. He looked quite handsome in a dark brown suit, white shirt, and plaid vest.

"Are you ready?" he asked.

"Yes," I said, smiling tentatively. "Where are the children?"

"I've hired a woman to care for them. You needn't worry about their safety. Mrs. Clancy has good references."

"I wasn't worried," I replied, "only curious."

Mr. Kincaid chewed the inside of his lip and I knew he was concerned over my lack of maternal interest in the little boy and girl.

We ate dinner at a lovely restaurant. Heavy green drapes were pulled back from the tall, leaded windows. A green patterned carpet covered the floor. The tables were covered with snowy linen cloths, the chairs were green damask. Crisp linen napkins, sparkling silverware and flowered china dishes were laid before us. Mr. Kincaid ordered a large steak with all the trimmings for himself, a smaller one for me. I shrugged when he asked if I cared for champagne. I could not remember if I had ever tasted it and, if I had, if I liked it.

Mr. Kincaid seemed at a loss for words as we dined. Sometimes I caught him staring at me, a worried expression on his ruggedly handsome face.

Later, over dessert, he said, hesitantly, "Hannah, I've made an appointment with a doctor for tomorrow at eleven o'clock."

"A doctor? For me?"

"Yes. Perhaps he can help you remember who you are."

"I'd like that."

Mr. Kincaid smiled. "Good. Shall we go?"

I was glad to return to my hotel room. I seemed to tire easily. At dinner, Mr. Kincaid had said I had been wounded, though he had not gone into detail. Now, undressing for bed, I saw the scar just under my left breast. The area was still sore, and I fretted over the scar. How ugly it was. As I studied the puckered flesh, it occurred to me that I was lucky to be alive.

But somehow it seemed unimportant. There was a nightgown on my bed and I slipped it over my head and crawled under the covers. The sheets were clean and smelled of sunshine and soap. I snuggled deeper into the blankets. Unaccountably, I began to cry.

It was a long time later when I fell asleep, only to have the same dream I had had earlier in the day.

When I woke in the morning, my cheeks were wet with tears.

* * *

The doctor, whose name was Lyman Whitehall, gave me a thorough examination and pronounced me physically healthy. His diagnosis came as no surprise. I had amnesia, he said, caused, in his opinion, as a result of the fall I had taken when I had been shot. Yes, he said, my memory would, in all probability, return in a matter of time. A word, a familiar face, a sudden shock, anything at all might cause my memory to return as suddenly as it had disappeared. On the other hand, there was a possibility that my loss of memory would be permanent. In the meantime, I was not to worry, nor was I to try and force myself to remember the past. Just relax, the doctor advised with a fatherly smile, and rest.

Easy for him to say, I thought irritably. He knew who he was. He wasn't the one feeling lost and alone and frightened.

Mr. Kincaid was quiet on the ride back to the hotel. He held my arm as I stepped from the hired carriage.

"You go to your room and rest awhile, Hannah," he said wearily. "I'm going to look in on Heecha and Mary."

I nodded and climbed the stairs to my room. Inside, I sat in the overstuffed chair near the window and gazed at the street below. People were coming and going, laughing and talking, carrying on with their lives while I sat in a strange room in a strange town, alone, and afraid. Why had my memory suddenly disappeared? Was there something so awful in my past that I had shut it out rather than remember? What if my memory never returned? Why couldn't I remember anything?

That night, at dinner, my father told me the story of my childhood, how we had lived in a beautiful place called Bear Valley. I had liked it there, he said, especially the pine tree forest near our home. Didn't I remember Rabbit's Head Rock? My old mare, Nellie? Shadow, the Indian boy who had been my friend?

"Surely you remember Shadow," my father coaxed. "He came to our house almost every day. Your mother taught him to read and write."

On the verge of tears, I shook my head. "I don't remember," I wailed in despair. "I'll never remember!"

"Calm down, Hannah," my father said kindly. "It will all come back to you. I know it will."

After dinner, we went for a walk around town. Mr. Kincaid bought gifts for Mary and Heecha, a new cream-colored stetson for himself, two dresses, a petticoat, a hat and a pair of shoes for me.

Heecha and Mary chattered excitedly as we went from store to store. They stared in wide-eyed wonder at two Chinamen standing in the doorway of a hand laundry, giggled at a scantily-clad tart leaning over the balcony of a tawdry saloon.

I tried to show some enthusiasm, but I failed miserably. How could I enjoy the sights and sounds of the city when I couldn't even remember who I was, or where I had come from? Heecha and Mary were supposed to be my children, blood of my blood and flesh of my flesh. How could I have born and nursed two children and have no memory of it? I thought of the dresses my father had bought me. One was the color of the sky at dawn, the other was a pale green. Maybe I didn't like blue. Or green. Maybe Mr. Kincaid wasn't my father. Maybe Heecha and Mary were not my children. Maybe . . .

"Say, look at that."

I glanced at the sign Mr. Kincaid was pointing at. It read:

"BUFFALO BILL'S WILD WEST AND CONGRESS OF ROUGH RIDERS OF THE WORLD . . . A congress of American Indians representing various tribes, characters and peculiarities of the wily dusky warriors in scenes from actual life giving their weird war dances and picturesque style of horsemanship."

"I'd like to see that," Heecha exclaimed.

"So would I," Mr. Kincaid agreed. "Says here that the show's coming to town tomorrow.What do you say, Hannah? Would you like to go? We could make a day of it."

"If you like," I said lethargically.

"Me, too!" Mary chimed in.

"Of course, you, too," Mr. Kincaid said enthusiastically. "I've read some of Ned Buntline's penny dreadfuls about Bill Cody. I'd kinda like to see how the man measures up to the legend."

I smiled, but I had no real desire to see William "Buffalo Bill" Cody, or his Indians.

"Did you ever meet Buffalo Bill?" Heecha asked his grandfather.

"No, never did. But I've heard a lot about him over the years. He was born in Iowa back in '46, but moved to Missouri when he was eight or nine. He rode for the Pony Express for a time. Later, he was chief of scouts for the Fifty Cavalry at Fort McPherson in Nebraska Territory. Made quite a name for himself fighting Indians. Of course, his real claim to fame was as a buffalo hunter for the U.P. Railroad. Killed better than four thousand buffalo." Mr. Kincaid laughed. "His favorite gun for hunting buffalo was named Lucretia Borgia. Guess I'm babbling," he said, smiling at me. "You go on upstairs and get some rest, and I'll go pick up some tickets for the show.

"Fine."

"Goodnight, Hannah."

"Goodnight, Mr. Kincaid."

"I wish you'd call me Pa, like you used to."

"Goodnight . . . Pa."

In my room, I undressed, bathed, and slipped into my nightgown. In bed, with the covers pulled up to my chin, I stared into the darkness, afraid to go to sleep. A distant clock chimed the hours—nine, ten, eleven. At last, I could fight it no longer and I closed my eyes.

The same man was in my dreams once again, and once again I was wandering alone in a dark land. Always, the man was ahead of me, just out of reach. I ran as fast as I could, ran until my lungs were on fire, but always he eluded me. Exhausted, I fell to the ground, my legs too weak to support me any longer. I closed my eyes, and felt his presence beside me. His hand touched my face, his mouth met mine. I tried to open my eyes, but my eyelids were so heavy, and I was so tired. His arms went around me, holding me tight, and I felt safe and warm. I knew if I could just open my eyes, I would see his face. I would know who he was, who I was.

With a strangled cry, I opened my eyes to find myself alone in my hotel room.

* * *

Buffalo Bill's Wild West Show was a spectacular event. It depicted the actual life of the Indians and the settlers who had lived in the west, fought for it and died for it.

There was a wigwam village, Indian war dances, chants and songs to the Great Spirit, the marching of soldiers, the building of frontier posts, the perilous life of scouts and trappers and settlers.

The grand entrance brought the crowd to its feet. Indians galloped by in war paint and feathers—Sioux, Cheyenne, Arapahoe. Mexicans and cowboys followed the Indians. There were black-bearded Cossacks and Arabs, German troopers, detachments from the United States Cavalry, Cubans and Puerto Ricans, Texas Rangers and rough riders.

And then, as the music picked up, Buffalo Bill made his entrance. He was handsome, broad-shouldered with long brown hair, a brown goatee, and brown eyes. He was indeed an awesome sight as he rode into the arena decked out in snowy white buckskins and wearing a white sombrero. Mounted on his favorite horse, Charlie, he cantered around the arena, the epitome of what a Western hero should be.

The show was exciting from beginning to end. I loved the color and majesty of the Indians. They sat on their spotted horses as if they were a part of the animal.

Sitting, standing, or hanging precariously over the horse's side, they rode magnificently. The most thrilling spectacle was when the Deadwood stage was attacked by a howling mob of Indians brandishing rifles and tomahawks. Just when the stage seemed doomed, the cavalry came to the rescue amid flashing sabers and thunderous rifle fire.

The show was a huge success. The audience cheered and clapped and stamped their feet when it was over. I, too, had found it highly entertaining and exciting. When my father asked if we would like to walk around the grounds, Heecha and Mary jumped up and down in their eagerness, so I said that I, too, would like to go exploring. And we did.

Heecha was fascinated by the Indians in their colorful native costumes and elaborate feathered headdresses. Mary, who seemed to be a shy, quiet little girl, held fast to her grandfather's hand, refusing to venture from his side.

We were standing at a concession booth, waiting to order some lemonade, when a tall blond man wearing a cavalry uniform happened by. He looked at me, turned away, and then looked at me again, his blue eyes wide with surprise.

"Hannah!" he exclaimed. "Hannah, it is you."

I glanced at my father. He was staring at the man in stunned disbelief, as if he had just seen a ghost. And then his expression grew hard and cold.

"Joshua Berdeen," my father said, his voice flat and unfriendly.

"Hello, Mr. Kincaid," the man called Berdeen replied amiably, never taking his eyes from mine. "Hannah, I've looked everywhere for you."

"Have you? Why?"

"Why?" Berdeen looked genuinely puzzled. "Why? For God's sake, you're my wife, that's why."

Wife! I felt the color drain from my face. Wife. I looked at my father. "You told me my husband was dead."

My father nodded, a troubled look in his eye.

"What the hell's going on here?" Joshua Berdeen demanded.

"Take it easy, Josh," my father admonished, conscious of the many people milling about. "Hannah's had an accident. She doesn't remember you, or anything else."

"Amnesia?" Berdeen mused skeptically. "How?"

"We're not sure. She was wounded a while back. She hit her head when she fell. The doctor said that may have caused it."

Several emotions flitted across Joshua's face and then he said, firmly, "Well, Amnesia or not, she's my wife and there's not a thing you can do about it."

The two men glowered at each other.

My father started to speak, glanced at me, and was silent.

"Listen, Kincaid, why don't we go someplace quiet and talk?" Joshua suggested, his tone and expression affable.

"I think that's probably a good idea," my father agreed. "We're staying at the Palace Hotel. They have a pretty fair dining room there. Does that suit you?"

"Right down to the ground," Berdeen said. "I'll meet you there in an hour."

My father nodded. Together, we watched Berdeen duck into one of the tents set up along the west side of the showgrounds.

"You said he was dead," I murmured, my voice faintly accusing. "Why did you tell me he was dead?"

"I thought he was," my father replied. "You told me he was dead."

"*I* told you?"

"Yes. Before your accident. Don't you remember?"

"No."

"It doesn't matter. Apparently, he's very much alive."

Our lemonade forgotten, we made our way to our carriage and drove back to the hotel. I dressed carefully for dinner. My dress, a pale cream-colored silk, had a square neckline, a fitted bodice and a flared skirt. I wore my hair down, pulled away from my face by a black velvet ribbon.

Dressing, I could think of nothing but my husband. I felt my cheeks flush as I remembered how he had looked at me, his eyes warm and possessive. What if Mr. Berdeen expected me to live with him? How could I live with a man who was a stranger?

Berdeen was waiting for us when we entered the hotel dining room. He was a handsome man. His dark blond hair was cut short, his skin was tanned from daily exposure to the sun. He was wearing a dark gray suit that emphasized his broad shoulders and long legs. His eyes were very blue, and I felt my cheeks grow hot as I read the desire lurking behind his cordial expression.

He rose politely to his feet as I approached the table. Smiling, he held my chair for me, complimented me on my dress and hair.

"How do you happen to be riding with Buffalo Bill's Wild West Show?" my father asked Berdeen after we ordered dinner.

"It's a long story," Joshua replied. He looked at my father, then at me.

"After the redskin kidnapped Hannah, I left the Army. I searched for her everywhere and when I saw Cody's show, I joined up, hoping that somewhere in our

travels, I'd run across Hannah." His blue
eyes danced merrily as he looked at me.
"As you can see, my hunch paid off."

My father nodded. "Yes."

"Naturally, now that I've found her,
I'll quit the show and start looking for a
house."

"A house?" I murmured.

"For us," Joshua said, patting my
hand. "We are married. You're my wife,
and I intend to take care of you from now
on, make a home for us."

"How long have we been married?"

"Seven years," Joshua answered.

"But Heecha can't be yours," I
mused, puzzled.

"No," Joshua replied thinly. "He's a
bastard whelped by the Cheyenne buck
who took you from me."

"Josh, mind your language," my
father admonished curtly.

"I'm sorry, Mr. Kincaid. Hannah. But
the thought of what that redskin did to
my wife makes my blood boil."

"What did he do?" I asked, frowning.

"Let's not talk about it now," Josh
said.

"Is Mary your daughter?"

"No." Joshua took my hand in his.
"Let's talk about something else, shall
we? The past is best left in the past. Isn't
that right, Mr. Kincaid?"

"I'm not sure," my father remarked
slowly. "I have a lot of questions that

need answers."

"I don't think this is the time or the place," Joshua said. "Hannah and I are together again, and that's all that matters."

"Perhaps you're right," my father said dubiously. He looked at me, and I knew he was worried that Joshua might say or do something that would upset me.

Our dinner came then and Josh steered the conversation around to the wild west show and Buffalo Bill. I ate mechanically, not really tasting anything. I was so confused. If only I could remember!

Joshua asked if I would go for a walk with him, alone. My father did not like the idea, but apparently he could think of no valid reason why I should not take a walk with my husband, so he kissed me goodnight, shook hands with Berdeen, and went upstairs to check on Heecha and Mary, who had dined in their room with Mrs. Clancy.

Joshua took my arm as we exited the hotel lobby. Turning left, we walked down the street.

"I've missed you," Josh said, squeezing my arm. "You'll never now how much. I didn't think I'd ever see you again."

There was no mistaking the love shining in his eyes, or the sincerity in his voice.

"Were we happy, Joshua?"

"Of course," he answered quickly.
"And we'll be happy again. You'll see."

"If only I could remember."

"It doesn't matter," Joshua assured
me with a benign smile. "We're together
again and that's what counts. We'll make
new memories, Hannah, and they'll be
good ones."

"Where are we going?" I asked as we
passed the last store and kept walking
into the darkened space beyond the town
proper.

"Nowhere. I just wanted a chance to
be alone with you. Hannah, I love you.
I've loved you ever since I first met you."

"Mr. Berdeen . . . Joshua."

"You've got to trust me, Hannah,
darling. I'll find a house for us tomorrow
and we can get on with our marriage."

"Tomorrow?"

"I can't wait any longer, Hannah."

With a low groan, he swept me into his
arms and kissed me deeply, passionately.
I returned his kiss because he was my
husband and because I didn't want to hurt
his feelings, but I felt nothing. Nothing at
all.

Josh was breathing deeply when we
parted. "Hannah, don't make me wait any
longer," he rasped, his hands caressing
my back and shoulders. "I want you so
much."

"We can't," I said quickly. "Not

here." The thought of letting him make love to me filled me with revulsion, but some primal instinct warned me not to let Joshua know I did not find him attractive sexually.

"You're right," he agreed, smiling wanly. He brightened suddenly. "The hotel! We can go there."

"Josh, please, this is all so sudden. I know you're my husband and have every right, but...I...I don't remember anything. It would be like making love to a stranger." I smiled up at him. "Please give me a little time."

Joshua let out a long sigh. I saw his hands clench at his sides. "Very well, Hannah," he said at last. "I'll try not to rush you. But don't make me wait too long."

"I won't," I promised. "Could we go back to the hotel now? I'm cold."

Later, alone in my bed, I wondered how I was going to live in the same house with a man who was a stranger to me. And yet, he seemed nice enough, his manners were impeccable, and he was quite handsome . . . still, if he were my husband, wouldn't I feel something for him?

Deeply troubled, I fell asleep.

The same dark, faceless man haunted my dreams.

X

Shadow

Rebecca Matthews stared, unbelieving, at the Indian seated on the edge of her bed. She opened her mouth, closed it slowly, too stunned to utter a word. He was here. After all these years, he was here. She had thought never to see him again. Bright color crept up her slender neck and flooded her cheeks as she recalled the intimacies she had shared with the handsome man who was staring back at her, a faint smile touching his lips.

"Hello, white lady," he said quietly, and Rebecca felt her heart flutter queerly. He had called her that when they first met. It had been a term of derision then, now it had the sound of an endearment.

"Hello," Rebecca replied tremulously.

Another long moment passed while they studied each other. Rebecca's eyes devoured the only man she had loved or desired since her husband died almost ten years ago. Two Hawks Flying. The name whispered through her mind, unlocking memories, conjuring up images of grassy prairies and hide-covered tepees scattered beneath a wild blue sky.

Two Hawks Flying. He looked strong and fit, even more handsome than she remembered. New color flooded her cheeks at the wicked thoughts that crowded her mind. She felt all her senses spring to life, kindling a sudden heat deep in the core of her being as she wondered, with shame, if he would make love to her again. She had not known a man that way since he left her so long ago and the hope of his touch stirred the passion that had lain dormant within her all that time. What was there about the man that aroused her so? She had been on fire for his touch the first time she saw him lying unconscious beside the road seven years ago.

Seven years, she mused. Where had the time gone? She wondered again why he affected her so strangely. She was thirty-six, seven years older than he was. She was a white woman, a good Christian; he was an Indian, a heathen savage. Yet the few nights she had spent in his arms had been the best, most fulfilling hours she had ever known. Even her husband had never aroused her to such a fever pitch, or satisfied her so completely.

Shadow's smile widened as he saw the

crimson flush staining Rebecca's cheeks.
So, he mused, she was also remembering
the nights they had shared in this house,
in this bed. He looked deep in her eyes and
saw the same wanting, the same loneliness, he had seen seven years before.

"Where is Beth?" he asked, referring
to Rebecca's daughter.

"Away. At school." It had been hard,
sending her fifteen-year-old daughter
away, but Beth had yearned to go to Miss
Elsbeth's School for Young Ladies, and
Rebecca could not refuse. "Would you like
some coffee?"

Shadow nodded. Rising, he followed
the woman through the parlor into the
kitchen. The house had not changed. The
same furniture still filled the rooms, the
same pictures decorated the walls, the
same worn Bible rested on a low table
beside the sofa.

He studied Rebecca as she busied
herself at the stove. She had not changed
much. There were a few strands of gray in
her hair, a few more lines around her
mouth and eyes, but the long brown hair
still framed a face that was lovely and sen-
sitive, the brown eyes were still warm and
serene, the figure beneath the simple
calico frock was still trim and pleasing to a
man's eye.

Rebecca took two china cups from the
sideboard and placed them on the table.
Her hand shook a little as she poured hot

coffee into the cups, then sat down at the table across from Shadow.

"Why have you come here?" she asked, unable to stifle her curiosity any longer.

"I need your help."

"My help." Concern darkened her eyes. "Are you hurt?"

"No. I need to go to New York."

"New York! Whatever for?"

"My woman is there. And my children. I must find them."

"Oh."

Shadow nodded as he read the unspoken question in her eyes. "It is the same woman."

"You said she belonged to another."

"She did, but now she is mine."

"You . . . you bastard!" Rebecca flung the words at him, her jealousy nearly choking her. Once, she had begged him to take her away with him and he had refused. And now he was asking her to help him find the very woman he had left her for, a woman she had grown to hate. It wasn't fair. She put her face in her hands, not wanting him to see her tears.

She didn't hear him move, but he was suddenly beside her, his hand on her shoulder.

"Please, Rebecca. I must find her."

Rebecca remained silent for several moments. If she refused to help Two Hawks Flying find his woman, he would

probably go away. If she agreed, she
would at least be with him until he
accomplished his goal. New York was a
big place, and far away. The journey
would take several weeks. Perhaps
months. Perhaps he would never find the
woman . . .

"I'll help you," Rebecca decided.

Shadow smiled. Impetuously, he
kissed her cheek, his nostrils breathing in
the clean sweet scent of her hair while his
memory replayed the nights he had made
love to her. With an effort, he put the
thoughts from his mind. Such a thing
must never happen again.

"How soon do you want to leave?"
Rebecca asked.

"In the morning."

"You can't go wandering around New
York dressed like that," Rebecca mused.

Shadow grinned ruefully as he glanced
down at his dusty buckskins and mud-
splattered moccasins. "I have nothing else
to wear," he said with a shrug.

"I . . . I still have the pants and shirt
you wore the last time you were here,"
Rebecca murmured. She flushed under his
probing gaze. She had kept the clothes
because they were a tangible reminder of
Two Hawks Flying, something she could
cling to. Somehow, they had brought her
comfort when she grew sad and lonely.
"You'll need some shoes," she said,
refusing to meet his eyes. "And a hat. And

you'll have to cut your hair."

"No."

Rebecca frowned. "Why not?"

"I am a warrior."

"I know that," she retorted, exasperated. "But if you don't cut your hair, you might as well wear a sign with the word 'Indian' in big black letters."

"No."

"Suit yourself. But if you walk around New York looking like that, you're just asking for trouble. Of course, it doesn't matter to me. I hope you never find her."

"Cut it," Shadow said curtly.

She had the grace not to gloat. But once she had the scissors in her hand, Rebecca hesitated. His hair was thick and black, longer than her own. It felt heavy in her hands, alive.

"Cut it," Shadow said again.

With a sigh, Rebecca picked up a lock of his hair. Shadow's face was grim as he felt the scissors move through his hair. A warrior never cut his hair except in shame or deep mourning. Yet, he knew he would have willingly shaved his head if it meant finding Hannah and his children.

A half hour later, Rebecca stepped back to take a look at her handiwork. "Not bad," she mused, then grinned at his look of utter dismay. "It will grow back," she assured him.

Shadow nodded, but he did not look convinced.

"I'll go to the store in the morning and get you a pair of boots and a hat," Rebecca said, thinking aloud. "And I'll ask Mrs. Phelps to keep an eye on my place until I get back." She met Shadow's eyes, then looked away, embarrassed because she knew he could read the wanting in her eyes. "Good night," she whispered, and fled the room.

Shadow bedded down on the parlor floor. Lying on his back, his arms folded beneath his head, he stared at the whitewashed ceiling, his expression thoughtful. It would not be easy, spending the long days and nights with Rebecca Matthews while he searched for Hannah. He had grown fond of Rebecca when he had stayed with her seven years ago. And she had been fond of him. Too fond. She had made no secret of the fact that she desired him, and he had satisfied her needs because she had saved his life and he had nothing else to give. She had begged him not to go back to his people, had begged him to take her with him when he left. Tonight, looking into her quiet brown eyes, he had seen her love for him was still strong, but his love and his heart belonged to Hannah, only Hannah. Perhaps it was cruel of him to ask for Rebecca's help in finding Hannah, but he had no one else to turn to.

They left early the next morning.

Shadow felt uncomfortable in the clothes of the white man. The boots on his feet were not so comfortable as his moccasins; the hat felt heavy on his shorn head. Only the rifle resting in the crook of his arm felt right.

Rebecca smiled warmly at Two Hawks Flying as she climbed into the buggy and picked up the reins. He looked very different from the man whose unexpected appearance had so surprised her the night before; different but still breathtakingly handsome. He would never pass for a white man but, with his hat pulled low, he might pass for a Mexican. It was a slim chance, but one he seemed willing to take.

She felt a swift surge of jealousy for the woman he loved so much, and then a surge of gratitude. If not for his woman, Two Hawks Flying would not be here now seeking her help.

Rebecca laughed happily as she contemplated going to New York with Two Hawks Flying. New York! Home of the Astors, J.P. Morgan, Commodore Vanderbilt, Jay Gould.

Her excitement mounted as she thought of going sightseeing in the city. New York had grown considerably since she left it to be married eighteen years ago. Perhaps Two Hawks Flying would take her for a drive along Fifth Avenue, which had been nicknamed Millionaires

Row because of all the mansions built there. The mansion built by Jay Gould was said to have thirty-five rooms! Perhaps they could visit Delmonico's Restaurant, where the beau monde wined and dined. Perhaps they could stop at Saint Patrick's Cathedral.

Eyes shining, Rebecca glanced at the handsome man sitting beside her. "Shall we go?"

Shadow nodded, eager to begin the journey that would take him to New York, and Hannah.

XI

Spring 1885

The house Joshua bought was more lovely than anything I had ever seen or imagined. It was two stories high, painted white, with yellow shutters. A wide porch spanned the length of the house, red and yellow flowers bloomed in a neat border around the front yard. Inside, there was a large parlor with a stone fireplace, a dining room and a spacious, airy kitchen. Upstairs, there were three large sunlit bedrooms.

I had many reservations about moving into the house with Joshua, even though he had convinced me that we were indeed man and wife and that we had once been blissfully happy until we had been cruelly separated by the savage warrior who had kidnapped and raped me. Heecha and Mary were the result of that horrible time, Josh said. His voice filled

159

with venom when he spoke of the Indian
who had abducted me. I was sure I had
never seen such implacable hatred in my
life.

It was Joshua's suggestion that we
leave Heecha and Mary in the care of my
father for the time being so that we could
get reacquainted. I had grown very fond of
Heecha and Mary, but I agreed with Josh
that it would be best for them to stay with
my father. The children were both a little
wary of me, and I didn't feel quite ready to
accept the full responsibility for their care
just yet. I had so many questions, so
many strange feelings. Often I burst into
tears for no reason; sometimes I simply
sat at the window and stared into the distance, plagued by a sense of loss, of
emptiness. Occasionally I felt as if I were
on the verge of some great discovery, but
each time I neared the brink, I found only
a dark empty void.

My father was as reluctant for me to
move into the house with Joshua as I was,
but there was little he could do. I was,
after all, Joshua's wife. He even produced
a marriage license to prove it.

"Joined in Holy Matrimony this 31st
day of January, 1878," the document read,
"Hannah   Kincaid   and   Joshua   Lee
Berdeen." It   was   witnessed   by   Dr.
Edward Mitchell and Colonel Grant Craw-
ford. The names meant nothing.

I was extremely nervous the day we

moved into the house. I had grown to care for Joshua a little since he had come into my life over a month ago. He was always kind and sympathetic, as patient as a saint. But now we were alone, just the two of us, and I was as nervous as a new bride.

Joshua seemed to understand. In the afternoon, he took me shopping, insisting I buy whatever caught my fancy. When I could not decide between a pale blue silk and a similar gown in jade green, he insisted I buy them both, as well as hats, shoes and gloves to match. We returned home with a dozen boxes filled with dresses, shoes, hats, gloves, petticoats, a lacy shawl, a delicate ivory fan, a dainty parasol, silk stockings, everything I could possibly need.

That night, we ate dinner by candle-light. The meal was prepared by a cook Josh had hired that morning; it was served by a young Mexican girl dressed in a crisp black uniform with lace cuffs.

Joshua smiled at me over his wine glass. "To you, my darling Hannah," he said, raising his glass.

I smiled back at him, not knowing what to say. Josh made small talk as we dined, commenting on Buffalo Bill's wild west show, and about the rumor that Sitting Bull and Annie Oakley were going to join the show. Sitting Bull had been a great Sioux war chief, Josh informed me, and Annie Oakley was a brilliant sharp-

shooter whose accomplishments bordered
on the supernatural. Now that the Indians
had been subdued, there was a great
curiosity to know more about them, Josh
said, not only here, but abroad. To that
end, Cody was planning a trip to England
in the future, to perform for the Queen.

"That would be exciting," I said.
"Won't you be sorry to miss it?"

"No." Joshua's eyes grew solemn. "I
never intend to leave you again, Hannah,"
he vowed. "Or be parted from you."

I suppose I should have been touched
by such a declaration of love and devotion,
but it filled me with dread.

After dinner, we went into the parlor.
Josh sat beside me, his eyes touching my
face again and again, as if to reassure himself that I was really there. We talked of
trivial things, of Joshua's plans for the
future, about New York, about my father.
Joshua had spent most of his life in the
west, out of doors, but he said he was tired
of that and ready to settle down. He had
several friends in the city and he was certain one of them would give him a job. In
the meantime, he had enough money in the
bank to take care of us. I wasn't to worry
about anything, just rest and take life
easy.

"It's hard to rest and take it easy," I
said impatiently. "Sometimes I feel that if
I could just remember one tiny thing that

happened in my past, I would remember everything."

"The past doesn't matter," Josh said as he put his arm around me and drew me close. "We're together now and that's what's important. The only thing you need to remember from the past is that I loved you, that I still love you."

His words did little to ease my mind. Instead of making me feel better, I had the odd impression that he didn't want me to remember anything.

About nine o'clock, Josh yawned. Stretching, he said, "Well, it's been a long day. I think I'm ready to turn in. How about you?"

Words failed me, so I nodded instead. Josh smiled at me as he took my arm and led me upstairs. The maid had turned back the covers. My nightgown was waiting.

I stood in the middle of the room, unmoving, as Joshua began to undress.

"Here, let me help you," he offered, moving toward me. I shivered with apprehension as I felt his fingers begin to unfasten the hooks on the back of my dress. His hands were warm against my skin, and I grimaced as I felt his rising manhood press against my buttocks.

When my dress was unfastened, Josh slipped it from my shoulders and let it fall around my feet. Then, hands on my shoulders, he turned me to face him. His

eyes glowed with a possessive light as his
fingers unlaced my chemise and untied the
tapes of my petticoat.

"You're so beautiful, Hannah," he
said huskily, his eyes burning into my
naked flesh. "So beautiful. I've dreamed
of this moment for years."

"Have you?" My voice was high and
shaky.

"Don't be afraid, Hannah," he
whispered. "I won't hurt you."

Joshua's eyes flamed with desire as he
lifted me into his arms and carried me to
bed. The clean white linen sheet was cold
as ice against my bare flesh as he put me
to bed. I lay stiff and unmoving as he slid
into bed beside me, his arms drawing me
close. A fine mat of dark blond hair
covered his chest and I felt a quick wave
of revulsion as his chest hair rubbed
against my breasts. His manhood burned
against my thigh.

"Josh, don't please," I begged, trying
to push him away. "Please."

Anger flared in Joshua's eyes, then
was gone. With an effort, he loosened his
hold on me, though he did not release me
completely.

"Don't make me wait, Hannah," he
rasped. "I've waited so long."

"I'm sorry," I said miserably, "but
please try to understand how I feel. I
know we're married, but you're a stranger
to me, someone I've just met. Can't we

please wait a little longer? I'd be so grateful."

"Very well," he growled tersely. Releasing me, he swung his legs over the edge of the bed and stood up. I kept my eyes averted from the sight of his aroused manhood, weak with relief that I had persuaded him to leave me alone, for the present, at least.

Josh let out a long disappointed sigh as he picked up a cigar and lit it. I studied him as he paced the dimly lit room. His face was in shadow so I could not read his expression clearly. His body was taut, with anger or desire I could not tell. His neck, face and arms were tanned a golden brown, the rest of his body was pale. Dark blond hair curled on his chest, arms, and legs. There was a deep purple scar on the side of his left leg, as though a hunk of meat had been gouged out. There were smaller scars on both of his arms, just below the elbow.

Feeling my gaze, he walked toward the bed. "Go to sleep, Hannah," he said curtly. "I'm willing to wait a little while before I claim my husbandly rights, but only a little while."

Nodding, I obediently closed my eyes. Surprisingly, I quickly fell asleep.

My life with Joshua should have been a happy one. He found a job at one of the banks, did well, and was soon promoted to a management position. I had a lovely home, a cook and a maid to do most of the work, more clothes than I could wear, a shiny black carriage to take me wherever I wanted to go. I made a few friends. My father came to see me daily, bringing Heecha and Mary.

Heecha had been enrolled in school and was fast becoming a problem. He did not like school. He did not like his teacher. He did not like the other children. He did not like the clothes he had to wear.

"I don't know what I'm going to do with him," my father lamented. "He won't try. And now he's starting to cut class. I'm afraid we'll never make a white man out of the boy. He's too much like his father."

"Tell me about his father," I said. "What was he like?"

"He was a good man, in his way. You grew up together, back in Bear Valley."

"Why are you so hesitant to tell me about him?"

"I'm not hesitant. It's just that, well, there's a lot I don't know."

"What do you mean?"

"Well, I'm not sure how you felt about Josh, before your accident, I mean, and I don't want to say anything that might ruin your chance for happiness. He is your husband, legally, and Shadow isn't."

"Did Shadow take me away from Joshua?"

"In a way."

"You're only confusing me more."

"I know, honey. I'm sorry. As far as I can tell, Josh blackmailed you into marriage because he loved you and couldn't get you any other way."

"Blackmail?" I exclaimed, shocked. "How?"

"Listen, Hannah, honey, let's not talk about it any more. I don't want to upset you, and I don't want to say anything that might not be true. I know Josh loves you and no matter what you think or how you feel, you're legally his wife. I think, for now, you had best hold onto that."

Later, alone, I pondered my father's words. What was he so reluctant to tell me? How had Joshua blackmailed me into marriage? Had I loved Joshua? If so, why had it been necessary for him to blackmail me into marriage? Had I loved the man called Shadow? Could I love an Indian? I thought of the Indians I had seen at the wild west show. They had looked savage and forbidding, yet I had been fascinated by them.

So many thoughts, so many questions, and no answers. No wonder I had a headache. With a sigh, I climbed the stairs to the room I shared with Joshua and curled up on the bed. There were so many things I longed to remember, but now, I wanted only to lose myself in sleep, to search for that elusive man of my dreams who was, in some ways, more real than reality.

XII

Shadow

Rebecca Matthews smiled as Two Hawks Flying materialized out of the shadows, a young deer slung over his broad, copper-hued shoulders. She had fallen deeper and deeper in love with him as the weeks went by. He was kind, thoughtful, a good provider. She marveled daily at his knowledge of the outdoors, at his ability to hunt and fish, to find water where there seemed to be none. He taught her about the plants and animals they saw in their travels, pointed out the tracks of deer and bear and coyote. To pass the time, he told her the stories and legends of the Cheyenne people.

Late one night, sitting side by side in front of the fire, he told her of Heammawihio, the Wise One Above, who was the chief god of the Cheyenne. In the beginning, Heammawihio made people to

live. When they died, they would be dead
for only four nights, and then they came to
life again. After awhile, Heammawihio discovered this was not a good idea. Knowing
he would live again made a man too brave,
too rash, and caused much needless
killing. Men were not afraid to die and so
they took foolish chances. They felt no
grief at death, no remorse in killing. What
harm was there in slaying a man when he
would live again in four days? That was
why people now died forever.

Rebecca smiled indulgently at the
story of Heammawihio. It was a heathen
belief, yet she found it charming. Two
Hawks Flying also told her about the
various animals that possessed mystical
powers. The badger was considered very
powerful. Often, the badger advised the
People what to do and how they should
live. The bear possessed spiritual powers.
Eagles, ravens, hawks, owls, and magpies
were birds which possessed powers in
matters of war. Often, the feathers of such
birds were tied into the tail of a war horse.
The skunk also held special powers.
Medicine men wrapped their herbs and
remedies in the skin of the skunk; its tail
was also tied to the tails of war horses. It
was believed that deer had power for good
or evil. The white-tailed deer was known to
have special power with affairs of the
heart. The antelope's power could only be
used for good. The lizard was considered

good luck and rawhide cutouts of lizards were often worn as charms by men going to battle. Such charms, made by the medicine men, were believed to give the wearer courage and the power to move quickly and avoid arrows or bullets. Prairie owls were believed to have protective powers. Owl feathers worn on the head and arms gave the wearer the ability to move silently in the night.

"Do you truly believe these things?" Rebecca asked, finding it hard to believe that a full-grown man could give credence to such superstitions.

"Yes."

Rebecca mulled that over for several moments. His name was Two Hawks Flying, and the Indians believed the hawks had power.

"Your name?" she asked, "does it hold some special significance?"

"Yes. I am called Two Hawks Flying because of a vision I had during the Sun Dance."

"Can you tell me what you saw in your vision, or is it forbidden to speak of it to a stranger?"

"You are not a stranger," Shadow said quietly. "The Sun Dance is our most sacred religious ceremony. In it, a man offers his blood and his pain to Maheo, the Great Spirit. Sometimes a man is granted a vision. Sometimes the vision is for the benefit of all the people. Sitting Bull offered a hundred pieces of his flesh to the Great Spirit shortly before the battle at the Greasy Grass. In his vision, he saw hundreds of white men falling into his camp.''

"Custer," Rebecca murmured. How well she remembered the horror of reading of the Custer massacre back in '76. It had been a terrible slaughter as thousands of Sioux and Cheyenne rode through Custer and the Seventh Cavalry, destroying everything in sight.

"Sometimes a vision is personal," Shadow went on. "I was in great pain as I hung suspended from the Sun Dance pole. The sun was hot against my flesh and my sweat mingled with my blood as I gazed into the sun. In torment, I offered a prayer to Man Above, begging him for help, and his answer came in a rushing of mighty wings as two red-tailed hawks swept out of the sunlight to hover near my head. They admonished me to be strong and brave and promised that I should be a mighty war leader, and that I should have everything I desired."

Rebecca gazed at him for several minutes, fascinated by his words. It was hard for her to understand such a heathen ritual and yet, sitting beside him, she could easily believe he posessed supernatural powers.

"And did the hawks speak the truth?" she asked, still mesmerized by his story.

"Yes."

There was a faraway look in his fathomless black eyes, and Rebecca knew intuitively that he was thinking of his woman. She felt her heart swell with jealousy as she thought of the woman who had won the heart of Two Hawks Flying. What kind of woman was she? Was she young and fair and beautiful? Did she love the man as much as the man loved her?

Rebecca knew somehow that the woman of Two Hawks Flying would possess more than mere physical beauty. She would have to possess great inner strength and peace to withstand the hardships of life in the west. The woman had ridden the war trails with Two Hawks Flying, had fought at his side. The thought made Rebecca shudder with horror, yet she knew she would have done the same to be with the man sitting quietly beside her.

Now, as she watched him skin the deer he had killed, she marveled anew at his lithe grace and easy strength. He was beautiful to watch. Powerful muscles rippled beneath his shirt as he sliced off a section of haunch. His face was strong and handsome in the glow of the fire, his movements were swift and sure as he spitted the meat and placed it over the fire to cook.

Rising, he towered above her, making her feel small and vulnerable and yet so safe, so protected. Each night she yearned for his touch, hoping he would come to her blankets and take her in his arms. And each morning she woke alone and unfulfilled, her secret woman's place still throbbing for his touch.

Rebecca's heart beat faster as he smiled down at her. Maybe tonight would be the night. Maybe tonight he would read the hunger in her eyes. Maybe tonight . . .

Shadow was silent as he turned the meat over the fire. He was well aware of the aching need in Rebecca's eyes. He heard her toss and turn in her blankets night after night, knew what she desired of him. He had read the love shining in her luminous brown eyes; the love, and the sadness.

Later, as they ate the succulent venison, the companionable silence of the previous nights was gone and in its place the tension grew, stretching taut as a bowstring between them.

As was his habit, Shadow moved into the darkness after dinner, giving Rebecca time to relieve herself and wash before crawling into bed.

This night, he prowled the darkness, his brow furrowed, his thoughts troubled. The wind was cold on his neck, and he lifted a hand to his butchered hair, mourning the loss. Like all Cheyenne males, he had been vain about his hair, yet it seemed a small loss if he could get Hannah back. Hannah. His arms ached to hold her, his mouth hungered for the taste of her sweet lips, his eyes longed for the sight of her beloved face.

He was constantly nagging Rebecca, urging her to push the team harder, faster, in his eagerness to cross the miles that separated him from the woman he loved above all else.

Rebecca. What was he to do with her?

When he returned to camp, he saw she had spread their blankets near the fire. Tonight, instead of spreading their blankets on either side of the fire, she had placed them side by side. He could see her body outlined beneath her blankets, saw her clothes and undergarments folded to one side.

With a sigh, he went to his bedroll. For a long moment, he stood staring down at her. Then, removing his boots and socks, he slid into his blankets and closed his eyes.

For a time, there was no sound in the night save for the hiss of the dying flames and the soft whisper of the wind moving through the trees. And then he heard the muffled sound of her weeping.

Turning his head, he saw that she had drawn the covers over her head. He could see her shoulders shaking beneath the blankets as she began to weep harder.

"Rebecca." He spoke her name softly, his voice filled with tender compassion.

"Leave me alone," she sobbed, though

that was the last thing in the world she wanted.

Shadow listened to her cry for a few moments more, willing himself to be strong, to ignore the pain he detected in her tears, but he could not callously disregard her sorrow, not when he was the cause of it.

Sitting up, he threw back the covers of his makeshift bed, reached across the narrow space that separated them, and drew Rebecca into his arms. She did not resist, only buried her face against his chest so he could not see her tears. Tenderly, he patted her back, gently smoothed the long brown hair.

"Do not weep, Rebecca," he said quietly. "I cannot bear the sound of your tears."

"I love you," she whispered tremulously. "Why can't you love me?"

"I could easily love you," Shadow replied heavily. "But you could never be first in my heart, and you would not be happy otherwise."

"I would," Rebecca argued petulantly. "Honest I would."

"Maybe," Shadow said dubiously. "But Hannah would scratch your eyes out."

"Hannah? Is that her name? I hate her!"

"No, you would like her. And she would like you."

Rebecca looked at him through tear-swollen eyes. "Please love me," she implored in a little-girl voice. "I've thought of no one else since you left."

"I cannot."

"Please." Throwing her arms around his neck, Rebecca pressed her lips to his, all the hunger and loneliness in her heart conveyed in her kiss. The heat of her breasts penetrated his shirt, searing his skin.

Shadow might have resisted the temptation of her lips had she not dropped her hand to his groin, covering his manhood. With a low groan, he bent her back, pressing her onto the blankets, his mouth taking possession of hers.

Rebecca was on fire for him, her hands eager as they explored his hard muscular flesh, stroking his arms and chest as she lifted her hips, arching upward, aching with the need to receive him. She was so willing, so eager, and he was just a man, after all . . .

Afterward, he was overcome with remorse, but the damage was done. How would he face Hannah? How would he explain what he had done?

For once, Rebecca had no trouble interpreting the expression on Shadow's face, and she was suddenly ashamed of the way she had thrown herself at him. No matter that she loved Two Hawks Flying with all her heart, he belonged to another and she had caused him to be unfaithful. She knew suddenly that what she had done had been wrong, very wrong.

Wrapping a blanket around her nakedness, she went to where Shadow was sitting, his eyes dark and brooding as he stared into the cold embers of their fire.

"I'm sorry," she said earnestly. "I was wrong. Please forgive me. Your woman, Hannah, need never know."

Shadow lifted tormented eyes to Rebecca's face. "I cannot live with a lie between us. I will tell her and hope she will forgive me a second time."

"You told her, about the other times?"

Shadow nodded. "She said she was grateful you had saved my life, that she did not begrudge you the hours we had spent together." He shook his head slowly. "I do not think she will feel that way this time."

"Please forgive me," Rebecca said again.

"It was not your fault. I am a grown man. You did not force me into your bed."

"Didn't I?" Rebecca asked with a rueful smile. "I threw myself at you. Practically raped you."

Shadow grinned at her, his black mood lifting a little. "Perhaps I shall tell Hannah that you raped me against my will. I will say I fought as hard as I could, but you were too strong for me."

Rebecca blushed, the laughter

bubbling in her throat at the picture his words painted in her mind. Then, as her laughter died away, she became serious once more. "It won't happen again, I promise."

Shadow rose to his feet, his hands cupping her slim shoulders. "If things were different, I would be proud to have you for my woman. But there is no place in my heart or my life for anyone but Hannah. She is a part of me."

Rebecca nodded. Blinking back her tears, she walked back to her bedroll and crawled under the covers. Sleep was a long time coming.

XIII

Joshua

Joshua Berdeen frowned when he stepped out of the bank building and found his father-in-law waiting for him. He had been avoiding a confrontation with Samuel Kincaid for weeks, but he could tell by the expression on Kincaid's face that the man wasn't going to be put off again.

Bowing to the inevitable, Joshua put a smile on his face. "Evening, Mr. Kincaid," he said pleasantly.

"Evening, Josh. I'd like a few minutes of your time, if you don't mind."

"Sure. Shall we step into the Crystal Palace for a drink?"

"If you like."

The two men were silent as they walked the two blocks to the saloon. Inside, Kincaid headed for a table in a far corner of the room. Joshua ordered a bottle of rye whiskey and two glasses, his

insides slowly knotting with tension as he
waited for Kincaid to say what was on his
mind. He didn't have to wait long. The
man came right to the point.

"I want to know what happened
between you and Shadow and Hannah,"
Kincaid said curtly. "All of it."

"How much did Hannah tell you?"
Joshua answered evasively.

"What Hannah told me is neither here
nor there," Kincaid retorted. "I want to
hear your side of the story, and I want the
truth."

Joshua licked his lips nervously, his
eyes darting around the saloon as he tried
to gather his thoughts.

"I . . . I was in charge of the men sent
out to hunt Shadow down and bring him
in," Josh began slowly. "I didn't know he
had Hannah with him. I thought she had
been killed back in Bear Valley when the
Sioux attacked your place. I couldn't
believe it when she came tumbling out of
that cave. She was pregnant, in labor, but
the baby was born dead. As soon as I saw
Hannah, I knew I still loved her. Knew I'd
always love her. But she was infatuated
with that damn Cheyenne buck, couldn't
talk about anything else."

"Infatuated?"   Kincaid   muttered
dryly.

"Okay, okay, she was in love with the
bastard. But the Army wanted him out of
the way. He was scheduled to be hanged

the first of the year. The thought drove
Hannah crazy. She came to me, begging
me to do something to save his life. Maybe
it was a rotten thing to do, I don't know.
But I loved her so damn much, so I told
her I'd set him free if she'd marry me. And
she did.''

Josh poured himself a drink, downed
it in a single swallow, and poured a second.

Kincaid ran one brown finger around
the rim of his glass, his eyes thoughtful.
"You didn't keep your end of the bargain,
did you?''

"I kept it,'' Josh answered harshly. "I
promised I wouldn't kill him, and I
didn't.''

Kincaid's blue eyes filled with disdain.
"But you cut him up and left him tied up
out in the woods, prey to the cold and
wolves.''

Joshua didn't answer, but his eyes
betrayed his guilt. Muttering an oath, he
emptied his glass.

"I should have killed the bastard,''
Josh murmured bitterly. "Every time I
took Hannah in my arms, I knew she was
thinking of him, dreaming of him,
pretending I was him. Wishing I was him!
It drove me wild. I loved her so much, I
would have done anything to make her
happy, anything to make her love me.''

"Is that why you threatened to give
Heecha away? Kincaid sneered. "To make
her love you?''

"You don't understand! What was I supposed to do, let everyone know my wife had slept with that filthy savage while he was in prison? Did you expect me to let her keep the brat, to look at it every day and know I wasn't the father? How could I face my men with that half-breed brat tagging at Hannah's skirts? How could I face myself?"

There was real anguish in Berdeen's voice and Kincaid felt an unwanted wave of sympathy for the man.

"When she ran away from the fort, I went after her," Josh continued in a hopeless tone, "determined to win her love, to make her know how much she meant to me. When I found her, I could have cried, I was so relieved. But she refused to go with me. She was going home, she said, home to the Cheyenne. I don't know, I guess I went crazy. I . . . I slapped her. And then that damned Indian showed up." Joshua's blue eyes turned dark and ugly at the memory. "He shot me twice, then staked me out and left me to die."

"As you had left him," Kincaid murmured.

Joshua nodded, his face contorted with rage. "The wolves came when the sun went down. They licked the blood from my arms. One of them took a chunk out of my left leg. I was nearly out of my mind with pain when a dozen troopers showed up. A few minutes more and they would have been too late . . ."

Sam Kincaid shivered as Berdeen's voice trailed off. The man had been through hell, there was no doubt about that. But so had Shadow. It was obvious both men were in love with Hannah, and equally obvious that neither one would willingly give her up to the other. Sooner or later, the two men would meet again. He hoped, for his daughter's sake, that the right man won the last battle.

With a sigh, Kincaid sipped his drink. Perhaps there wouldn't be another confrontation. Shadow had been wounded back in Nebraska Territory, and might, even now, be lying dead out on the prairie.

"So what now?" Kincaid queried. "What are your plans?"

"I plan to stay right here," Josh answered, staring bleakly into his empty glass. "I've got a good job, a nice house. As soon as Hannah's feeling better, I plan to give her sons. Lots of sons."

"What about Mary and the boy?"

"I don't know. I guess I'll cross that bridge when I come to it."

Kincaid leaned forward, his face only inches from Berdeen's. "You're at it," he said evenly. "Those kids are my grandkids, and if anything happens to either one of them, anything at all, I'll come after you. You savvy my meaning?"

Joshua swallowed hard. "I understand."

"Good. I'll be going now, but before I go, I've got just one more thing to say. It's about my girl. You make her happy, Berdeen. You give Hannah anything she wants, and if she wants those kids living with her, you let her have them. Hannah deserves that much. And she sure as hell deserves someone better than you."

Josh nodded, intimidated by the fierce expression in Kincaid's eyes. It would not be wise to cross the man, that was certain.

Josh stayed in the saloon for a long time, methodically working his way to the bottom of the bottle. Sam Kincaid was a meddlesome old fool, Josh mused. Who the hell did Kincaid think he was, anyway, to tell Joshua Berdeen what to do? Old windbag, full of dire threats and warnings. But as long as Kincaid was around, Hannah would never be completely his. And as for that Indian brat, Josh had no intention of having the little bastard underfoot now or ever. Or the girl, either, though she could easily pass for white. No, there was only one thing to do—take Hannah and leave New York for good.

Josh smiled crookedly at the thought. He had always had a secret yearning to see California and the Pacific Ocean. Perhaps he would take Hannah to Los

Angeles or San Francisco. Let the old man keep the kids. He wanted Hannah, only Hannah.

XIV

I was sitting in the parlor, mending a pair of Joshua's socks, when Heecha came storming through the door, his handsome young face dark with anger and frustration.

"I will not have a white man's name!" he cried, stamping his foot. "My father said I did not have to have one, and I won't!"

"Heecha, calm down." I laid my mending aside and drew the boy close. "Who said you must have a white man's name?"

"My teacher, Mr. Patten. He said if I did not pick one out by tomorrow, he would give me one. Can he do that? Why must I have a white man's name? I am Cheyenne!"

"You are white, too!" I reminded him gently. "Your mother is white."

"You are my mother," he said with an exasperated sigh. "Why do you not remember?"

"I don't know. I wish I could."

"I want to come and live with you. Why can't I?"

"You ask difficult questions."

"Don't you love me any more?"

"I do love you, Heecha," I answered slowly, realizing it was true. "It's just that I'm so confused. I don't know what to do. I don't know who I am. But I do love you. You are a fine, brave boy."

Heecha's dark eyes regarded me solemnly, reminding me of other eyes, but I could not remember whose. It was all so frustrating. Every time I thought I was on the verge of remembering something, the memory faded, leaving me sadly disgruntled.

"I'll talk to Joshua soon," I promised. "I'll ask him tonight if you and Mary can come and live with us."

"Mary would like that. She cries for you at night."

"Does she?"

"Yes. She is very lonely for you, and for our father."

"Do you know where your father is?"

"No. He was shot the day you were hurt."

"Shot? How? By who?"

"He killed the man who hurt you. My grandfather told my father to run away.

My father did not want to go, but Namshim said he must or he would be arrested for killing a white man. We did not see him again. Namshim said my father might be dead, but I do not believe that. I know he is alive. He will come for me one day. I told Mary this, but she does not believe me."

"I hope you're right, Heecha. I'm sure he is a fine man."

Heecha nodded gravely, and I thought how grown up he was for a boy his age.

"Have you decided on a name?"

"No. I will not take a white man's name."

"How about a Cheyenne name, only in English?" I suggested.

Heecha frowned, and then smiled. "I shall be called Hawk!" he said resolutely. "It is my father's special spirit."

"Hawk." I repeated the name, wondering why it sounded so familiar. An image danced in the back of my mind, an indistinct image of a tall, dark-skinned man and a soaring red bird. Frowning, I tried to bring the blurred image into focus. Almost, I could see the man's face and I felt as if I were on the verge of remembering something vitally important when Josh called my name and the moment was gone.

Heecha left the house a few minutes after Joshua came home. Heecha did not

like Josh. And Josh did not like Heecha. I
thought that was odd, because I knew
Joshua liked children. He had told me
often that he was eager for us to have
sons, lots of sons. Nevertheless, I knew
Josh would not want Heecha to live with
us, but I was determined to have my son
and daughter with me. I did not remember
having children, but I had grown to love
the solemn-faced boy and the sweet shy
girl, and I meant to give them a home and
all the love they would ever need.

I mentioned as much to Joshua at
dinner that night.

"Perhaps, in time," he said coldly.
"For now, I don't want to share you with
anyone else."

I did not like the tone of Joshua's
voice, or the look in his eyes, and so I let
the matter drop, at least for the time
being.

After dinner, we went into the parlor.
Josh picked up his pipe and the newspaper; I sat beside him on the sofa to
finish mending his socks. We sat in companionable silence until, by chance, I
glanced at the front page of the paper.

There, in bold black print, I read,
"NINE YEARS SINCE CUSTER
MASSACRE" and below there was a
replica of the headlines the paper had
featured on July 6, 1876:

"A Bloody Battle."

"General Custer Killed."

"The Entire Detachment Under His Command Slaughtered."

"Seventeen Officers Slain."

I leaned forward, all else forgotten as I read a detailed account of the massacre of General George Armstrong Custer and his men. I read names, many names: Boston Custer. Alfred Terry. Medicine Tail Coulee. Lonesome Charlie Reynolds. Sundance Creek. Mitch Boyer. Varnum, Custer's chief of scouts. Bloody Knife, the Arikara scout. The steamer, "Far West." Captain Keogh's horse, Comanche, the only survivor of the battle. Mark Kellogg, the newspaper reporter. Isaiah Dorman, the Negro interpreter. Tom Custer. Crazy Horse. Gall. Sitting Bull. And there, in among all the others, was the name of Two Hawks Flying, war chief of the Cheyenne.

I felt as if a veil was suddenly taken from my mind and I remembered clearly the battle that had taken place at the Little Big Horn on June 25, 1876. I remembered being desperately afraid the man I loved more than my own life would be killed, and when his big red roan horse came back from the battle without him, I knew a terrible, heart-wrenching fear. I remembered climbing aboard the big red stallion, hoping the animal would carry me to its master.

And he did . . .

I found Shadow standing atop a high

*bluff, a pensive expression on his hand-
some face. Blood was leaking from a
jagged gash in his right side; his leggings
were covered with it. He did not seem
aware of my presence as I drew rein beside
him.*

*Following his gaze, I saw the cold,
unmoving forms of Custer's men scattered
below us. Stripped naked, they made an
eerie sight in the dusky twilight. Many of
the bodies had been scalped. Others had
been mutilated with the Cheyenne cut-arm
sign or the Sioux cut-throat sign. Ribbons
of dried blood made dark stains against
their pale waxy flesh.*

*A single horse grazed in the
distance . . .*

"Shadow." I whispered his name, felt
my heart leap with joy as I remembered
who he was. And who I was.

Joshua looked up, his eyes narrowed
to mere slits. "What did you say?"

"You!" I recoiled in horror as I
recognized the man who had lied to me.
The man who had wanted to kill my son.
Had I gone mad? Joshua was dead, long
dead.

"So," Joshua mused ruefully. "You
remember."

"Everything," I said bitterly. I looked
at the sock I had been mending and threw
it to the floor. I did not want to touch anything that belonged to Joshua Lee

Berdeen.

I stood up, my eyes flashing defiantly. "I'm leaving," I said tersely. "Don't ever try to see me again."

In a quick movement, Joshua was off the sofa, his hand biting into my arm. "You're not going anywhere, Hannah Berdeen. Yes, Berdeen! You're my wife, all nice and legal, and I intend to be your husband. In every way."

Joshua's face was close to mine, his blue eyes alight with the heat of his desire. I struggled wildly, trying to loosen his hold on my arm. Shadow needed me. Heecha said he had been wounded, might be dead. But he couldn't be dead. I couldn't live without him. Or Heecha. My heart swelled with love and my arms ached to hold my son and daughter again.

"Let me go!" I shrieked. Lifting my knee, I rammed it into Joshua's groin, felt a quick satisfaction as he groaned and doubled over, releasing my arm.

Triumphant, I headed for the door, screamed as I felt Joshua's hand close around my ankle. I fell face down, scraping my cheek against the edge of a table. We grappled on the floor for several minutes, but I was no match for Joshua's strength and he soon had me pinned to the floor, his hands trapping my arms above my head, his body straddling my hips. I did not like the smile that twisted his lips, or the lust burning in his eyes.

"You're mine, Hannah," he said huskily. "Only mine."

I shuddered at hearing those words, for they were similar to what Josh had said on our wedding night just before he ripped my wedding gown from my body and forcibly made me his. Only I had never been his. And I never would be.

I cringed as he unfastened the bodice of my dress and ripped away my chemise. His hand was hot against my flesh, his mouth hard and unyielding as he kissed me.

Knowing it was useless to fight, I closed my eyes and summoned Shadow's image to mind—eyes like a dark flame, a wealth of thick black hair, muscles that rippled like silk beneath smooth, copper-hued skin . . .

I felt nothing that night as Joshua possessed my body, nothing at all. In my mind, I was far away in Bear Valley, warm and safe in the arms of the only man I had ever loved.

XV

Shadow

Rebecca Matthews sighed as she spread her blankets beside the fire. Tomorrow, they would reach New York and Two Hawks Flying would be reunited with his woman. How could she bear to watch him with his precious Hannah? Just thinking of him holding someone else made her want to scratch the woman's eyes out. It was so unfair!

She put her unhappy thoughts from her as she heard footsteps coming through the brush behind her. This was her last night with Two Hawks Flying. She would not spoil it by brooding about the future.

Putting a smile on her face, Rebecca turned around, felt the smile fade as she saw three men riding toward her. Rebecca knew, by the look of them, that they were the kind of men decent women avoided. She took a step backward as the three men reined their horses to a halt. Dismounting, they walked toward her, their eyes taking in the blankets spread before the fire, the wagon parked in the shadows, the horses grazing nearby. and the woman standing alone.

"Well, now, looky here," mused the tallest of the three. "Just what the doctor ordered. A warm fire, a little food, and a woman to cuddle."

"Settle down, Lem," cautioned a ruddy-faced man with a full black beard and a scarred face. "Let's find out just who the little lady is, and what she's doing out here all by her lonesome." The man walked closer to Rebecca, his close-set eyes traveling up and down her body. "Who are you, missy? What are you doing out here by yourself?"

"Who I am is none of your business," Rebecca answered haughtily. "And I am not alone. My . . . my husband is due back any moment. He . . . he went into the woods to . . . to relieve himself."

"That right?" the man called Lem said with a leer. "Just the two of you here alone. Romantic, ain't it, Harv?"

The third man grinned, revealing stained yellow teeth. "Yeah," he agreed. "I could use a little romancin' myself."

"All in good time," the ruddy-faced man said cheerfully. "All in good time. Lem, you go search that wagon, see if there's any money or liquor under the seat. Harv, you search the woman."

Rebecca's eyes widened with fear and revulsion as the man called Harv laid his rifle down and walked purposefully toward her. Her mind screamed for her to run, but fear held her frozen to the spot. She gasped as Harv reached out and ran his dirty hands over her breasts and thighs and buttocks. She cringed as his foul breath filled her nostrils, cried out as he pushed her down on the ground. She began to thrash wildly as the man lowered himself over her, his mouth tasting her lips.

"Hold on, Harv," growled the ruddy-faced man. "I'm the ramrod of this here outfit. I figure that gives me first crack at the woman."

Harv reared up, his eyes flashing in protest. "Shit, Hooper, don't stop me now!"

The man called Hooper opened his mouth to reply, but whatever he was going to say died with him. There was a sharp retort and Hooper fell backward, blood spurting from a hole in his chest. Rebecca screamed as his blood sprayed over her. A second gunshot killed Lem as he reached for his rifle.

Harv sprang to his feet, his hands over his head, his face pale as death. "Don't shoot!" he cried. "Don't shoot. I give up."

Rebecca scrambled to her feet and ran

to Shadow's side. Now that the danger
was past, she felt suddenly weak. She
glanced at Shadow, gratitude in her eyes,
but he was glaring at the man called Harv.
His black eyes were ablaze with fury, his
mouth was parted in a feral snarl. He
looked suddenly savage and merciless and
she took a step backward, more afraid of
the man beside her than she had been of
the three strangers.

"Listen, there was no harm done,
mister," Harv said, speaking rapidly. "Me
and others just got carried away a little,
but we didn't do nothing. Honest!" He
looked at Rebecca pleadingly. "Tell him
nothing happened, lady." His voice rose
shrilly. "Tell him, lady! For God's sake,
tell him before it's too late."

"It is already too late," Shadow said
coldly, and pulled the trigger a third time.

Rebecca turned away as Harv lurched
forward, a hand pressed against his chest.
Blood trickled through his fingers. "Help
me," he begged, his voice faint. And then
he fell forward to move no more.

Rebecca stared at the three bodies in
horror. Only moments ago they had been
alive and now they were dead. She looked
at Two Hawks Flying out of the corner of
her eye. His face was hard, cold, and cruel.
A look of satisfaction lurked in his deep
black eyes.

He had killed three men, and he was
glad. The thought frightened her and she

turned on her heel and began running, away from the man who had become a stranger, away from the bodies lying in the dirt.

She heard Two Hawks Flying call her name, but the sound of his voice only spurred her on and she ran blindly into the woods, running as if the devil himself pursued her. She had to get away. Away from Two Hawks Flying. Away from her own desire for a man who was a heathen, a savage, a coldblooded killer.

She screamed as she felt his arm close around her waist, and then he was pulling her close. She struggled wildly, her nails raking his cheeks as she kicked at his shins. He grunted once as her knee slammed into his groin, but he did not release his hold and in a few minutes she stopped fighting, suddenly too tired to care what happened.

"Rebecca, do not be afraid. I will not hurt you."

His voice was kind, tender with concern. Lifting her face, she looked into his eyes. The savage killer was gone. Relief washed through her and then the tears came, washing away the nameless fear that had sent her fleeing into the night.

Lifting her in his arms, Shadow carried Rebecca back to the fire, placed her carefully onto her bedroll, covered her as if she were a child.

"Sleep now," he said, stroking her hair. "I will keep watch."

Rebecca nodded wordlessly, knowing if she tried to speak, she would beg him to share her bed again, to hold her one last time. Knowing that if she asked, he would refuse.

The thought hurt worse than anything else.

In the morning, the bodies were gone, all traces of them completely erased.

That evening, they arrived in New York.

It was a big city. Shadow looked around in awe. He had forgotten how strange the white man's dwellings were, how noisy the city was. There was the shrill sound of a woman hawking vegetables, the constant clatter of iron-shod hooves, the creak of numerous carriages and buggies and wagons, the chiming of a distant clock as it struck the hour. People crowded the sidewalks, all of them apparently in a hurry to be somewhere else.

Rebecca reined the team to a halt before one of the many hotels, draped the lines around the brake. "Well, we're here."

Shadow nodded. He felt strange in the white man's city clad in the clothing of a white man.

"This place looks nice," Rebecca remarked, nodding toward the hotel. "We

might as well stay here for the night, if
that's all right with you. Tomorrow we'll
start looking for your woman. Do you
know where she's staying?"

"No."

"Well, I guess we'll just have to ask at
every hotel and boarding house in town
until we find her." Rebecca climbed down
from the carriage and followed Two
Hawks Flying into the hotel. She did not
say what she was thinking, but she was
hoping he never found Hannah. Perhaps
then he would turn to her for the love and
comfort every man needed.

The clerk standing behind the front
desk frowned as Rebecca informed him
they would like a large room with a double
bed and a bath.

"How much will that be, please?" she
asked politely.

"It's . . . uh, excuse me, ma'am," the
clerk said, running a nervous finger
around the inside of his starched white
collar. "You see, we're . . . uh, full up just
now."

Rebecca drew herself up to her full
height. "And would you still be full up if
my . . . my husband were a white man?"
she demanded, her brown eyes flashing
angrily.

The clerk grew red around the ears.
"I'm sorry, ma'am, but it's company
policy not to rent rooms to Indians."

"I assure you my husband won't run

wild and scalp you in the night," Rebecca said, her manner regal. "I'd be willing to make it worth your while if you let us stay."

The clerk licked his lips. His salary was nothing to brag about, and he was not averse to taking a little money under the table now and then.

"Well, I, uh, perhaps we do have an empty room." He reached under the counter and withdrew a large brass key. "Room 22, top of the stairs to your left."

Rebecca smiled sweetly. "Thank you."

Shadow followed Rebecca up a winding staircase, keenly aware of the desk clerk's curious eyes on his back.

Room 22 was large, decorated in various shades of pink and green. Flowered paper covered the walls.

Shadow placed Rebecca's valise at the foot of the bed. "Now what?"

"I'd like to change my dress, and then go out for something to eat. Tomorrow morning, we'll inquire at every hotel and boarding house in town. If that doesn't work, we'll have to check all the doctor's offices. Don't worry," Rebecca said, laying a hand on Shadow's arm. "I'm sure we'll find her."

Shadow nodded. Somehow, he would find Hannah, no matter how long it took.

"I think we should buy you some city clothes," Rebecca suggested.

"Why?"

"So you won't look so out of place. That shirt and those pants are all right for the country, but they're out of date and a little ragged. We don't want people staring at you too hard."

Shadow nodded ruefully. It was useless to argue with the woman. What she said made sense, even if he didn't like it.

They dined at a small restaurant. In hushed tones, Rebecca instructed him to hold her chair until she was seated. He grinned wryly as he followed her instructions. While they studied the menu, she told him the proper way to order dinner. He was aware of the many curious glances sent in his direction. The word "Indian" was whispered at many tables, but no one caused any trouble and the meal passed without incident.

Back in their hotel room, he stripped off his shirt and flexed his muscles. The white man's clothing was tight, restricting, and he longed for his comfortable buckskins.

"I . . . uh, I need to get ready for bed," Rebecca said, suddenly shy. "Would you put out the light, please?"

Shadow nodded. Pulling a blanket from the foot of the bed, he spread it out on the floor. Snuffing the lamp, he stretched out on the floor, his hands folded beneath his head. He could hear

Rebecca undressing in the dark, the whisper of cotton against her flesh as she slipped into her nightgown.

"Goodnight," she murmured.

"Goodnight."

Rebecca was soon asleep, but Shadow lay awake for a long time, listening to the sounds of the city. Somewhere, Hannah was hearing the same sounds. Soon, she would be beside him again. Soon.

Rebecca smiled as Shadow stepped from the tailor shop. How handsome he looked in a black suit and tie. The crisp linen shirt emphasized his dark good looks, the cut of the suit showed off his broad shoulders and long legs. Several women paused to stare at him as they passed by, their eyes openly admiring what they saw. He was very male; few women could see him and not take a moment to appreciate his rugged good looks and muscular build.

With an air of proud possession, Rebecca stepped up and slipped her arm through his. "Shall we go?" she asked brightly, and grinned as she felt the envious glances of the other women.

They started at the near end of town and stopped at each hotel, and always the answer was the same: "Sorry, no one here by that name."

When they reached the end of the main street, they crossed to the other side

and began working their way back down.
Finally, at the Palace Hotel, the clerk
nodded.

"Yes, we have a Kincaid registered
here, a Mr. Samuel Kincaid."

"What room?" Shadow asked, unable
to keep the excitement out of his voice.

"Room 29."

"Thank you," Rebecca said, and
hurried after Two Hawk Flying, who was
already racing up the stairs. She caught up
with him outside the door of room 29, her
heart hammering at the thought of
meeting the woman of Two Hawks Flying.
Now that they had reached the end of
their search, Two Hawks Flying would
have no further need of her help. The
thought filled her with sadness. His
presence had cheered her days, giving
purpose to her life. The thought of going
back to her lonely house was suddenly
depressing; her life, once so serene, now
seemed empty.

She glanced at the door as it swung
open to reveal a big man dressed in brown
twill pants and a tan shirt.

"Shadow!" the man exclaimed,
grinning broadly. "Well, I'll be damned.
Come on in, son. Damn, but I'm glad to see
you."

Kincaid ushered his visitors inside
and closed the door.

"Nehyo!" A young voice shrieked the
Cheyenne word for father as Heecha

hurled himself into Shadow's arms.

"Naha," Shadow said in a choked voice. Sweeping his son into his arms, he hugged him tight.

Mary came out of her bedroom, wiping sleep from her eyes. At the sight of her father, she flew to his side, her hands clutching at his pant leg. "Nehyo! Nehyo!"

Bending, Shadow scooped his daughter into his other arm.

Rebecca blinked back tears as she watched the children hug and kiss their father, both chattering a mile a minute as they poured out a dozen questions.

"Hold on, little ones," Shadow said. "Where is your mother?"

"She is living with a white man," Heecha said, his joy ebbing.

Shadow's eyes sought his father-in-law's face. "What white man?"

"Berdeen," Kincaid answered.

Disbelief showed in Shadow's eyes. "Berdeen is dead."

Kincaid shook his head. "No. He is alive and Hannah is living with him. They have a house not far from here."

Rage flamed in Shadow's eyes. Slowly, he put Heecha and Mary down. His hands curled into tight fists.

"Shadow, before you get yourself all worked up, let me explain. Hannah has amnesia."

"What is amnesia?" Shadow asked in

a tight voice.

"It's a sickness. When she got hurt back on the reservation, she hit her head. She doesn't remember anything."

Shadow frowned. "What do you mean?"

"She doesn't remember you, or the children, or anything that happened before the accident. We ran into Joshua here in New York. She *is* his wife."

"No! She is mine."

"Not according to the white man's law. She belongs to Berdeen."

Rebecca pressed a hand over her mouth as she saw Shadow's face grow black with anger and jealousy. She was reminded of the three men who had tried to abuse her and she felt a sudden pity for the man called Joshua Berdeen. If Shadow had coldbloodedly killed men who had tried to attack a woman who was only a friend, what would he do to the man who had taken his wife?

"Where does Berdeen live?"

"I'll take you there myself," Kincaid replied.

"I do not need any help in taking back what is mine."

Kincaid grinned ruefully. "I know. I just want to be there in case Hannah needs me."

Shadow nodded. There was always a chance that Berdeen would emerge victorious. Hannah would need her father then, because no matter who won the coming battle, Berdeen would not survive.

"Shall I wait for you here?" Rebecca asked.

She put the question to Two Hawks Flying, but it was the older man who replied. "Please stay until we return," Kincaid said, smiling at Rebecca. "I'm Hannah's father, Sam Kincaid. Forgive my bad manners for not introducing myself sooner."

"Of course," Rebecca said. In the excitement of their arrival, no introductions had been made. Now she held out her hand. "I'm Rebecca Matthews."

"Pleased to meet you, ma'am."

"Call me Rebecca, please."

Kincaid nodded. He had many questions he wanted to ask, but he was unsure how to phrase them. Who was this lovely woman, and how did she happen to be with Shadow? Was she married? How long was she going to be in town? Was she married?

Rebecca smiled. "Shadow is an old friend," she said, answering one of Kincaid's unspoken questions. "I helped him once, a long time ago, when he was in trouble."

"I see." Kincaid glanced at Shadow.

"When I found out Hannah was alive, I went to Rebecca and asked her to help me find her."

Kincaid nodded. It was easy to see

that Shadow felt only friendship for the woman, and just as easy to see that the woman was in love with Shadow.

"Please wait here," Kincaid said to Rebecca. "Perhaps you'd let me take you out to dinner later on?"

"Yes," Rebecca said. "I think I'd like that."

"Good. Shadow, let me tell Mrs. Clancy we're leaving. She's been looking after the children for me."

Shadow nodded impatiently. He was eager to see Hannah, to hold her in his arms. And almost as eager to put his knife into Berdeen's flesh.

Kincaid returned moments later, a sixgun shoved into the waistband of his trousers.

"Nehyo, take me with you."

Shadow dropped to one knee before his son. "Not this time, naha. I will be back soon, and then we will all go back home."

"You will come back? You promise?"

"I promise." Shadow hugged his son tightly, kissed his daughter on the cheek, and then walked briskly out of the room.

With a sigh, Kincaid followed him.

Kincaid knocked on the door of the Berdeen home three times, then shrugged. "I guess they're not home."

"I will wait," Shadow said. "Inside."

"Door's locked," Kincaid said, trying

the latch.

Pivoting on his heel, Shadow went down the porch steps and rounded the corner of the house. There was the faint sound of breaking glass; a moment later, Shadow opened the front door.

Kincaid stepped inside, whistled under his breath. The house was empty. He could feel it even before they checked the closets and rooms upstairs.

Shadow's rage exloded then. Grabbing a fireplace poker, he lashed out in fury, smashing lamps, pictures, bric-a-brac, breaking windows and mirrors.

Kincaid stayed out of the way, letting Shadow vent his frustration. Only a fool would have drawn Shadow's anger to himself, and Kincaid was no fool.

Finally, Shadow dropped the poker. He stood in the center of the parlor, surrounded by broken glass and furniture, his sides heaving, his dark eyes smoldering.

"Damn," Kincaid murmured. "I wonder what spooked him."

"Where would he go?" Shadow asked.

"I don't know. He could have gone anywhere. You go back to the hotel. I'll check the train station. Maybe somebody wll remember seeing them. If I don't have any luck there, I'll try the livery stable."

"I will go with you."

"No. It'll be better if I go alone. If anybody thinks you're after Berdeen, they won't tell us a thing. There's murder written all over your face."

"You go," Shadow said with a wry grin. "I will wait for you at the hotel."

Rebecca was sitting on the sofa with Heecha and Mary when Shadow returned to the hotel. One look at his face told her everything she needed to know.

"Where is Nahkoa?" Mary asked.

"I do not know, little one," Shadow answered heavily. "The white man has taken her away. But I will find her. I promise."

Looking at him, Rebecca knew he would not fail.

Rebecca Matthews smiled shyly at Sam Kincaid the following morning. It was a little unsettling, sharing a hotel suite with a man she had only met the day before. The children could not be considered adequate chaperones, and she knew her reputation was ruined. A single woman sharing a suite with two men? It simply wasn't done. But only dynamite could have blasted her from the hotel. She had to stay, had to know the final outcome of Shadow's search for his woman.

Kincaid had returned to the hotel the night before with the news that a man answering Joshua Berdeen's description had bought an old Conestoga wagon and four good horses. The man at the livery barn did not recall seeing a woman with

Berdeen. Two Hawks Flying—she never could remember to call him Shadow like everyone else—had left early this morning. Rebecca was at a loss to know how Two Hawks Flying would ever find Berdeen when he had no clue as to the man's destination. Berdeen could be headed for Mexico or Canada or any of the states and territories in between. And yet, despite the monumental odds involved, Rebecca knew deep within her heart that Two Hawks Flying would not give up until he found Hannah.

Hannah. What attributes did this paragon of womanhood possess that two men were so determined to have her?

"Good morning, Mrs. Matthews," Kincaid said cheerfully. "Would you care to go downstairs and have some breakfast?"

"Yes, I'd like that," Rebecca said, putting all thoughts of Hannah and Two Hawks Flying aside for the moment.

"Good. Shall we go?"

"Will the children be dining with us?"

"No. They were up early this morning to see Shadow off. They've already eaten and gone back to bed."

Breakfast was a congenial meal. Rebecca told Sam about her home, about Beth, and about the time she had saved Shadow's life. Sam told Rebecca about his wife, Mary, and how she had been killed by Indians back in '76. He told her how he had barely escaped with his own life, and how he had been reunited with Hannah and Shadow at the Rosebud Reservation.

Unbelievably, two hours passed.

Later, they walked through the town, pausing now and then to window-shop. Rebecca exclaimed over the latest fashions; Kincaid grumbled about the high price of tobacco.

When they tired of walking, they stopped at a sweet shop for a cup of coffee and a slice of rich French pastry. Rebecca smiled at Kincaid as he held her chair for her. He was a charming man, she thought as she sat down and gracefully spread her skirts around her. She could not remember when she'd had a nicer time, or felt more at ease with another person. He was so easy to talk to. He was not as handsome as Two Hawks Flying. Not so young, not quite so fascinating. And yet she had no complaints. He was big and strong, nice-looking for a man his age, which she judged to be about fifty. They were never at a loss for words. Surprisingly, there was never any awkwardness between them as there was so often between strangers.

In the afternoon, they picked up Heecha and Mary and went for a drive along Millionaire's Row. It was difficult to say who was more dazzled by the splendid mansions, the children or the adults. They all gazed in wide-eyed admiration at the beautiful homes, most of which had been copied from medieval castles, palaces, or chateaus.

Rebecca thought the homes looked grand. The turrets reminded her of stories about England and Robin Hood. The Vanderbilt mansion at Fifth Avenue and Fifty-Eighth Street looked more like a cathedral than a home. It was rumored that it took the combined efforts of thirty servants to cater to its needs.

"This is where the kings live," Kincaid told Heecha and Mary as they drove along the street.

"Kings?" Heecha repeated. "What kind of kings?"

"All kinds. Oil kings, railroad kings, sugar kings, silver kings, tobacco kings."

"What kinds of kings are those?" Mary wanted to know.

"The rich kind." Kincaid smiled at his grandchildren. They had no real concept of money. They had been raised where money was virtually nonexistent.

It was a good way to grow up, he thought, but how much longer could they live that way? Civilization was spreading across the face of the land. First there were only a few houses, then someone opened a small store and the next thing you knew, you had a bank and a church and soon you had a new city on your hands.

Kincaid frowned as he looked at the monstrous houses along Millionaire's

Row. Given a choice, he thought he much
preferred the little place he had built with
his own two hands back in Bear Valley to
these pretentious houses with their lofty
ceilings and leaded windows and crystal
chandeliers.

That night, they ate an early dinner
and then, after seeing the children off to
bed, they went to the Metropolitan Opera
House.

Rebecca tried to concentrate on the
play, but she was too conscious of the man
sitting beside her. She was drawn to him,
and she wondered how she could find him
so attractive when she was in love with
Two Hawks Flying. She must be in love
with Two Hawks Flying, why else would
he have the power to stir her desires to
such a high peak?

She was so lost in her thoughts that
she failed to realize it was intermission
until Kincaid tugged gently on her sleeve.

"Mrs. Matthews?"

"What? Oh, I'm sorry, I guess I was
daydreaming."

"The play is a little silly," Kincaid
remarked. "Do you want to stay for the
rest of it?"

"Do you?"

"Not really. I'd just as soon go somewhere and have a cup of coffee."

"If you like."

Kincaid took Rebecca's elbow and
guided her up the aisle. "Hard to believe

the Goulds and the Vanderbilts shelled out sixty thousand dollars for a box in this place when it opened back in '83," he remarked as they stepped outside. "Of course, I guess sixty thousand is just a drop in the bucket when you're a millionaire."

"I guess," Rebecca agreed, laughing softly. "Although sixty thousand sounds like a million to me."

"Yeah," Kincaid allowed. He smiled down at her. "Nice night."

"Beautiful."

"I hate to see it end."

"Me, too."

Rebecca returned his smile and Kincaid felt like throwing his hat into the air and shouting out loud. By damn, she was a pretty woman and when she smiled at him, he felt like he was sixteen and in love for the first time all over again.

They walked for hours, oblivious to the other people on the streets, oblivious to the time or the place. It was well after midnight when they returned to the hotel. And still they were reluctant to part.

"I guess it's getting late," Kincaid lamented.

"Is it?"

"Yeah."

"I had a wonderful time tonight," Rebecca said, giving him a radiant smile.

"I'm glad. Would you, ah, mind spending tomorrow night with me, too?"

"Mind?" Rebecca laughed happily. "I'd love it."

"Good. Well, goodnight then,"

They were standing at the door to Rebecca's bedroom, but she made no move to open the door. She didn't want to leave him, did not want the night to end.

"Rebecca." Kincaid breathed her name like a sigh. Then, slowly, but knowing he would not be rebuffed, he kissed her goodnight.

They could part then. The words hadn't been said, no questions had been asked, but both knew that their lives would be entwined from that night on.

XVI

Summer 1885

The wagon creaked softly as it lumbered across the rough ground. I tried to find a more comfortable position, but the ropes binding my arms and legs didn't allow much movement. A wide strip of cloth covered my eyes, a bandana was tied over my mouth.

With a sigh, I stifled the urge to weep. Crying would not help; it only made my eyes itch and my throat sore. We had been on the road for over a week, and I was convinced that Josh was out of his mind. He was obsessed with the thought that I was his, only his, and he viewed everyone as a threat to our happiness together. When I said I did not love him, he did not hear me. When I begged to go back to my father, he flew into a rage.

I was tormented by the thought that I might never see Shadow or my father or

my children again. Shadow. I did not know
if he were dead or alive, but I prayed constantly that he was alive and well, that
somehow he would find me.

Daily, I hoped I might find a chance to
escape, but Joshua was very cautious. He
never untied my hands or my feet, only at
night did he remove the kerchiefs that
covered my mouth and eyes. I was
dependent upon him for everything. He
fed me, he lifted my skirts when I needed
to relieve myself, he bathed me. It was
degrading and humiliating, and I wondered if he intended to keep me bound and
gagged the rest of my life. It was a dismal
thought.

Josh spoke to me as if we were very
much in love, as if I were with him of my
own free will and completely happy to be
in his company. He called me tender
names and told me constantly of his love,
assuring me of his devotion, telling me he
could not live without me. He promised to
give me sons, many sons. Sons who were
the "right" color.

I felt as if I were caught in the jaws of
a nightmare from which I could not
awake.

It was just after sundown when the
wagon came to a halt. Moments later,
Joshua climbed into the back of the wagon
and removed the bandana from my mouth,
then removed the one over my eyes.
Taking me by the arm, he helped me to my

feet, guided me to the back of the wagon, helped me to the ground. Taking a rope from his back pocket, he looped it around my neck and secured the end to a tree. I was not going anywhere.

"Joshua, why don't you let me fix dinner tonight," I asked, hoping this time he would agree, hoping that, if he freed my hands and feet, I would be able to escape.

But he only smiled knowingly and shook his head. "I'll fix dinner, darling. You know how I love to wait on you."

Resigned, I sat down, my back against the tree, while Joshua laid a fire, sliced some meat into a pan, added beans and some chopped onion. He filled the coffee pot with water and placed it over the coals, then unhitched the team and led the horses to a nearby stream. When the horses had been watered, he hobbled them and turned them loose to graze along the stream bank.

Soon dinner was ready and he came to kneel beside me, a plate in his hand. A bite for me, a bite for him. I shuddered as he put the spoon in my mouth. It was disgusting, being forced to eat from his plate, having to use the spoon he used. I cringed as his hand reached out to stroke my arm and cheek.

"You're so lovely, Hannah," he said. "So lovely. I always knew you loved me more than you loved Orin."

I nodded, not daring to argue, afraid

to remind Josh that his younger brother was dead, killed by Indians almost ten years ago . . .

Orin. I remembered the day I saw a bear cub and asked Joshua to get it for me. I was thirteen at the time. Joshua had been sixteen then, Orin fourteen. Josh had refused to get the cub for me, but Orin had gallantly volunteered. He had no sooner picked up the cub than its mother came charging out of a nearby thicket. Orin had dropped the cub and the three of us had run until we couldn't run any more, then collapsed on the ground . . .

"Oh, Orin," I giggled. "You should have seen your face when that fat old sow reared up in the bushes."

"Pretty funny, huh?" he asked good-naturedly. "Would you have cried if she'd ripped me to pieces?"

"You know I would have," I said. "Why, I'd have cried buckets every night!"

"See, Josh, it's me she's crazy about," Orin had boasted. Falling to one knee, he grabbed my hands and said, with mock gravity, "Hannah, thou art fairest of all the fair. For one smile from thy ruby lips, I would climb the highest mountain, swim the deepest river, defend thee to the death, but please, please, don't bid me fetch any more bear cubs."

Josh scowled as I burst into laughter.

Always the serious one, Josh was...

When we finished eating, Joshua laid the plate aside. Going to the stream, he filled a large pot with water and set it over the fire to heat. He was going to wash me, something he did every night.

I had learned not to fight. The slightest protest filled Josh with rage, making him violent and abusive. I looked away as he raised my skirts and began to wash my bare legs. My stockings had been a nuisance and he had thrown them away days ago. My petticoats had gone the way of my stockings.

Josh chattered constantly as he washed me, telling me how glad he was that we were together again, saying how happy we would be when we reached our new home.

"Where will it be?" I asked, trying to sound enthusiastic.

"It's a secret, my darling, but I know you'll love it there." He dried my legs and began to wash my arms. Next, he unbuttoned my bodice and washed my neck and breasts.

"There," Josh said as he dried me. "Doesn't that feel better?"

I nodded, blinking back tears of frustration. If only I could get away. If only I could see Heecha and Mary and my father. If only I could hide from the hunger lurking in Joshua's eyes.

Later, after the dishes were washed
and put away and the fire was low, Joshua
spread his blankets on the ground and
drew me into his arms.

"Hannah, my Hannah." He mur-
mured the words over and over again. "I'll
never let you go, darling, I promise. We'll
always be together, just the two of us."
He laid his hand over my stomach as he
smiled at me. "Just the two of us until the
babies come. How many sons do you want
me to give you, my darling? Three? Six? A
dozen?" He put his face close to mine, the
madness shining in his eyes. "How many
sons, darling Hannah?"

"As many as you like, Josh," I
answered meekly.

He smiled, pleased with my answer.
And then he made love to me as he did
every night. Later, with Josh snoring
softly beside me, I stared up at the stars
wheeling high overhead, determined not to
give way to despair or discouragement.
Josh couldn't keep me tied up forever.
When we reached a town, he would have to
release my hands and feet. We would be
with other people. Sooner or later I would
find a way to escape from Joshua. I fell
asleep clinging to that thought.

We traveled steadily westward. Josh
stayed off the main roads, avoiding
contact with other people. My wrists and
ankles became sore and swollen from the

constant chafing of the rope. My shoulders ached and my legs cramped from being in one position for so long, but when I complained to Joshua, he just nodded and said things would be better soon.

I lost track of the days as we traveled across the wilderness. I had no idea where we were, was no longer certain of our direction. Josh kept the wagon cover securely fastened so that I could not see outside. At night, it was impossible to discern landmarks of any kind.

Fall was in the air when Josh ran out of supplies. That night he tied my wrists to a slat in the wagon, checked twice to make sure my bonds were secure, and then gagged me. Then, giving me a hearty kiss on the cheek, he rode off to town for provisions.

The total darkness inside the wagon, the melancholy wail of a distant coyote, and my own helplessness weighed heavily upon me. Sunk in despair, I began to cry, long wracking sobs that burned my eyes and tore at my throat. I cried until I had no tears left and then I lay there, the tears drying on my cheeks. I could not remember ever feeling so depressed, so helpless.

In an effort to overcome my despair, I thought of my children. My amnesia must have been hard on them. I smiled faintly as I thought of my sweet little Mary. She was such a warm loving child. Everytime I looked at her, I saw my mother's face. Thinking of my mother brought fresh tears. She had been the kindest, sweetest woman I had ever known. Closing my eyes, I could see her standing before me, her lovely chestnut hair worn in a severe bun at the nape of her neck, her lovely gray eyes glowing with love and a zest for living. I never heard my mother raise her voice in anger. I remembered how kind she had been to Shadow when he was a young boy. She had taught him to read and write, but she had been careful not to try to influence him too heavily in our ways. It would be hard for him to be a warrior, she had said wisely, if he acquired too many American habits.

And Shadow had openly adored my mother. He had frequently brought her gifts: a pair of soft doeskin moccasins, an exquisite necklace of turquoise and silver, a set of delicately carved wooden combs for her hair. I knew he would have walked barefoot over hot coals if my mother had asked him to. But now she was gone, and Shadow was far away, perhaps dead . . .

Shadow. How I missed him. How I longed to know if he were still alive. I was so starved for the sight of his beloved face, for the sound of his voice, the strength of his presence.

"Oh, God," I prayed silently, "please let him be all right. Please bring him back to me."

I had no sooner finished my prayer than the wagon cover was thrown open and a tall figure stepped into the bed of the wagon. My heart lurched with fear and then with joy as I recognized the outline of the man standing before me. Shadow! I would have shouted his name if not for the gag stuffed into my mouth.

In minutes, I was free and in his arms.

"Do not cry, Hannah," he said. "Everything is all right now." His lips moved against my hair, his arms held me in a grip of iron, as if he would never let me go. Indeed, I would have been content to remain in the warm circle of his embrace forever. I felt the tears well in my eyes again as I endeavored to press myself still closer to his solid strength and deeper into the safety of his arms.

For a few minutes we just sat there, not speaking. What heaven, to be in his arms again, to feel the strength of his arms around me, to breathe in the heady masculine scent that was his alone, to know that nothing could hurt me so long as he was near.

"Hannah." His voice was a choked whisper as he buried his face in my hair. "I thought I had lost you forever. When I saw you fall, I thought you were dead."

I held Shadow tight, deeply moved by the depth of his feelings. I knew Shadow loved me but, like most men, he rarely

spoke the words. I did not need to hear
them now to know he cared.

"Promise me," he said lifting his head
and staring into my face intently.
"Promise me you will never do anything
like that again."

"I promise."

"You say the words," he accused,
"but your heart is not in them."

"I know, but I can't make a promise
like that. I would rather die myself than
see anything happen to you or my
children."

"I know," he said with a wry grin. "I
feel the same."

"You were wounded that day. Heecha
said he didn't know if you were dead or
alive."

Shadow nodded. "I took a bullet in the
side, and another in the arm."

"Are you all right now?"

"Yes."

"Mattlock might have killed you."

Shadow shrugged. "I thought you
were dead, and I did not care if I lived or
died. But then I thought of our little ones,
and I knew one of us must survive for
their sake."

"Heecha said you killed Mattlock."

"Yes. I was sorry I could only kill him
once."

I shuddered, chilled by the hatred in
Shadow's tone. I had never known anything but tenderness at Shadow's hands.

Sometimes it was hard for me to believe
that the man cradling me in the shelter of
his arms was the same man who could kill
violently and without mercy.

A sudden image of Joshua lying
staked out in the dirt flashed into my
mind, and I was suddenly anxious to be
gone from this place.

"Shadow, let's get out of here," I said,
trying to keep the urgency out of my
voice.

"Not yet."

I had heard that tone of voice before
and I knew there was no point in arguing.
Shadow was not going to leave. Not until
Joshua returned.

"You're going to kill him?" It was not
a question. I already knew the answer. I
had seen it in Shadow's eyes.

"Yes. No one will save him this time."

We sat together for an hour, waiting,
but Josh did not return.

"Let's go outside," I suggested. "I
need to stretch my legs."

Shadow helped me to my feet, held my
arm as we crossed to the rear of the
wagon. It felt good to be outside, to be
able to walk and stretch my cramped
muscles, to move about as I pleased after
being tied up for so long.

There was a pot of coffee sitting on the
coals and I poured myself a cup while
Shadow added some wood to the fire. The
coffee was barely lukewarm, but I drank it

anyway and then poured a second cup for
Shadow. I studied him in the light of the
flames as he drank the thick bitter brew.
He was dressed in dark twill pants and a
brown wool shirt. Brown boots hugged his
feet. A .44 Colt was shoved into the waistband of his pants, a knife was sheathed on
his belt.

"Your hair!" I exclaimed, noticing for
the first time that his long hair had been
cut short. "What happened to your hair?"

Shadow grinned ruefully. "Rebecca
Matthews cut it so I would look more like
a white man."

Rebecca Matthews. The woman who
had once saved his life. I had been grateful
to her then. I was still grateful, but I could
not stifle the little flare of jealousy that
burned in my heart when I thought of
Rebecca and Shadow together.

"Why did you go see Rebecca?"

"Your father left a message at the
reservation saying he was taking you to a
doctor in New York. I asked Rebecca to
help me find you."

"Oh."

"She was very helpful."

"Where is my father?"

"In New York, with Heecha and
Mary."

"And Rebecca?" Some inner demon
would not let me ignore her. "Is she
waiting for you in New York?"

"I do not know."

I was about to say something decidedly shrewish about Rebecca Matthews when Shadow put his hand over my mouth.

"Someone is coming," he warned softly.

I gazed at Shadow. I didn't hear a sound, but he did. His narrowed eyes probed the darkness, his flared nostrils tested the wind like a wolf on the scent of fresh meat.

"Four horses," Shadow said.

Moments later, four mounted men materialized out of the darkness. They were all middle-aged men dressed in serviceable denim pants and cotton shirts. One of them had a five-pointed star pinned to the pocket of his shirt.

I drew my gaze from the four men and turned to face Shadow, but he was no longer standing beside me. Ghostlike, he had disappeared into the underbrush.

"Ma'am." The sheriff urged his horse ahead of the others, touching his hat brim respectfully. "Would you be Hannah Berdeen?"

"Yes."

There was an awkward silence as the sheriff and his men eyed me strangely.

"Is something wrong?" I asked.

"Your husband said you were, uh, insane. He said he had to keep you tied up in the wagon to keep you from hurting yourself."

"I'm quite rational, I assure you. It's my husband who's mad."

The sheriff chewed on his lower lip, his hooded brown eyes troubled.

"Where is my . . . husband?"

"I'm afraid he's in jail. He got into a dispute over a card game and killed a man."

I felt a swift surge of relief. Joshua was in jail! Now Shadow and I could go back to New York and get Heecha and Mary. I wouldn't have to worry about a showdown between Shadow and Josh.

"I'm afraid you'll have to come with me, ma'am," the sheriff said.

I took a wary step backward. "I'd rather not."

"I'm afraid it's for your own good, ma'am. I can't leave you out here alone. Anyway, I'm sure you want to see your husband. Maybe get him a lawyer. And I, uh, I think old Doc Wayfield should take a look at you."

"There's nothing wrong with me," I said quickly. "And I have no desire to see my husband."

I had spoken too hastily. The sheriff was looking at me oddly, apparently finding it peculiar that I did not want to see Josh. His face was set in determined lines as he stepped from his horse and walked toward me.

"Sorry, ma'am," he said, grabbing me by the arm. "But I'm afraid you're going into town whether you like it or not."

He was lifting me onto the back of his horse when Shadow's voice sliced through the air.

"Let her go."

Startled, the sheriff whirled around, his hand going for his gun. A shot rang out in the stillness of the night and the sheriff lurched forward, then fell face down in the dirt. The other three men were out of their saddles before the echo of the gunshot died away. Drawing their weapons, they began firing into the darkness.

I slid from the sheriff's horse and dropped to the ground, my arms over my head, as gunfire rent the air and then abruptly ceased.

Raising my head cautiously, I saw that two of the sheriff's men were lying dead on the ground only a few feet away. The third member of the posse had been wounded in the arm. He stood beside his horse, blood soaking his shirt sleeve, his eyes peering anxiously into the night.

"White man."

Shadow's voice sounded from behind the remaining deputy. I could see the sweat dripping down the man's face, see the fear that haunted his eyes as he whirled around, blindly firing his gun in the direction of Shadow's voice as panic took hold of him. The deputy grunted softly as Shadow's knife swished through the air and pierced his heart.

And then Shadow stepped out of the darkness.

I scrambled to my feet and ran to his side, my heart hammering wildly as I saw the blood oozing from a narrow gash along the side of his head.

"It is nothing," Shadow assured me. "A bullet creased my scalp. It is not serious."

I murmured a quick prayer of thanks as I tore a strip of material from the hem of my dress and wound it around Shadow's forehead.

"We've got to get out of here," I said urgently. "Someone will come looking for the sheriff before long."

Shadow frowned. He did not want to leave until he had finished with Joshua, but he knew I was right. We might be near a civilized town and its citizens might consider themselves to be well-bred, well-mannered Christian people, but they would not hesitate to lynch an Indian who had dared to shoot down four white men, especially when one of the men killed had been an officer of the law.

I gathered a few of my things together while Shadow slipped a makeshift bridle over the head of one of the horses Josh had left behind. Shadow's horse, a piebald stallion, was tethered about twenty yards away.

It was nearing midnight when

Shadow lifted me onto the back of the horse he had chosen for me.

"Where are we going?" I asked, patting the horse's neck.

"Chicago."

"Chicago!" I could not disguise my astonishment. "I thought we were going back to New York."

"No. I told your father I would send him word as soon as I found you. Chicago is the next big city. He will meet us there as soon as he can."

Our trip was uneventful; even so, I never let Shadow out of my sight. He was all the security I had in the world and I did not intend to be separated from him again. We traveled cautiously over the countryside, aware of the possibility that another posse might be sent out to avenge the men Shadow had killed. But no one ever came, and I breathed a sigh of heartfelt relief as we rode down Chicago's main street.

Our first stop was at the telegraph office where Shadow sent a short message to my father, informing him that we had arrived safely, and then we went to the biggest hotel in the city. I could only watch in amazement as Shadow walked boldly to the front desk and quietly demanded a room with a double bed and a bath.

The desk clerk, a wizened old man with pale gray eyes and a grizzled goatee, did not offer the slightest protest as Shadow signed the register and paid for our room in advance. Then, taking my arm, he escorted me up the stairs to the second floor as if he had been doing such things all his life.

Moments after we arrived in our room, two young boys brought in buckets of steaming hot water and filled the zinc tub. I was luxuriating in a hot bubble bath twenty minutes after we arrived in town. It was wonderful.

Shadow's eyes, as black as polished ebony, burned with a deep and passionate fire as he watched me bathe. A quick intake of breath shook his whole body and then he took the cloth from my hand and dropped it on the floor. Slowly, deliberately he lathered his hands and began to wash me. He started at my shoulders, slowly soaping my skin, his hands moving lazily down my arms. My breasts were next, and I could feel his hands tremble as he washed first one and then the other. My whole body was aquiver as his soapy hands strayed down to wash my belly; I moaned out loud as he gently lifted my left leg and washed it from ankle to thigh. I was on fire with longing when his hand moved to my right leg, and as his fingers stroked the soft flesh of my inner thigh, I was certain I would burst into flame. I whispered his name, wanting him, needing him.

With a low groan, Shadow rinsed the soap from my skin, then lifted me, still dripping wet from the tub, and carried me to the bed. I watched, quivering with longing, as he pulled off his boots, stripped off his shirt and pants. For a moment, he stood naked beside the bed, his dark eyes burning into mine. I could not take my eyes from Shadow and I thrilled at the sight of him—all hard muscled bronze flesh and throbbing desire.

I sighed with pleasure as he lowered his body over mine, his skin smooth and warm, his mouth hungrily seeking mine. He kissed me until I was breathless, and then he began kissing my neck and my breasts, his mouth trailing fire, until I could wait no longer. For a moment, he hovered over me, his eyes caressing my face, and then he thrust into me, the warm hardness of him filling me with delight. We moved together, sweat-sheened flesh against sweat-sheened flesh, mouths fused together, until we reached that magical moment when two people become one.

Drifting back to earth, I smiled as I realized this was the first time we had made love in a bed between clean sheets, like any other married couple. We had made love in a hide lodge, in a damp cave, out in the open under a starry sky, in the bowels of a smelly prison cell, but never in a real bed with linen sheets.

Later, we bathed together and this time I washed Shadow, loving the feeling of power it gave me to know I could arouse him as he aroused me, to know that the touch of my hands upon his hard male flesh turned him into a quivering mass of desire. When he reached for me, I splashed water in his face and jumped out of the tub, laughing as I slipped on the water-slick floor.

With a growl, Shadow bounded out of the tub and came after me. I eluded him by crawling over the bed and running behind a table, but he continued to pursue me. I could not stop laughing and finally, breathless, I collapsed on the floor. Shadow dropped down on top of me, his strong hands pinning my shoulders to the floor, his long legs straddling my hips.

With a low growl, he kissed me, a hard kiss full of fire and promise. Still laughing, I struggled against him, my hands pushing ineffectively against the un-yielding wall of his chest.

"Woman," he growled, aroused by my struggles. "Do not fight me."

"Beast!" I cried in mock fury.

"Beast, am I?" Shadow mused. "Only a few moments ago you were eager for my touch, begging for more."

"That was then," I retorted mischievously. "This is now."

Shadow nodded. "And now it is I who want more."

"Would you ravage an unwilling woman?" I asked, my fists pummeling his chest.

Shadow smiled wickedly. "Perhaps."

"Let me go this instant!" I demanded, intrigued by the game.

Slowly, Shadow shook his head. His dark eyes burned into mine, and I could see he was excited by my resistance. He bent to kiss me, but I turned my head away. With an oath, Shadow grabbed a handful of my hair and forced me to face him. Then, very deliberately, he bent down and kissed me, his hands and mouth assaulting my senses as they traveled at will over my face, breasts, belly and thighs. I struggled in his grasp, but it was only a sham and in the end I surrendered willingly to the urgings of my heart and body, glorying in Shadow's easy strength, wondering, in the back of my mind, if he would have taken me by force if I had truly been unwilling. The thought was scary, intriguing and exciting all at once.

Later, we bathed again, the cool water refreshing on our heated flesh. Our eyes met continually, and we could not seem to stop smiling. I was happy and content, deliciously satisfied. Lazily, I let my hands roam over Shadow's body as I dried him with a fluffy towel, loving the touch of his skin, and the way my touch aroused him.

"We will never get out of this room if

you are not careful," Shadow warned, and
I tossed him the towel and began to dry
myself.

Later, we went for a walk through the
town. We ate dinner at a fine resturant,
went shopping for clothes in a rather
elegant shop, stopped for dessert at a
quiet cafe.

People gawked at Shadow wherever
we went, and the word Indian followed us
like smoke, but no one made any trouble
for us. Men stared at Shadow, awed and
envious of his dark good looks and strong
physique; women openly admired him
with their eyes, drawn to the raw, animal-
like sexuality lurking beneath the surface
of his calm exterior. I only smiled and held
tight to his arm. He was mine, this rare
and wonderful man. All mine.

The next day we went shopping again.
Shadow bought me three new dresses, lacy
underwear, a pair of high-heeled shoes, a
perky white bonnet, a feather fan, a box of
chocolates in a heart-shaped box, a bottle
of fragrant perfume.

Joshua had taken me shopping in New
York, but it had been a chore, not fun, as it
was now. I basked in the love I read in
Shadow's ebony eyes, felt myself blush
under his approving gaze when I modeled
a dress that was cut shockingly low in
front.

That night we went to the theater.
The play was a drama about a timid city

girl, a bloodthirsty Indian who abducted her and carried her off to his tepee, and the handsome Mountie who rescued the girl from the Indian's savage clutches. Shadow snickered at the sight of a white man pretending to be an Indian.

We spent a week in Chicago and did everything there was to do, saw everything there was to see. By the end of the week, my curiosity was near the breaking point. We were sitting side by side on the bed in our room when I asked Shadow where he had learned to register in a hotel, order a full-course meal in a fancy restaurant, and do all the other "civilized" things I had been watching him do. I was soon sorry I asked.

"Rebecca Matthews instructed me in the fine art of being a gentleman," Shadow answered, shrugging nonchalantly. "She taught me the social graces, as she called them, while we were in New York looking for you."

"Did she give you all the money you've been spending, too?" I asked, my voice a trifle sharp.

"No. It was a gift from your father. He said it was a late wedding present, and that when I found you, we were to have a second honeymoon."

Shadow looked deep into my eyes, his expression solemn. "Do not be jealous of Rebecca," he said quietly. "She is only a good friend. Nothing more."

It was uncanny, the way that man always knew exactly what I was thinking and feeling.

"Hannah."

I knew, from the tone of his voice, that something was wrong. Very wrong. Thinking back, I realized something had been bothering Shadow for several days. More than once I had caught him looking at me oddly. Several times he had started to say something and then changed his mind. I knew intuitively that whatever Shadow was about to tell me was something I would not want to hear.

Suddenly nervous, I began to fidget with the folds of my skirt. What was he going to say? My imagination went wild. Heecha had been hurt. Mary was dead. My father was sick. He didn't love me any more . . .

"What is it?" I asked abruptly. "What's wrong?"

"There is something I must tell you."

"About Rebecca?" I could not hide the fear in my voice. My hands were suddenly cold, and I felt my throat constrict as I waited for Shadow to explain.

He did not speak for several minutes and the cold knot forming in the pit of my stomach grew larger with each second that slipped by. I glanced around our hotel room as if seeing it for the first time. The bed was covered with a flowered print spread. The wallpaper was attractive. A green and gold carpet covered the floor. Lace curtains hung at the windows. A large armoire took up most of one wall.

I glanced in the mirror hanging on the wall across from the bed and saw Shadow watching me intently. Our eyes met and held in the glass.

"I was unfaithful to you," Shadow said.

"With Rebecca?" I could hardly say her name.

"Yes."

I made no effort to hold back my tears, or to wipe them away. I was hurting inside, hurting so bad I thought I might die. Hurting as I had never hurt before.

"Hannah, I did not mean for it to happen." Shadow's voice was raw and edged with pain. "I do not blame her for what happened. It was all my fault. I could have said no."

"Why didn't you?" I lashed out at him, wanting to hurt him as I was hurting. "Did she force you into her bed. Is she so bewitching you couldn't say no?"

"She loves me, Hannah," he said without conceit. "Or thinks she does. There has been no other man in her life since her husband died."

I turned so we were face to face. "Too bad we're not living with the Cheyenne," I said bitterly. "You could make her your number two wife."

"I want no other wife."

"Just a lover!" I spat the words at him, saw his eyes grow dark with pain. Good! I thought. That hurt him. But I took no pleasure in his unhappiness.

"Hannah, you know in your heart there is no other woman for me. Only you."

"And Rebecca," I said miserably. "Why did you have to tell me?"

"I cannot live with a lie between us. I have wanted to tell you for a long time."

"Why? Why did you do it?"

Shadow raised his eyes from mine and stared out the window. "She was lonely and unhappy. Every day we were together, I could see that she wanted me in the way a woman wants a man. I pretended I did not notice. But one night I could not pretend, and when I ignored her open invitation to her bed, she began to cry." His eyes sought mine again, begging me to believe him, begging me to understand. "I only meant to comfort her, Hannah, nothing else. Afterward, we were both ashamed. Rebecca begged my forgiveness. She said you need never know, but I could not live with you and not tell you what I had done." His voice went soft, so filled with pain I wanted to cry. "I could not see the trust in your eyes and know I did not deserve it."

Why did he have to be so honest? Why did I have to love him so very much? The pain in his eyes was more than I could bear., I knew, deep in the core of my being, that Shadow might have been unfaithful to me with his body, but never with his heart. And deep in the back of my mind, I was glad he had told me. Our love would have been sorely tarnished if I had learned the truth from someone else.

"We won't speak of it again," I said, laying my hand on his arm.

Shadow smiled at me, the love in his eyes washing over me like sunshine as he took me in his arms.

"I am sorry, Hannah," he whispered fervently. "Please forgive me."

I nodded, unable to speak.

Shadow made love to me that night as never before. Each touch of his hands, each kiss, each caress was an affirmation of his love for me. Our joining was more than flesh meeting flesh, it was heart speaking to heart, and soul touching soul. I felt sorry for Rebecca Matthews then, because I knew that whatever she and Shadow had shared had been of no more substance than a puff of smoke caught in a high wind.

Shadow and I spent the next day in our room, locked in each other's arms. We made love, slept, ate, and made love again.

That night, walking hand in hand down the street after a late supper, I realized that my childhood dream had come true. I laughed softly as I glanced at Shadow, who looked regal and terribly

handsome in a gray frock coat, black
cravat, and dove gray trousers.

"What is funny?" he asked, frowning
at me.

"You," I said, laughing the harder.
"Once, a long time ago, I dreamed of going
to a big city, but I could never imagine
you in evening clothes. Now I know why."

"I am wearing this silly outfit to
please you," Shadow said gruffly. "And
now you tell me you do not like it?"

"Oh, I like it, but it isn't you. I think I
like you better in buckskins. Or in nothing
at all."

A wicked light danced in Shadow's
dark eyes as he ripped off his cravat and
tossed it into the street. His coat went
next, and then the soft black shoes on his
feet. He was unbuttoning his shirt when I
cried, "Shadow, stop! You'll be arrested."

We were at the entrance to our hotel
now. Suddenly sober, Shadow opened the
door for me. Then, taking my arm, he
guided me up the staircase to our room. I
could feel the clerk staring after us, mouth
agape, until we were out of sight.

My father arrived in the city the next
day just after noon. With him were
Heecha and Mary. And Rebecca
Matthews. My children and I shared a
noisy, happy, tearful reunion and then
Shadow introduced me to Rebecca
Matthews. She was a pretty woman, a few

years older than I was. Her long brown hair was swept away from her face and gathered in a neat coil at the nape of her neck. Her figure was trim beneath a dark brown skirt and pale yellow shirtwaist. She seemed very nice, a little embarrassed to meet me, but I suppose that was to be expected since she was in love with my husband. Her mild brown eyes lingered on Shadow's face whenever she thought no one was looking, and it was all I could do not to punch her in the nose even though I felt sorry for her. It was sad to love someone and know that love would never be returned.

When everything settled down to some semblance of quiet, I glanced at my two favorite men. "Well, where do we go from here?"

Shadow and Pa grinned at each other. "Bear Valley," they answered in unison.

I had been standing beside a chair. Now I sat down, hard, too stunned to speak. Bear Valley! In my mind, it had always been home.

Pa nodded, his grin stretching from ear to ear. "Yep. I've decided to go back and try my hand at raising cattle. Mighty pretty country back there. Sorta gets in a man's blood."

I looked at Shadow and he nodded. "It is time to go home. Your father has asked for my help in getting started, and I have agreed to work with him, if it is what you want."

"What I want? Oh, Shadow, it's what I've always wanted." I jumped up from the chair and threw my arms around my husband's neck. "I think it's wonderful. When do we leave?"

"First thing in the morning," Pa said. "We'll take the train as far as we can, then go by wagon to Steel's Crossing. I hear it's a good sized town by now. We should be able to get everything we need to get started there."

My eyes slid toward Rebecca Matthews. She smiled at me tentatively, then sent a pleading glance in my father's direction. Pa cleared his throat a couple of times, turned red around the ears as he draped one big arm around Rebecca's slender shoulders.

"I . . . I, uh . . ." He coughed again. "I asked Rebecca, here, to marry me and she, uh, she said yes. The wedding's tomorrow morning at eight o'clock at the Baptist Church. We'd like you all to be there," Pa finished in a rush, then looked at me, his eyes seeking my approval and understanding. "Your mother's been dead a long time," he said quietly. "I've been lonely. Real lonely. I'd like your blessing, Hannah. It would mean a lot."

I looked at my father and then at Rebecca. They looked well together, I thought. I could see that Pa loved her, and she loved him. Could I have been mistaken about Rebecca's feeling for Shadow? I didn't think so. But if Rebecca loved Shadow, why was she marrying my father?

"Hannah?"

"Congratulations, Pa. Mrs. Matthews. I hope you'll both be very happy."

Rebecca murmured her thanks while Pa swept me into his arms. Then everyone was talking at once, voices merging into a happy cacophony as we planned for the future. Heecha and Mary were excited at the idea of seeing the place where I had been born, of seeing where their father had once lived. They talked excitedly about exploring the woods, about visiting Rabbit's Head Rock where I had first met Shadow.

Later, after Heecha and Mary were in bed and the men were hunched over a table making plans about cattle and fences and how many animals to start with, Rebecca took me aside.

"I'd like to talk to you, Hannah," she said quietly.

"About what?"

"About the future. About Two Hawks Flying. He told you what happened between us, didn't he? He said he would."

"Yes," I said stiffly. "He told me."

"He's a wonderful man."

"Yes, I know."

"Hannah, I'd like for us to be friends.

What happened between your husband
and myself was all my fault. I threw
myself at him, practically begged him to
make love to me."

"I don't want to hear this," I said
brusquely.

"Please. I married my husband when I
was very young. Martin and I had a good
life, and he loved me very much. But I was
a preacher's daughter and Martin treated
me like a saint, even in bed. I never knew
what real passion was until Two Hawks
Flying entered my life. When he left, I
thought of nothing else. I know now that
what I thought was undying love was just
loneliness and..." Rebecca's cheeks
turned crimson. "And lust."

"You don't have to tell me this. It's
none of my business."

"Yes, it is. I want you to know how
sorry I am for what happened. And I want
you to know that I love your father very
much. He's a wonderful man."

"Yes, he is." I wanted to dislike the
woman who had caused me so much heartache, but I couldn't. I knew how hard it
must have been for her to confide in me
about her marriage and her infatuation
with Shadow. Knowing her for even this
short time, I was certain she was ashamed
of her passion for my husband, yet she had
felt it necessary to face me and apologize.
I admired her courage.

"I hope we can be friends," Rebecca said.

"I think we are."

The wedding was small and informal, just the family and the minister. Pa looked handsome in his dark suit, Rebecca was radiant in a peach-colored silk that high-lighted her fair skin and chestnut hair. Her face fairly glowed with happiness as Pa slipped a plain gold wedding band over her finger. Looking at the two of them, I knew I need never be jealous of Rebecca again.

Heecha and Mary giggled behind their hands when their grandfather bent down and claimed his first kiss as Rebecca's husband. I dabbed at my eyes, hoping no one would see my tears, but Shadow never missed anything going on around him. I assumed he would think I was just being female and that I was crying because that's what women did at weddings, but in truth I was crying because Shadow and I could never be legally wed in the eyes of the law. True, we had been married accord-ing to Cheyenne custom, but such a marriage was not considered legal or binding among my people.

I sniffed as I recalled the day I had married Shadow . . .

It was in mid-May when Shadow came

to me, a grave look in his deep black eyes.

"What is it?" I asked anxiously. "Is something wrong?"

"Yes," he said. "Very wrong."

"What's wrong?" I asked hoarsely. A dozen dreadful thoughts crowded my mind. The soldiers had found us. Someone had died. He didn't love me any more . . .

"We have not been properly married, Hannah," Shadow said. "I want you to be my wife. Will you marry me according to Cheyenne custom?"

Relief washed over me in great waves. "Marry you," I breathed. "Oh, yes, yes, yes!"

The next evening, just after sunset, Shadow and I stood together before Elk Dreamer, surrounded by all the Cheyenne people. I wore a doeskin dress that had been bleached white and tanned to a softness like velvet. It had been a gift from Fawn, and was, in fact, the dress she had worn when she married Black Owl. Foot-long fringe dangled from the sleeves; hundreds of tiny blue beads decorated the bodice. New Leaf had stayed up the night before to make me a pair of moccasins. They were beautiful, as intricately designed and crafted as any evening slippers I had ever seen. My hair fell free about my shoulders, adorned with a single white rose.

Shadow stood straight and tall beside me, looking more handsome than I had *ever seen him. He wore a white buckskin shirt that was open at the throat, white leggings heavy with fringe, and white moccasins. A single white eagle feather was tied in his waist-length black hair.*

Elk Dreamer raised his right hand for silence. "This is a special day for our people," he began. "One of our warriors has chosen a woman to share his life. Though she is not of our blood, her heart is good for our people. From this day forward, she will be one of us." Pausing, Elk Dreamer drew his knife. Taking Shadow's right hand, he made a shallow cut in his palm, and then did the same to my right hand. Caught up in the beauty of the moment, I did not feel the pain.

Taking our hands in his, Elk Dreamer pressed them together, palm to palm. "Now their blood is mixing, and they are one. From this time forward, all pain will be divided, all joy will be doubled . . ."

I brushed my tears aside as I kissed Pa's cheek and then gave Rebecca a hug.

Shadow took me aside while Rebecca collected the marriage license and Pa paid the preacher.

"Someday, Hannah," Shadow said so only I could hear. "Someday I will marry you in the white man's way."

I looked in his eyes. How did he always know what I was thinking? It was uncanny, the way that man could read my mind.

"Am I never to have any secrets from you?" I asked.

"Never," Shadow stated emphatically. "You are as much a part of me as my arms and legs. I will always know what you want and what you need."

"It doesn't matter, really, about the wedding, I mean."

His eyes told me he knew I was lying. "Someday," he said again. "I promise."

And I believed him, because he had never lied to me, but I was a little frightened by such a promise because I knew Shadow and I could never be wed so long as Joshua Berdeen lived. I did not like to think what would happen if Shadow and Joshua ever saw each other again.

Thirty minutes later we were on a train bound for home.

GET YOUR 4 FREE BOOKS
NOW — A $21.96 Value!
Mail the Free Book Certificate Today!

Get Four Books Totally FREE — A $21.96 Value

PLEASE RUSH
MY FOUR FREE
BOOKS TO ME
RIGHT AWAY!

Leisure Romance Book Club
65 Commerce Road
Stamford CT 06902-4563

AFFIX
STAMP
HERE

XVII

As Pa had expected, Steel's Crossing had grown a great deal in the nine years since we had been away. The town that had once consisted of little more than a general store and saloon now took up three long blocks. I was surprised to see a large bank, a telegraph office, a newspaper office, a barber shop, a whitewashed church, and four saloons. There was even a dentist located at the end of the town.

Our first stop was Sheets Livery Barn where Pa bought a big flatbed wagon, a team of chestnut geldings to pull it, and a bay quarter-horse mare for riding.

At Blankenships Mercantile, Pa and Shadow purchased a variety of merchandise: hammers, nails, saws, canned goods, harness, blankets, cooking pots and utensils, two shovels, candles, a couple of lanterns. The list went on and on. Pa put

in an order for window glass for the cabin
we were going to build; Rebecca picked
out material for curtains. Pa and Shadow
bought new Winchester rifles and plenty
of ammunition. The West might be
settling down, but there were still outlaws
to contend with. And game to be hunted.
Heecha begged to have a gun, too, but
Shadow said no, not until he was older,
and I breathed a sigh of relief. I did not
like to think of my baby owning a gun.

At Norquist's Feed and Tack Store, Pa
bought a dozen chickens, a milk cow and
several sacks of grain for the livestock.

"Come spring, we'll start looking for
cattle," Pa remarked to Shadow as he
tossed a sack of feed into the back of the
wagon.

Shadow nodded as he tossed a second
sack of oats into the wagon. The sacks
weighed one hundred pounds each and
Rebecca and I smiled at each other as we
watched our men toss the heavy sacks
around like they weighed no more than a
few pounds.

Shadow drew a lot of curious stares as
he helped Pa load the wagon. Indians
weren't a common sight in Steel's Crossing, nor a welcome one. People had long
memories and they still remembered the
Custer massacre and the Indian wars that
had kept things stirred up in this part of
the country just a short ten years ago.

Shadow ignored the derisive looks and

derogatory comments thrown his way until he took me by the arm to help me into the back of the wagon and a man standing nearby made a crack about a white woman living with an Indian.

With the speed of a striking snake, Shadow released my arm and lunged at the man who had dared to insult me. They hit the ground rolling over and over as they scrabbled for a hold on one another. Naked fury burned in the depths of Shadow's eyes as he pinned the man to the ground, his long legs straddling the man's thighs. Whipping a knife from his belt, Shadow laid the finely-honed blade against the man's throat.

The man remained perfectly still, arms outstretched, his eyes glazed with fear as he looked into Shadow's eyes and saw death lurking there.

The sound of a rifle being cocked drew my attention and I saw Pa come up behind Shadow, his rifle covering the crowd that had gathered around the two men brawling in the dusty street.

"You will apologize to my wife," Shadow told the man cowering beneath him, "or you will not draw another breath."

The man started to nod his head, but stopped as the blade at his throat cut into his flesh. A single drop of blood trickled down the man's neck.

Slowly, Shadow withdrew his knife

from the man's throat. Rising, he allowed
the man to stand up.

"I apologize, ma'am," the man said,
his eyes seeking mine, but not quite
making contact. "I didn't mean no dis-
respect."

I accepted his apology with a quick
nod of my head, then scrambled into the
back of the wagon. Rebecca was there, and
she put her arm around my shoulders, her
eyes sympathetic.

Shadow's eyes swept the crowd, his
expression as hard and cold as ice, before
he climbed onto the front seat. Pa sent the
crowd a similar look before he, too,
climbed into the wagon.

Moments later we were heading out of
town.

Bear Valley was as lovely as I remembered. The trees were green, the grass
was high, the river was low and sluggish
this time of year. A thousand memories
came out of hiding as the wagon came to a
halt near the site of our old homestead.
But there was no time for reminiscing. Pa
and Shadow went off in search of game
while Rebecca and I pitched the tent that
would serve as our home until a cabin
could be built. Mary gathered wood and
twigs for a fire; Heecha unhitched the
team and took the horses down to the river
to drink.

By nightfall, we were comfortably

settled around a small fire. Heecha and
Mary stared into the flames until they fell
asleep, their heads pillowed on my lap. Pa
and Rebecca were sitting with their arms
around each other, dreaming about the
future. It seemed strange to think of my
father married to Rebecca. I could
remember how happy he had been with my
mother. I had never known two people so
right for each other or so much in love. Pa
had told me once that he met Mother on
Thursday, courted her on Friday, kissed
her on Saturday, and married her on Sunday. Mother always insisted things didn't
happen quite that fast. Almost, but not
quite. Sometimes, as a child, I had felt a
little left out, they seemed so wrapped up
in each other. Long before I had been old
enough to know what such things meant, I
had noticed the way they looked at each
other, the little touches, the secret smiles.
Did Pa feel the same way about Rebecca?
A part of me was jealous that he could
give his love to another woman and yet
the older, wiser part was glad that he had
found someone to share the rest of his life
with.

Pa was leaning forward, his lips
brushing Rebecca's, when Shadow moved
Heecha and Mary and pulled me to my
feet.

"Let us go for a walk," he suggested.
"I think Rebecca and your father would
like to be alone."

Shadow held my hand as we walked away from the fire. I knew immediately where we were going.

Our secret place had not changed. How many times had I met Shadow under "our" tree? It was at this very spot that I had purposefully seduced him. I slid a glance at Shadow and saw that he, too, was remembering that day.

Wordlessly, I stepped into his arms, sighed as his arms slid around my waist and his mouth slanted over mine. Gently, he lowered me to the ground, his mouth never leaving mine. Time slipped away and I was sixteen again, desperate to be with the man I loved, not caring that my friends and neighbors would ostracize me for loving an Indian, not caring about anything but the magic of Shadow's touch. His skin was firm and warm beneath my fingertips, the muscles flexing and relaxing as his hands kneaded my back. He was so strong, so beautiful to look at. I had never ceased to marvel that he was mine.

We made love leisurely, lingering over each kiss, each caress. There was no need to hurry now, no fear of discovery. My skin felt vital and alive, attuned to every sensation. The sweet summer breeze was cool, the grass beneath us was soft and damp, but the fire in Shadow's touch was more than enough to keep me warm. His hands, big and brown and strong, moved gently over my body, lingering on my breasts to stroke and tease before moving on to caress the inside of my thigh. His touch, soft as butterfly wings, exploded through me like lightning. His mouth covered mine, his tongue softly dancing over the inside of my lower lip.

My hands were busy, too, roaming lazily over his hard muscled flesh, marveling anew that the male body could be so beautiful to see, so thrilling to the touch. I reveled in the breadth of his shoulders, the length of his legs, the powerful muscles in his arms and thighs. Boldly, I let my hand wander down to grasp his manhood, which quivered with a life all its own.

We petted and played, arousing each other until we were filled with a wild primal need that could no longer wait to be satisfied.

Shadow rose over me, his dark eyes afire as his flesh merged with mine, two people now made one. I strained upward, wanting all of him, loving the old, yet always new experience of being a part of the man I loved.

Later, happy and content, I fell asleep in Shadow's arms.

Something was tickling my ear. I tried to swat it away, but it came back again and again. Irritated, I opened one eye to see Shadow leaning over me, a blade of grass in his hand.

"We had better go back to camp," he said regretfully. "It will be daylight soon."

His words brought me wide awake. What a sight we would make if Pa or one of our children came looking for us. Jumping to my feet, I grabbed my clothes and began to dress, only to have Shadow pluck my chemise from my hands and carry me toward the river. The water looked very cold and I locked my arms around his neck as I began to realize what he had in mind.

"You said we should get back to camp!" I shouted, hoping to avoid what I knew was coming.

"Soon," Shadow grinned wickedly as he stepped into the waist-deep water.

I squealed as the icy water closed around us. And then we were splashing each other, yelping as the cold water sprayed over our bare skin. Later, breathless, we fell into each other's arms and I prayed that all our days in the future would be as carefree and filled with laughter.

Rebecca had breakfast waiting for us when we returned to camp. Her cheeks turned pink when she saw us, and I smiled to myself, knowing that she and Pa had likely spent the night much the same way as Shadow and I. Pa grinned like a new bridegroom and then he and Shadow exchanged satisfied smiles while Rebecca and I secretly did the same.

Breakfast was a happy meal as we planned the day's work. There was so much to be done, I wondered how we would ever accomplish it all before winter set in. We worked from dawn til dark seven days a week and before long, the cabin walls were up, a winter garden was planted, and we had a small corral to hold our stock.

Pa and Rebecca urged us to share the cabin with them, even though it was just a shell at present, but Shadow said no. He did not want to live within four walls. I understood his feelings and I didn't argue. In truth, I enjoyed living Cheyenne style. We had stopped at the reservation on our way to Bear Valley so Pa could visit Sunbird, only to learn that the old woman had died peacefully in her sleep the day before we arrived. Pa had gone to visit her grave. Sunbird had no relatives and no one had touched her lodge. Pa gave her belongings away and then I dismantled the lodge. We had brought it was us to Bear Valley, and now Shadow and I shared it.

After our separation, it seemed like we could never be together enough again. Sometimes Shadow left whatever he was working on to be with me. Sometimes he only stayed a moment. Sometimes he helped me finish whatever chore I was engaged in.

I was just as bad. I caught myself reaching out to touch him, to make sure he was really there. My eyes looked for him constantly, the sight of him making my heart tingle with gladness.

Sometimes, as now, I ignored the task at hand just to watch him. He had discarded the trappings of civilization and wore nothing but his buckskins and moccasins. His hair, though still short, was growing longer. His muscles rippled like silk under his tawny skin as he chopped down a large tree. He was beautiful to watch. His movements were smooth, economical, rhythmic. A fine sheen of sweat covered his face and chest, and the sight of his sweat-dampened body made my insides turn to mush.

Feeling my gaze, Shadow stopped in mid-swing, the ax suspended in mid-air as he turned to face me. I felt my cheeks grow hot under his knowing grin. His mouth formed the word "later," and then he was swinging the ax again.

I felt all keyed up as I went back to work, rather like a schoolgirl anticipating the arrival of her first beau.

The feeling stayed with me all day, whether I was helping Rebecca wash clothes, preparing our midday meal, or washing a pound of mud from Mary's face.

With the coming of darkness, I could barely keep from singing with excitement.

I felt Shadow's eyes on mine all through dinner, felt his eager desire as I put the children to bed a half hour early.

Pa flashed us a knowing grin as we mumbled something about going to the river for water.

Out of sight of the cabin, Shadow took my hand and we ran toward the river crossing. When I would have stopped, Shadow shook his head and we went past the crossing and into the pine tree forest where I had played as a child. I had never ventured into the forest at night. It was eerie, walking among the tall trees, hearing the sounds of the night all around us. A full moon hung low in the sky, its pale light making grotesque shadows on the trees. Alone, I would have been afraid, but not with Shadow beside me.

As a little girl, I had pretended the forest was an enchanted fairyland, and I was the fairy queen. The frog on the river-bank had been a handsome prince under an evil spell, the masked raccoon had been a wicked witch in disguise. The distant mountains had been a crystal palace filled with riches.

With a grin, I glanced up at Shadow. My prince had come to me disguised as a Cheyenne warrior. No real prince could have pleased me more.

Shadow came to a halt, and I saw that we were at Rabbit's Head Rock. It was an unusual hunk of granite, gray in color and

shaped like the head of a jack rabbit with
its ears laid back. It was here that I had
first met Shadow.

"Look," he said, pointing toward the
grassland that stretched away before us.

I looked in the direction he indicated.
At first, I saw nothing but a sea of grass
but then, to my delight, I saw a dazzling
red flower illuminated by the soft glow of
the moon. It was the same kind of flower
that had lured me into the forbidden
grassland the day I saw Shadow for the
first time.

I felt tears prick my eyes as Shadow
picked the flower and handed it to me. No
gift had ever been sweeter.

"Hannah." He murmured my name,
his voice deep, husky with longing. His
eyes were as soft and black as midnight
velvet, his mouth warm as the summer
sun as it covered mine.

I kissed him back with all the love in
my heart. My hands were eager to touch
his flesh and I delved under his buckskin
shirt, glorying in the hard strength of his
back and shoulders. Our bodies strained
together, needing, wanting, as we slowly
sank down in the tall yellow grass.

Shadow's eyes seared my flesh as he
removed my clothing, and then his own. I
stared at him, my pulse beating wildly, my
heart pounding in my breast like the beat
of a Cheyenne war drum.

Memories assaulted me, driving me to

hold him closer, tighter. There had been so many times when I had almost lost him, so many times when we had been apart. But never again, never again.

The words were a prayer in my heart as Shadow lowered his lean body over mine. There were no preliminaries this night, no leisurely explorations. Shadow possessed me boldly, masterfully, and I basked in his strength. He was Man, provider, protector, and I was Woman, helpmeet and mate, and we came together in a glorious rush, our bodies uniting, joining as they were meant to be joined.

I closed my eyes, lost in a web of pleasure as Shadow thrust into me, making me complete. I locked my legs around Shadow's waist, my hands clutching his back, as the rhythm of our love grew stronger and more intense.

Shadow growled my name as his life poured into me, filling me with sweet, sweet ecstasy.

XVIII

Fall-Winter 1885

By late October, Pa's cabin was completed inside and out. It was a rough structure by city standards, but Rebecca seemed pleased. There was a large parlor with two windows and a stone fireplace, two bedrooms, a sunlit kitchen with a large pantry. Cheery curtains covered the windows, rag rugs covered the plank floors. There was no furniture as yet save for a table and six chairs that Pa built with his own two hands.

Pa and Rebecca took a trip to Steel's Crossing to order a sofa and two chairs, a brass bed, an armoire, a bathtub and a cook stove from a mail order house back east. Rebecca thought it was a little foolish to buy a houseful of new furniture when she had everything they needed at her house back in West Virginia, but Pa said he wanted to start off fresh.

271

"No hand-me-downs," Pa said adamantly. "No reminders of the past. This is our life, yours and mine. Besides, I can afford it."

So Rebecca wrote her neighbor, Mrs. Poulson, and asked her to keep an eye on her house, then wrote a second letter to her daughter, Beth, advising her of her new location and her marriage to Pa.

When the cabin was finished, Pa and Shadow started work on a barn to shelter the cow and the horses during the coming winter. It was hard work, and Pa and Shadow were bone weary at the end of the day.

"I'll be glad when that bathtub arrives," Pa grumbled one evening. "I'd sure like to soak in a hot tub. These cold baths in the river are making my old bones brittle as kindling."

Rebecca laughed softly. "I'll warm you up," she murmured, then blushed when she realized I had overheard her remark.

Shadow shook his head ruefully. He did not approve of hot baths. Cold water was invigorating, stimulating. Hot water drained the strength from a man and left him weak and sluggish.

We didn't often disagree, Shadow and I, but I was eager for a hot bath myself. There was nothing more peaceful or relaxing than a leisurely soak in a hot bubble bath.

I wasn't thinking of a hot bath now, as I washed in the river. I was thinking of the child growing under my heart. I had suspected for some time that I was pregnant, but I had put off telling Shadow about my condition because I didn't know if the child was Shadow's or Joshua's, nor was I certain when the child had been conceived. My monthly flow had been erratic for some time, ever since the day I had been shot by Joe Mattlock. Since then, my life had been in such turmoil, I had scarcely paid attention. From the way I felt, I was certain I was at least four months pregnant. The child could easily be Shadow's. It could just as easily be Joshua's.

I pondered how to break the news to Shadow. Would he be glad? How would he feel if the child had been fathered by Joshua Berdeen? How would I feel?

Suddenly depressed, I sat down in the water and watched it swirl and eddy around me. Why couldn't my life flow as calmly as the water rolling past?

"Hannah."

I glanced up, startled, as I heard Shadow's voice calling me. I was drying off when he reached the riverbank, and I felt my cheeks grow hot as his dark eyes perused my body from head to heel. Shadow knew every inch of my flesh as well as I did. Would he notice the slight swelling in my abdomen? Would he notice my breasts were larger, heavier?

Guilt washed over me, making me feel as if I had betrayed Shadow even though I had never willingly let Joshua touch me.

Refusing to meet Shadow's eyes, I wrapped the towel around my middle and climbed the muddy bank to the flat ground above. I could feel Shadow's eyes on my head, compelling me to face him. Slowly, I raised my eyes to his.

"Why didn't you tell me?" he asked, his voice quietly accusing. "We have never had any secrets between us."

"Tell you what?" My voice was a choked whisper, my scarlet cheeks an unspoken admission of guilt.

"About the baby. How far along are you?"

"I'm not sure. About four months, I think."

"I thought you wanted another child."

"I did. I do."

"Then why do you look so unhappy?"

"Oh, Shadow," I wailed miserably. "I don't know if it's yours."

I stood there, feeling awful, as I watched Shadow's face. He did not need any explanation. He knew what I was saying. I saw his eyes grow dark with implacable hatred for Joshua Berdeen, saw the bloodlust burn like an evil flame, making his countenance dark and ruthless. His jaw clenched and his hands balled into tight fists. And then, miraculously, his face softened and he drew me into the snug security of his arms.

With a sigh, he rested his cheek against the top of my head. "It does not matter who the father is," he said quietly. "You are the mother and I will love the child for that reason alone."

Tears filled my eyes and ran down my cheeks. What had I ever done to deserve such a man? I knew what those few words had cost him. Shadow was a proud man; sometimes stubborn, almost arrogant in many ways. I knew how jealous he could be, how it outraged his sense of pride and honor to know another man had possessed me, and yet he was willing to love this child because it was mine.

Shadow held me tight while I cried, his long body pressed close to mine, his arms lovingly enfolding me.

"Come," he said after awhile. "Let us go tell the others."

The news that I was pregnant put a smile on everybody's face. Pa was thrilled at the thought of another grandchild, Rebecca was thrilled with the idea of a baby to love. Heecha and Mary thought it would be fun to have a little brother or sister to play with.

Shadow and I had decided not to mention that the baby might not be his,

and sometimes even I forgot that I didn't
know who the father was. At those times,
I was glad that I was pregnant again. I
loved children and looked forward to
another. But, too often, thoughts of
Joshua penetrated my mind. I did not
want to be carrying his child. I did not
want his baby. I did not want anything
that would remind me of Joshua Berdeen
or the unhappiness he had caused me.

The days were busy and passed
quickly. The barn was almost finished, we
had laid in a good supply of firewood, and
we had enough meat to see us through the
winter. In the evening, Pa worked on the
cradle he was making for the baby while
Rebecca and I sewed sacques and gowns
and quilts. While the rest of us were
making baby things, Shadow entertained
Heecha and Mary with games and stories.

I knew Shadow was not pleased with
the idea that the baby I was carrying
might be Joshua's, but he was unfailingly
kind and considerate during my pregnancy. He comforted me when I felt blue,
refused to let me do any heavy work,
insisted that I rest for an hour or two each
afternoon. He never referred to the coming
child as anything but "our" baby.

Winter came in a flurry of snow and
rain, turning our valley into a pristine
world of unblemished white. The furniture
and the window glass Pa had ordered
arrived a week ahead of the first big snow

storm and the cabin was snug and comfortable.

I was eagerly anticipating Christmas this year. It would be such fun to spend the day with my father again, to reminisce about holidays past, to hear him tell Heecha and Mary the stories he had once told me.

Pa and Shadow made snowshoes for all of us so we could go outside when the weather permitted. We took long walks between storms, looking around for the perfect Christmas tree.

It was on one of our walks that Rebecca was attacked by a mountain lion. She had fallen behind to fix one of her snowshoes when a terrible roar filled the air. I turned in time to see a large tawny shape drop from a snow-covered branch onto Rebecca's back. I quickly grabbed Heecha and Mary and pushed them out of sight behind a large fir tree.

With a wordless cry of alarm, Pa raised his rifle but couldn't fire for fear of hitting Rebecca who was vainly trying to avoid the cat's claws and teeth.

It was then that Shadow sprang into action. The shrill, ululating war cry of the Cheyenne echoed through the wooded hills as Shadow hurled himself at the snarling cat, his powerful arms locking around the animal's throat.

In an instant, the cat turned from Rebecca to defend itself against this new threat. I watched in horror as Shadow and the mountain lion rolled back and forth on the snow-covered ground. The cat's angry growls and Shadow's labored breathing seemed extraordinarily loud.

I glanced anxiously at my father who was still sighting down the barrel of his rifle, waiting for a clear shot.

Shadow grunted with pain as the mountain lion's razor-sharp teeth sliced through his shirt and into his back. I felt suddenly sick to my stomach as Shadow's blood turned the snow from white to red.

There was a sharp retort as Pa fired a round at the mountain lion. The bullet took the animal clean between the eyes, killing it instantly.

I ran to Shadow's side while Pa hastened to help Rebecca. Shadow was bleeding from a multitude of cuts and scratches on his face, neck, shoulders, back and chest. He groaned softly as he pushed the mountain lion off his legs and stood up. I knew he was in pain, but his first thought was for Rebecca.

"How is she?" he asked.

"I don't know."

Together, we went over to where Pa was kneeling beside Rebecca. Her eyes were glazed with pain, and I could see she had been hurt much worse than Shadow. The cat's claws had gouged a deep gash in her right shoulder and it was bleeding profusely. She had a dozen minor scratches on her face and neck, several deep claw marks on her back.

Pa took a handful of snow and pressed it against the wound in Rebecca's shoulder, then wrapped his scarf around her shoulder. She whimpered pathetically when he lifted her in his arms.

The sight of so much blood made Mary cry. I picked her up, my heart heavy with concern as we made our way back to the cabin. Heecha ran ahead to open the door.

Inside, Pa placed Rebecca on their bed.

"We need some warm water," I told Heecha. "Mary, bring me all the clean cloths you can find. Pa, get Rebecca out of that dress and put a blanket over her so she doesn't get a chill. Shadow, you sit down before you fall down."

As I searched for our medicine kit, I sorely wished there was a doctor close by, but the nearest one was in Steel's Crossing over a hundred miles away.

While I waited for the water to heat, I took a closer look at Shadow's wounds. None appeared to be serious and I offered a silent prayer of thanks to Man Above as I wiped the blood from Shadow's cuts. Later, I would disinfect them, but for now Rebecca must come first.

Her eyes were closed and I thanked God she was unconscious as I began to wash the wound.

"It'll need stitching," Pa said, his eyes searching mine. "Can you do it, or shall I?"

"I'll do it. You'll have to hold her down."

I disinfected a needle and some silk thread, poured disinfectant over the wound in Rebecca's shoulder, took a deep breath, and began to sew. The years melted away and I recalled standing in our old cabin while my mother deftly stitched a nasty wound in Shadow's leg, her needle drawing the raw edges of skin together with the same neat even stitches she used to mend Pa's shirts. Now, as I did the very thing I had seen my mother do, I wondered how she had managed to remain so calm as she pushed a needle through living tissue. Sweat dripped from my brow and I flinched each time the needle pierced Rebecca's ivory skin, each time she groaned with pain.

Pa spoke to her in a low voice, telling her to stay calm, that everything would be fine, just fine. I prayed he was right, that I would not do more harm than good, that Rebecca's arm would not get infected. So many things could go wrong, and we were so far away from a doctor.

I sensed Shadow's presence behind me even before I felt his hand on my shoulder. He didn't say a word, only smiled reassuringly, but some of his strength seemed to flow into me, giving me the courage to do what had to be done.

At last, I was finished. I placed a piece of gauze over the wound, bandaged it lightly. Rebecca lay quiet on the bed, her eyes closed. Pa's eyes were wet with tears when Shadow and I left the room.

In the parlor, Shadow sat down on a chair while I poured some water in a bowl and cleaned his wounds. He winced a little when I began to daub disinfectant on the many cuts and scratches the cat had inflicted on him. I hated to add to his pain, yet the thought of infection spurred me on and I applied more of the stinging medicine than was probably necessary.

It was dusk when I finished. Admonishing Shadow to stay put, I went into the kitchen to prepare dinner. It was a sober meal. Heecha and Mary were solemn and quiet, their eyes reflecting concern for Rebecca, whom they had grown to love in the past several months. Pa could not eat at all. He swallowed three cups of strong black coffee and then went back to sit at Rebecca's side.

I washed the dishes and put Heecha and Mary to bed in the spare bedroom, and all the while I was conscious of Rebecca's shallow breathing and her occasional moans of pain.

"I think we should stay here tonight," I told Shadow. "In case Pa needs us."

Shadow nodded and I spread some blankets on the floor near the fireplace. He sighed heavily as he sank down beside me.

"Are you all right?" I asked. "Are you in pain?"

"Do not worry about me, Hannah. I will be all right. I am afraid for your father. He loves Rebecca very much."

"Yes." I knew what Shadow was thinking. It would break my father's heart if Rebecca died.

In the morning, Rebecca had a high fever. She tossed restlessly, sometimes crying out, sometimes mumbling incoherently. Once she called for her daughter. Pa refused to leave her side. As gently as a mother tending a loved child, Pa bathed Rebecca's face and body with cool water to bring her fever down. He spooned broth into her mouth, coaxing her to eat just a little more when she said she was full. He held her hand while she slept, talked softly to her even though she couldn't hear him. He begged her to get better, pleaded with God to make her well.

Rebecca's fever was worse that night. About midnight, Shadow left the cabin. He returned a short time later carrying a small otter-skin bag, a bowl, and a handful of damp tree moss. Lifting the bandage from Rebecca's shoulder, he packed the raw, angry-looking wound with the moss. Then he poured the contents of the sack into the bowl, and placed the bowl on a box near the head of the bed. Striking a match, he dropped it into the bowl, igniting the contents. Immediately, a pungent aroma filled the room. Standing beside the bowl, Shadow passed his hands through the whitish-blue smoke, drawing it in Rebecca's direction while he uttered a soft Cheyenne chant.

Pa looked up, frowning. Then, recognizing the chant as a prayer, he smiled faintly and bowed his head. Heecha and Mary entered the room on quiet feet. Going to Shadow, they stood on either side of him, their heads bowed.

When the smoke died away, Shadow raised his arms toward heaven and offered a prayer to Maheo, beseeching the Great Spirit to heal Rebecca. Bowing my head, I added my own prayer to Shadow's.

In the morning, Rebecca was much improved. The fever was gone, the wound was no longer red and angry-looking.

I looked at Shadow with new respect.

"My people have lived in this place for a long time," he explained with a grin that was a trifle smug. "We were healing our sick long before the white man crossed the Missouri."

I nodded, but secretly I wondered what had brought about Rebecca's miraculous cure. Had it been the healing power in the green tree moss, Shadow's mysterious herbs and prayer smoke, or our heartfelt prayers to the gods both red and white? I concluded it was probably a combination of all three.

The glow in Pa's eyes could have lit up the city of New York, he was that pleased with Rebecca's miraculous recovery. He gave Shadow a bear hug, then apologized profusely when he realized he was causing Shadow's wounds considerable discomfort.

"Shadow, I . . . hell, what can I say? I'm beholden to you for what you did for Rebecca. And you too, Hannah. You'll never know how grateful I am. If there's ever anything I can do . . ."

Shadow dropped a hand over Pa's mouth. "That's enough, Sam," he said, grinning.

"Enough, hell!" Pa exclaimed. "Let's go skin that cat before the scavengers ruin the hide."

Christmas was special that year. I was with those I loved and we were all strong and healthy. Rebecca's shoulder was nearly healed, though still tender to the touch, and Shadow's wounds had healed without a scar. We had a beautiful tree, good food, and a promising future. Life was perfect.

We were sitting in front of the fireplace, singing Christmas carols, when there was a knock at the door. We looked at each other, startled by the idea that we were not alone in the valley.

"Who could it be?" Rebecca asked, frowning.

"Beats me," Pa said. "But there's only one way to find out." And taking the rifle from its place over the mantel, he opened the door.

A man and a woman and a girl of about seven stood on the porch. They were bundled up in heavy coats, mittens, scarves and hats against the cold. Beyond them, I could see a small wagon hitched to a slat-sided gray mare.

"Afternoon, folks," the man said, smiling broadly. "We were out for a ride when we saw the smoke from your chimney and thought we'd come check it out. We live about ten miles east of here. Didn't know we had any neighbors."

Pa put out a big hand. "Glad to meet you folks. Come on in before you freeze. This here's my wife, Rebecca. This is my daughter, Hannah, and her husband, Shadow. These are my grandkids, Heecha and Mary."

There was an awkward moment of silence when our new neighbors realized Shadow was an Indian. They glanced at me and then at Heecha and Mary, and I could see them wondering if Heecha was mine.

The man cleared his throat. He was short and stocky, and bowlegged. His hair and eyes were brown, his features nondescript.

"I'm Porter Sprague," he said. This is my missus, Helen, and our girl, Nelda."

Pa and the man shook hands. Shadow did not offer his hand to the stranger, and Sprague didn't seem to expect it.

Rebecca asked the Spragues to join us for pie and coffee and they accepted. Helen Sprague was a shade taller than her husband. She had curly red hair, brown eyes, and a wide mouth that was rarely still. She gushed over everything and eagerly offered to help Rebecca in the kitchen, more out of curiosity to see the rest of the house than to be of help, I thought uncharitably.

I sat in the parlor beside Shadow, feeling my anger grow as Porter Sprague chatted with my father and totally ignored my husband. Mary and Nelda sat on the floor in front of the fireplace playing with Mary's doll. Heecha had gone into the spare bedroom to work on a new bow he was making.

The Spragues stayed for an hour or so and seemed like nice enough people. They had come out from Illinois the year before, bound for California, but they had fallen in love with Bear Valley and decided to make their home here instead.

They didn't say anything about Shadow being an Indian, but every now and then Helen or Porter would glance at Shadow, a hint of disdain in their eyes.

Shadow ignored them both. He sat beside me, his face impassive, his dark eyes unfathomable as he gazed at the fire crackling in the hearth. Indeed, he might have been alone in the room, for he seemed to be oblivious to what was going on around him.

It was Nelda who finally brought up the subject of Indians. Pa and Porter Sprague were discussing cattle, hay and barbed wire, Rebecca and Helen Sprague were making a date to get together in the near future to make a quilt when Nelda Sprague's high-pitched voice caught everyone's attention.

"Why does your brother have such dark skin?" Nelda asked brashly. "He looks like an Indian."

Mary gave the girl a look that would have scorched green grass. "He is an Indian," she said haughtily. "And so am I."

"Well, I wouldn't brag about it if I were you," Nelda Sprague replied scornfully. "Everybody knows Indians are no good."

My daughter's face clearly reflected the hurt Nelda Sprague's words had caused. It took every ounce of self-control I possessed to keep from reaching out and slapping Nelda's freckled face.

"Nelda, hush!" Porter Sprague glanced at Pa apologetically. "I'm awfully sorry, Kincaid," he said gruffly. "You know how kids are."

Pa's face was as dark as a thundercloud. "I know kids that age generally repeat what they hear at home," Pa said tersely. "That's what I know. I think you'd better leave now."

Sprague nodded, his face and neck turning beet red with embarrassment. Helen Sprague mumbled a quick goodnight as they put on their hats and coats and hurried outside.

Pa slammed the door behind them. "I'm sorry, Shadow," he said. "I know how they feel. I felt the same way about Indians myself not too long ago, and I'm sorry."

"It is not your fault," Shadow said stiffly, and left the house.

I looked at my father and Rebecca, uncertain as to whether I should go after Shadow or leave him alone for awhile. The bitterness in my husband's eyes was like a knife in my heart. He was a good man, a proud man, and yet people like Helen and Porter Sprague could not see past the color of his skin. For a moment, I wished I were a man so I could curse and holler and slam my fist into the wall.

"Go to him, Hannah," Rebecca advised. "he needs you."

With a nod, I pulled a shawl around my shoulders and went to find Shadow. He was nowhere in sight, but a dazzling full moon clearly illuminated his tracks in the snow. His trail led me to the river crossing. I saw him standing near the water's edge, staring across the river at the vast stretch of land that had once belonged to the Cheyenne. His face was dark with anger; his hands were balled into tight fists.

He heard me long before I reached him. As he swung around to face me, I saw the hatred burning in his eyes, hatred for the whole white race. I could not blame him for his feelings. Many whites had wronged him. Joshua Berdeen had left him bleeding in the wilderness to die. Clyde Stewart and Barney McCall had saved his life only to take him back East and put him on exhibit in a traveling tent show. It had been a humiliating experience for Shadow. Men and women and children had stared and pointed at him as if he were some new species of wild animal. Clad only in a brief clout, moccasins, and an ankle-length warbonnet of Crow origin, he had been forced to stand before gawking crowds while Barney McCall spun a wild tale depicting the atrocities Two Hawks Flying had perpetrated against helpless women and children, then went on to extol the virtues of Clyde Stewart who had, single-handedly and with great daring and courage, captured Two Hawks Flying, thereby ridding the west of a great menace. Before he had managed to escape from the tent show,

Shadow had been cruelly whipped to settle a foolish bet. He had been shot in the arm by an irate father whose son and daughter had been killed by Apaches. He had been poked, prodded, mocked and spat upon.

Looking at him now, I could see that he was remembering it all. The force of his angry gaze stopped me in my tracks and I shivered, more from the ominous expression in Shadow's black eyes than from the cold.

"Shadow . . ." I whispered his name and then fell silent. What could I say to erase the bitterness from his eyes?

"Some things will never change," Shadow said acridly. "There will always be white men who hate Indians, just as there will always be Indians who hate whites."

"I love you," I said. "I will always love you."

Shadow's eyes lost their angry look as he held out his arms. "It is good that some things do not change," he murmured, drawing me close.

We stood there together for a long time, content to be quietly close. The night was beautiful, quiet and peaceful. The sky was clear and inky black, the stars twinkling like lights in a dark house.

I gasped as the child stirred beneath my heart.

"What is it?" Shadow asked, concerned.

"The baby moved. Here, feel." I placed Shadow's hand over my swollen abdomen, smiled as the child moved beneath his palm. "I had forgotten how it feels," I said wonderingly.

"It was a good strong kick," Shadow remarked. "Perhaps we will have another son."

"I hope he looks like you."

Shadow shook his head, his good mood gone again. "I think the child will be better off if it looks like you."

I knew why he felt that way, but I could think of nothing to say in reply. Perhaps Shadow was right. Perhaps the Indian would never be accepted by the whites. I stared into the distance, wondering what the future would hold for our children. Would they be shunned and ridiculed because of their Cheyenne blood, never accepted because they were half-breeds? It was a dismal thought, one that haunted me for many days to come.

XIX

Spring 1886

With the coming of spring, we learned there were four other families in the valley. Pa and Shadow spotted their cabins during one of their forays across the valley in search of game and Pa, being a friendly, outgoing man, took off one day to meet them.

The family nearest us was from Vermont. Their name was Smythe and they had eight sons ranging in age from nineteen months to seventeen years. The Bannermans lived beyond the Smythes near the bend of the river. They had a daughter, Victoria, who was six years old.

Fred and Myrtle Brown lived across the river. They had a sixteen year old son named Jeremy. The last homestead belonged to George and Ruth Tippitt. The Tippitts were an elderly couple with no children at home. Their son had been killed at Shiloh, their daughter lived in Rhode Island.

I dreaded the thought of meeting the rest of our neighbors after our encounter with the Spragues. I was certain Helen Sprague had already informed anyone who would listen that there was a real, honest-to-goodness Indian living in the valley. I was equally certain she had encouraged everyone to avoid Shadow, and perhaps myself, like the plague.

It was on a lovely clear day in March that the invitation I had been dreading arrived. The Bannermans were having a party so we could all get acquainted. Everyone in the valley was invited. Shadow immediately said he would not go.

"Then neither will I," I said, relieved.

"Don't be silly," Pa admonished. "You can't spend the rest of your life holed up here. These folks are our neighbors and if we're going to make our home here, then we've got to get to know them, and they've got to get to know us. Especially Shadow. Once they learn he's not going to scalp them in their beds, they'll come around." Pa directed his gaze at Shadow. "Most folks are pretty decent if you give them half a chance."

Shadow looked doubtful.

"It's up to you," I said, hoping he would say no.

"Perhaps your father is right," Shadow said thoughtfully.

I was terribly nervous as I dressed for the party. I was eight months pregnant and I felt fat and unattractive as I pulled a pale blue dress over my swollen belly and smoothed the full skirt over my hips. As I brushed my hair, I prayed that Shadow, my children and I, would be accepted by our neighbors as I had been accepted by the Cheyenne years ago. People could be cruel and unforgiving, and it was with that thought in mind that I urged Shadow to wear the dark pants and shirt he had worn in Chicago, but he refused.

"I am Cheyenne," he said as he pulled on a pair of buckskin pants and a long sleeved buckskin shirt. "What I wear will not change what I am."

Why would anyone want to change him? The thought ran around in my mind as I looked at Shadow. His hair, freshly washed, hung black and shining past his shoulders. The buckskin shirt, fringed at the sleeves and across the back, outlined his broad shoulders. The pants, fringed along the outer seams, covered long muscular legs. He was a perfect example of what a man should be, and I loved him dearly.

"You look very handsome," I said.

"And you are beautiful."

"Am I?" I looked in the mirror. I had never thought of myself as being attractive but it pleased me to know that Shadow thought so. I had always thought

my nose was a trifle too small and my
mouth a little too wide. My hair was my
best feature. It fell in soft waves around
my face. Most women wore their hair
gathered in a bun or a braid, but I wore
mine loose because Shadow preferred it
that way.

My stomach was in knots when we
arrived at the Bannerman's cabin. I took a
last hasty look at our children. They had
been scrubbed from head to toe, their hair
neatly brushed and combed. Mary wore a
bright yellow dress that Rebecca had
made especially for this occasion. Heecha
wore brown pants and a red shirt. Looking
at them, I knew they would make a good
impression.

I smiled nervously at Rebecca and she
patted my arm reassuringly. Rebecca
looked lovely in a long blue skirt and long-
sleeved white blouse. Her hair was swept
high on her head, a single chestnut curl fell
over one shoulder. Pa looked handsome in
a pair of black pants and a crisp white
shirt. I took a deep breath as Pa knocked
on the door.

We were the last to arrive, and I felt
every eye swing in our direction as we
entered the house.

Mrs. Bannerman broke the silence
before it grew awkward. "Welcome," she
said, smiling cordially. "I'm Lydia, and
this is my husband, Horace."

Pa made our introductions to Lydia

Bannerman, and she introduced us to the rest of her guests. Mattie Smythe was a woman with dark hair, gray eyes, and a figure that remained trim in spite of eight pregnancies. Her husband, Leland, was tall and lean, with brown hair and brown eyes. Their children, named alphabetically, were Abel, Benjamin, Cabel, David, Ethan, Frank, Gene, and Henry. They were as nice a bunch of boys as I had ever met.

Ruth Tippitt was a rather tall angular woman with gray hair and twinkling blue eyes. She loved to talk and as I got to know her better, I discovered she had a fine hand with a needle and loved to sew, crochet, knit and embroider. She made lovely shawls and quilts and doilies and gave them away as gifts to all her friends.

George Tippitt was a crusty old man with a fringe of white hair and a shaggy gray beard. He rarely said more than two words at a time and was a little hard of hearing. I thought George and Ruth made an odd couple, Ruth being so charming and polite and George being so crotchety and kind of scruffy-looking, but they seemed very happy together.

Fred Brown was a jolly sort. He had graying blond hair, green eyes and always wore a plaid vest and a derby hat. His wife, Myrtle, was short and plump. She had a mass of curly light brown hair and deep blue eyes. Their son, Jeremy,

was tall and blond and more than a little
arrogant about his looks.

Lydia Bannerman had auburn hair
which she always wore piled high on her
head. It was obvious she was accustomed
to being in charge and she quickly became
the social leader and trend-setter in the
valley. She came from a fine Boston family
and it showed. Her manners were impeccable, her voice was always carefully
modulated, her table always correctly set.
Lydia had violet eyes and frequently wore
dresses of lavender and purple to bring
out their color.

Horace Bannerman was a rather
paunchy man with a shock of black hair
and deep brown eyes. He looked more like
a gentleman farmer than a settler, and
acted like one, too.

Dinners at the Bannerman home were
always formal occasions, putting everyone
on their best behavior. The men were
careful of their language and their cigars,
the women always wore their best dresses,
and the children were careful to mind their
manners.

Victoria Bannerman was the image of
her mother. Her long auburn hair was
always neatly combed, and I never saw
her in a dress that wasn't freshly
laundered and ironed. It was easy to see
that one day she would be a beautiful
young woman, poised, well-mannered and
eagerly sought-after.

I smiled and shook hands with everyone I was introduced to, feeling as nervous as a cat in a roomful of rocking chairs. I felt as if everyone was judging me, wondering what kind of woman would marry an Indian and bear his children.

Shadow seemed at ease. He shook hands with the men, smiled pleasantly at the women, and promised the children he would not scalp them until he knew them better.

Our neighbors were all polite and friendly, save for Helen Sprague, who remained cool and standoffish. During the course of the evening, I occasionally noticed someone staring curiously at Shadow, but I couldn't blame them. After all, he was different from the rest of us and few whites had ever seen an Indian up close. Heecha and Mary were soon involved in a game of hide-and-seek with the other children and I breathed a sigh of relief. They seemed to be having a good time in spite of Nelda Sprague's presence.

It was a lively party. George Tippitt played the fiddle and there was dancing and singing out in the lantern-lit yard. I smiled as Pa and Rebecca danced by. Rebecca seemed to grow more lovely every day, and I was glad Pa had found her. They made a handsome couple and it was easy to see they were very much in love. Pa had been lucky twice, I mused, first with my mother, and then with Rebecca. I realized suddenly that Rebecca and my mother were very much alike, and I wondered if that was one of the reasons Pa had been drawn to Rebecca in the first place.

Shadow was not familiar with most of the songs or dances, so I stayed close to his side, knowing he felt out of place. We were sitting on the porch steps, watching the Bannermans and the Smythes do the polka, when Fred Brown sat down on the step next to Shadow.

"Haven't we met someplace before?" Fred Brown asked, frowning thoughtfully. "You look familiar."

"I do not think so," Shadow replied.

Mr. Brown shook his head slowly. "I'm sure I've seen you somewhere before," he insisted, and then his green eyes lit up with recognition. "Damn!" he exclaimed in a loud voice. "You're the Indian from the carnival. I saw you in Jersey City back in '77. Well, I'll be gone to hell, imagine you being here!"

"Yes," Shadow said through clenched teeth. "Imagine."

"It was a hell of a show," Fred Brown went on, slapping his thigh gleefully. "Me and the missus purely enjoyed it. And Jeremy near busted a gut when Clyde Stewart himself invited him to come on stage. The boy talked about it for weeks afterward. Hey, Jeremy, come on over here a minute."

"What do you want, pa?" Jeremy Brown asked impatiently. "We're playing tag and the kids are waiting for me."

"You remember that trip we took to Jersey City when you were a kid? I knew you would. This is the Indian you and your cousin, Marynell, slapped all that war paint on."

"No kidding? Nice to meet you," Jeremy said politely. "I had a good time that night. Can I go now, Pa?"

"Sure, son, run along," Fred Brown said, giving the boy an affectionate slap on the rump before turning to Shadow again. "Yep, that was some show. I don't know what Stewart paid you to wear them chains and strut around the stage pretending you were Two Hawks Flying, but it wasn't enough."

"I was not pretending," Shadow said quietly.

Fred Brown's face went gray, as if he had just been punched in the stomach. "Two Hawks Flying." He breathed the name aloud. "I'll be damned."

Two Hawks Flying. The name drew everyone's attention and all other conversation around us came to a halt as people turned to stare at Shadow.

Two Hawks Flying, war chief of the Cheyenne.

Two Hawks Flying, one of the Indians responsible for the Custer massacre.

Two Hawks Flying, a name that

stirred fear in the hearts of men and women.

"He killed Custer!" Helen Sprague jabbed an accusing finger in Shadow's direction. "I read his name in the newspaper. He was there!" Her voice rose hysterically. "He'll kill us all!"

"Calm down, Helen," Horace Bannerman advised curtly. "The man isn't even armed." Bannerman shot an inquiring look at Fred Brown. "What the hell's going on, Fred?"

"Nothing. I, uh, I was just surprised to learn that Shadow, here, is really Two Hawks Flying. I didn't mean to start a ruckus."

Horace Bannerman's gaze shifted to Shadow's face. The name Two Hawks Flying had been prominent in the newspapers back east when General George Armstrong Custer was killed at the Little Big Horn. There had been a lot of speculation about which Indian had killed the general. Had it been Crazy Horse or Gall, Sitting Bull or Two Hawks Flying? Had it been Rain-in-the-Face, who, according to one grisly rumor, was said to have cut out Custer's heart and eaten it?

I knew for a fact that none of the Indians usually credited with Custer's death had actually killed him. While living with Shadow's people, I had heard it said that a young warrior named Hawk had killed Custer, while the Sioux claimed one of their braves, Flat Hip, had killed the general.

It was my opinion that no one really knew who ended the flamboyant career of George Armstrong Custer. He had cut his long yellow hair prior to the battle and without his well-known trademark to identify him, he probably looked like any other white man. It was my guess that the Indian who killed Custer didn't even know it was Custer.

In the years since the Custer massacre, other theories had come to light. One theory held that Custer committed suicide, another contended that the body identified as George Custer had actually been the body of his brother, Tom, and that Custer had been captured alive by the Sioux and tortured to death. Another theory claimed that Custer had somehow managed to escape from the battlefield and was even now living in obscurity in some little town, afraid to come forward for fear of being branded a coward.

But none of that was important now. What mattered was the way our neighbors were staring at Shadow, wondering if he was the man who had killed a legend. Custer had been a hero in the eyes of many whites, a man whose life had been held in high esteem.

Horace Bannerman cleared his throat as he took a step closer to Shadow. "Did you kill Custer?''

Was I imagining it, or was everyone holding their breath?

The night grew suddenly still, as if the whole world was waiting for Shadow's reply. I saw Pa move closer to the end of the porch, his face set in angry lines, and I knew if trouble started, Pa would step in and take a place at Shadow's side.

"Well?" Horace Bannerman said, his voice sounding loud in the quiet of the night.

"I did not kill Custer," Shadow answered with regret. "But I was at the Little Big Horn the day he died." Shadow stood up, his dark eyes sweeping the crowd. "I am Two Hawks Flying of the Cheyenne," he announced proudly. "I am not ashamed to be Indian. I have killed many white men in battle, but that is over now. I have come to this place to live with my wife and her family. If my presence is going to cause trouble, say so now, and I will leave."

There was a moment of silence, then everyone began talking at once.

"No need to leave," Fred Brown said emphatically. "The war's over as far as I'm concerned."

"That's right," Lydia Bannerman agreed. "There's room in the valley for everyone, red or white."

"We're happy to have you here," Ruth Tippitt said, laying her hand on Shadow's arm. "Sounds to me like you've had some bad experiences with white folks in the past, but we're not all like that."

I felt my heart swell with gratitude as our neighbors flocked around Shadow, urging him to stay, assuring him that he was welcome. Only the Spragues remained aloof, their faces showing their disapproval.

There was a new feeling of friendship in the valley after that night. We got together as often as possible to sing and dance or just talk about crops and cattle and kids. We had a barn raising for the Tippitts when their old one burned down, and after the work was done, we had a party to celebrate.

I was pouring lemonade in the Tippitt's kitchen when I overheard Helen Sprague and her husband talking outside the window.

"Kind of strange, that barn burning down," Helen said.

"Not so strange when you think nothing like that ever happened until that redskin moved into the valley," Porter Sprague replied.

Helen Sprague smiled maliciously. "Why, that's right. I'll bet he did it out of pure cussedness."

They moved away from the window, their heads together as though they were plotting some mischief. I didn't mention the incident to Shadow. I didn't want to

spoil the day for him. He was having a
good time, talking and laughing with the
other men while they ate the dinner the
women had prepared. It was good to see
him enjoying himself instead of remaining
apart from the crowd, good to know that,
except for the Spragues, our neighbors
had accepted him as an equal.

It was shortly after the barn raising
that the trouble began. Horace Bannerman found one of his bulls with its throat
cut. The Tippitts went out to their chicken
coop and found three hens missing. The
Spragues announced the loss of one of
their goats. Fred Brown complained that
someone was stealing his milk. Leland
Smythe lamented the loss of one of his
prize roosters.

It was at one of our gatherings that
Helen Sprague pointed out that our place
was the only one that hadn't been
bothered.

"I think that's awfully strange," she
remarked, staring at Shadow. "Don't
you?"

"It is odd," George Tippitt agreed,
"but it probably doesn't mean anything.
The Kincaids live quite a ways out from
the rest of us."

"I think it could mean a lot," Porter
Sprague argued.

"Just what are you hinting at,
Porter?" Pa demanded angrily.

Porter Sprague glanced at Shadow,

his eyes filled with accusation. "I'm not stealing my own goats," he said with a shrug. "And I know Bannerman didn't slit his bull's throat. Why hasn't anything happened at your place?"

"I don't know," Pa answered testily. "But I'd be damned careful before I made any accusations I couldn't prove if I were you."

Porter Sprague swelled up like an angry gobbler. "Is that a threat, Kincaid?"

"You're damn right!" Pa said. "And don't you forget it."

Sprague looked at Shadow. Apparently he did not like what he saw reflected in Shadow's eyes because he didn't pursue the matter further. But the damage had been done. Even though no direct accusations had been made, I knew our neighbors were wondering if Shadow was guilty of stealing livestock and killing Bannerman's bull.

In the next few weeks, there were more thefts. Porter Sprague bought a new shotgun and threatened to shoot anything that moved in his yard after dark and ask questions later. Three families, all from Philadelphia, moved into the south end of the valley. They had no more than gotten settled when they began to notice things were missing—a harness, a spotted calf, a pair of shoats, a new Winchester rifle.

It was in the midst of this turmoil that

my third child made its entrance into the world. I was alone in Pa's cabin when my labor began. Pa and Rebecca had taken Heecha and Mary and gone to Steel's Crossing to pick up some supplies. They would be gone several days. Shadow had gone hunting early that morning, but had promised to be back before dark.

I tried to ignore the pains as I finished a batch of bread and washed up the breakfast dishes. About noon, my water broke and the contractions grew harder. I had forgotten how bad the pain was, and I groaned softly as another contraction left me breathless.

When it passed, I went into the spare bedroom and stretched out on the bed, my fingers worrying the bedclothes as another pain came, and then another.

It was going on five o'clock in the evening when I began to suspect something was wrong. The contractions were coming closer together, but no matter how hard I pushed, the baby would not be born. I was sobbing now, and badly frightened, my fears intensified by the gathering darkness and the fact that Shadow had not returned home.

I crawled out of bed during a lull in the pains and made my way through the dark rooms toward the kitchen. If I was going to die, I didn't want to die in the dark. I was groping in the cupboard for a match when the worst contraction of all knifed through me and I fell to the floor, my arms folded across my stomach as I cried Shadow's name.

Where was he? Why didn't he come home? Had he been hurt? I remembered the time long ago when Shadow had been badly beaten by our neighbors simply because he was an Indian and a new fear burned into my brain. What if Porter Sprague and some of the others had found Shadow and decided he was responsible for the thefts that had been taking place in the valley? What if they killed him?

Fear for Shadow's life, combined with the awful pains tearing me in half brought fresh tears to my eyes and I curled up on the floor, sobbing, on the verge of hysteria. I tried to pray, but the pains were coming too fast and I couldn't concentrate, could only murmur Shadow's name over and over again.

Lying there, unable to expel the child from my womb, I began to imagine that Death was all around me. He was lurking in the dark corners of the room. He was watching me from the doorway. He was watching me through the windows. Soon he would come for me and I would never see Shadow or my father or my children again. Soon, I would feel his cold clammy hand on my arm and there would be nothing I could do. I was too weak to fight, too tired to resist . . .

I screamed as a hand closed over my

arm.

"Hannah, be still. I am here."

It was Shadow. The sound of his voice chased all my fears away and I felt my body relax as he picked me up in his arms and carried me into the bedroom. There was a sudden light as he touched a match to the lamp on the bedside table. His face was dark with concern as he removed my dress and covered me with a clean sheet.

"The baby," I gasped. "It won't come."

"When did the pains start?"

"This morning."

Shadow mouthed a vague obscenity as he lifted the sheet, and I felt his hand probe gently between my thighs. I cried out as another contraction urged me to push, but pushing brought no relief.

"Hannah, relax," Shadow's voice cut through the pain. "The baby's arm is over it's head. I am going to try and move the arm out of the way. Do not push."

I nodded, but it was an effort not to bear down as the contractions kept coming. I stared at the top of Shadow's head as his hand slipped between my thighs. His hushed whispers reached my ears and I knew he was praying to the Great Spirit of the Cheyenne to let the child be born healthy, to ease my pain.

I focused all my attention on the sound of Shadow's voice, letting the rich deep tone surround me like loving arms, comforting me, its strength giving me strength.

Shadow gave a triumphant cry as he succeeded in moving the baby's arm so that it no longer blocked the birth canal.

"Push now, Hannah," he urged when the next contraction came.

I pushed with what little strength I had left and the child's head appeared. Moments later, my newborn child was cradled in Shadow's hands, whimpering softly.

"It is a boy," Shadow said, his voice thick with emotion.

He held up the child so I could see it and our eyes met. Whose child was it? I peered anxiously at the infant in Shadow's hands. The baby had a thatch of dark brown hair and dark blue eyes. Was it Shadow's son, or Joshua Berdeen's? There was no way to be sure.

Shadow placed the baby on my stomach while he cut and tied the cord, then he washed the infant and wrapped it in a blanket.

"It does not matter who fathered the child," Shadow said as he placed my son in my arms. "From this day forward, he will be my son, and I will be his father." Shadow smiled then, and I marveled anew at how handsome he was as he brushed a wisp of damp hair from my face. "Rest now."

"I love you," I murmured sleepily.

"Thank you for a beautiful son."

I fell asleep with our child cradled against my breast.

XX

Spring-Summer 1886

I was on my feet again a few days after our son was born. We named him Samuel Black Elk, after his grandfathers, but everyone called him Blackie and as he grew older, and his brown hair turned the color of obsidian, it seemed a fitting nick-name.

Pa and Rebecca returned home nine days after his birth. Rebecca lamented the fact that she had not been present to help with the delivery, but I assured her that Shadow had been a perfect midwife.

"Really?" Rebecca said. She grinned at Shadow, her brown eyes sparkling with amusement. "Perhaps Mary Crowley would like your assistance when her time comes."

"Very funny," Shadow muttered. Mary Crowley was one of the new people from Philadelphia. She was rather plump, in her late thirties, and very pregnant.

"It might start a whole new trend," Rebecca went on. "You should think about it."

Shadow glared at her as he left the room, and Rebecca and I burst into gales of laughter. Shadow, acting as a midwife to an eastern-bred lady, it was too funny for words.

A cry from Blackie sent us to his cradle.

"He's darling," Rebecca crooned. "So sweet and soft. You forget how precious babies are when your children grow up."

It was true, I thought wistfully. They grew up so fast. One minute you were carrying them in your arms, and the next minute they were exploring the world. I thought of my own children. Heecha was already eight, Mary was seven. Where had the time gone?

Big changes were taking place in our valley now. Horace Bannerman decided to give up farming and build a blacksmith shop. It was how he had earned his living back east and he discovered he was not really happy doing anything else.

George and Ruth Tippitt said the quiet life didn't suit them and they converted their new barn into a general store which they stocked with merchandise and provisions purchased from Steel's Crossing. Their store turned out to be a blessing for everyone in the valley, as it was no longer necessary to make the long trek to Steel's Crossing to buy salt, sugar, cloth, canned goods, or any of the other items we could not easily grow or produce ourselves.

Clancy Turner and his wife raised pigs and chickens, adding a welcome change frm beef and venison. In their spare time, they printed a one-page newspaper carrying the latest news in the valley, as well as news from the east when they could get it. It was a popular paper; men advertised animals or crops for sale, women exchanged recipes and patterns.

Christopher and Sarah Thorsen were another family from Philadelphia. Sarah was a retired schoolteacher; Christopher was an ordained minister in the Methodist church. Mr. Thorsen conducted his church services out in the open until Lydia Bannerman decided we needed a building to meet in and everyone agreed.

Every family in Bear Valley contributed something to the building of the church, whether it was cash or labor or both. Mattie Smythe donated a beautiful silver candlelabra that had belonged to her mother. Ruth Tippitt crocheted a lace cloth for the altar that was as light and fine as a spiderweb. Horace Bannerman ordered a bell for the steeple.

It was agreed that the building site should be near the river in a grove of aspens, halfway between the two outlying homesteads. When it was completed, it became a favorite meeting place for social gatherings.

Late that spring, Pa and Shadow went to the railhead to pick up the herd of cattle Pa had bought from a rancher in Fort Worth. They were gone almost three months.

I missed Shadow terribly even though I had Heecha and Mary and Rebecca for company. And Blackie, of course. He took up a good deal of my day so I rarely had time to fret. He was a darling child. At two months, he was already smiling and cooing. And since he was the only baby in the valley, for the moment, he was terribly spoiled. Ruth Tippitt was forever sewing him something new to wear; Fred Brown carved animals out of wood for him to look at; many of the women and older girls offered to sit with him if I felt the need of some time alone; Leland Smythe promised to give us the pick of the litter when his hound had puppies so that Blackie could have a dog to grow up with.

It was on a beautiful day in early smmer when Pa and Shadow returned. I ran outside and threw myself into my husband's arms, crying and laughing in my happiness to see him again.

As always, just looking at Shadow filled me with joy. He was so handsome, I was certain Man Above had created him as the perfect example of what a man should be. His skin was smooth and clear, the color of old copper. His hair, grown long again, was as black and sleek as a raven's wing. His eyes were as black as ten feet down, warm with love as he drew me close, his lips moving in my hair as he hugged me tight.

Pa's cabin was filled with happy laughter that night as Pa and Shadow recounted their journey to Fort Worth and back, joking about the long drive, cattle that were not trail broken, and the lack of female companionship. Heecha and Mary danced around, waiting for the gifts they knew their father had brought them. They were not disappointed. With a grin, Shadow pulled three packages from his war bag. He handed the first to Heecha, and our son crowed with delight as he unwrapped his gift and found a new hunting knife and a whetstone. Mary was equally pleased with her gift of a new dress and a ribbon for her hair. The third present was a toy for Blackie.

"Didn't you bring anything for nahkoa?" Heecha asked.

"I would not forget your mother," Shadow assured the boy, and dipping into his war bag one more time, he withdrew a small square box and handed it to me.

With eager hands, I opened the box. Inside, nestled against a bed of tissue paper, was a lovely enameled music box.

"Oh, Shadow," I murmured, "it's

beautiful."

"What is it, mama?" Mary asked.

"A music box," I said, winding it up. "Listen."

Mary's eyes grew wide as a lovely waltz tune filed the air. Heecha laughed aloud as Pa swept Rebecca into his arms and twirled her around the room.

All in all, it was a lovely evening and the trip was deemed a success.

Shadow and I went for a walk along the river that night after the children were in bed. We stopped now and then to kiss in the moonlight until kissing wasn't enough, and we found a secluded spot screened by flowering shrubs and vines. The grass was soft as velvet as Shadow lowered me to the ground. His eyes moved over my flesh like fire, warming me through and through. We had not made love since Blackie was born and I was eager for Shadow's touch. Only in his arms did I feel complete.

Wrapping my arms around his neck, I pulled him toward me, wanting him to be closer, closer, until we were one flesh, one heart. I reveled in his touch. He was such a magnificent man, so strong, so virile. I loved the way his skin felt beneath my fingertips, the touch of his legs on mine, the solid wall of his chest crushing my breasts.

"Ne-mehotatse,   Hannah,"   he whispered huskily. "I love you."

"And I love you." I breathed the

words as wave after wave of rapture
washed through me, lifting me up, up, to
that wondrous peak of pleasure where
only Shadow could take me.

That night, we slept under the starry
sky. Like Adam and Eve in the Garden of
Eden, we were the only two people in our
world and we slept peacefully in each
other's arms, blissfully unaware that the
serpent waited in the future.

I looked at Shadow in astonishment.
"A house? You want to build a house?"

He shrugged a trifle sheepishly.
"Don't you want one?"

"Well, yes, I guess so, but I thought
you liked living in our lodge."

"I do," he said with a wry smile. "But
it makes us different from our neighbors,
and we are different enough. I think we
should build a house and live like everyone
else. I do not want the other children in
the valley sneering at Heecha and Mary,
or making jokes about them because they
live in a Cheyenne lodge. It is time to
change."

"Do the thefts in the valley have anything to do with your decision?"

"No. I have been thinking about it for
a long time. If we start building now, we
can have the house completed before the
first snowfall."

It would seem strange, living in a
house again, with wood for walls instead

of hide and a roof overhead. Though we spent a good deal of time in Pa's cabin, we did the major portion of our living in our own lodge. Now, seemingly out of the blue, Shadow had decided to build a house.

Once I got used to the idea, I began to get excited. Pa drew the plans, and I selected the site. Shadow's only requirement was that the front door face the east. Pa argued that the view facing west was a better one and would offer shade in the morning, but I told him the door would have to face east. It was a custom among the Cheyenne that the door of their dwelling always face the rising sun.

Our cabin would be quite large. Three bedrooms, a kitchen, a parlor, and a small porch in the back. Our neighbors came as often as possible to help. The men brought their tools and put up the framework while the women brought baskets of food and cider and lemonade. While the men toiled on the house, the women quilted or tore rags into strips to be made into rugs.

It was exciting to watch our house take shape. It had been a long time since I had lived within four walls, and I was suddenly eager to begin decorating.

The only bit of unhappiness in our life was the continued thefts in the valley. A week never went by that someone complained they were missing something. Often the items stolen were of little value: a pie cooling in the window, a man's shirt taken from a washline, a rag doll. Our homestead continued to be the only one untouched by the thief.

I knew our neighbors suspected Shadow of being the thief, but no one dared openly accuse him. He was well-liked by most of the valley people and no one wanted to believe he would steal from his friends.

Shadow knew he was innocent and he managed to keep his temper under control whenever Porter or Helen Sprague made some vague reference to Indians being sneaky and untrustworthy. Shadow was no thief. Let the others think what they liked.

In late August, there was a sudden increase in the amount of goods that turned up missing. The Smythes lost a milk cow, the Thorsens lost a horse, the Turners lost a pig and six chickens.

Who the thief might be was the main topic of conversation at every gathering in the valley, as well as after church on Sunday. On this particular Sunday, the adults stood around in small groups, pondering how to catch the elusive thief, while the children played tag or cooled themselves in the shade.

Shadow did not attend church with the rest of the family. It was the one aspect of the white man's life that he could not accept. He usually spent the time down by the river, worshipping

Heammawihio in his own way. This day
was no different.

Shadow was sitting in the shade on
the riverbank when a cry for help reached
his ears. Gaining his feet, he searched the
area for some sign of the person in distress
and it was then that he saw Nelda Sprague
race by on the back of her father's horse.
The animal, obviously spooked, had the
bit between its teeth and was running flat
out, heading for the open prairie across the
river.

Instinctively, Shadow vaulted onto
the back of his stallion and took off after
the runaway horse.

"Help me! Help me!" Nelda's
frightened cries grew louder as her horse
plunged into the river and scrambled up
the opposite bank.

I wasn't there when Shadow drew his
horse alongside Nelda's and leaped from
the back of his horse to hers, but I
pictured it in my mind many times after
that day. With ease, he reined the
frightened animal to a trot and then a
walk, his quiet voice soothing the nervous
horse until it stood with its head down, its
lathered sides heaving mightily.

Dismounting, Shadow lifted Nelda
from the saddle and placed her gently on
her feet. She was sobbing with fear and
didn't resist when Shadow took her in his
arms.

"It is all right, little one," he said,

patting her back. "You are safe now."

"A snake spooked my horse," Nelda said, wiping the tears from her eyes. "Pa will whip me sure when he finds out I took old Duke."

"I think he will be too happy to see you are safe to whip you," Shadow told her. "Come, I will take you to your father."

I was the first one to see Shadow riding up. Nelda was sitting in front of him, her eyes still red, her hair blown by the wind.

"My baby!" Helen Sprague ran toward her errant daughter. Pulling Nelda from Shadow's horse, she glared up at him. "You savage!" she shrieked. "What have you done to my baby?"

All eyes turned in Shadow's direction. Angry murmurs could be heard as people gathered around Shadow and Helen Sprague.

"Shadow didn't do anything to me," Nelda said, wriggling out of her mother's arms. "I snuck out of church to ride Duke and he ran away with me. Mr. Shadow rescued me." There was a new gleam of admiration in Nelda's eyes when she looked at Shadow. "You should have seen him, mama. He jumped from his horse to the back of old Duke, just like the man in my circus book!"

Helen Sprague blushed to the roots of her hair. "I'm ... I'm sorry." She mumbled her apology, her eyes not meeting Shadow's. "Forgive me. I thought . . ." Her cheeks turned scarlet. "Forgive me," she said again.

Shadow nodded, his face void of expression.

When Helen explained what had happened to Porter, there were more thank you-s and then the Spragues went home.

There were no more thefts in the valley after that day and the sudden cessation caused even more speculation than the thefts had. I don't know what anyone else thought, but I knew deep in my heart that the Spragues had been responsible for the thefts in Bear Valley. They hadn't wanted Shadow around because he was an Indian, and they had tried to convince everybody that he was a thief in the hopes that Shadow would be driven from the valley. But then he saved Nelda's life, and suddenly the fact that he was an Indian was no longer important. At any rate, the Spragues were suddenly as friendly as could be. Helen brought a gift over for Blackie, apologizing for taking so long to be neighborly. Porter was the first one to show up to work on our cabin in the morning and the last to leave at night.

By summer's end, our valley had all the makings of a town. Other families had taken up residence in the southern end of the valley, and who could blame them? The land was beautiful, the soil fertile, the water cold and clear, the sky a deep azure blue.

It was about this time that Sarah Thorsen decided to start holding classes for the valley children. Surprisingly, most of the children were eager to go to school, eager to learn to read and write, or to further the knowledge they already had.

Mary was especially excited about school. She was very fond of Sarah Thorsen, and the thought of spending a part of each weekday in her presence made school even more attractive. Our Mary was turning into quite a little lady. She took great pains with her appearance, refusing to wear anything that was dirty, stained, torn, or too small. Quite a change from the little tomboy who had loved to climb trees and play in the mud. Rebecca and I sewed three new dresses and a pinafore for Mary so she would have some nice clothes to wear to school.

Heecha was another matter entirely. At the mature age of almost nine, he was tall and slender and stubborn. He already knew how to read and write, he stated emphatically, and he did not wish to learn any more. He wanted to go hunting and fishing with Shadow. He wanted to become a warrior like his father and nothing I could say would change his mind.

I turned to Shadow for help. "You've got to make him go to school," I urged. "He needs to associate with the other children, and he needs to learn more of the world."

"I do not think you will make a white man out of Heecha," Shadow said with a wry grin. "The blood of the Cheyenne is too strong in his veins. Already he is looking forward to the day when he can go out and seek his vision."

"How is he going to seek a vision with no medicine man to guide him?"

"I will instruct him when the time comes," Shadow replied, no longer smiling.

"What good will a vision do him?" I asked, becoming exasperated with the whole conversation. "The time of the warrior is past."

"I am still a warrior," Shadow said, his voice strong with pride. "And if Heecha desires it, he, too, will be a warrior."

There was no arguing with the man or the boy and from that day forward Heecha spent a good part of every day in his father's company. He learned the ways of the Cheyenne, the songs and the chants and the stories. He learned to hunt and fight, to use the bow and the knife and the rifle. He learned to track anything that moved, to lie quiet for hours without food or water, to disappear into the country-

side. Some nights Heecha returned home
bone weary, too tired to do more than
swallow a drink of water and fall into bed.

As the days passed, I watched my son
grow strong physically and spiritually and
my doubts about what he was doing began
to dwindle. He began to develop the same
strong sense of self-assurance and
confidence that I so admired in his father,
the same inner strength that set Shadow
apart from other men.

As the days and weeks and months
went by, I realized Shadow had been right.
Heecha would never be a white man. He
was not ashamed of his white blood, but it
was his Cheyenne blood that would always
prevail. Heecha would never wear a suit
and tie, nor would he ever be content to
live in some crowded city, prisoner to
clocks and conventions and the limits of
civilization. A part of Heecha would
always yearn for the open prairie, for new
adventures and new horizons. Heecha was
truly his father's son and I knew deep in
my heart that if Heecha proved to be half
the man his father was, the woman who
married him would never be sorry.

XXI

1889-1892

A year passed. Two. Three, and it was the spring of 1889. Our valley had grown from a sprinkling of crude cabins into a small town occupied by more than thirty families. We had a schoolhouse now, a bank, a doctor, even a small saloon where the farmers could go for a cold beer on Saturday night.

My children were growing faster than I cared to admit. Heecha was going on eleven, Mary was almost ten, and my baby was already three. Shadow was raising horses now, using his spotted stallion as stud, and the people in the valley bought his horses eagerly, for they were choice animals with flashy coats, good confor- mation, and staying power. Pa's herd was thriving and his cattle provided meat and milk for many of our neighbors. I had never been happier. Our cabin was large

and comfortable, the furniture well-made
and pleasing to the eye. Shadow did not
seem to mind living within four walls, but
he refused to sleep on a mattress,
declaring they were too soft, so we made
our bed on a pile of warm furs instead.

Our lodge was still standing and
whenever Shadow felt the need to get out
of the house for a little while, he went
there to be alone and meditate. The rest of
the family respected his need to be alone,
and we never disturbed him. In the
summer, Heecha and Blackie often slept in
the lodge, but Mary preferred a soft bed
and clean sheets.

It was early in the spring of 1890 that
we began to hear rumors that something
big was in the wind, something that was
stirring fresh hope in the hearts of the
reservation Indians. The news flew from
tribe to tribe, from the Utes and the
Bannocks to the Arapahoe and the
Cheyenne and the Sioux.

Overcome with curiosity, Shadow left
Bear Valley to see what he could find out.
He returned two weeks later with startling
news.

"There is a new Messiah," Shadow
told us at dinner that night. "His name is
Wovoka, and he lives in Nevada. He has a
sacred dance the people must learn, and
songs they must sing. He has promised
that the Indian dead will live again if the
people sing and dance as he directs, and

that the white men will be destroyed."

Pa snorted derisively. "You don't believe that nonsense?"

"I would like to believe it," Shadow said. "For the sake of my people, I would like to see it happen."

Mary was unusually quiet when I tucked her into bed that night. She didn't ask to stay up just a little longer. She didn't ask for a story. When I asked her what was wrong, she began to cry.

"I don't want Rebecca and Namshim to be destroyed," she said between heart-rendering sobs. "And what will happen to Heecha and Blackie and me? We are part white. Will we be destroyed, too?"

"Of course not," I said, taking Mary into my arms and holding her close. "You must not believe what this man, Wovoka, says. He is not the Messiah. Singing and dancing will not bring the dead back to life, or destroy the people who are now alive. The Indians are bitter and unhappy living on the reservation, and they are hoping for a miracle to bring back their old way of life. But the old way is gone forever."

I sat with Mary until she fell asleep. My heart was heavy for Shadow's people. It was tragic that a once proud and free people had been reduced to living in misery on reservations where, as wards of the United States, they were supposed to learn to farm and raise cattle. The Indians were even losing a part of the land that was reservation property as government agencies urged the Indians to sell off so-called excess acreage to land-hungry whites for as little as fifty cents an acre. It was no wonder they clung to the memories of the old days; no wonder that they would grab at any straw that promised hope and a return to the old ways.

Little more of the new religion was heard about until late in October. And then we learned that Sitting Bull had become a believer. He had been made a priest in the new religion, which was called the Ghost Dance because some of the dancers had seen visions of their dead. Sitting Bull painted the faces of his people in the sacred patterns set forth by Kicking Bear, one of Wovoka's apostles. And the people danced.

Shadow left Bear Valley again, drawn to the reservation to see for himself what was going on. He was gone for a month this time, and when he returned, he was deeply troubled.

We did not discuss what he had learned in front of the children this time.

"The Indians are eager to believe in the Ghost Dance," Shadow told me when we were in bed that night. "A Cheyenne called Porcupine said he had spoken to some Paiutes who claimed that Christ had appeared on the earth again. Porcupine saw the man identified as Christ, and the man was Indian."

"That's impossible. Surely you don't believe it?"

"No. But there is a Sioux, Kicking Bear, who claims to have met a man dressed like an Indian, but who had long golden hair. Kicking Bear claims the Messiah took him up a ladder of clouds into heaven. There Kicking Bear met the Great Spirit and his wife. In heaven, Kicking Bear saw the devil, who claimed half the people on earth belonged to him. At first the Great Spirit would not let the devil have the people because he loved them so much, but then he decided to let the devil have the whites because the Indians were his chosen people. The Great Spirit promised to renew the earth. According to Kicking Bear, a great wave of new earth is going to crush the whites, but the Indians will be suspended in the air if they learn the spirit dance and sing the sacred songs."

I stared at Shadow, my emotions in turmoil. Surely he did not believe such a story? It was so preposterous it was almost comical. But I did not laugh. What if Shadow became a believer? What would happen to our life, our children, our marriage? I knew Shadow missed his old way of life. Did he miss it badly enough to become one of Wovoka's followers?

"The Sioux are desperate," Shadow mused aloud. "They have been living in misery for so long, they need something to believe in, something to hope for. There are stories of Indians who have gone to see Wovoka who have seen friends long dead in his camp. There is a story that someone killed a buffalo, but it came to life again, as Wovoka had promised it would.

"Some of the dancers are wearing ghost shirts which the Indians believe will turn away bullets. The Sioux have given up wearing anything made of metal because it comes from the white man."

"You don't believe in this Ghost Dance, do you?" I asked tremulously. "You're not going to Pine Ridge to join in the dancing?"

"No. Once I would have believed," Shadow said, and I caught a note of sadness in his voice, a longing for the old ways. "Now I think this dance will only bring more trouble for the Indians. The whites are getting scared. Some of the Indians are carrying guns when they dance. Wovoka preaches only peace, but Sitting Bull has broken the peace pipe he has kept since the day he surrendered to the whites. He wants to fight. He is old and tired and ready to die. When I was at the reservation, the agent, McLaughlin, told Sitting Bull that the dancing must stop. But Sitting Bull would not listen."

I knew then that Shadow was right.

The Ghost Dance would surely bring the Army down on the Indians.

In the days that followed, Heecha pestered his father for news of Wovoka and the Ghost Dance. The subject got a lot of attention in the newspapers and our neighbors speculated on what would happen if the Indians decided to leave the reservation. Men began to carry their rifles with them wherever they went, and women insisted their little ones stay close to home. Everyone remembered what it had been like when the Indians roamed free. Homesteads had been raided and sometimes burned to the ground. Children had been taken. Men and women had been killed. Were those days about to return?

There were several incidents in the valley that were caused by men with jumpy nerves. The worst happened when Cotton Tanner went hunting and accidentally shot his neighbor, Hugh Sloan, whom he mistook for an Indian. Mr. Sloan lived, but the incident only proved how upset the whites were becoming. There was talk of calling in the Army for protection, of setting up our own militia, just in case the Indians went wild.

Heecha was in a perpetual state of excitement. Though he had never lived with the Cheyenne, he had heard countless tales of the old days when the Indian ruled the land and the buffalo covered the earth.

He longed to be a warrior like his father, to seek a vision, to participate in the Sun Dance. In his mind, he would have a chance to experience all these things if Wovoka's prophecies came true.

I didn't realize how badly my son wanted to believe in the Ghost Dance until the cold December morning when I woke up and found his bed empty. His knife and his bow were missing. I knew without a doubt that Heecha had gone to find Sitting Bull, that he wanted to be a part of the Ghost Dance.

Numbly, I left my son's room and went to find Shadow.

"He has taken one of the horses," Shadow said, coming back from the barn. "The tracks are about nine hours old."

"He's only twelve," I wailed. "Oh, Shadow, please find him."

"Do not worry, Hannah. I will bring him back."

"I'm going with you." Until this moment, I had no intention of leaving Bear Valley. I had other children to think of, and I knew Shadow could travel faster alone. But suddenly I knew I had to go with him.

Shadow looked deep into my eyes, and then he nodded. We left Mary and Blackie with Pa and Rebecca. An hour later, Shadow and I rode out of Bear Valley toward the Sioux Reservation.

The Plains were barren, the trees

naked beneath a cold winter sun. Once I had seen beauty even in a bleak December landscape; now I saw only death and loneliness.

Heecha knew how to survive in the wilderness alone, he knew how to find food and water and shelter, thanks to his father's teachings. And yet, he was still only a boy of twelve.

When Shadow decided it was time to bed down for the night, I urged him to go just a few more miles, when he paused to rest the horses, I nagged at him to hurry. I could not sleep at night, could only think of my son traveling across the vast prairie alone. There were still outlaws roaming the west, still an occasional Indian on the prowl, wild animals to contend with. My imagination, always fertile, conjured up awful images of my son lying dead on the plains, his body mutilated by scavengers.

When we arrived at the reservation, the place was in turmoil. Agent McLaughlin wanted to arrest Sitting Bull. With the old chief out of the way, it was hoped things would quiet down and the Ghost Dance would die out, at least at Pine Ridge. Eight troops of the Seventh Cavalry had arrived at the reservation. One had only to look at the soldiers to know they had not forgotten what the Sioux had done to Custer at the Little Big Horn fourteen years earlier. But this was now, and three thousand Indians had left

the reservation and gone into hiding in the
Bad Lands. But Sitting Bull had not run,
and the dancing went on.

We made it onto the reservation un-
detected. Shadow had stripped down to
his loincloth and moccasins. A single eagle
feather was braided into his hair. I wore
my old buckskin dress and kept an Indian
blanket over my head to cover my red hair
and hide my face.

The Indians were dancing when we
arrived. We stood far back in the shadows,
watching, as the Indians circled slowly
from right to left, their hands joined as
their bodies swayed back and forth, hardly
lifting their feet from the ground. I had
expected to see frenzied posturing and
shouting, but the dancers were quite
subdued. There were no drums echoing in
the night, only the sound of many voices
lifted in song.

I felt Shadow's hand tighten around
mine and then I saw Sitting Bull. Here
was Tatanka Iyotanke, the great Sioux
medicine man, the Indian who had offered
one hundred pieces of his flesh to the
Great Spirit during the Sun Dance and
was granted a vision prophesying Custer's
defeat. Sitting Bull carried an eagle
feather in his hand and he watched the
dancers as they circled from right to left. I
saw him stare intently into one man's face
while he twirled the feather, grunting,
"Hu! Hu! Hu!" until the man's eyes

glazed over and he fell to the ground. When the man awoke, he stood in the center of the dancers to tell the others what he had seen while his spirit went into the After World. He said he had seen great herds of shaggy buffalo feeding on a grassy plain. A woman proclaimed that she had seen her dead son. Another man shouted that he had seen his parents.

I listened in awe as the Indians came out of their trances to speak of what they had seen. Was it possible that they had actually gone to the Spirit World, as they claimed, or did they believe such fantastic things had occurred because they so desperately needed something to believe in, something positive to cling to?

The Indians danced through the night and into the next morning, dancing for hours and hours without food or water or rest.

It was shortly after dark when Shadow spied Heecha talking to Sitting Bull. My son's eyes were bright, filled with awe and adulation as he listened to the old chief speak. Moments later, the two of them entered Sitting Bull's cabin.

I started to go to Heecha, but Shadow grabbed my arm. "No, Hannah. We will wait until dawn. If we are discovered, there could be trouble. The Indians will be angry if they know a white woman has seen the dance."

I slept fitfully that night. I was

hungry and worried and my dreams were filled with nightmares, but none of my dreams was as bad as the very real nightmare that erupted at daybreak as forty-three Indian police and one hundred cavalrymen rode into the reservation to arrest Sitting Bull.

The old chief began to dress while a hundred Indians or more milled around outside the cabin. The door opened and he stood there, flanked by two Indian police. Another stood behind him. A low roar rose from the Indians assembled at Sitting Bull's cabin. It was an angry sound, filled with menace. One of the Indian police was leading a horse to the cabin.

Abruptly, Sitting Bull decided he would not go with the Indian police, he would not mount the horse, and he called for help. Panic ensued. A shot was fired. There was a moment of utter silence and then all was pandemonium. Voices were raised in fear and anger. Horses snorted and whinnied nervously as people scrambled about. Soldiers fouled the air with their profanity, while the Indian voices were raised in the age-old cry of war.

I watched in horror as bullets riddled Sitting Bull's cabin. My son was inside that cabin, and only Shadow's iron-like grip on my arm kept me from bursting out of my hiding place and running into the midst of the battle. Blinded by my own tears, I did not notice the moisture in my husband's eyes.

The battle was quickly over. Sitting Bull was dead, along with his son, Crow Foot, and twelve other Indians.

"Hannah, stay here," Shadow said, his voice harsh. "Do not move."

I nodded dumbly and he gave me a quick kiss and a hug and then he walked boldly into the middle of the crowd gathered around the old chief's cabin.

"Hey, redskin, where do you think you're going?" The words belonged to a ruddy-faced cavalryman. He jabbed his rifle barrel into Shadow's stomach as he spoke.

"My son is inside," Shadow answered calmly. "He is just a boy."

The cavalryman ruminated for a moment and then gave a quick nod of his head as he lowered his rifle. There had been enough killing for one day.

I held my breath as Shadow entered the cabin. Time stopped and stood still as I waited for him to reappear, and all the while I sent urgent prayers to God and Maheo, begging them to let my son be alive. Over and over again I whispered the words, "please let him be alive, please let him be alive."

Fresh tears welled in my eyes as Shadow appeared in the doorway of the cabin, our son in his arms. There was blood splattered across the front of

Heecha's shirt, and his eyes were closed. I
could not tell if he was breathing.

Shadow's face was wiped clean of
emotion as he walked past the soldiers and
the Indian police. A look of sympathy
crossed the face of the ruddy-faced
cavalryman. No one spoke to Shadow or
tried to stop him as he walked away from
the scene of death.

When Shadow reached my hiding
place, he did not speak, but kept on
walking until he came to the place where
we had left our horses. Fearing the worst,
I trailed after him, not ready to face the
fact that my oldest child was dead.

I watched as Shadow spread a blanket
on the ground and gently placed Heecha
upon it.

"Nehyo." Heecha called for his father,
his voice weak and filled with pain.

"I am here, naha," Shadow replied.

With a cry, I fell to my knees, too
weak with relief to stand. He was alive.
Thank God, my son was alive.

"I want to go home," Heecha said.

"Soon," Shadow promised. "But first
we must clean and bandage your wound.
You must be very brave and not cry out."

"A Cheyenne does not show pain,"
Heecha said, smiling bravely at his father.

Shadow nodded, and then he turned to
me. "Hannah, I will need your help."

Wiping the tears from my eyes, I went
to kneel beside my son. Heecha smiled at

me. "I will be a brave warrior," he said, gritting his teeth against the pain. "Sitting Bull himself has told me so."

"You're already a brave warrior," I said, taking his hands in mine. "You must lie still now and not talk."

Heecha nodded, his eyes full of trust as he looked at his father.

"The bullet is still inside," Shadow said. "It must come out."

"I am not afraid, nehyo."

"I know," Shadow said, his voice thick with unshed tears. Rising, he went to his war bag and withdrew a thin-bladed knife. His eyes met mine, and I shook my head. I could not dig the bullet out of Heecha's side. Shadow understood, and no words were spoken.

I leaned across Heecha, my hands on his shoulders, my body blocking his view of the ugly wound in his right side. I heard Shadow murmur a quiet prayer to Maheo, felt my son's body go rigid with pain as Shadow began to probe the wound for the bullet. I choked back my tears as my son struggled not to cry.

It took only a few minutes for Shadow to remove the slug from our son's flesh, but it seemed like hours. We had nothing but water to clean the wound, and Shadow washed it several times before packing the wound with moss. He bandaged Heecha's middle with strips of cloth torn from his shirt.

I held Heecha's hand until he fell asleep, and then I began to cry, the flood of tears releasing the strain and worry of the past two days. As my sobs tapered off, I offered a prayer of thanks to the gods, both red and white, for preserving my son's life.

"He might have been killed and it is all my fault," Shadow said, his voice bitter with remorse. "I filled his head with stories of the old days because I wanted him to know who he was. I wanted him to be proud of his Indian blood. I did not want him to feel inferior to the whites because of his mixed heritage."

The anguish in Shadow's voice tore at my heart. Rising to my feet, I went to stand beside him. "It is no one's fault," I said. "He has always been more Cheyenne than white. It would not have mattered what any of us said or did, Heecha's heart would still have reached out for the Cheyenne. Now he has known Sitting Bull. It is something he will remember for as long as he lives."

If he lives. The words sounded in the back of my mind and I bit down on my lower lip to keep from crying. Heecha looked so young, so helpless. His face was pale, his breathing shallow and uneven.

Shadow and I stayed close to Heecha's side the whole night. Our son slept fitfully, moaning softly in his sleep, tossing restlessly when his dreams grew troubled. I gladly would have suffered in his place.

Slowly, the night turned to day. The eastern sky began to grow light as the sun peered over the horizon. Broad slashes of gold and crimson streaked the sky like paint splashed by a careless hand.

As the sun cleared the hills, Shadow moved away a few paces. Then, head and arms raised toward heaven, he began to pray. What a rare and wonderful sight he made standing there with the prairie stretching endlessly behind him and the first bright rays of the sun shining down on his copper-hued flesh. Naked save for his loincloth and moccasins, he looked like a statue carved from bronze as he lifted his voice to Maheo, pleading with the Great Spirit of the Cheyenne to heal our child.

He stood there for a long time, and I let my eyes feast upon the sight. His arms and legs were long, the muscles well-defined. His flanks were lean, his shoulders broad, his stomach hard and flat. Thick black hair hung to his waist, shining like polished onyx in the sunlight.

After perhaps ten minutes, Shadow lowered his head and arms and returned to Heecha's side. We spent the day nursing our son, offering him drinks of cool water when he was awake, bathing his body with cold cloths when the fever came.

At sundown, Shadow again went off

to pray and I added my own prayers to
his. Kneeling beside my son, I was filled
with a sense of peace and I knew that
Heecha would be all right.

Heecha's fever was gone in the
morning and I wept tears of joy and
gratitude as I thanked God for my son's
life. By midafternoon, he was much
improved, and the following morning,
Shadow made a travois to carry Heecha
and we started the long journey home.

Our cabin had never looked more
inviting. Mary and Blackie ran out to meet
us, chattering excitedly when they saw
the bloody bandage wrapped around
Heecha's middle. Later that day, the
family listened as Heecha related his
story, telling how he had found Sitting
Bull's camp on the Grand River, and how
the old medicine man had taken him into
his house as though he were a member of
the family. Heecha wept softly when he
told how the soldiers had come and killed
Sitting Bull. Mary looked at her older
brother with admiration and respect as
Shadow related how brave Heecha had
been when the bullet was removed from
his side.

I felt my heart thrill with love when
Shadow took the eagle feather from his
hair and placed it in Heecha's hand.

"Today you are a man," he said
proudly. "From this day forth you shall be

known as True Hawk, for your heart is as brave as the eagle and as strong as the hawk.''

Hawk recovered quickly and I thanked God daily that he had spared my son's life. I felt a keener appreciation for all my children, a deeper gratitude for the good husband I had been blessed with.

In late December, the last chapter of the Ghost Dance was written. The Indians who had fled into the Badlands were hunted down by the Seventh Cavalry and herded toward Wounded Knee Creek. There were four hundred and seventy soldiers armed with four Hotchkiss guns against one hundred and one warriors and a number of women and children.

Two weeks after Sitting Bull's death, the Indians were ordered to surrender their weapons. A few of the warriors surrendered their old guns. Dissatisfied troopers searched the Indian lodges for more weapons and ammunition, looking into packs and parfleches, scaring the women and children as they stormed through their tepees. The tension grew thicker. The warriors, most of them wearing the forbidden Ghost shirts, grew more and more angry and disgruntled. A medicine man named Yellow Bird walked through the camp promising the warriors that the soldiers could not hurt them. He had made medicine, he said. The soldiers were weak. Their bullets could not penetrate the sacred Ghost shirts.

When one of the soldiers tried to take a blanket from an Indian, Yellow Bird gave the signal to fight. An Indian fired at the soldiers, and then the massacre began as the soldiers opened fire with the four Hotchkiss guns. Three hundred Indians were slaughtered as two-pound shells rained terror on helpless women and children. Bodies were found two miles away from the field of battle. Thirty-one soldiers were killed. The Seventh Cavalry's defeat at the Little Big Horn had been avenged at last.

It was a horrible story and I wept bitter tears as I read it. I had seen death on the battlefield; I knew how awful it was. I remembered Little Big Horn, and yet even that was not so awful as the battle at Wounded Knee Creek. Helpless women and children had not been cut down at the Little Big Horn.

Shadow said little of the massacre, but his eyes held a lingering sadness for the loss of Sitting Bull and his people. Truly the day of the Indian was over.

And yet, in our cabin, the spirit of the red man burned strong and bright in our son, True Hawk. He was determined to seek a vision and in the fall of 1892 he set out to commune with the spirits.

It was hard for me to let him go. He was only fourteen, and though he was tall and strong and wise in the ways of the Cheyenne, he was still only fourteen years old. As his father before him, Hawk took nothing to sustain him in his quest, only a small pouch filled with tobacco. He would be gone for four days and during that time he would fast and pray, beseeching the gods for a vision to guide his steps through the hills and valleys of life.

It was a very long four days. I tried not to let my concern for Heecha show. I did not want Mary and Blackie to worry. I did not want Shadow to think I was weak, but it was hard for me to concentrate on tasks at hand when all I could think about was Hawk, hungry and alone in the hills.

"He will be all right, Hannah," Shadow assured me as we walked hand in hand along the river. "Maheo will watch over him. Do not be afraid."

With a sigh, I laid my head against Shadow's chest and closed my eyes. His heart beat strong and steady beneath my ear. I trusted Shadow. He had never been wrong. He had never let me down. He was always there when I needed him, a pillar of strength to lean on when times were hard.

He stroked my hair and I snuggled closer to him. We had known a great deal of heartache in our life together, a good share of unhappiness, and yet I did not regret a moment of the time I had spent with this man who knew me better than I knew myself.

Hawk came home after four days, and
he was no longer a boy, but a man. There
was a new sense of pride in his step, a new
look of confidence in his eye. I prepared
his favorite meal that night, and then
Shadow, Hawk and I went into our lodge
behind the cabin. I sat in the back of the
lodge, glad that Hawk was willing for me
to be there. Had we been living in the old
days, Hawk would have gone to the
shaman with his vision, but there was no
medicine man here.

"I did as you said, Nehyo," Hawk
began after Shadow had lit the sacred pipe
and offered it to the four directions and to
the earth and sky. "Each day I offered
tobacco to the gods and then I prayed for
a vision. I grew hungry and thirsty and
cold, but I did not give up, and on the
third morning a yellow hawk appeared in
the sky. As I watched, the hawk landed on
the ground and came toward me. And as it
grew nearer, it changed from a hawk to a
man with yellow hair. 'I am waiting for
you,' the hawkman said, and then he
turned and walked away and as he walked,
he turned into a hawk again and disappeared into the sky. Do you know what
it means, nehyo?"

"Yes, naha," Shadow said quietly. "I
know wht it means, but you may not want
to hear it."

"I am a warrior," Hawk said proudly.
"I can accept anything."

"Then accept this. In your heart, you are Cheyenne, but the day of the Indian is over. If you wish to survive in this land, you must do so as a white man. You may hold fast to our beliefs and to the qualities that make a man worthy to be a warrior and a Cheyenne, but you will not be able to live as an Indian. The man with the yellow hair is you, just as the hawk is you. The hawk-man is a symbol of your mixed blood."

Hawk nodded slowly, and I could see that he was trying to understand what his father was saying. My son's eyes, so like those of his father, took on a wistful look as he accepted the fact that he would never be able to live the life he had always dreamed of. The Indians no longer roamed the vast prairies and hills, they no longer made their camp along the Powder and the Tongue, the Sioux no longer gathered in the Pa Sapa, the sacred Black Hills. There were no more coup to be counted, no more buffalo to hunt, no more war dances, or raids against the Crow and Pawnee. Hawk had dreamed of these things for years and now he had to face the fact that he could never fulfill his dream. It was a hard thing for a boy of fourteen to accept.

"I will walk in the white man's path if that is the only way," Hawk said thoughtfully. "But before I become a white man, I want to participate in the Sun Dance. I must know for myself if I would have been able to endure it." He looked deep into Shadow's eyes. "It is a sacrifice I must make."

"We must have a shaman," Shadow said, frowning. "There are things you must be taught, special payers that must be said. I cannot guide you through the Sun Dance alone."

Hawk smiled faintly. "But you will find a way," he said confidently.

"Yes," Shadow promised solemnly. "When the time comes, I will find a way."

XXII

It was a warm day in late August when Mary came running into the house. She was thirteen now, and as lovely a girl as any mother could hope for. Her hair was a dark rich brown, her skin the color of fresh cream, her eyes a beautiful shade of gray. Already, her figure gave promise of the woman she would become.

But now she was a young girl, her cheeks flushed with excitement as she burst into the house. "Come quick!" she cried, grabbing my arm. "Hawk is riding the blue roan!"

Blackie let out a whoop of excitement as he bolted out the door. Putting down the iron, I took Mary's hand and we ran out of the house, following Blackie to the south pasture where Shadow kept the horses he was breaking to ride. The blue roan was a young, high-spirited stallion that Shadow had chosen for Hawk. The horse was big-boned and wild, and yet Shadow said he would make a fine mount once he was broken to the saddle. I didn't like to think of my son astride that wild-eyed roan, yet Shadow was a good judge of horseflesh and if he said the roan would make a good mount, then it was so.

Breathless, Mary, Blackie, and I plopped down on the grass outside the breaking pen. Hawk was already in the saddle and the roan was bucking and pitching for all it was worth. I watched with a real sense of pride as my son stuck to the saddle like a fly to flypaper, his face shining with exhilaration as he showed the horse who was going to be the boss.

Shadow's eyes glowed with pride and affection as the blue roan gave up the fight. With a triumphant grin, Hawk slid to the ground, his hand giving the roan a couple of hardy pats that said "well done." Hawk attempted to look proud and haughty, as a warrior would, but he could not help laughing aloud with excitement. It was a happy moment for us all.

"The Cheyenne are still the best horsemen in all the world," Shadow exclaimed, clapping Hawk on the shoulder. "No seasoned warrior could have done better."

Hawk's sensational ride was the main topic of conversation when we went to dinner at Pa's house two nights later.

Mary and I helped Rebecca set the table and prepare dinner while the menfolk gabbed in the parlor. Rebecca and I had become close friends over the years, and I was truly glad my father had married her. I had made many friends in the valley, but Rebecca was special, and not just because she was married to my father.

Rebecca had done wonders with their cabin. There were ruffled curtains at every window, a rug on every floor. There was always a vase of wildflowers on the table in the summer, a sprig of colorful leaves in the fall. There was always something good to eat in the kitchen and lots of happy laughter under her roof. She was a favorite in the valley, and the women flocked around her, for she was easy to talk to and had a talent for making everyone feel welcome.

While serving dinner, Rebecca and I discussed the upcoming harvest festival. It was always a happy occasion, a time when everyone in the valley got together for a good time. There was always an abundance of food, games for everyone, a community sing, and square dancing for those so inclined. The climax of the day was a horse race. Shadow had won the race three years running, and was favored to win this year as well.

"I am going to enter the blue roan in the race," Hawk announced after Pa blessed the food.

"What blue roan?" Pa asked.

"I have a new horse," Hawk said proudly. "I broke him myself."

Pa leaned forward, his eyes alight with interest. If there was one thing my father loved, it was a good horse and a good race.

"Is that Appy stud of yours the blue's sire?" Pa asked Shadow.

"Yes," Shadow replied.

"How old is the blue?" Rebecca wanted to know.

"Three," Shadow replied.

"He is fast as the wind," Heecha boasted.

"And just three years old," Rebecca mused. She grinned at Shadow. "Sounds like you might have some real competition this year," she said.

"Smoke and I welcome the challenge," Shadow answered solemnly, and we all laughed.

Everybody in the valley was gathered at the church for the harvest festival. Long trestle tables were set up in the shade, heavily laden with fried chicken, roast beef, potato salad, assorted vegetables, and a wide variety of cakes, breads, and pies.

The Reverend Christopher Thorsen blessed the food and asked for the Lord's protection on the day's activities, and then the fun began. There were sack races and foot races for children and adults

alike, a wrestling match, shooting con-
tests, a greased pig to chase, a hog-calling
contest, bull and bronc riding, and a corn-
shucking contest.

Blackie won several races against
boys his age. Mary came in second in the
sack race. Hawk won the bull riding
contest, but refused to have anything to
do with chasing the greased pig, claiming
such conduct was beneath the dignity of a
warrior. Shadow, that man among men,
won every contest he entered. I shouted
and clapped as he won the bronc riding
contest, a mile-long foot race, and the
wrestling contest. It was so good to see
him accepted as an equal by the other
men, to see the women look at him with
envy and know he was mine.

There was square dancing after lunch.
I watched Mary dance with one of the
Smythe boys. Her face was flushed, her
eyes shining as she smiled up at her
partner. The boy, Frank, said something
that made her laugh merrily and I felt a
peculiar catch in my throat. Mary was
growing up so fast. Soon she would be
married and raising a family of her own. I
studied her critically, but could find no
fault in her. She was lovely, polite, warmhearted and fun-loving. No doubt she
would make a good wife and a wonderful
mother. She was already popular with the
boys and it was a fact that gave Shadow a
lot of concern. He had threatened to

horsewhip any boy who dared lay a hand
on her. He was very proud of his only
daughter, and very protective. I glanced
at him now, and saw him scowling as
Frank Smythe twirled her around the
floor. I almost pitied the man who would
have to ask Shadow for Mary's hand.

As the next set got under way, I was
surprised to see Hawk lead Victoria
Bannerman onto the floor. Somehow, I
had thought Hawk would consider
dancing in the same light as chasing a
greased pig. My son didn't look
particularly happy to be dancing, but he
went through the steps and smiled
frequently at Victoria. And then Rebecca
called my name and I forgot about Hawk
as I went to help her at the food table.

It was late afternoon when the call
went out that the race was about to begin.
There were ten riders entered this year,
Shadow and Hawk among them. Horace
Bannerman had recently purchased a
quarter-horse mare and there was heavy
betting that he would win. In looks,
Bannerman's new horse could not be
faulted. She was a blood bay, with wide-
set eyes, a sleek coat, and near-perfect con-
formation. Shadow's Appaloosa did not
look so fine. It had the sparse mane and
rat-tail typical of the breed, but it also had
a deep chest, wide nostrils to drink the
wind, and plenty of speed and bottom.

The   air   fairly   crackled   with

excitement as the riders lined up. I looked at Shadow, sitting easily aboard his wide-eyed Appaloosa, almost a part of the horse. I looked at Hawk, sitting proudly erect, his black eyes shining and eager for the race to begin. How did a wife and mother choose between a husband and son? I wanted Shadow to win, and I wanted Hawk to win, and that was impossible. There could only be one winner.

George Tippitt had been selected to start the race and there was an audible gasp of anticipation as he stepped forward and lifted his arm. The crowd seemed to surge forward. A few of the horses pranced nervously, their hooves raising small clouds of dust.

A moment later, the starting shot was fired and the horses were off. Shadow and Smoke quickly took the lead, closely followed by Hawk on his blue roan, and by Horace Bannerman astride his bay Quarter Horse mare. Frank Smythe swept by mounted on a rangy gray gelding, followed by his brother, Ethan, who was mounted on a flashy black mare.

For a time, the riders were out of sight as they went around the schoolhouse and across the river. Then we could hear the thunder of pounding hooves as they came around the bend in the road on their way back to the churchyard.

Shadow was still in the lead, and what

a sight he made. He was riding bareback, his body moving in perfect time with the horse. They made a beautiful picture etched against the clear blue sky. Shadow's hair hung long and loose, flowing behind him like a skein of black silk. He was riding low over Smoke's neck, and I felt a thrill of excitement run through me. How handsome he was! Now, for this brief moment, he looked like a warrior again.

Slowly, I pulled my eyes from my husband and found Hawk. My son was riding close on the heels of his father's horse. His face was set and determined, and he rode with the same natural grace as his father. As they drew near the finish line, the two horses were almost neck and neck and then, in a sudden burst of speed, Hawk put his horse across the finish line, winning by barely half a length.

Hawk's face lit up like a Christmas tree as people cheered, and then Ruth Tippitt came forward and handed him a silver cup and a twenty dollar gold piece.

I ran up to my son and hugged him, as pleased and proud as I had ever been. Hawk turned a little red around the ears at my show of affection, so I quickly stepped back, making room for the young men and women who crowded around him, eager to offer their congratulations.

Smiling, I walked over to where Shadow was rubbing down his horse.

"Nice race," I said.

"Not bad. Bannerman's horse almost caught up with us a time or two."

"You let Hawk win, didn't you?"

Shadow grinned crookedly. "I never could fool you, could I?"

"Not often."

Shadow shrugged. "I just couldn't beat him. He wanted to win so much, not just to prove he could beat Smoke, but to show off for Victoria Bannerman."

"Show off for Victoria Bannerman!" I exclaimed. "Whatever for?"

Shadow nodded in Hawk's direction. "Haven't you noticed how often he looks at her?"

"No, I guess not," I said. But I was noticing now, and remembering how they had danced together earlier. Victoria Bannerman was blossoming into a lovely young woman. A cloud of auburn hair framed a heart-shaped face that was smooth and unblemished. A smattering of freckles only added to her beauty. Just now, she was smiling up at Hawk, her blue eyes wide with admiration as she complimented him on winning the race. Hawk's face was faintly flushed with pride, and I could see he was more than pleased with Victoria's rapt attention.

"A man likes to look good in his woman's eyes," Shadow remarked.

"A man! Hawk is just a boy."

"He will not be a boy much longer,"

Shadow pointed out. "He grows taller and stronger each day. Soon he will be old enough for the Sun Dance, and then he will truly be a man."

The Sun Dance. I had pushed my son's desire to participate in that sacred Cheyenne ritual far out of my thoughts, hoping that as time passed, Hawk would change his mind. He had not mentioned it since the time of his vision, and I secretly hoped he had forgotten all about it.

Shadow smiled faintly as he laid his hand on my shoulder and gave me a small squeeze. "He has not forgotten, Hannah," Shadow said quietly. "He does not speak of it because he knows you do not fully approve. But he has mentioned it to me, and his desire to prove himself worthy to be a warrior grows stronger every day."

"I'm not sure I will be able to bear it."

"We must both be strong when the time comes," Shadow said. "It is a thing he must do."

"I know. I guess I just hate to see him growing up so fast. Before you know it, Hawk and Mary will both be getting married and having children of their own."

Shadow nodded as he cupped my chin in the palm of his hand. "You will be as beautiful to me when you are a grandmother as you were that day I saw you swimming in the river."

I felt my cheeks grow warm with the memory. I had turned sixteen that day. I had gone to the river crossing to swim and had been sitting on the grassy bank when Shadow rode up. It was the first time I had seen him since he had reached manhood. I remembered every detail of how he looked that balmy afternoon. He had been clad in moccasins and the briefest of deerskin clouts; the closest thing to a naked man I had ever seen. His legs had been long and well-muscled by years of riding bareback; his belly had been hard and flat, as it was even now. Like a bird hypnotized by a snake, I had stared at him, awed by his proud carriage, mesmerized by his savage yet utterly fascinating appearance. Was this the same boy who had eaten at our table and shared our laughter only a few years ago, I had thought, the same boy who had taught me to warble like a thrush and coo like a dove. A raw animal-like power had radiated from him, causing my heart to pound with such force I had been certain he could hear it.

"That was a long time ago," I murmured.

"Almost twenty years," Shadow mused. "You were wearing a blue gingham dress."

"Yes. And you were practically naked." He had been terribly handsome then, I thought, but no more so than now.

Shadow laughed softly. "Let us go home and get naked together now," he whispered. His hand slid down my arm, sending a shiver of delight coursing through me. My blood seemed to turn to warm honey as he kissed me, and then he was lifting me onto Smoke's back and we were riding for home.

That afternoon, lying wrapped in Shadow's arms, I was sixteen all over again.

XXIII

In the fall of 1894, Hawk turned sixteen and the time I had been dreading for so long was upon us. Early in the summer of 1895, Shadow went to the Cheyenne reservation and found an aged medicine man who was willing to sneak off the reservation and make the long trek to Bear Valley to instruct a young Cheyenne in the ritual of the Sun Dance. Three other warriors, all well into their sixties, asked if they might accompany Shadow and the medicine man to the valley. With them, they brought the sacred emblems necessary, a drum, and the knowledge of what needed to be done.

The shaman, whose name was Eagle-That-Soars-in-the-Sky, was a wizened old man with long gray braids, skin the texture and color of old saddle leather, and black eyes that missed nothing. He wore a worn elkskin shirt, leggings, loincloth and moccasins. Though he was old and bent, he still possessed an aura of power and quiet dignity and I knew that once he must have been a proud warrior among his people.

The four Indians settled into the lodge behind our cabin and soon after they arrived Hawk began spending many hours each day with Eagle-That-Soars-in-the-Sky, learning from the aged shaman those things he needed to know in order to accomplish his goal.

Shadow and Blackie went into the woods to find a tree that would be suitable for the Sun Dance pole. Not just any tree would do. It must be tall and straight and strong. When Shadow found one that pleased him, he cut it down and carried it to a small clearing deep in the midst of the pine tree forest. The Sun Dance would take place in secrecy, for our white neighbors would probably not approve, nor would they be likely to understand. One had to be an Indian, or Indian in heart and spirit, to understand and appreciate the significance of the Sun Dance.

The following day, the shaman painted the Sun Dance pole with four different colors, each color representing one of the four corners of the earth. When that was done, cutouts of a male buffalo and an Indian warrior, both depicting beings with exaggerated genital organs, were placed in a fork in the tree. And then Shadow and the four venerable warriors did a war dance around the pole.

I sat, enthralled, with Hawk, Mary and Blackie at my side. My children gazed, wide-eyed, at their father as he danced around the sacred pole. This day, this hour, Shadow was all Indian. His long black hair flowed loose about his shoulders, adorned with a pair of snowy white eagle feathers. His skin was sheened with a fine layer of sweat as he moved his feet in the intricate steps of the dance.

"He's beautiful," Mary whispered.

And he was. He moved with a smooth, animal-like grace, his muscles rippling in the sunlight, his dark eyes glowing as he lost himself in the ancient magic of the dance.

The next day, just before dawn, we gathered at the Sun Dance pole. The sky was a pale blue-gray, the forest quiet and damp with dew. From high in the treetops, a bird scolded us for disturbing his rest.

Hawk stood beside the Sun Dance pole. He wore only a loincloth. His face was set in determined lines, his eyes riveted upon the face of Eagle-That-Soars-in-the-Sky. Shadow stood beside Hawk; he was also dressed in a loincloth and nothing else.

Eagle-That-Soars-in-the-Sky lifted his arms above his head and began to chant a sacred prayer song as the sun rose above the trees. One by one, the other aged warriors joined their voices with his. The chant, sung in a minor key, seemed to penetrate my very soul. Images of warriors long dead flashed before my eyes: Crazy Horse, Calf Running, Black Elk. In my mind's eye I saw buffalo grazing on the grassy plains. I saw the Sacred Black Hills, the wild roses that grew along the banks of the Rosebud River, the valley of the Little Big Horn. I felt tears well in my eyes as I grieved for a way of life that was gone, and for my son, who had been born too late to live the life he yearned for.

Hawk stood straight and proud as the old medicine man approached him. My son did not flinch as the shaman pierced the muscle over his left breast with a sharp knife. A slim wooden skewer was inserted into the opening made by the knife, and then the procedure was repeated on the right side. Rawhide thongs were attached to the skewers in my son's chest, the loose end was then attached to the Sun Dance pole. Hawk would pull against the thongs until his flesh gave way, freeing him from the pole.

The ceremony was one I did not fully comprehend. I knew only that the Cheyenne believed that through their willingness to endure pain they would ensure prosperity for their tribe for the year to come. It was a chance for a man to prove his bravery, a chance to obtain a vision from Maheo.

I took a deep breath as the medicine man moved to stand in front of Shadow. I had not been surprised when Shadow told me he was going to participate in the Sun Dance with Hawk. I knew he was doing it to give Hawk courage, to share his son's pain.

It seemed to me that there was a subtle transformation in my husband as the medicine man pierced his flesh. It was no longer Shadow standing before me, but the Cheyenne warrior and chief, Two Hawks Flying.

The medicine man completed his preparations and stepped away from Hawk and Shadow and now the drumming began, a constant throbbing that was like the beat of the Cheyenne heart, strong and invincible.

Shadow and Hawk danced back and forth, moving toward the pole, moving away, bodies straining against the rawhide thongs that held them bound to the sacred pole. Faces lifted, they stared into the sun and when the pain grew unbearable, they blew upon eagle bone whistles. The notes were high-pitched and long, floating in the air like ghostly shafts of pain.

Slowly, the sun climbed higher and higher in the sky. The air grew warm. Sweat poured from the faces and bodies of the dancers as they shuffled endlessly back and forth. Blood trickled from their wounds, mingling with their sweat.

My heart ached for their pain, especially for Hawk. He did not have his father's rigorous upbringing to sustain him, he had only his tremendous desire to prove he was worthy to be a warrior in the old way.

The hours passed. Blackie fell asleep, his head pillowed in my lap, but Mary remained awake, her eyes riveted on her father and her brother. Tears welled in her eyes as the minutes went by. And still Shadow and Hawk danced back and forth. Hungry, weary, in pain, they danced and they prayed, never hesitating, never stopping.

Once Shadow's eyes met mine and I felt such a surge of love it was almost painful. I knew he had decided to participate in the dance not only to bolster Hawk's courage, but to beseech the spirits to bless our family. The tears came then, but they were tears of joy.

It was just before sundown that Shadow's flesh gave way and he fell back, exhausted. Eagle-That-Soars-in-the-Sky went to him, chanting softly while he washed Shadow's wounds and then sprinkled them with healing herbs and sacred pollen.

Moments later, Hawk pulled against the thongs with all his strength and his flesh tore free of the skewers. He fell to the ground, his eyes glazed with pain. He lay in a semi-stupor for several minutes and then fell into a deep sleep.

Eagle -That -Soars -in -the-Sky tended Hawk's wounds and then Shadow bundled our son in a robe and lifted him onto Smoke's back. Swinging up behind Hawk, he started for home. Mary, Blackie, and I followed Shadow, leaving the four warriors to dismantle the sacred pole and erase all evidence of what we had done in the clearing.

Later that night, when everyone else was in bed asleep, Shadow and I sat on the front porch holding hands.

"Are you all right?" I asked.

"I am fine," Shadow said, squeezing my hand. "It is a good kind of pain."

"I was very proud of Hawk today, and of you, too."

Shadow nodded. "He is a fine young man. He would have made a good warrior."

"Did you have a vision?" I asked, unable to wait any longer.

"Yes, Hannah. My old friends, the hawks, came to me. We will live to a ripe old age, you and I. And our children will all find happiness. This is what the hawks promised."

"Do you believe it?"

"Yes. They have never been wrong."

"Do you think Hawk also had a vision?"

"I am sure of it."

The next day Shadow gave each of the Cheyenne warriors a horse for their time and trouble in preparing the Sun Dance ceremony and the men went back to the reservation.

Later that day, Hawk felt like getting out of bed. I fixed him some hearty beef stew and he told us of his vision while he ate. The same yellow-tailed hawk had appeared to him. As before, the hawk had changed into a man. But this time a woman came out of a dark mist to stand beside the hawk-man. The woman's face was in shadow, but Hawk knew he would recognize the woman when he saw her, and that she would be his wife. Then the man was transformed into a hawk again. Rising into the air, the hawk disappeared into the sun. A single feather remained where he had been.

My son held the feather in his hand now, a look of wonder on his handsome young face.

"The hawk said I should always know happiness so long as I remained true to the things I had been taught by my father and Eagle-That-Soars-in-the-Sky. He said I should never be afraid to do what I know is right."

Shadow nodded, his eyes warm with affection. "If you do as the hawk has said, you will always have peace in here."

Shadow placed his hand over his heart. "If you are at peace with yourself, you need never be concerned with what other people think or say, for no one can destroy you except yourself."

"I understand, nehyo," Hawk said. "I thank you for helping me to achieve my goal."

There was a new bond of love and solidarity in our home after the Sun Dance. Mary and Blackie had gained a keener appreciation and respect for their father and elder brother, as well as new insight into their Cheyenne heritage. Though I had not participated in the dance itself, I, too, felt a deeper sense of inner peace.

As the sweet summer days passed by, I knew the gods, red and white, were indeed smiling down on our home, blessing us with peace and happiness.

XXIV

1895-1896

A few weeks after the Sun Dance, Rebecca received a letter from her daughter, Beth. The letter was long, filled with a glowing description of a young man Beth had met at a church social. His name was Jason Chatsworth. He was studying to be a lawyer. His parents were quite wealthy and lived in Pennsylvania. He was six feet tall, had black hair and gray eyes, a darling dimple in his chin, and was, in fact, the most wonderful man in the whole world.

Six months later, a second letter arrived telling of Beth's engagement to her young man and asking Rebecca to please come back east for the wedding, set for June.

"You've got to go," I said as I finished reading the letter. "After all, she is your only daughter. You don't want to miss her wedding, do you?"

"Of course not, but I don't know how I'll get Sam to leave the ranch, and I wouldn't dream of making the trip without him."

"Shadow and Hawk can look after the ranch while you're gone," I said. "Oh, Rebecca, just think, a chance to go east!"

Rebecca smiled broadly. "It would be fun," she mused. "I'd love to go shopping and get some new things. I saw a darling hat advertised in one of the catalogs. And it would be wonderful to see Beth. I haven't seen her for such a long time."

We spent the rest of the afternoon daydreaming about the trip back east and discussing what to buy Beth for a wedding present.

It took some persuasive talking on Rebecca's part, but Pa finally agreed to go with her to Pennsylvania. Hawk said he would stay at the ranch while they were gone, and Blackie said he would stay and help, too.

In the spring of '96, Pa and Rebecca left for Steel's Crossing to catch the train back east. Hawk and Blackie moved into Pa's cabin, and Mary decided to go along and keep house for the boys.

Our own place seemed suddenly empty, and for the first time in years, I found myself with time on my hands. I spent a few hours each day riding with Shadow when he went to check on the horses. Our herd was growing every year, and Shadow's horses were eagerly sought after by our friends and neighbors. People came from miles away to buy a horse sired by Smoke and trained by Shadow. He broke each horse himself, and I never tired of watching him ride. Most of the horses we raised were gentle, tractable creatures. They were used to Shadow, used to being handled, and they didn't buck and pitch the way the horses caught wild off the range did. There was always an exception, however. Hawk's blue roan had fought man and saddle every inch of the way, but now he was a good reliable horse, just as Shadow had said he would be. Shadow was wonderful with horses. He never lost his temper, never grew impatient, never pushed a horse too far too fast.

Now, riding through a pasture that held mares and their foals, I felt blissfully content. I smiled as a handful of colts and fillies began to chase each other, squealing loudly as they pranced around, heads and tails high. They were beautiful horses, no two alike. I was particularly fond of a little filly that was red with a white blanket and red spots.

After checking the herd, Shadow and I went to the river crossing for lunch. I had packed a basket and we spent a lazy hour resting in the shade while we ate.

"Hawk has been spending a lot of time with Victoria Bannerman," Shadow remarked, skimming a flat stone across the river.

"I know. Do you think its serious?"

"At this age, everything is serious."

I nodded. That was true enough. It was hard to imagine my children growing older and getting married. Somehow, I always thought of them as youngsters, yet Mary was fifteen already and far too beautiful for her own good. Her skin was flawless, her dark brown hair thick and wavy, her gray eyes clear and innocent. Already, the boys in the valley were finding excuses to visit her, to be with her. At church on Sunday, the young men scrambled to see who would sit beside her. At socials, they argued over who would have the first dance, who would fetch her supper, who would have the last dance. Mary basked in all the attention but then, what girl wouldn't? I worried about her constantly, afraid she would give her heart too soon. Next year she would be sixteen, the same age I had been when I fell hopelessly in love with Shadow. I only hoped my daughter would find the same happiness I had found. Shadow adored his daughter, and I wondered if he would consider any man good enough for her.

And Hawk—the Sun Dance had indeed turned him into a man. At sixteen, he was the image of his father: tall and strong and handsome. He was endowed with an air of self-confidence few boys his age possessed, and it made him seem far older

than his years. He wore his straight black
hair long, as befitted a warrior, and
though he usually wore blue jeans and a
cotton shirt, no one ever mistook him for
anything but an Indian. His heritage was
clearly stamped on his features and in his
attitude toward life and I could not help
but wonder if his Cheyenne blood had
somehow swallowed up the white.

Blackie was nine. He seemed to have
inherited the best of both worlds. His skin
was a golden brown, his hair was black, his
eyes were dark. He was a lively, happy boy
who made friends wherever he went. He
rarely lost his temper, and had a warm and
tender heart that could not stand to see
suffering of any kind. He brought home
countless stray animals that were hurt or
sick or lost and nursed them back to
health. Most of the coons and birds and
squirrels eventually went back to the wild
after they recovered, but a few of his
orphans hung around our place and you
never knew what would turn up in his
room next.

Pensive, I stared into the slowly
moving river. Shadow had never treated
Blackie any differently from Hawk or
Mary, and yet sometimes I caught him
staring at the boy and I knew he was wondering if Blackie was truly his son, or if he
had been fathered by Joshua Berdeen. In
my heart, I was certain Blackie belonged
to Shadow, and yet I knew the answer

would always remain a mystery.

"You seem far away," Shadow remarked, reaching for my hand. "Is anything wrong?"

"No." I turned to smile at him. "I was just thinking about our children and wondering what it will be like when they're all married and gone. It made made me a little sad."

"You cannot keep them from growing up any more than you can stop the days from passing," Shadow said matter-of-factly. "Nothing lives long but the earth and the mountains."

"And my love for you," I said, scooting over to lean against him.

Shadow smiled down at me as his arms went around my waist, the love in his fathomless black eyes making my pulse beat faster and my blood run hot and sweet, like melted honey. How I loved him!

Rising, Shadow lifted me into his arms and carried me into a shady glen. It was a lovely place for a rendezvous. A leafy green umbrella blocked the sun, pine needles layered the ground like a soft carpet, ferns and wildflowers grew in profusion, creating a miniature garden of Eden in the heart of the wilderness.

Gently, Shadow lowered me to the ground, his black eyes aglow as he knelt beside me and began to unfasten the bodice of my dress. His hands trembled slightly as reached for the narrow blue ribbon that laced my chemise. His hands moved lazily over my bared flesh as he removed my clothing, the touch of his fingers thrilling me down to my toes.

He stood with fluid grace and I watched through heavy-lidded eyes as he stepped out of his buckskin pants, clout, shirt and moccasins to stand naked before me. The sight of him quickened my desire. Age had not marred his perfect form. He was still tall and lean, his copper-hued flesh firm and sleek. He had many scars and I touched each one as he knelt beside me.

The scars on his broad chest were souvenirs of the two Sun Dance rituals he had participated in. The marks on his back were from a severe beating he had received while a prisoner of Stewart and McCall back east. The long scar on his right leg had been inflicted by angry homesteaders in Bear Valley in the spring of 1875. There was a small scar on his upper left arm and another low on his left side, both caused by bullets when he had fled the reservation the day I had been injured by Joe Mattlock. So many scars, I mused, and each one like a badge of his love and courage.

I shuddered with pleasure as Shadow lowered his long body over mine. I loved the feel and the scent of him, loved the touch of his hands moving lovingly, intimately, over my flesh and through my hair, loved the deep throaty sound of his voice as he whispered, "Ne-mehotatse, Hannah. I love you."

"Ne-mehotatse," I replied, my voice barely audible as I buried my face in the hollow of his shoulder, my hips arching up to meet him as he thrust into me, possessing me, completing me, making me whole at last. I surged upward, my hands cupping his buttocks, pulling him closer, closer, knowing I could never get enough of him.

And then we were one flesh, our hearts and souls soaring upward, ever upward, reaching for the stars.

XXV

Hawk

Fall 1896

He paced up and down beside the river crossing, wondering if she would come. They had been meeting secretly a couple times a week for over two years, their affection for one another growing steadily stronger, deeper, more compelling. In private, they kissed and caressed, always careful not to go too far. In public, they were only friends. They danced together at socials, went riding together, sought each other out at parties, always careful to keep things light and above suspicion. Victoria saw other young men; Hawk occasionally courted other girls, but he did not like the worried looks parents cast in his direction when he came to call on their daughters and he rarely saw the same girl twice.

He glanced over his shoulder, impatient with the need to be alone with her, and suddenly she was there, her long auburn hair curling around her lovely, heart-shaped face, her sky blue eyes shining eagerly as she jumped from her horse and ran toward him.

Hawk's heart thudded loudly in his chest as he caught her in his arms, their bodies straining together as they kissed.

"Oh, Hawk," Victoria murmured breathlessly. "You make my heart soar with happiness."

"With me it is the same."

Victoria gazed up at the handsome young man holding her tight in his arms. "I love you." She blurted the words, speaking them aloud for the first time.

"Do you?" Hawk asked, astonished. His hand caressed the soft curve of her cheek. She was so beautiful, so sweet and kind. Every unmarried man in the valley looked at her with longing. Many had courted her. Many professed undying love and devotion, promising to make her happy all the days of her life. And yet she loved him. It was a miracle.

"I love you very much," she whispered, unable to keep her feelings bottled up inside any longer. "Love you, love you, love you!"

Hawk's blood seemed to be on fire, his throat suddenly constricted as he rasped, "I love you, too, Vickie."

Victoria smiled up at Hawk, the wonder of it glowing in her eyes. Of all the young men who had courted her, only Hawk made her insides swell with joy; only Hawk fired her imagination, making her yearn for the unknown, making her long to be held closer, tighter, more intimately.

"You are ever in my thoughts," Hawk confessed. "Sometimes, I want you so much I can't sleep, and I get up and run to your house, just to be near you."

"Really?"

"Yes. One night I slept outside, near your bedroom window."

Victoria's smile was radiant. "I think about you all the time, too," she admitted.

She studied the face of the man she loved, and found no fault in it. Every feature was perfect, from his fathomless black eyes to his strong proud chin. His nose was long and straight, his mouth full, his forehead high. Her fingers stroked the nape of his neck, toyed with a lock of his hair. She loved his hair. It was long and thick and straight, black as pitch, just like his father's. Hawk was, in fact, very like Shadow and that pleased Victoria, for Shadow was a man she admired and respected.

Hawk gazed lovingly into Victoria's beautiful blue eyes. She was soft and warm and so very feminine. Her skin was the color of a ripe peach, her hair reddish-

brown, like the leaves of autumn, her lips
were softer than velvet, sweeter than
honey. And her breasts, ah, they were high
and firm, large enough to fill his hand. His
groin grew tight as he thought of holding
her close. His dreams were tormented with
visions of Victoria lying beside him, her
sapphire eyes alight with desire, her
golden flesh pressed against his. More
than anything else in the world, he longed
to possess her, to make her his woman in
every sense of the word. But a warrior did
not defile the woman he loved, and so
Hawk kept a tight rein on his desires. It
was the most difficult manhood test of all,
one he was in great fear of losing. Each
time he held her, it was harder to let her
go. Each day saw his longing for her grow
deeper, more intense.

   "I wish we could be married," Victoria
murmured, and Hawk nodded as she
expressed the desire of his own heart.

   "Is it true that Cheyenne men used to
buy their brides with horses?" Victoria
asked. She laid her hand on his chest. The
warmth of her palm seemed to burn
through his thin cotton shirt, branding the
skin beneath.

   "Yes, but I don't think there are
enough horses in all of Bear Valley to buy
you from your father."

   "I know," Victoria agreed grimly.
"My parents like you well enough as a
friend, but . . ."

"But they do not want their only daughter to marry a half-breed," Hawk finished bitterly.

"We could run away," Victoria suggested hopefully. "I'd go anywhere with you."

Hawk shook his head. "No. We will not run away as though there were something shameful about our love."

Victoria nodded, secretly glad that he felt that way. "I'll be eighteen next year," she said brightly. "They can't stop me from marrying you then, but it seems like such a long time to wait. Such a long time, when I want you now."

The last few words emerged from her lips in the softest of whispers, but they rang in Hawk's ears like thunder.

"And I want you," he said huskily. "But we must wait."

"Hawk." His name was a low moan on her lips as she pressed her body against his.

Her breasts were soft, warm, as they flattened against his chest, her lips moist as she kissed him, pulling his head down to meet hers. His response was immediate, his manhood swelling with desire, pushing against her belly.

The willpower he had exercised so valiantly in the past fled and somehow they were lying side by side on the grass, their bodies close, their mouths fused together. Eager hands touched, explored, caressed. Clothing was removed, cast carelessly aside in their haste to be one. Curious hands fondled bare flesh, stroking, tasting. Sensations blossomed and burst into being as the novelty of discovery urged them to kiss a little more intimately, probe a little deeper, until they had passed the point of no return.

Hawk's hands slid down Victoria's rib cage, caressed her slim waist, a waist so tiny he was sure he could easily span it with his hands. His breathing grew erratic as he went on to stroke the gentle swell of her hips, her buttocks, the satin smoothness of her thighs, and he was lost, gloriously lost as his mouth roamed over her breasts and belly.

Victoria's fevered response to his touch of her hands upon his skin drove him touch of herhands upon his skin drove him wild with wanting. And then Victoria cried his name, begging him to quench the fire he had ignited. She lifted her hips, her slim white thighs parting to receive him, her arms holding him close, and he was lost, gloriously lost . . .

They met at the river crossing the next day where Hawk's parents had met so many years before. Hand in hand, they walked through the pine tree forest, penetrating deeper and deeper into the woods until they came to Rabbit's Head Rock.

"Let's rest awhile," Victoria

suggested, and they sat down on the grass
beside the huge gray boulder. Hawk put
his arm around Victoria's slight shoulders
and gave her an affectionate squeeze. She
was his now, truly his, and he felt a
tenderness and protectiveness toward her
that he had never experienced before.

"I wish my parents cared for you as
much as I do," Victoria lamented.
Plucking a bright yellow wildflower, she
twirled it back and forth between her
fingers. "Maybe, if they got to know you
better, they wouldn't object to my seeing
you more often," Victoria suggested.
"Why don't you come for dinner next
week?"

Hawk grimaced with distaste. He did
not like Lydia Bannerman, or her rotund
husband, Horace. He did not like the way
they looked at him, distrusting him, con-
temptuous of him because he was a half-
breed. Their attitude was doubly hard to
accept because Horace and Lydia both
liked his mother and father, and even
Mary and Blackie. It was only Hawk they
disliked, and he wondered if it was because
he cared for Victoria.

Hawk stared into the distance. All his
life he had lived with the prejudice of the
whites. He remembered going to school at
the fort on the reservation and how the
white boys had beat him up because he
had an Indian name. Here, in Bear Valley,
there were those who disliked him simply

because of the color of his skin, but he had
learned to live with it. He did not tell his
parents of the many slights and
derogatory remarks he received when he
went into town, knowing it would cause
them pain, nor did he mention the half-
dozen street fights and saloon brawls he
had been involved in because he wouldn't
back down when he was provoked. Once,
he had almost killed a passing stranger
with his bare hands because the man had
called his mother an Injun-loving whore.

Things were not so bad for his sister,
Mary. She did not look so decidedly
Cheyenne, nor did she yearn for the Indian
way of life. The girls Mary's age liked her
because she was outgoing and friendly,
the boys idolized her because she was
pretty and vivacious. His brother, Blackie,
lived in a world all his own. People were
not important to Blackie, though he made
friends as easily as Mary. Animals filled
Blackie's world.

Hawk sighed heavily. He did not fit in
the white man's world, and the Indian
world was gone.

Heavy-hearted, he drew Victoria into
his arms and kissed her, needing to hold
her close, to know there was one person
who loved him unconditionally for who
and what he was.

A burst of amused laughter drew
Hawk's attention and he sat up, a guilty
look on his face as he released his hold on

Victoria. He scowled at the girl peering around Rabbit's Head Rock.

"What are you doing here?" Hawk demanded angrily.

"I live here."

Hawk glared at Mercy Tillman. She was a short blond girl with generous breasts and wide hips. Her father, Morgus, ran a whiskey still in a remote part of the woods.

Mercy sneered as she glanced at Victoria. "Lordy, lordy," she said with a smirk. "Wouldn't your daddy have a conniption fit if he knew you was diddling a buck in the woods!"

Victoria looked stricken. Hawk sprang to his feet, his eyes blazing. He lifted his hand, wanting to lash out at the girl who had insulted Victoria, but, mad as he was, he couldn't strike a female.

"Shut up, Mercy," Hawk warned.

"Don't worry," Mercy said, puffing out her chest. "I won't tell anyone." She smiled a knowing smile. "When you get tired of sweet Victoria there, you come see me, and I'll pleasure you for free."

"Get out of here, Mercy," Hawk growled, "or I'll slap that silly grin off your face."

Mercy Tillman laughed impudently. "I'm not afraid of you," she retorted saucily. "You're just like all the other Valley boys. Sooner or later, you'll come knocking at my door." She threw Victoria a malicious grin, and smiled beguilingly at Hawk. Then, with a swish of her hips, she was gone.

Victoria looked at Hawk, a question in her eyes. "You wouldn't go to visit a girl like that, would you?"

"Of course not."

Victoria's cheeks grew hot and she looked away as she recalled how she had let Hawk make love to her in a secluded glade near the river crossing.

"Do you think I'm like Mercy Tillman?" she asked, her head down so he couldn't see her eyes.

"Victoria!"

"Do you?"

"Dammit, Vickie, what are you trying to say?"

"I let you make love to me. Maybe I'm no different than Mercy. Maybe I'm just as bad as she is."

"Vickie, stop it. You're nothing like Mercy Tillman." Hawk groaned low in his throat, hating himself for making Victoria feel cheap because she had given him her love without benefit of marriage. "Vickie, Mercy Tillman has lifted her skirts for just about every man in the valley. You're not like that. You could never be like that. I'm sorry what we did has made you feel dirty." He swore softly as tears welled in Victoria's eyes. "I'll never touch you again, never see you again, if that's what you want. But don't hate yourself for what we did."

"I'm not sorry for what we did," Victoria murmured, blinking the tears from her eyes. "I love you. I was only afraid you'd think I was no good, that you didn't respect me any more."

"Vickie." He took her in his arms and held her tight, knowing he'd rather cut off his arm than hurt her. "We'll never do it again," he said, stroking her hair. "Not until we're married. Please don't cry."

"I love you, Hawk." She sniffled a little, wiping her eyes dry with the hem of her skirt. "You never answered my question," she reminded him with a captivating smile. "Will you come for dinner next week?"

"Yes," Hawk answered with a sigh of resignation. "I'll come next week and every week after that if it will make you happy."

As promised, Hawk arrived for dinner at the Bannermans a week later. It was an ordeal he dreaded, and one that proved to be every bit as bad as he had expected.

Lydia Bannerman welcomed him at the door, a superficial smile on her face. "Good evening, Hawk," she said, trying to inject a note of warmth into her voice, and failing miserably. "Won't you come in?"

Horace and Victoria were waiting in

the parlor. Vickie smiled at Hawk fondly, her eyes aglow with the depth of her feelings. Horace Bannerman shook his hand as if he were shaking hands with a leper.

The first meal was the worst and would have been the last if not for Victoria's constant pleading that he return again and again. To please her, he endured several evenings at the Bannerman home, subjecting himself to Horace Bannerman's suspicious glances and Lydia Bannerman's barely concealed disapproval. The Bannermans had welcomed Hawk's parents into the community, insisting there was room in the valley for all, red and white alike. But that had been before Hawk became a man, before Victoria began to talk and think of Hawk and no one else.

The Bannermans never left them alone, a fact that both angered and amused Hawk. Always, Lydia or Horace remained in the parlor with them, stifling conversation, forestalling any show of affection. And because the Bannermans watched them so closely, Hawk and Victoria met more and more often at the river crossing.

It was inevitable that what had happened before would happen again. Their love was young, impatient and demanding as only young love can be.

Hawk was torn with guilt. He was a warrior. He had seen a vision. He had

endured the agony of the Sun Dance. It
was wrong for him to make love to
Victoria out of wedlock, but he loved her
with all his heart, and his blood ran hot
with desire. Perhaps, if she had refused
him, he could have kept a tight rein on his
emotions, but she was as eager for his
touch as he was for hers. He vowed each
time he took her that it would be the last,
that he would wait until she was his wife,
but Victoria had only to touch him, her
clear blue eyes alight with desire, and he
was lost . . .

They made plans to go to the next
social together, but Lydia Bannerman had
other ideas. Ethan Smythe had recently
returned from the East where he had gone
to school to study law. He was back now,
ready to begin his practice, ready to settle
down, and Lydia Bannerman considered
Ethan a much better match for her only
daughter than a half-breed boy who would
never amount to anything.

"What shall I do?" Victoria wailed to
Hawk. "I don't want to go to the dance
with Ethan Smythe. I want to go with
you!"

"Go with him," Hawk advised, not
wanting to cause trouble between Victoria
and her mother. "Just because you go
with him doesn't mean you have to stay
with him."

The monthly socials were held at the

grange. Most of the families in the valley attended. After a month of hard work, everyone looked forward to an evening of music and dancing. It gave the women a chance to get together to discuss recipes and quilting, to learn who was in a family way, and who had given birth, to laugh and talk and think about something besides chores and housework. The men discussed crops and cattle, pondered world events, or bragged about who had the best bull or the fastest horse.

Hawk dressed with care for the dance that night. He wore a blue shirt, black pants, a black vest, and black boots. His shoulder-length hair was squeaky clean.

Several girls took notice of him when he walked into the Grange Hall, wishing they had the nerve to defy their parents and flirt with him. He was so handsome, and his Indian blood made him exciting, different. And the fact that he was forbidden made him even more intriguing.

On a dare, Kitty Mason broke away from her circle of friends and walked boldly to where Hawk was standing.

"Dance with me, Hawk?" she asked, fluttering her lashes at him.

With a nod, Hawk followed Kitty onto the dance floor, only half listening as she chatted animatedly about her sister's upcoming wedding. He clenched his teeth when he saw Victoria and Ethan Smythe waltz by. It was galling, to see the girl he loved in another man's arms.

Hawk glared at Ethan Smythe. Ethan was of average height with broad shoulders, brown hair and brown eyes. He wore a dark blue city suit, a string tie, and black boots. He smiled as he twirled Victoria around the room, obviously enchanted by the girl in his arms.

And no wonder, Hawk thought sourly. Vitoria looked lovely in a dress of pale green muslin. A dark green sash circled her tiny waist, a ribbon of the same color was twined through her reddish-brown hair.

When the music ended, Hawk returned Kitty to her friends, politely thanked her for the dance.

The musicians struck up a lively polka and Hawk scowled blackly as he saw Ethan lead Victoria onto the dance floor again. Taking a deep breath, Hawk strode across the floor to cut in on Ethan Smythe.

Ethan surrendered Victoria with a tight smile and the next half hour saw the two young men vying for her attention. Lydia Bannerman's mouth thinned with disapproval every time she saw her daughter dancing with Hawk.

About nine o'clock, the musicians took a break and Hawk and Victoria slipped outside for a few moments alone.

Horace and Lydia Bannerman peered anxiously around the room, searching for Victoria, and when they couldn't find her, Horace left the building. He gasped aloud as he rounded a corner of the Grange and saw Victoria and Hawk standing in the shadows, their bodies pressed close together. Rage exploded in Horace Bannerman's heart as he saw Hawk's head descend toward Victoria, saw Hawk kiss his daughter deeply, passionately.

Growling an oath, Horace rushed forward. Grabbing Hawk by the shirt collar, he pulled him away from Victoria. Spinning Hawk around, Horace drove his fist into Hawk's face.

"Daddy, stop!"

"Keep out of this, Victoria!" Horace Bannerman said sharply, and drove his fist into Hawk's face a second time.

Twisting out of Bannerman's grasp, Hawk backed away, his hands clenched at his sides, his eyes blazing with anger. Blood oozed from his lower lip and trickled from his nose.

Horace Bannerman raised his fists. "Come on, you dirty half-breed," he challenged. "I'll teach you to lay hands on a decent white woman."

Hawk glared at Victoria's father, the urge to fight back strong within him. The words "half-breed" rang in his ears like thunder.

Horace Bannerman laughed derisive-

ly. "I didn't think you had the guts to
fight like a man," he sneered.

Hawk took a step forward, his face
dark with fury. It would be so easy to beat
Horace Bannerman to a bloody pulp. So
easy, and so satisfying.

"Hawk, don't!"

Victoria's voice reached through the
red haze of anger, and Hawk knew he
could not fight her father, no matter how
tempting it would be to smash his fist into
Horace Bannerman's flaccid face.

Taking a deep breath, Hawk threw
Victoria a quick look, then turned on his
heel and stalked off into the night.

Horace Bannerman swung around to
face his daughter. "You little tramp," he
hissed. "Is that the way your mother and
I raised you? To sneak around in the
shadows with a dirty half-breed?"

"We weren't sneaking," Victoria
replied sullenly. "I love Hawk."

"Love," Horace Bannerman sneered.
"What do you know about love? You're
just a child."

"I am not a child, and I wish you'd
stop treating me like one," Victoria
retorted. "I'm seventeen." Tears welled in
her eyes. Her father had never yelled at
her before, never treated her with anything but love and affection. The scorn she
read in his eyes cut her heart like a knife.
"I'm sorry, daddy," she said contritely.
"Please don't be angry."

Horace Bannerman melted like butter in a hot pan. "I'm sorry, too, angel," he murmured. "Let's not mention this to your mother. We'll pretend it never happened."

They met late the next afternoon at the river crossing and after a quick embrace, they stretched out on the grass, gazing up at the sky. For a while, they did not speak, neither of them wanting to mention what had happened the night before.

"I see a ship," Victoria remarked, pointing at a large white cloud that resembled a ship under sail. "And there's a whale." She turned to face Hawk, her eyes thrilling at the sight of him. "What do you see?"

"I see trouble," Hawk answered glumly.

"I don't want to talk about it," Victoria said. "Not now."

"Ignoring the problem won't make it go away."

"I don't care. It's a lovely day. Let's not spoil it." Turning on her side, she pressed her mouth to his.

Hawk kissed her as though the touch of her lips was the only thing that could save him.

"I love you," Victoria murmured. "I don't care what anyone says or thinks. I love you."

Hawk's hand slipped through the layers of her clothing to close on the warm mound of her breast. Victoria gave a little gasp of pleasure, loving his touch, loving the way he made her feel all warm and tingly inside.

"Vickie." Hawk groaned low in his throat as his hand kneaded her soft flesh. "Vickie, stop me before it's too late."

"Don't stop," she murmured against his neck. "Don't ever stop."

His hands were shaking as he quickly stripped away Victoria's clothing and then his own. He was on fire for her, wanting her as never before, desperately afraid that her parents would find some way to keep them apart. He stroked her slender alabaster body, awed by the beauty and perfection of each inch of satin flesh. He drew her close, whispering to her in English and Cheyenne.

Victoria clung to Hawk, her body arching up to meet his, her hands cupping his buttocks, drawing him closer, closer, her fingers clawing at his strong back and shoulders as he emptied his life into her.

XXVI

1897

Pa and Rebecca came home in January, bringing presents for everyone, regaling us with tales of life in the east.

Rebecca was bubbling with news about her daughter, Beth. "She was a beautiful bride," Rebecca said, laughing, "and I'm not saying that just because I'm her mother."

Pa agreed that Beth had indeed been beautiful, though not as beautiful as her mother. The wedding, he said, had been first-class all the way. A sit-down dinner for over a hundred people, a wedding cake four feet high, champagne that flowed like water. He added that Jason Chatsworth was a likeable enough fellow, handsome as the very devil, with a good head on his shoulders.

"Likely be a rich man in his own right before too long," Pa mused. "If not, it won't matter. His father has more money than one man can spend."

It was good to have Pa and Rebecca home again. I had missed their company, missed knowing they were nearby.

I glanced up from the shirt I was mending as Mary entered the room. She was a lovely girl, I thought proudly. Her long brown hair was pulled away from her face by a pink ribbon, her gray eyes were serene and happy and I guessed Frank Smythe was coming to call.

Frank and Mary had been made for each other. They had been childhood friends and that friendship had grown and flowered into a deep and abiding love that was beautiful to see. Frank Smythe was a young man with ambition and I knew he would not long remain in Bear Valley. On more than one occasion he had expressed a desire to go east and make something of himself. Mary was excited by the idea of living in the east, of going to the theater and dining in fine restaurants, of being surrounded by the bustle of a big noisy city.

Now, watching her as she primped before the mirror, it occurred to me that my daughter would likely wind up living the life I had once dreamed of before Shadow entered my life.

Frank arrived a few minutes later and Mary kissed me goodby, saying they were off for a walk in the snow. They made a handsome couple as they went off together, smiling and laughing.

With a sigh, I turned my attention back to the mending in my lap. Mary had found a good man, and I knew in my heart that life would be good to her.

During the first part of March, I began to suspect something was worrying Hawk. He was quiet and subdued. He often took long rides on the blue roan. Once, when I asked him if there was something troubling him, he shook his head and said everything was all right. But it was not all right. He continued to be sober and withdrawn. When I mentioned it to Shadow, he told me not to worry.

"Hawk is a big boy, Hannah," Shadow remarked. "He will tell us what is wrong when he is ready."

Things came to a head one dreary morning about a week later when Lydia Bannerman came to call. She came right to the point.

"We think Hawk is a very nice young man," she said. "As you know, we have had him to dinner in our home several times, but we ... that is, well, Horace and I feel it would be better if Hawk did not call on Victoria in the future. Victoria is getting much too fond of Hawk and ..." Lydia took a deep breath, her eyes not quite meeting mine. "There just isn't any nice way to say it, Hannah, dear. We like your family very much, but we don't want their relationship to go any further. You understand?"

"Perfectly," I said in as calm a voice as I could manage. "You don't want a half-breed in the family."

"I'm sorry, dear," Lydia said. She fidgeted with the cuff of her immaculately white glove. "I don't know just how deep my daughter's feelings are for Hawk, but I don't want it to go any further. We have great plans for Victoria's future. College back east, marriage into one of the better families in the valley . . ." Lydia's voice trailed off and she had the decency to blush. "You will speak to Hawk, won't you? I wouldn't want to hurt his feelings."

"I don't see how it can be helped," I retorted, wishing I were a man so I could punch Lydia Bannerman in the nose.

Lydia rose to her feet. "I am sorry, Hannah, truly I am. But I must do what I think is best for my daughter. You're a mother. Surely you can understand how I feel?"

"Yes," I said coldly. "I understand. Good day, Mrs. Bannerman."

I stared out the window long after Lydia Bannerman had gone. I was not surprised at how she felt, not surprised that she did not want Hawk for a son-in-law. Old prejudices died hard, old suspicions ran deep, so deep you never knew they were still alive until something like this happened and then all the old feelings surfaced.

I could understand how the Bannermans felt only too well. Hadn't my own parents once felt the same way about Shadow?

My husband scowled blackly when I told him about Lydia Bannerman's visit. There was a trace of his old bitterness in his voice as he murmured, "Some things will never change."

I didn't say anything, but I knew he was right.

We didn't speak of Lydia Bannerman's visit during dinner, but it was much on my mind and I paid little attention to Mary, who was telling about her date with Frank, or to Blackie, who was chattering excitedly about the orphan calf he was caring for. Hawk was quiet, never speaking unless spoken to, and I wondered what the future held for my son. Mary had no trouble being accepted by others, but then her Indian heritage was not so pronounced and she rarely reminded people that she was half Cheyenne. Blackie was still a child, but I knew he would fit in wherever he went because he loved all living things, and they responded to that love, animals as well as people, friends and strangers alike.

But Hawk was his father's son. He was Indian and proud of it, and he never let anyone forget it. I knew he loved

Victoria, yet I wondered if they were right for each other, wondered if Victoria could be happy married to a man who would always be a little wild, who would never be completely "civilized." Hawk would always have a need to explore, to be free, just as his father did. It was something I could live with, something I had accepted. Could Victoria do the same?

After Mary and Blackie had gone to bed, Shadow and I told Hawk what Lydia Bannerman had said. Hawk's temper flared with all the heat and intensity of a forest fire. He ranted and raved and threatened and then he sat down, his head cradled in his hands, all the fight gone out of him.

"I love Victoria," he said quietly, sincerely. "She is the woman in my vision. I have known it for months. Nehyo, what shall I do?"

Shadow shook his head. In the old days, a warrior sometimes kidnapped the girl he loved when her parents did not approve the match. Sometimes the parents relented after such a drastic act, but more often than not, the couple had to take up residence elsewhere.

"Does Victoria feel the same about you?" Shadow asked.

"Yes."

"Perhaps, in time, the Bannermans will change their minds."

"Time!" Hawk exclaimed. "How much time? I will soon be nineteen. Victoria is seventeen. We cannot wait forever."

"You are both still young," Shadow said. "It will not hurt to wait. If your love is real, it will last."

Hawk's gaze shifted from his father's face to the floor. "We do not want to wait," he murmured. "My mother was not much older than Victoria when she went away with you to live with the Cheyenne."

"That was different," Shadow replied. "Our people were at war. Kincaid knew I was your mother's only chance for survival."

"The feelings are the same," Hawk argued.

I looked at my son, my heart aching. Hawk and Victoria had been seeing each other steadily since the harvest festival several years ago. They had gone riding together, taken walks in the woods. They met each other at dances and socials. Sometimes Victoria came to our house for dinner after church on Sunday. As the years went by, I had noticed the way Hawk and Victoria looked at each other, the secret smiles, the frequent touches when they thought no one was looking. I had seen and not wanted to believe.

I took a deep breath, and let it out slowly. "Is Victoria pregnant?"

Hawk's head jerked up. Slowly, his eyes met mine. "Yes." His voice was thick with shame. "We did not mean for it to happen."

I had been standing near the fireplace. Now I sat down hard, feeling like my heart would break. And yet I could not chastise my son for what he and Victoria had done. I could not lecture him and tell him how wrong he was. I could not unbraid him for his lack of self-control and tell him he should have waited for marriage, not when I had once shamelessly seduced his father.

I saw the disappointment in Shadow's eyes. And the love. "You must go to Victoria's parents and tell them what you have done," Shadow said. "It will not be easy, but it must be done immediately."

Hawk nodded. "I will go tomorrow." He looked at his father, and then at me. "I am sorry. I have shamed you, and Victoria. I am not worthy to be a warrior."

Shadow's eyes filled with compassion as he looked at his son. "You are not the first man who could not wait until the wedding night, nor will you be the last. Do not spend the rest of your life regretting what cannot be changed. What is done is done. Your mother and I will help you in any way we can."

Hawk nodded. "I know. Thank you, nehyo."

Shadow and I were about to go to our room when Victoria Bannerman ran into the house, her eyes red with tears.

"Oh, Hawk!" she wailed, hurling herself into his arms. "My parents won't let me see you any more. They said if I dared, they would send me back east to school. What will we do?"

She dissolved into tears, her red-gold head pressed against his shoulder, her arms around his waist.

"I will speak to your parents tomorrow," Hawk said. His hand stroked her hair soothingly. "I will tell them about the baby, and we will be married."

"No! You can't tell my parents about the baby. My father will kill you!" Victoria's voice rose in panic. "They wouldn't understand. Promise you won't tell!"

"Your parents must be told," Hawk insisted. "I have already told mine."

"What did they say?"

"Ask them yourself."

Victoria stiffened in Hawk's arms. Slowly, she swung her head around. Her face reddened with embarrassment when she saw us. "Good evening," she mumbled. "I didn't see you."

I smiled at her, uncertain as to what to say. I could not help glancing at her stomach. How far along was she? Two months? Three?

Victoria did not miss my curious gaze and her cheeks grew even redder.

"It's all right, Victoria," Hawk told

her, giving her shoulders a comforting squeeze. "They understand."

Victoria began to cry then, and my heart went out to her. She was so young. They were both so young.

The Bannermans were beside themselves with anger when Hawk and Victoria told them Victoria was three months pregnant. Lydia Bannerman burst into tears, sobbing hysterically that the family name was ruined. Horace Bannerman pulled a gun on Hawk and ordered him out of the house. Hawk left because he knew it would only cause more trouble if he refused, but he did not go far, in case Victoria needed him.

"You'll be on the train east tomorrow," Horace Bannerman thundered. "Pack your bags."

"No." Victoria stood up to her father for the first time in her life. "I love Hawk. I'm pregnant with his child, and I'm going to marry him."

"But you can't stay here," Lydia Bannerman wailed. "What will people say?"

"I don't care what anybody says," Victoria retorted.

"How can you be so ungrateful after all we've done for you?" Horace Bannerman shouted. "We've given you everything you ever wanted and this is how you repay us? By sneaking off with that dirty

half-breed like a damn squaw! Get out of
my house, you harlot!''

"Daddy!''

"Get out," Horace repeated. "You've
made your bed, now go lay in it.''

I was appalled by the Bannerman's
behavior and even more stunned when
they sold their house and moved out of
Bear Valley, leaving Victoria behind.

I had never heard of anything so cruel.
Naturally, Hawk brought Victoria home.
We all welcomed her with open arms.
Mary gave her a hug and a smile and
assured Victoria that she didn't mind
sharing her bedroom with her future
sister-in-law.

Victoria was deeply hurt by her
parents' actions and she needed Hawk's
reassurance that he loved her, that everything would be all right. I did my best to
make Victoria feel at home, to let her know
we didn't think she was terrible. But it
wasn't until Shadow took her aside and
told her we would be her family from now
on that her spirits picked up.

It was late on a Friday night shortly
after Victoria had moved in with us that
we were roused from bed by the sound of
someone pounding on the door. I followed
Shadow to the front door, my heart in my
throat. Only bad news or a calamity of
some kind would send someone to our
home so late at night. Good news could

wait until morning.

Shadow called, "Who's there?" then opened the door when Morgus Tillman identified himself.

I threw Shadow a worried glance. Morgus Tillman was a big man. He stood six feet eight inches tall, had stringy brown hair, yellow eyes, and a temper said to rival that of a grizzly roused from its winter sleep. What could he possibly want at our house in the middle of the night?

I stared at Morgus as he pushed Hawk into the house ahead of him, gave a small cry of alarm when I saw my son's face. He had been badly beaten. His left eye was swollen shut, his whole face was bruised and discolored.

As Morgus loosened his hold on Hawk's shirt collar, Hawk dropped to his knees, and I screamed as I saw the blood crusted on my son's back.

Shadow's face was like granite, his eyes like black pools of death. "Who did this?" he demanded.

"I did it," Morgus replied blandly. "My daughter's pregnant, and your boy's responsible."

I stared at Hawk. He was still on his knees, his body trembling with pain.

"Hawk?" Shadow's voice was low, commanding.

My son raised his head and met his

father's eyes. "I never touched her," Hawk said clearly.

A small cry drew our attention. Turning, I saw Victoria standing in the bedroom doorway, her face almost as white as the demure cotton nightgown that billowed around her ankles.

Hawk's eyes met Victoria's, begging her to have faith in him. "I never touched her, Vickie, I swear it."

Morgus lifted a meaty fist. "Damn you, you son-of-a-bitch, stop your lying! Morgus swung around to face Shadow. "I caught him kissing my little girl in the woods not two hours ago. It's true!" Morgus swore, seeing the doubt in Shadow's eyes. "Ask him yourself."

"It wasn't how it looked," Hawk said stonily. "I was worried about . . ." He glanced at Victoria and quickly looked away. "About something and I went out for a ride. I stopped at Rabbit's Head Rock, and I was sitting there when Mercy showed up. We started talking and she told me she was in trouble and had to get married. I told her I was sorry, and she begged me to marry her. When I refused, she started to cry, and then she started kissing me, saying she would do anything if I'd marry her before it was too late. That was when Morgus showed up."

"He's lying!" Morgus roared. "I know all about your son. Mercy told me how she saw him diddling that prissy Bannerman girl in the woods, how he was hot for any white girl he could get his hands on. Mercy told me Hawk got her alone in the woods and when she refused to do what he wanted, he raped her. Then, tonight, when she told him about the baby, he refused to do the right thing by her."

"That's a lie!" Hawk shouted. "Mercy was terrified of what you'd do to her when you found out she was pregnant. She would have said anything." Hawk looked up at his father. "I tried to tell Morgus I wasn't the one, but he pulled a gun on me, and when I still wouldn't confess, he hit me a couple of times and then whipped me with his belt. I never touched Mercy, nehyo, you must believe me."

Shadow nodded. "I believe you."

Morgus Tillman's face turned ugly. "I don't give a damn what you believe, Indian," he snarled. "My little girl wouldn't lie and I don't aim to see her shamed. That boy of yours is gonna do the right thing by my girl, or else."

Shadow laughed, a short ugly laugh tinged with bitterness. "Won't marrying a half-breed shame your daughter?"

"Not as much as giving birth to a bastard," Morgus retorted. "You have that boy at my place next Sunday, or I'll come after him again, and this time I'll finish what I started tonight."

"Morgus." Shadow's voice stopped

the big man in his tracks. "If you ever lay a hand on my son, or anyone else in my family again, I will strip the skin from your bones an inch at a time."

"Next Sunday," Morgus repeated tersely, and stalked out of the house.

For a moment, no one moved. Victoria looked like she might faint. Her eyes, so big and blue, never left Hawk's face. I knew she was wondering who to believe, Morgus or Hawk.

Shadow looked grim. His eyes glittered with a deep and implacable hatred that I had not seen in years, and I knew that he would not hesitate to kill Morgus Tillman if the man dared laid a hand on Hawk again.

Slowly, Hawk gained his feet and went to Victoria.

"It isn't true," he said fervently. "You must believe me."

"I want to," Victoria said, not meeting Hawk's eyes. "But I keep remembering that day in the woods. Mercy said you would come knocking at her door, just like everyone else."

"Vickie . . ."

"I don't want to believe her," Victoria said with a sob. "Tell me you never touched her, and I'll believe you. Only don't lie to me, Hawk. I couldn't stand that."

"I never touched her. I swear it."

"Oh, Hawk," Victoria cried, and buried

her face in the hollow of his shoulder.

Hawk put his arms around her, wincing as the movement pulled against his torn flesh.

I looked at Shadow, standing near the fireplace, his face grim. What was he thinking? I remembered how willing everyone had been to believe Shadow was a thief just because he was an Indian. If Morgus went around telling people Hawk had raped his daughter, they would likely believe that, too, especially when it became apparent that Victoria was also pregnant.

Hawk flinched as I swabbed the cuts on his back with carbolic, and I silently raged inside, furious with the man who had dared take a belt to my son. Victoria hovered near Hawk, her face mirroring his pain.

Later, when everyone had gone to bed, Shadow and I sat together on the sofa before the fireplace.

"What are we going to do?" I asked. "He can't marry them both."

Shadow snorted. "Why should he marry Mercy Tillman? Every man old enough to crawl between her thighs has done so."

I glanced pointedly at Shadow, one eyebrow raised. "Every man?" I asked dryly.

Shadow grinned at me. "You know what I mean. Mercy probably does not know who the father is. I think she picked on Hawk because her father would be quick to believe he was guilty."

"Because he's a half-breed," I added glumly.

"Yes."

I did not like the twinge of guilt I saw lurking in Shadow's eyes. I knew what he was thinking, knew he was thinking this would never have happened if I had married a white man instead of a Cheyenne warrior.

"Don't you dare say it," I warned, my voice stern. "It's not our children who are at fault for being part Indian. It's the stupid prejudice of some people who are too blind to see what fine children we have, and nothing more. And if you dare say I should have married a white man, I'll punch you in the nose!"

Shadow laughed softly as my tirade came to an abrupt halt. "Are you through?"

"Yes, but it makes me so mad. Shadow, what are we going to do?"

"Tomorrow, you and I and Hawk will go out to the Tillman place and see Mercy. I want to hear it from her own mouth that Hawk is the father of her child. I want to hear her say it in front of Hawk."

It was shortly after noon when we arrived at the Tillman place. I was amazed that anyone would live in such a hovel.

The house, if it could be called that, was made of unfinished wood, the roof was made of sod. There were no windows; the door was hanging at an odd angle. A few chickens scratched in the dirt, a pig was asleep under a tree, several dogs were stretched out in the sun. A pair of faded overalls hung on a wash line.

Mercy was obviously surprised to see us. Her mouth made a little "o", her eyes grew wide.

"May we come in?" I asked, my nose wrinkling at the smell emanating from the inside of the house.

"Why?"

"We'd like to talk to you, Mercy, if you don't mind."

Mercy Tillman shook her head, her eyes worried as she tried to close the door. Shadow stepped forward, blocking the way, and Mercy took a step back. Hawk and I followed Shadow into the house.

It was the dirtiest place I had ever seen. Unwashed dishes were stacked on the kitchen table, a cat napped on the wood-burning stove, the furniture, what little there was, was shabby and worn.

"What do you want?" Mercy asked, sounding scared. She was dressed in a ragged red skirt; a man's shirt covered her ample breasts.

"Why did you tell your father I raped you?" Hawk's voice was tight, angry, his eyes accusing.

Mercy glanced at Shadow, who was standing against the door, his arms folded over his chest. She licked her lips nervously. "I . . . because it's true, and you've got to marry me."

"Mercy, it's a lie, and you know it."

"Hawk, please marry me. I've got to get married. I'll make you happy." She was crying now, her sobs wracking her body.

"I can't," Hawk said coldly. "Why don't you tell your father who's responsible? Or tell the father of your baby?"

Mercy shook her head, her hands worrying a lock of her hair.

Shadow stepped forward. "Mercy, who is the father of your child?"

Mercy took a step back, her fear of Shadow plain in her face. "Leave me alone."

"We both know Hawk is not the father."

"He is, he is!" she cried. "You've got to believe me!"

"Let's get out of here," Hawk said disgustedly. "She's never going to admit she's lying."

Shadow stepped closer to Mercy, and Mercy looked at me, her eyes pleading for help. "Don't let him hurt me, please!"

"Do not talk nonsense," Shadow said tersely. "I am not going to hurt you." Reaching out, he took Mercy in his arms and held her close. Mercy struggled wildly until she realized she could not escape, and then she stood passive in his arms, her attitude one of defeat. "Mercy, you would not want Hawk to marry you when he loves Victoria. You would not be happy with a man who does not love you. Have you told the father of your child that you are pregnant?"

"I don't know who it is," Mercy wailed unhappily.

My heart went out to the girl. I had never wanted to believe the stories about Mercy Tillman were true, but I believed them now.

"My father doesn't know about me," Mercy said, staring at the floor. "He thinks I'm a good girl. He'll kill me when he finds out what I've done. How can I tell him I don't know who the father is?" She looked up at Shadow, her eyes wild with fear. "Please make Hawk marry me."

"Hawk has troubles of his own," Shadow said ruefully. "He has an obligation to marry Victoria Bannerman."

Mercy frowned, and then she began to laugh hysterically. Shadow gently stroked her hair as her laughter turned to tears.

It was then that Morgus Tillman stomped into the house.

Morgus took in the scene at a glance: Mercy sobbing in Shadow's arms, Hawk staring out the window. He looked at me, and then at Shadow and Mercy.

"What the hell's goin' on here?" he roared.

Mercy jumped at the sound of her father's voice. Her face paled as she saw the rage in his eyes, and she clung to Shadow, hoping he would protect her.

Morgus glared at Shadow, his expression fierce. "No wonder you didn't want your boy to marry up with my girl," Morgus growled. "You're sweet on her yourself."

"Don't be silly," I said, astonished at Tillman's ridiculous accusation. "We came here to talk to Mercy, to see if she'd tell us who the real father of her baby is."

"Hah! Looks to me like the father's right here."

"Do not be a fool, Tillman," Shadow said curtly.

"A fool, am I? I'll show you who's a fool," Morgus gritted through clenched teeth. Dropping the rifle and sack he had been holding, he reached for the knife sheathed on his belt. "You dirty bastard!" He hissed, "I'll teach you to come around sniffing after my girl!"

Shadow pushed Mercy out of the way, then took a quick step to the side, his hand closing on his own knife, his dark eyes wary as he dropped into a crouch, knees slightly bent, knife arm thrust forward, stomach tucked in.

Morgus grinned as he darted a glance at Hawk. "You're next!" he growled, and

lunged forward, his knife driving for
Shadow's heart. I gasped as Shadow
danced out of the way, his own blade
striking out to nick Morgus on the arm as
he stepped in range.

Morgus Tillman was a big man, solid
as a tree. He was not fast, but he was
determined, and my heart was in my
throat as I watched Shadow and Morgus
circle each other, looking for an opening.
They came together in a rush, grunting
with exertion as steel met steel. Tillman's
reach was longer, Shadow was faster,
more agile. Tillman drew blood, his
knife catching Shadow just under his
right arm. Shadow grunted and dodged
out of the way as Tillman struck again.
Shadow was ready this time, and he
ducked under Tillman's knife arm and
plunged the blade into Tillman's side. The
big man grimaced as his free hand struck
Shadow in the back, knocking him to the
floor.

Hawk uttered a strangled cry as he
ran toward Tillman's rifle, but Mercy got
there first, and the two of them began
struggling over the gun. My eyes were
torn between my son and my husband. I
clenched my hands, my nails biting into
my palms, drawing blood, as Shadow
scrambled to his feet. The two men stood
facing each other, panting, bleeding, while
Hawk and Mercy continued to fight over
the rifle.

Suddenly Morgus rushed forward, his arms thrown wide, trapping Shadow in a bear hug. Morgus gave a cry of victory as he lifted his blade, intending to drive it into Shadow's back.

There was a sudden explosion of noise as the rifle went off, and then everything seemed to move in slow motion. Morgus took a step back, his arms falling to his sides, a blank expression on his face. Shadow fell to his knees, and I screamed as the fear became too much to bear. Mercy cried, "Daddy, no!" and then Morgus Tillman crashed to the floor. It was then I saw the blood pumping from the wound in his back.

Mercy threw herself over her father's body, sobbing hysterically, as I rushed to Shadow's side.

"I'm all right, Hannah," Shadow said. "His blade just creased my side. It isn't serious."

I nodded, unable to speak. The wound, though not deep, was bleeding profusely. I glanced around the Tillman cabin, looking for a bit of clean cloth and found none. Hawk came to stand beside me, his dark eyes filled with concern.

"I'm all right," Shadow said. "Look after Mercy."

With a nod, Hawk went to kneel beside the girl. Gently, Hawk lifted her away from her father's body and held her in his arms while she cried, his hand stroking her blond hair while he murmured to her, assuring her that everything would work out for the best.

Turning my attention back to my husband, I tore a strip of cloth from my petticoat and wrapped it around the wound in Shadow's side, then bandaged the shallow gash under his right arm.

We took Mercy home with us. Victoria glanced worriedly at Hawk as Mercy stood uncertainly in the middle of the parlor. Mercy's eyes were still red; there were bloodstains on her skirt.

"There was an accident," Hawk explained to Victoria. "Mercy's going to stay with us for awhile."

"She's going to stay here?" Victoria exclaimed, aghast.

Mercy Tillman stiffened her spine as she glared at Victoria. "Don't give yourself airs, Victoria Bannerman," she warned. "I know all about you."

Victoria's cheeks turned scarlet. "Know what?" she asked hoarsely.

"I know all about that baby you're carrying," Mercy sneered. "You're no better than I am, after all."

"At least I know who my baby's father is," Victoria retorted cruelly. "Do you?"

"That's enough," Shadow said sternly. "I do not care how you two feel about each other, but I will not have you spitting and clawing like two cats under my roof. Is that understood?''

Victoria and Mercy nodded sullenly.

Later, Victoria and Mary prepared dinner while I took Mercy into my room to clean her up. Dressed in one of Mary's everyday cottons, her hair washed and her skin freshly scrubbed, Mercy Tillman looked like a different girl.

Dinner was a strained meal. Victoria and Mercy glared at each other, Hawk looked uncomfortable. Blackie, usually so full of chatter, was silent.

Mercy went to bed immediately after dinner. Hawk and Blackie would sleep in the lodge while Mercy stayed with us.

My father was a big help in the next few days. He helped Hawk bury Morgus Tillman in the deep woods and advised us not to say anything about the fight between Shadow and Morgus. There was no lawman in Bear Valley to ask questions that no one wanted to answer, Pa said with a shrug, and it was best to keep everything quiet.

I wasn't sure we were doing the right thing, but Mercy begged us not to tell anyone what had happened. She told people her father had died in his sleep, and no one seemed to doubt her. Few people in Bear Valley cared for Morgus Tillman. He had been a gruff, mean-spirited man, and most of those who knew him seemed relieved that he was gone.

A week later, Hawk drove Mercy to

Steel's Crossing where she caught a train back East. She had a cousin there who would look after her, she said. Pa had given Mercy twenty dollars spending money, Mary had given her a couple of dresses so she would have something decent to wear, and I had packed her a lunch to take on the train. Mercy took it all as her due, offering no thanks in return. We never heard from Mercy Tillman again.

Two days later, Hawk and Victoria were married in our parlor by the Reverend Thorsen. The Smythes, George and Ruth Tippitt, and the Browns came to the wedding, bringing gifts and good wishes.

Victoria's best friend, Jenny Lee McCall, was her maid of honor. Jenny Lee wore a dress of light blue and carried a bouquet of yellow daisies.

Victoria looked lovely in Mattie Smythe's wedding gown. The dress was of Ivory satin, with a high neck, long sleeves, and a bustle adorned with flowers. Delicate ivory lace edged the stand-up collar and cuffs. The bodice was tight, the skirt long and full. Victoria carried a bouquet of wildflowers. I thought she looked like a princess out of a fairy tale.

Hawk wore a black suit and vest, starched white shirt, and a gray tie. He looked quite uncomfortable and quite handsome. His face was solemn as he took

Victoria's hand in his and recited the vows that made Vickie his wife.

I stood beside Shadow, my eyes damp with tears as Victoria Bannerman became my son's wife. Despite the circumstances, it was a lovely ceremony. The bride was beautiful, the groom was undeniably handsome, and they were very much in love.

I saw Pa give Rebecca's hand a squeeze as Hawk kissed Victoria, and then the ceremony was over and Blackie and Mary gathered around, eager to kiss the bride and hug the groom. I hoped with all my heart that Hawk and Victoria would be as happy together as Shadow and I had always been.

As Hawk and Victoria thanked the Reverend Thorsen, Shadow turned to me and whispered "Someday" in my ear, reminding me that he had not forgotten his promise that someday we would be married in the white man's way.

We had a small party after the ceremony. Ruth Tippitt gave Victoria and Hawk a lovely tablecloth she had crocheted. The Browns gave them a quilt, the Smythes gave them a clock.

It was a pleasant afternoon. We ate cake and drank champagne that Pa had brought back from Pennsylvania. Mattie Smythe and Lorna Clancy got a little tipsy and began to warn Victoria about men and their peculiar quirks. It was sundown when our guests went home.

Hawk and Victoria had decided to live in the Cheyenne lodge until they could build a cabin of their own. Shadow and Hawk had moved the lodge the day before to a place Victoria had chosen. It stood on a flat piece of ground, shaded by trees. A stream gurgled nearby.

Shadow had given Hawk and Victoria fifteen acres of land adjoining ours, as well as five good mares and a young Appaloosa stallion, for a wedding gift. Pa and Rebecca gave them a twenty dollar gold piece and a set of dishes. It wasn't much to start a life on, I thought, but Shadow and I had started on much less.

I knew life would not be easy for Victoria, although Hawk was looking forward to living in the lodge. He had plans to raise and train horses, like his father, and he was young and eager. He would not mind the hardships of living in a crude Indian lodge, of having to do without. He loved the land, loved the freedom of the outdoors.

But what of Victoria? How would she adjust to living in a hide lodge? As an only child, she had been pampered and spoiled by her parents all her life. I knew she was accustomed to a nice house, nice furniture, a soft bed. There would be no luxuries now, no extra money to spend on fancy hats or dresses or pretty nick-nacks, no time to fritter away. She would have to learn to cook over an open fire, she would have to sleep on a pallet on the ground, carry water from the stream, cook and clean and sew. And soon there would be a baby to care for.

I saw her smile up at Hawk, her eyes brimming with love. Would her feelings for Hawk survive the first few months of hard living until they could build and furnish a cabin of their own? In my heart, I felt certain their love would endure, but I knew only time would tell.

XXVII

Hawk

They had said goodbye to Hawk's parents and the wedding guests and now they were standing in the shadow of the Cheyenne lodge that was to be their home. The night was dark and warm, the sky awash with a million twinkling stars and a yellow moon. In the distance, a coyote bayed at the moon.

"I love you, Vickie," Hawk said in a voice that was thick with emotion. "People will say I married you because of the baby and for no other reason, but it isn't true. I married you because I love you very, very much."

"And I love you," Victoria murmured fervently. "Very, very much."

"If you were an Indian girl, your male relatives would have put you on a blanket and carried you into my lodge," Hawk said, smiling wryly. "But since we were

married the white man's way..." He
shrugged as he swung her up in his arms
and carried her over the threshold of the
lodge. "Welcome to your new home, wife."
He lingered over the last word, savoring
the sound of it.

"This is all new to me," Victoria said,
gesturing at the lodge and its meager
furnishings. "But I'll try my best to make
you happy. I promise."

"You've already made me happy,"
Hawk said quietly. His breath was warm
on her neck as he carried her toward the
buffalo robes spread at the rear of the
lodge. Gently, he placed her on the soft
robes, his eyes caressing her face. She was
his now, truly his. He could hold her and
love her without feeling guilty, without
fear of discovery. He could enfold her in
his arms all night long, kiss her sweet lips
at the beginning of each new day. A fierce
surge of possessiveness swept over him.
She was his woman, his wife, and he would
live and die for her.

Victoria smiled up at Hawk, feeling
unaccountably shy. They had been alone
before, but never like this. She was
Hawk's wife now, and he could do to her
whatever he wished. She could not go
running home if things did not work out.
Her father's words rang in the back of her
mind: "You've made your bed," he had
declared spitefully. "Now lay in it."

Suddenly apprehensive, she gazed

around the lodge. It was large, roomy and alien. There was a firepit in the center of the lodge, a pair of willow backrests, a wooden crate that held a blue enamel coffee pot and several iron cooking pots, as well as some mismatched silverware, towels, and glasses. A large trunk held her clothes and a few personal belongings. Hawk's rifle was propped against one of the lodgepoles, his clothing was stacked in a neat pile beside his rifle.

Victoria glanced down at the furry robe that would be her bed until they could afford a regular one, then lifted her eyes to Hawk's face. The love in his eyes reached out to her and her doubts evaporated like morning dew. She could endure any hardship, any deprivation, so long as Hawk was at her side.

How tenderly he made love to her that night, his hands gentle as they pleasured her in ways only he knew. He treated her as if she were a fragile flower that might wilt and die if not handled with the utmost care, and Victoria was deeply moved by Hawk's tender concern. His gentleness, his patience, made her feel as though they were making love for the very first time, and surely no one else in all the world had ever known such bliss.

The next few days were paradise. They made love and slept and made love again. They bathed in the stream. At first, Victoria was shy about bathing in front of

Hawk, embarrassed to stand naked before him in the full light of day, but she soon overcame her modesty. She liked having Hawk admire her, liked the way his dark eyes moved lovingly over her bare flesh. And she liked looking at him. He was tall and lean, sleek and muscular as a panther. Looking at him as he emerged from the stream shaking the water from his long black hair, she could easily visualize him as a warrior, for he was very Indian in his appearance and beliefs. Each morning, he went alone to the stream to meditate. He was respectful of all life: the animals that lived in the hills, the fish in the streams, the squirrels and jays that sang in the trees. He was a very religious man in his way, but he refused to go to church with her on Sunday, declaring Heammawihio could not be found within the four square walls of the white man's house of worship. However, he did not object to her going, and Victoria went to church on Sunday with Hannah.

Hawk's love for Victoria grew with each passing day. She was cheerful and good-natured, a little embarrassed because she did not know how to cook over an open fire, or how to skin the game he brought home. But she was eager and willing to learn. She never complained about living in a Cheyenne lodge, or lamented the fact that they sat on the ground and slept on a pile of furs.

Often, he placed his hand over her abdomen, his heart swelling with love for the child she carried beneath her heart. He refused to let her do any heavy work, insisted she take a nap each afternoon.

They had been married less than a week when Helen and Porter Sprague came to offer their congratulations. The Spragues gave them a pair of silver candlesticks as a wedding gift.

They did not stay long, and Hawk knew it was because, even though they wanted to be friendly, they were uncomfortable visiting in a hide lodge.

"We have to be getting back," Helen explained as they started for the door. "Porter's mother is living with us now and she doesn't like to be left alone for too long."

"She's almost sixty," Porter added with a shrug. "You understand?"

"Yes," Victoria said graciously. "Thank you for coming, and thank you for the lovely gift."

Hawk grinned at Victoria when they were alone. "Silver candlesticks," he muttered, shaking his head. "What are we going to do with silver candlesticks?"

"Use them," Victoria replied.

And that night, they ate dinner by candlelight.

Later, Hawk made love to Victoria in the dim glow of the candlelight. His hands gently caressed her smooth skin, lingering on her breasts, imagining what it would be like when her breasts were swollen with milk. His mouth nuzzled her sweet flesh while his hands stroked the hidden valley between her slim thighs, and when he could no longer hold back, he plunged into her, giving himself over to the wonder of being enveloped in her warm womanly softness . . .

The next day, Sam and Rebecca brought them a milk cow, a pail, and a stool.

"How are you getting along?" Rebecca asked Victoria while the men were outside building a corral for the cow.

"Fine," Victoria said, making light of the rough housing and lack of creature comforts she had known with her parents. "Come on, I'll show you where we're going to build our cabin."

Victoria was all smiles as they walked through the rooms they had planned. "Here's the kitchen," Victoria said, indicating a large area in the back. "This will be our bedroom, and the baby's room will be here." She moved toward the front of the proposed house. "This will be the parlor."

Rebecca nodded, glad to see that Victoria was happy. "It's going to be very nice," she said. "I notice the front door faces east."

"Yes, Hawk insisted on it. He said all

Cheyenne lodges face the rising sun."

"I'm glad you're happy, Vickie."

"I am. Hawk is so good to me. I love him very much. I only wish . . ."

"What?"

"I wish everyone knew how wonderful he is. We went into town to the mercantile the other day to buy a few things and Hawk almost got into a fight when someone made a nasty remark about white women who marry half-breeds." Victoria's eyes flashed angrily. "Why do people care who my husband is? Hawk is the most wonderful man I've ever known. He's honest and caring and reliable. Why should the color of his skin make any difference?"

"I can't answer that, Victoria. I guess people are always a little afraid of someone who's different. And you've got to remember there are a lot of people living in Bear Valley who lost loved ones during the Indian wars. People are slow to forget that kind of thing. And slow to forgive."

"But the Indian wars have been over for twenty years!" Victoria exclaimed.

"I know. You'll just have to be patient."

"Like Hannah?"

"Yes. Sooner or later, people will realize what a good man Hawk is. Many of the people in the valley who once thought Shadow was a savage have become his friends."

"I guess you're right," Victoria allowed. "The Spragues came to congratulate us on our wedding just yesterday. And when we were in town, Mrs. Turner gave us six quarts of preserves and two loaves of bread." Victoria smiled. "Mr. Smythe volunteered to help us build our cabin. He said he'd bring David, Ethan, Frank, Gene, and Henry out to help next Saturday morning and they'd have the frame up by nightfall."

"That's wonderful!" Rebecca said enthusiastically. "Hannah and I will bring lunch so you won't have to cook."

Leland Smythe was as good as his word and he had his five boys hard at work by seven o'clock Saturday morning. His two older sons, Benjamin and Cabel, were also there. Ben and Cabel were both married now with children of their own. The Smythe's oldest son, Abel, had gone to California several years ago. He lived in San Francisco and was the president of a bank. His mother was very proud of him.

It was a busy day. The men worked steadily until noon, then broke for lunch. Hawk, usually reserved around everyone but family, seemed happy and relaxed, pleased that some of his neighbors had come to help with the cabin raising. Sam had brought a jug and the men passed it around while the women looked on, frowning. Victoria was pleased when Hawk let the jug pass by.

When the men went back to work, Rebecca, Mary, Hannah and Victoria did the dishes, then sat in the shade, quilting a pink and blue quilt for the baby.

It was a lovely, productive day and as Leland Smythe had promised, the frame was up before nightfall.

"We'll be back next week to put the roof on," Frank Smythe hollered as he climbed into his father's wagon. "See you bright and early."

Leland Smythe waved as he took up the reins. "Hey, Sam!" he called jovially. "Don't forget the jug!"

XXVIII

Summer 1897

It was summer in Bear Valley. Wildflowers bloomed on the hillsides, trees and bushes were heavy with fruit, my garden yielded an abundance of squash and tomatoes and beans, carrots and radishes and onions. Eight of Shadow's mares had dropped Appaloosa foals. I could see them romping in the pasture near the house as I hung a load of wash on the line to dry.

It had been a good year after all. Hawk and Victoria seemed to be more in love with each passing day. Their cabin was almost completed and they were excited about their new home, and about the baby which was due late in September. Pa and Rebecca were thrilled with the prospect of being great-grandparents. Most of the families in the valley had accepted Victoria's marriage to Hawk without much thought, though I knew

some of them would not have been so
tolerant and understanding if it had been
their own daughter who had married a
half-breed. There were a few skeptics who
predicted dire consequences from such a
match. And when it became obvious that
Victoria had been pregnant before the
wedding, the town gossips had a field day.
The couple had only gotten married
because of the baby, some said, love had
nothing to do with it. Hawk had raped her,
others declared with conviction. That was
why the Bannermans had been so upset.
No, others insisted, Victoria had been all
too willing to take up with a half-breed and
that was why the Bannermans had been so
ashamed, why they had left the valley.
Victoria was no better than a harlot,
whispered others, and it served her right
to be in the family way and married to a
half-breed.

Fortunately, no one was foolish
enough to say such things when Shadow
or Hawk were within hearing distance.
Gradually, the gossip died away. Who
could possibly believe Victoria had been
raped when she looked at her new husband
with such adoration in her eyes? Who
could find fault with a couple who were so
obviously in love, so eager to make a home
for their child?

A child. I would be a grandmother
before the year was out.

I smiled, amused at the thought. Was

it possible I was old enough to be a grandmother? The years had flown by so
quickly, yet I still felt the same as I had at
twenty. It didn't seem possible that Hawk
was a man, married, and about to become
a father.

I thought of Shadow. At 41, he was
still strong and virile, more handsome now
than when I had first fallen in love with
him. I remembered the day Elk Dreamer
had married us in the Cheyenne way. We
had been camped along the Big Bend of
the Rosebud River, waiting for Custer. It
had been May, 1876. I had worn a white
doeskin dress decorated with long fringe
and hundreds of tiny blue beads. A single
white rose had been my only adornment.
Shadow had worn a white buckskin shirt,
white fringed leggings and moccasins. A
white eagle feather had been tied in his
long black hair.

I was not the same girl I had been that
day so long ago, and Shadow was not the
same man. Time and circumstances had
changed us, matured us, strengthened our
love.

So many things had changed in the
last twenty years. The Indians no longer
roamed wild and free, the buffalo were
almost gone. Bear Valley had grown into a
good-sized town. We had a telegraph office
now, a small hotel, a newspaper, a
restaurant, even a lawman. Progress was
making itself felt. Steel's Crossing had a

telephone. Pa and Rebecca had a phono-
graph. There was talk of the railroad
coming to Bear Valley.

So many changes . . . and yet, sometimes at night, I missed the happiness of
the old days when Shadow and I had
shared a hide lodge in the wilds of Dakota.
Our grandchildren would never know the
peaceful quiet of a night in the Black Hills,
or know the wonder of seeing a herd of
buffalo stampede across the open prairie,
heads low, tails flying like flags. Our
grandsons would never hear the sound of
drums, or know the thrill of riding after
buffalo, or experience the pain and ecstasy
of the Sun Dance. Our granddaughters
would never court beneath a big red
blanket, or hear the plaintive call of the
flute played by a bronze-skinned warrior.

With a sigh, I picked up my laundry
basket and walked back to the house.
Shadow had left early that morning to
help Pa round up some cattle that had
broken down a fence and wandered off into
the hills. Blackie had gone with his father.
Mary had gone to spend a few days with
Patience Osborn, who had just had a baby
girl and needed help with her other three
children while she recuperated from a
difficult birth.

I paused to admire our house as I
drew near. It didn't look the same as it had
ten years ago. The trees we had planted
had grown and now gave shade to the

house. There were flowers blooming on either side of the porch. A white picket fence surrounded the front yard. Shadow had built it for me last year just because I had always wanted one. Three cats napped beside the front door. A squirrel, one of Blackie's strays, chattered at me from the roof as I started up the porch steps.

I knew, the minute I opened the front door and entered the house, that something was wrong. I stood inside the doorway, suddenly tense all over as a coldness swept over me.

Chiding myself for being foolish, I closed the door and started for the kitchen.

"Hello, Hannah."

His voice stopped me in my tracks and I felt an icy chill slither down my spine as I turned to face him.

"Hello, Joshua."

He smiled at me, a decidedly possessive smile. He had not changed much in the eleven years since I had last seen him. He was a little thinner, perhaps, his hair was gray, but other than that, he looked much the same as always. And yet he was not the same. There was a hint of madness lurking in his bright blue eyes, and it frightened me more than I cared to admit.

"Are you ready?" Josh asked.

"Ready?" My heart was pounding wildly in my breast. I tried to think, to stay calm, but I could think of nothing except that Joshua was here to take me away. His next words confirmed my worst suspicions.

"Surely you knew I would come for you, darling," he said huskily. "Don't I always come for you?"

"Yes, you do." My thoughts raced, going nowhere. I was alone in the house. Shadow would not be home until late, if at all.

"Pack your things, Hannah, dear. It's time to go."

"Go where?" I was stalling for time, wondering how I could keep Josh here until Shadow came home.

"California," Joshua replied. He came toward me, his hands reaching out to clasp my shoulders. "I've missed you," he murmured, and kissed me, his lips grinding against mine as his hands drew my body closer to his. I cringed as his fingers moved through my hair, down my neck, along my back, over my hips. His mouth moved over my face, kissing my eyes and cheeks, returning to cover my mouth. I longed to push him away, but some inner voice warned me not to fight him.

I smiled at him when he finally let me go. "Would you like something to eat, Josh? I was just about to have lunch."

His eyes mirrored his indecision and then he said, "Sure, why not. You always were a good cook."

I smiled woodenly and went into the kitchen. He followed me, of course. I put the coffee pot on the stove, began to slice some roast beef for sandwiches. Josh sat at the table, his eyes watching my every move.

I served Josh, then sat down across from him. If only Shadow would come home early. If only I could get my hands on the pistol I kept in the bedroom. And yet, even as the thought crossed my mind, I knew I could not kill Josh.

"That was good, darling," Joshua said. Pushing away from the table, he stood up. "Let's go. We've got time to put some miles behind us if we start now."

"I'll just do the dishes . . ."

"No need," he said. "Just pack your things."

"All right. I won't be a minute. Why don't you have another cup of coffee?" I kissed Josh on the cheek. Perhaps he wouldn't follow me if he thought I was eager to go with him. Trying not to run in my haste to get away from him, I turned and walked toward the bedroom I shared with Shadow. If I could sneak out the window, I could run down the valley and stay with the Smythes until Shadow came home.

"I'll help you pack," Josh said, coming up behind me.

I nodded, unable to speak. He wasn't going to let me out of his sight for a moment. Despair dropped over my shoulders as I recalled the days I had spent gagged, bound hand and foot in the wagon. Was that what waited for me now? How would I stand being Joshua's prisoner again? The thought of his hands touching me filled me with dread. Oh, God, please don't let me have to live through that nightmare again.

Taking a valise from the armoire, I began to pack my belongings. My hands were shaking so badly I could hardly fold my clothes.

"Where have you been all this time, Josh?" I asked, not liking the silence, or the way he was staring at me.

"Prison," Josh answered bitterly. "I spent over ten years in that damn jail. But I'm here now." He laughed softly and without humor. "I had to kill four men to get out of that damn jail, but it was worth it. We'll be happy now. No one will find us in California." Joshua's blue eyes narrowed darkly as he noticed Shadow's clothes hanging in the armoire next to mine. "That redskin," he growled. "Are you still shacked up with him?"

I hesitated to answer, yet I knew it was pointless to lie. "Yes."

Josh grunted. "How many bastards has he given you?"

"I have three children."

"Where are they?"

"They went to Steel's Crossing with

my father," I lied. "They'll be gone for several days."

"And the redskin?"

"He's hunting."

Joshua nodded and I felt a shiver of apprehension as he began to stroke the butt of the gun shoved into the waistband of his pants.

"I always meant to kill that Injun," Josh mused. "Maybe I'll just wait around and bushwhack him when he gets back."

"Let's not waste time waiting for him," I said quickly. "He could be gone for days." I laid my hand on Joshua's arm and smiled at him, forcing as much warmth as I could into my expression. "California sounds exciting, Josh. Let's hurry."

Joshua looked at me hard, his blue eyes probing mine. Then he grinned. "Let's go," he said. He closed my valise, and then he kissed me. "California," he murmured. "We'll make it this time."

XXIX

Shadow

It was nearly eight o'clock that night when Shadow returned home. He, Blackie, and Hawk had put in a hard day rounding up three dozen cattle that had broken down a section of fence and wandered into the hills south of Kincaid's cabin. Eight hours in the saddle made for a long day, and chasing a bunch of cattle that didn't want to be caught was never easy. Neither was repairing the fence the cattle had trampled in their clumsy haste to reach the grass on the other side.

Shadow grinned ruefully as he rode toward the corral behind the house. Who would have thought the day would come when Two Hawks Flying, the last fighting chief of the Plains, would be chasing the white man's cattle instead of the shaggy-haired buffalo? Who would have dreamed that a Cheyenne warrior would abandon a

snug hide lodge for a square house made of
wood?

But then, his life had changed in so
many ways. He lived, ate, and spoke like a
white man. He kept the white man's time,
purchased supplies with the white man's
currency, lived surrounded by white men
who were once his enemies. His long black
hair and dusty buckskins were the only
visible sign that he was different from his
neighbors—that, and the color of his skin.

So many changes. No longer did he
live within the sacred circle of the
Cheyenne. No longer did he hunt and live
and fight in the old way. And yet, he was
not unhappy. He had three fine, healthy
children, a lovely daughter-in-law. Soon he
would be a grandfather. The thought
brought a smile. But best of all, there was
Hannah. Her sweet smile brightened the
darkest days and the dreariest nights. His
love for her remained a vital force in his
life.

Dismounting outside the corral, he un-
saddled Smoke and threw the rig over the
top rail of the corral. He gave the horse a
quick rubdown, turned the stallion loose in
the corral, forked it some fresh hay.

Tired as he was, his steps quickened
as he headed for the house. He was eager
to see Hannah, to hold her in his arms. It
was something that still amazed him, the
way he missed her when they were apart
for more than a few hours. Even after all

the years they had lived together, he looked forward to being with her at the end of the day.

He knew the house was empty the minute he opened the door. Walking noiselessly through the dark parlor, he struck a match and lit the lamp beside the sofa. There was no note waiting for him on the table to tell him where she had gone. Frowning, he picked up the lamp and crossed the parlor to the bedroom he and Hannah shared.

He paused in the doorway. The armoire was open and he could see that some of her clothes were gone. Nothing else was missing.

Turning on his heel, he went to the kitchen. The room was empty, clean except for a few dishes left on the table. His frown deepened. Hannah never left dirty dishes on the table.

He went into Mary's room. His daughter was staying with one of the women in the south end of the valley. Mary's bed was neatly made. A vase of wildflowers stood on the small oak dresser.

He felt a twinge of unease as he left Mary's room and went into Blackie's room, searching for some clue as to Hannah's whereabouts. Blackie's room was cluttered. A cage held a pair of young sparrows that had fallen from a nest. A tortoise slept in a box beside the bed.

Returning to the parlor, Shadow felt a moment of relief that Blackie had decided to spend the night with Hawk and Victoria because something was wrong, very wrong.

Placing the lamp on the table, he surveyed the parlor, his keen eyes taking in every detail. There was no sign of a struggle, everything was in its usual place. It looked as if Hannah had tidied up the house, packed her clothes, and walked out. But why?

It was too dark to scout her trail and he spent the long hours until dawn pacing from one end of the cabin to the other. He would have preferred to be outside, but he dared not walk in the yard for fear of erasing Hannah's tracks.

Hannah. In his mind, he pictured her ready smile, the smooth creamy skin that remained smooth and unblemished despite the passage of time. He remembered the way her eyes lit up when she met him at the door, the way she always melted into his arms, lifting her face for his kiss.

Damn! Where was she?

The hours passed by slowly and his thoughts were filled with the woman who had been the best part of his life since he first met her almost thirty years ago. Thirty years. Where had the time gone?

He remembered the day he first saw Hannah out at Rabbit's Head Rock. He had been twelve that day; Hannah had been a skinny child of nine. Even then he had been drawn to her, captivated by the color of her hair and the warmth in her gray eyes. The times he had spent with her family were some of the fondest memories of his childhood.

When he turned sixteen, he had stopped going to the Kincaid cabin and spent all his time preparing to be a warrior. But he never forgot Hannah, nor would he ever forget the day he had seen her, quite by accident, walking along the riverbank with Joshua and Orin Berdeen. The sight of her had taken his breath away and he had known at that moment that he would never be happy with any other woman. He had gone south to spend the winter with his people and when they returned to Bear Valley, he had but one thought in mind: to see Hannah again.

He had gone to the river crossing every day for the next month, hoping to find her alone, and his patience had been rewarded. He would never forget that day. It had been Hannah's sixteenth birthday and she had gone to the river early in the morning for a swim. Even now, some twenty-two years later, he could clearly recall how the sun had danced in her flaming red hair and the way the water had glistened on her smooth ivory skin. Naked and unaware she was being watched, she had been the most beautiful creature he had ever seen as she swam in the clear water and then stood, drying, on the bank afterward. He remembered how her cheeks had burned with embarrassment when he had made his presence known. They had spoken only a little that day, but there had been no need for words. He had known from that brief meeting that Hannah would be his, and Hannah had known it, too. They had met at the river crossing the next morning at first light and gone straight into each other's arms. Hannah had begged him to kiss her, and when he hesitated, she had pulled his head down and pressed her lips to his. He had been unprepared for the rush of desire her kiss aroused . . .

He swore aloud. Where was she? Why had she left without a word? Hannah. He remembered how she had seduced him into a proposal of marriage, how tenderly she had cared for him when the settlers had attacked him and left him for dead, how eagerly she had accepted his way of life when he had taken her to live with his people after her home was attacked by the Sioux.

With the coming of dawn, he was outside, his keen eyes searching the ground. It took but a moment to find the tracks of a man wearing city shoes. Sitting on his heels, Shadow easily read the sign left in the soft dirt. The man had gone into the house. Later, Hannah had entered the house. Sometime later, Hannah and the man had left the house together. They walked side by side. There was no sign of a struggle, no scuffed prints to indicate Hannah had tried to run away from the man.

Rising, Shadow followed the twin set of tracks some distance into the brush, and there he found the prints of two shod horses.

Muttering an oath, he returned to the house and left a short note for Blackie, telling him to stay with Hawk until someone came for him. That done, he turned out the stock that was penned in the corrals, saddled Smoke, and began to trail the man who had come for Hannah.

Who was the man? The thought pounded in his brain as the miles went by. Who could show up at the house and take Hannah away without a struggle?

With an oath, Shadow put the spotted stallion into an easy lope. Hannah and the stranger had about a sixteen hour lead, judging by the tracks. Later that morning, he found the ashes of the fire where they had spent the night. He stirred the ashes, studied the horse droppings. They still had a good lean on him, but he would catch them. Of that, he was certain.

Riding on, his mind continued to play back scenes of his life with Hannah, and he remembered how she had ridden the war trail at his side, never complaining.

How she had nursed the sick and comforted the dying. How bitterly she had wept when their first child had been born dead. How she had married a man she didn't love to save his life . . .

Like a bolt of lightning slashing through blackened skies, the answer came. Joshua Berdeen. Somehow, the man had found Hannah and forced her to go with him. Forced her? A niggling doubt surfaced in the back of Shadow's mind. There had been no sign of a struggle back at the house, no indication that Hannah had been made to leave against her will.

A sharp pain tore at Shadow's heart. Had she gone willingly with Berdeen? Had she been waiting for the man to come for her all along? No! There had to be another answer.

Driven by his growing anger and frustration, he swung into the saddle, gave the stallion a sharp kick. The horse broke into a run, its long easy stride carrying him quickly across the miles. West, the tracks went. Always west.

At dark, he reined the stallion to a halt in a copse of aspens. Hobbling the stud, he sank down on his heels and stared into the darkness. He had not taken time to pack food or water, but he felt no need for sustenance. Anger was his meat, hatred his drink.

As the sun began to rise in the sky, he stripped off his buckskin shirt and pants and tossed them aside. With his clothing went the thin veneer of civilization he had worn for the past twelve years. Now, clad only in a wolfskin clout and moccasins, he swung aboard the stallion's bare back and picked up Berdeen's trail.

He pushed the stallion hard, closing the distance that separated him from his woman. He stopped at noon to breathe the stud, let the animal drink from a shallow stream. Plucking a handful of berries from a bush, he crushed them in his hand, then applied the color to his cheeks and chest in broad crimson slashes. This day, he was a warrior on the hunt, and his prey was man. This day, a man would die. If it was his enemy, he would take his scalp and rejoice; if it was to be his enemy who emerged from the battle victorious, then he would go to meet Heammawihio dressed as a warrior, with paint on his face and a weapon in his hand.

Kneeling on the ground, he raised his arms toward heaven. "Hear me, Man Above," he cried in a loud voice. "Give me strength to overcome my enemy."

He knelt in the gathering dusk for almost an hour, his head thrown back, his arms stretched upward, a prayer on his lips.

In the distance, he heard the cry of a hawk. "Be strong," the bird seemed to say. "Be strong, and everything you desire shall be yours."

Face set in determined lines, Shadow swung aboard the stallion and resumed his search.

It was the last hour before dusk when he found Joshua Berdeen's night camp. Dismounting, he left Smoke tethered to a live oak some twenty yards away, and then walked boldly forward to meet Joshua Berdeen for the last time.

XXX

The days I spent with Joshua were filled with tension. He was clearly mad, and I feared to say or do anything that might spark his anger. So long as I agreed with him, he was easygoing and quick to laugh, but the moment I disagreed with him, his temper flared and he grew angry and violent.

As before, he kept my hands bound at all times. I was never allowed a moment alone. While riding, he tied my hands to the pommel of my saddle; my horse's reins were looped over Joshua's saddle horn. At night, when it was time for bed, he tied my feet together, slipped a noose over my neck and tied the end to his belt, or to a tree limb.

My thoughts were ever with Shadow. What had he thought when he arrived home and found me gone? I knew he would come after me. Perhaps, even now, he was in pursuit. Joshua had made no effort to cover our tracks. A novice warrior could have trailed us with no difficulty at all. Was Josh deliberately making it easy for Shadow to follow us? Was he still determined to kill the man he considered a rival for my love?

I had just poured Josh a cup of coffee when Shadow stepped noiselessly into the firelight. For the brief moment before Joshua became aware of Shadow's presence, there were just the two of us. Shadow's eyes met mine across three feet of barren ground and a flood of warmth suffused my whole body. He had come for me, just as I had known he would. I smiled at him. In spite of my fears for his safety, in spite of Joshua sitting an arm's length away, I smiled, my heart swelling with joy because Shadow was near. He looked tall and formidable in the light of the flames. The firelight cast golden highlights on his bronzed flesh. The paint smeared on his cheeks and torso looked like blood.

Shadow came to a halt a short distance from where Joshua was sitting on the ground, his back propped against a tree. Josh sprang to his feet when he saw Shadow, his hand grabbing for the gun tucked into the waistband of his pants. I gasped and took a step backward. I knew Joshua would not hesitate to kill Shadow, and I could not bear to watch. Yet I could not turn away.

"You!" Josh breathed in disbelief. "What are you doing here?"

"I have come for my woman."

"She's my wife, you dirty redskin, not yours," Josh shouted. "I've got the paper to prove it." He pulled a crumpled piece of parchment from his pants pocket and waved it at Shadow triumphantly. "See?"

"She is my woman," Shadow repeated quietly. "The mother of my children. She will never be yours."

Joshua stared at Shadow for a long time, a trace of fear surfacing in his eyes. Shadow loomed tall and savage in the light of the flickering flames. I could see all of Joshua's old hatred for Indians swelling within him and I knew he was remembering that his parents and his brother had been killed by the Sioux in Bear Valley back in 1875. Josh had gone off to Fort Lincoln to join the Army after his family was killed, determined to fight against the Sioux and the Cheyenne, to avenge the death of his loved ones by shedding as much Indian blood as possible. He had been with Reno at the Little Big Horn on the fateful day in June, when his hero, General George Armstrong Custer and his men had been slaughtered. Josh had never forgiven the Indians for Custer's death, either.

And now, here stood Shadow, the epitome of all that Joshua hated and feared. Shadow's hair, long and inky black, fell to his waist. Red paint was streaked across his cheeks and down his broad chest. His firm copper-hued flesh glistened in the firelight, while his eyes, black as the bowels of hell, burned bright with his own hatred, and a lust for blood.

"She's mine," Joshua said. "I'll kill you and her before I let you have her!"

Shadow's eyes narrowed ominously as Joshua threatened my life.

"Go away," Josh cried, his voice edged with panic. "Go away!"

But Shadow did not go away and Joshua raised his gun and leveled it at Shadow's chest.

I pressed my hand over my mouth to keep from screaming out loud as Shadow took a step forward, closing the distance between himself and Joshua.

Joshua took a step backward, and then another, his eyes wild. "I'll shoot!" he warned, his voice rising hysterically. "I'll shoot if you don't go away."

But Shadow moved steadily forward. There was no fear in his face, none in his eyes. Slowly, he walked toward Joshua, and Joshua panicked.

With a cry, Josh jerked the trigger. The bullet, meant for Shadow's heart, went wide and grazed his left shoulder. Blood dripped onto the red paint daubed on his chest, and still he came steadily forward. Josh fired his gun a second time, but again his panic spoiled his aim and the bullet plowed into the ground several feet behind Shadow. Again and again, Josh fired and missed. And now Shadow was only inches away, his dark eyes blazing with anger as his hand closed over the gun, wresting it from Joshua's grasp.

"Go ahead, you dirty red bastard," Josh rasped. "Go ahead and kill me."

Shadow nodded, his eyes filled with contempt as he tossed Joshua's gun into a thorn bush. Then, with a ghost of a smile playing over his lips, he withdrew two long-bladed knives from his belt.

Hope flickered in the back of Joshua's blue eyes as Shadow thrust one of the knives into his hand.

"You always were a stupid bastard," Josh hissed, and lunged forward, driving the blade toward Shadow's mid-section.

But Shadow moved easily out of harm's way, his movements as lithe and graceful as that of a cat on the prowl. Lips pulled back in a feral snarl, Shadow lashed out at Joshua, and he did not miss. His blade opened a long gash the length of Joshua's left arm. And then, before Josh could strike back, Shadow's knife was flashing through the air again, swift as a serpent's tongue, the sharp blade biting into Joshua's left side just above his

waist. Joshua loosed a harsh cry of pain
and rage as he began slashing wildly, but
Shadow eluded the blade with ease.

Shadow. He was Two Hawks Flying
now, and beautiful to watch. Never had he
looked so primitive, or so deadly. Years of
living as a white man had not dulled his
reflexes or dampened his skill with a knife.
His lean bronze body was as fluid as water
as he parried Joshua's thrust. He moved
lightly, agilely, on the balls of his feet, as
graceful as a ballet dancer, as elusive as
smoke in a high wind. An exultant cry
rose in the air as his blade drew blood yet
again.

Joshua fought heavily, his feet
moving as though weighted down with
lead. Anger and fear spoiled his judgment
and ruined his aim. Once, when Shadow
pulled back, Joshua looked at me, his blue
eyes mirroring his despair.

"He knows," I thought sadly. "He
knows he can't win."

I bit down hard on my lower lip as the
fight went on and on. Shadow was toying
with Joshua, and it was a cruel and
terrible thing to watch. Joshua's blade
lashed out again and again, and each time
it sliced harmlessly through empty air.
Tears of rage and frustration glistened on
Joshua's cheeks as he tried to break
through Shadow's defenses.

Shadow's smile was ruthless as he
lunged forward and dragged the edge of

his blade across Joshua's right cheek,
cutting through flesh to the bone. A
second flick of the sharp blade opened
Joshua's left cheek.

I had wondered why Shadow did not
carry a gun, and now I knew. He wanted
to kill Joshua slowly, wanted to feel the
blade of his knife slice into flesh, wanted
to feel Joshua's blood on his hands.

Tears welled in my eyes as I watched
Joshua grow steadily weaker, slower. He
seemed to be bleeding from every part of
his body, and still he fought, his hatred
giving him strength and endurance when
he should have been defeated.

Then, in a desperate rush, Joshua
hurled himself at Shadow. His arm went
up and slashed downward and I gasped as
the point of his blade sank into Shadow's
back, just above his right shoulder blade.
With a low grunt of pain, Shadow twisted
sharply to the left and with one swift
thrust, he buried his knife in Joshua's
heart. For a timeless moment, they stood
together, faces only inches apart. Then
Shadow jerked his knife free and stepped
back.

Joshua stayed on his feet, swaying
slightly, for the space of a heartbeat; then,
murmuring my name, he fell face down in
the dirt.

I stared at him, clearly remembering
the boy he had been long ago. I
remembered how he had courted me,

remembered how he had told me his plans
for the future, how he wanted to have a
spread of his own and raise cattle and
horses and a couple of kids. I remembered
the day I had told him I was in love with
Shadow. I had been sixteen, Josh had been
almost twenty. He had been shocked and
dismayed but he had promised to keep my
secret.

"I won't tell," he had said. "But you
had better think this over careful before
you go off and do something you'll likely
regret. I . . . I love you, Hannah. I guess
you know I'll always be here if you need
me."

I had liked Josh better at that
moment than ever before, and now he was
dead. Because he had loved me. I began to
weep softly. Joshua Berdeen had caused
me so much heartache, so much pain and
yet, long ago, I had cared deeply for him.

Shadow's quick intake of breath drew
my attention and I ran toward him, tears
of relief streaming down my cheeks. He
stared at the knife in his hand and then at
my bound wrists. The bloodlust was still
shining in his midnight eyes as he raised
the knife, the same knife that had killed
Joshua, and cut my hands free.

Shadow sighed heavily and I saw pain
and weariness wash the rage from his eyes
as he tossed his knife aside.

"Shadow, sit down," I urged.

With a nod, he sat cross-legged on the ground. Joshua's blade was still embedded in Shadow's back. I looked at Shadow, saw his hands ball into tight fists.

"Do it," he said through clenched teeth.

Biting down on my lower lip, I took hold of the knife hilt and pulled the blade from Shadow's flesh, then tossed the knife into the darkness. Tearing a ruffle from my petticoat, I pressed it over the wound to staunch the flow of blood.

And now, with the fighting over and Shadow safe, my knees grew weak. I must have looked faint, for Shadow drew me down beside him and put his arm around my shoulders.

"Are you all right?" he asked, his concern evident in the tone of his voice.

"Fine, now that you're here."

"Did he hurt you?"

"No."

"I cannot blame him for wanting you," Shadow murmured, squeezing my arm. "You are as beautiful and desirable as you were on your sixteenth birthday."

I smiled faintly. I remembered that day as though it had been yesterday. We had met at the river crossing and our hearts had reached out to one another.

"Will you be here tomorrow, Hannah?" Shadow had asked, and I had known even then that my whole future rested in my reply. There were a hundred reasons why I should have said no, but they all seemed shallow and unimportant with Shadow gazing down at me, waiting for my reply.

I had agreed to meet him the next day, and our lives had been entwined ever since. I had never been sorry.

Now we sat side by side in front of the fire as the flames burned low, our hearts and hands touching, content to be quietly close.

We buried Joshua beneath a live oak tree, smoothed the dirt so there was no telltale mound, then scattered leaves and twigs over the burial sight.

"It is all over now, Hannah," Shadow whispered, his lips brushing my cheek. "Nothing, no one, will ever part us again."

Nothing will ever part us again. I sighed as Shadow held me close, feeling again that wondrous sense of peace and contentment that permeated my very soul whenever Shadow held me in his arms.

We never spoke of Joshua Berdeen again.

XXXI

A persistent knock aroused me from a deep sleep and I woke to see Shadow padding out of our room.

Rising hastily, I pulled on my robe and followed Shadow to the front door. It was Hawk. Victoria was in labor, he said. Could we come right away? Shadow and I dressed quickly and twenty minutes later we were entering Hawk's cabin. It was solid and well-built, though sparsely furnished.

Victoria was in the bedroom, her eyes frightened, her face drawn and pale. I bid Shadow and Hawk stay in the parlor, and I went to sit by Victoria. She had been in labor about two hours, and her pains were five minutes apart.

Victoria smiled weakly as I took her hand in mine. "I didn't know it would hurt so bad," she said, squeezing my hand at the onset of another contraction.

"Try to relax," I advised. I brushed her hair away from her face, my heart going out to her. Childbirth was rarely easy.

The time passed slowly. Between contractions, we spoke of Victoria's plans to decorate the cabin, her hopes for the baby, her disappointment that her mother was not present.

At daybreak, Victoria's water broke and the contractions came harder and faster. Victoria cried out as the pains grew stronger. Her hair and face were damp with perspiration, as was the blanket beneath her.

"Hawk," she groaned. "I want Hawk."

"I'll get him."

My son's face was lined with worry as he followed me into the bedroom. Victoria reached out for him, her eyes begging for relief.

"Vickie." Hawk murmured her name as he kissed her cheek, his hand stroking her hair and neck.

"It hurts, Hawk," Victoria said plaintively. "Make it stop hurting."

She screamed as a pain knifed through her, and Hawk's face went white.

"What's wrong?" he asked, agitated. "Why is it taking so long?"

"Nothing's wrong," I assured him. "Most women go through a long labor with their first pregnancy."

"But it's been eight hours."

"It might take eight more," I said so only Hawk could hear me. "Don't let Victoria know how worried you are. It will only make her more tense."

"Vickie, get on your knees," Hawk urged. "That's how the Indian women deliver their babies."

"My knees?" Vickie repeated dubiously.

"Try it, Vickie."

Victoria looked at me, and I nodded. "It can't hurt, and it might help."

Hawk helped Victoria to her knees, knelt before her for the next half hour, murmuring to her, telling her he loved her, that everything would soon be over. Victoria squeezed his hands when the pains came, squeezed and clawed until Hawk's hands were red and swollen. He did not seem to notice.

It was just before noon on September 30th when Victoria gave one final push and Hawk caught his son in his hands.

"Push again, Victoria," I urged, and she dispelled the afterbirth, then lay back, exhausted, while I cut and tied the cord and wrapped the baby in a clean blanket.

Hawk stared in wonder at the tiny, black-haired infant cradled in Victoria's arms, his face aglow with love and pride for his wife and his son.

I was going to call Shadow when

Victoria let out a low groan and then
began to writhe in pain. Hawk looked up
at me, his eyes dark with worry.

"What's wrong?" he cried, his voice
edged with panic.

"I don't know."

Victoria gave a low cry of pain and
Hawk and I stared in amazement as a
second child made its appearance in the
world.

"Twins," Hawk murmured.

"Twins," I echoed as I laid the infant
on Victoria's stomach. "Vickie, look,
you're the mother of twin sons."

Victoria smiled, the pain forgotten, as
I laid the second child in her arm.

"Twins," I said again, smiling hugely.
"I'm the grandmother of twins!"

"They're beautiful!" Victoria exclaimed, examining each child's fingers
and toes. "Just beautiful."

"So are you," Hawk said. "Thank you
for giving me two fine sons."

"Thank you," Victoria murmured.
Her eyelids fluttered down and she was
asleep.

I saw a flicker of doubt in Shadow's
eyes when he saw the twins for the first
time. The Indians were a superstitious
people. In the old days, twins were often
taken away and killed. Sometimes a man
left his wife, believing the birth of twins
signified she had become pregnant by two
men and had therefore been unfaithful.

But the doubt was quickly gone from Shadow's face and he smiled proudly. The boys had straight black hair and dark blue eyes and everyone made a fuss over them, even Blackie.

The news that Hawk and Victoria had twins spread quickly through the valley, and the women came to help Victoria, cooing with delight over the adorable babies. The men slapped Hawk on the back, declaring that he must be a hell of a man to father twin boys.

In October, Mary announced her engagement to Frank Smythe. The announcement came as no surprise, and the wedding was set for the following spring.

In December, just three days before Christmas, Shadow and I were married, just as he had promised we would be. Shadow had wanted us to be married soon after his fight with Joshua, but I had needed some time to pass between that awful day and the day of our wedding.

I had assumed we would have a small informal ceremony at home, but Shadow had other plans. He got together with Mary and Rebecca and the three of them planned a wedding that would have done credit to the Vanderbilts. Everyone in the valley was invited. Mattie Smythe and a dozen women prepared great quantities of food, Ruth Tippitt baked three large cakes, each one a masterpiece, Mary and Rebecca decorated the church with flowers and white satin bows.

I wore a white satin gown, complete with a veil and matching slippers. Shadow wore a black suit and tie. It was indeed a rare occasion.

The strains of the wedding march filled the air as my father walked me down the narrow aisle to the altar. Rebecca, Frank Smythe, Blackie, and Victoria sat on the front pew, their faces shining with love. Rebecca and Victoria held the twins. Hawk stood at the altar beside his father; Mary was my maid of honor. The church was filled with our friends and neighbors, but I had eyes only for Shadow.

Hand in hand, we stood before the altar. Tears of joy welled in my eyes as the Reverend Thorsen spoke the solemn, beautiful words that made me Shadow's lawfully wedded wife. No words had ever sounded sweeter, or been more welcome.

"Hannah." Shadow smiled down at me as he lifted the veil from my face. "Long life and happiness," Shadow murmured so only I could hear. "That was what the hawks promised. Remember?"

I nodded as I lifted my face for his kiss, and as Shadow's mouth closed softly over mine, the distant cry of a red-tailed hawk echoed in my ears, its exultant cry like a benediction on our love.

LAKOTA RENEGADE

MADELINE BAKER

Handy with six-guns and fists, Creed Maddigan likes his women hot and ready. But the rugged half-breed isn't used to innocent girls like Jassy McCloud who curtsy and make ginger snaps. Then Creed is falsely jailed for a crime he didn't commit, and he can think of nothing besides escaping to savor Jassy's sweet love.

Alone on the Colorado frontier, Jassy can either work as a fancy lady or hope to find a husband. But what is she to do when the only man she hopes to marry is a wanted renegade? For Jassy, the decision is simple: She'll take Creed for better or worse, even if she has to spend the rest of her days dodging bounty hunters and bullets.

_3832-3 $5.99 US/$7.99 CAN

Dorchester Publishing Co., Inc.
65 Commerce Road
Stamford, CT 06902

Please add $1.75 for shipping and handling for the first book and $.50 for each book thereafter. NY, NYC, PA and CT residents, please add appropriate sales tax. No cash, stamps, or C.O.D.s. All orders shipped within 6 weeks via postal service book rate. Canadian orders require $2.00 extra postage and must be paid in U.S. dollars through a U.S. banking facility.

Name _____
Address _____
City _____ State _____ Zip _____
I have enclosed $_____ in payment for the checked book(s).
Payment <u>must</u> accompany all orders. ☐ Please send a free catalog.